TAHITIAN PEARL

TAHITIAN *pearl*

from the gritty dune....
   ...to an oasis in the Sun

a novel by author ESAUREN PHYER

Library of Congress Control Number (LCCN): 2009934906

Fiction: Contemporary Women
Fiction: African American—General
Self-Help: Motivational & Inspirational

ISBN: 978-0-9842188-0-6

ISBN: 0-9842188-0-7

Grateful acknowledgment is made to Hal Leonard Inc., for granting permission for the use of the song lyrics contained in this work.

"Used To Love"
WORDS AND MUSIC BY STEPHEN HUFF

Copyright © 2001 by Universal Music—Z Songs LLC and Tuff Huff Music
All Rights in the United States and Canada Administered by Universal Music—Z Songs LLC
International Copyright Secured All Rights Reserved

"No More Rain (In This Cloud)"
WORDS AND MUSIC BY ANGELA STONE, JAMES WEATHERLY AND GORDON CHAMBERS

Copyright © 1999 Universal—Songs of Polygram International, Inc., Lady Diamond Music, Universal—Polygram International Publishing, Inc. October 12th Music and Hitco South
All Rights for Lady Diamond Music Controlled and Administered by Universal—Songs of Polygram International, Inc.
All Rights for October 12th Music and Hitco South Administered by Music of Windswept
All Rights Reserved—Used by Permission

Cover design by: Savant Marketing, Inc. Baltimore, Maryland
Interior design by: Arc Manor Publishing Rockville, Maryland
Printed In the United States of America

This book is dedicated to My Lord and Savior,

Jesus, The Christ.

Thank you, Lord, for allowing me to write this book. It is also dedicated to my late husband Randy who believed I could, to my late mother Gladys, and to my grandchildren Allicea, Dominique and Shawn for their individual and collective inspiration.

Contents

Acknowledgments

I want to thank my editor, Elliot Bratton for his attention to detail. Your talent is superb. Thank you for holding my hand through this. I also want to thank Zina Casey, Linda Foster, and Maria Ray for cheering me on and catching my vision and excitement day after day. Leslie Carter, you're amazing. Thank you *soooo* much for your sharp eye and your critical reading of and input to the manuscript. Much thanks to Savant Marketing for listening to the concept and designing a cover that captured the entire essence of what I had in mind— Outstanding! Thank you. To my son Anthony for enduring reading after reading after reading and for the creditable insight you gave me from a male perspective. Thank you, Readers Digest Book Club of Boston, Massachusetts (Imelda Price, Linda McKenzie, Edna Mathieu and Grace Hammonds), for allowing me to be a part of your circle. To my friends and supporters—Diane Edwards, Janice Grant, Jeannette Brantley, Saundra Askew, Jacqueline Jackson, Ron Barner, Peggy Sue Missett, Cherry English, Valerie Watkins, Karen McCray, Louisa Brinson, Alma Goodwin, Mary Blanton, Patricia Jones, my hairstylist, Shawn, owner of Dynasty Hair Salon in Baltimore, Maryland, and all the other wonderfully supportive people there, Gavin Johnson, Carol Thompson, Shakina Martin and K. Tramaine Watson, for any part you played, big or small, as readers of the manuscript, listeners to every detail of the project as it developed, and your never-ending encouragement along the way. Victoria Christopher Murray, a distinguished author of many novels, thank you for always responding with grace to my many inquiries. You've been a tremendous blessing. I've been supported and encouraged by those who are too numerous to mention, but I know in my heart who you are and I thank you. To my son Damien, thank you for being you and helping me to "be easy," my stepsons Randy and Anderson, for teaching me some very important life lessons, my nephew Robert for aiming for and reaching the stars and always telling your "Auntie" I love you. Thank you. I give a shout-out of love and respect to all of my family. I pray that God's blessings of life, peace, love and abundance follow you all of your days. Finally, Curtis Bunn, President and Founder of The National Book Club Conference (NBCC) in Atlanta, Georgia, thank you for encouraging me to participate in the conference as a novice novel writer in 2005. I learned, as you promised, that this outstanding event was not just for book club members but an invaluable treasure to aspiring authors as well. Thanks to each of you and, from the bottom of my heart, I send you love.

I want to give special mention and acknowledgment to my father William, Sr. for your strong example of a man and a father. Thank you for your sacrificial love.

Thanks especially to all the book readers and book buyers.

ESAUREN PHYER

PUBLISHERS NOTE:

It's with great sadness that we acknowledge the passing of Esauren's father, William Sr. prior to this work going to print.

When I was 12 years old, it pleased God to alarm me by a remarkable dream. At midday, when the cattle went under the shade of the trees, I dreamt the world was on fire, and that I saw the supreme Judge defend on his great white Throne. I saw millions of millions of souls; some of whom ascended up to heaven; while others were rejected, and fell into the greatest confusion and despair. This dream made such an impression upon my mind, that I refrained from swearing and bad company, and from that time acknowledged that there was a God; but how to serve God I knew not.[1]

BOSTON KING—
A Fugitive Slave turned Missionary Preacher (1760-1802)

Prologue

Naiyah (Ni-ah) and YaYa's Story, The Beginning...

I was so terrified, I trembled. The huge gray train, as if on a deadly mission, sped directly towards Mr. Johnny. My knees weakened, my heart raced, yet I felt paralyzed and was rendered speechless as I watched his car straddle the tracks at the railroad crossing. I opened my mouth to scream, but there was no sound. Why wasn't Mr. Johnny moving? Why was he just sitting there? Was he afraid? Too scared to move and cross safely to the other side? Didn't he see the huge train about to hit him?

The train barreled faster and faster down the tracks. *Oh no!* Naiyah thought, it wasn't going to stop in time! And she was right. The train plowed right through Mr. Johnny's car, slicing through its front half like a knife in hot butter. Naiyah couldn't see where the rest of his body went, but there, rolling down the street, went Mr. Johnny's head, which stopped abruptly when it collided with the curb.

The year she turned thirteen, Naiyah Isabella Harland dreamed of Mr. Johnny's horrible decapitation. On the night of her dream, the moon was so full, it blazed as bright as the daylight. When night passed and she was fully awake and conscious, she had no voice and was unable to speak for days. The dream was so terrifying it produced a tremendous sense of shock in her and the weight of it was something she carried for weeks, like dumbbells pressed heavily upon her shoulders. Had Naiyah been able to speak, it wouldn't have mattered, because there were no words to express the terror that overcame her. The horrifying image played over and over in her mind, and each time it did, she shuddered, thinking that somehow, it seemed more real, not like a dream at all.

Naiyah's grandmother, Big Sadie Harland, or "YaYa" to those she knew, wanted to name her, Isabella. On the twelfth of February, when Naiyah, (lovingly called Izzy) was born to Big Sadie's son Lemuel, also called Lucky, and his wife Jade, the former Jade Diamond, Big Sadie looked at her with knowing eyes and said to Jade, "Honey, she's special, chosen to do liberating work for the glory of the Lord. Now, what you and Lucky decide as far as naming her, I don't have a say, I know." Then she whispered, "But this little one should be made holy unto the Lord and maybe giving her a special name may help her remember her special calling. That's what Isabella means—to be consecrated to God, so, as her grandmother, please honor me and give her that name, please?" she pleaded sweetly.

"Mama Sadie," Jade said while staring down at her precious daughter, "we had our hearts set on naming her Naiyah Alexis."

"Lucky," Big Sadie said, smiling sweetly, "excuse me, I'm going to step out so you and your wife can talk privately." Lucky considered his options. He knew Big Sadie didn't give up easily when she wanted something, but he also knew how much Jade liked the name they'd chosen together. Never having disagreed with Big Sadie before, he didn't know what to do.

Moving over to the bedside, Lucky bent down and kissed both his girls tenderly on the cheek, "Jade, sweetheart," he began "you know Big Sadie's tight with the Lord, right? And I don't want to go messin' with that, do you?" he asked with an anxious smile.

"Lem, you're not asking that I give in to Mama Sadie's wishes, are you? What about what I want, what you and I have already decided?" she said peevishly.

"Please, sweetheart," Lucky pleaded, "there's nothing wrong with adding a little sanctification to our household, if only in a name..." he laughed.

"Don't go there," Jade replied, rolling her eyes. "If you ask me, that holy rollin', Jesus shoutin', sanctified Mama of yours is asking for too much."

Lucky's mouth fell wide open. Did his conservative Catholic wife just say that? He wondered, looking at her sideways.

It was so comical that they both burst into uncontrollable laughter. "Okay," he said, still chuckling in his sexy bass voice. "But say you'll agree to what Big Sadie's asking. Do it for me," he said softly and, before she could protest further, Lucky leaned over his sleeping baby daughter and covered Jade's mouth with a passionate kiss.

"This will cost you," she said smiling, knowing full well that Lemuel Harland could get anything from her he wanted, all he had to do was ask. And he knew it too.

"Thanks baby, it'll be well worth it, you'll see." Flashing a megawatt smile, he continued, "You're my best and favorite girl, well, after my little Naiyah that is" he said, leaving the bright flower-filled nursery to share the good news with Big Sadie.

Jade and Lucky were truly blessed. As an accomplished fast track professional, Jade was a Professor of Linguistics at New York's Adelphi University on Long Island and a part-time English tutor. Lucky made a very comfortable living as a top investment executive at a prestigious brokerage house in Manhattan. In addition, Jade, who was also a skilled tailor, thanks to her grandfather, owned a small fashion boutique, *'Diamond Designs,'* which had created quite a buzz among Long Island's elite.

Surprisingly, Jade and Lucky's affluence only caused them to love each other and their family more. Two years after Naiyah was born, they welcomed the birth of their son Nathan. Oddly, the children called their parents, Mum and Poppy but Jade and Lucky weren't sure why. As their children grew up, some adjustments in lifestyle had to be made, but still, Jade was an extravagant girl and Lucky's was an extravagant world, so they were a good match and made a great team, in the beginning...

Naiyah, a happy, outgoing child, was always a flurry of activity, whether spending endless hours in sports activities, daydreaming with her best friend Imani, playing chess at the local Y, or participating in equestrian competitions with her friends at Choice Ranch. She was energetic, with strong lean legs, and excelled at everything she tried. Because of this effluent energy, Big Sadie sometimes called her "Butterfly." With the enormous love she had for her grandchildren, Big Sadie showered them with lots of attention. In return, Naiyah and Nathan lovingly called her "G-Ma." However, Naiyah started calling Big Sadie "YaYa" after she overheard a classmate use it when talking about his grandmother from Greece. She fell in love with it immediately, and from the sparkling gleam in Big Sadie's eyes the first time she called her YaYa, Naiyah knew, that Big Sadie loved it too.

Big Sadie had come a long way since leaving the life she had, working as a maid. Now as a successful personal chef and caterer, she spent as much time with Naiyah as she could, making up for the many winters spent in Florida working for the "rich white folks." Whenever YaYa went away, Naiyah's heart literally ached from missing her, and on many nights she cried herself to sleep.Theirs was an unbreakable bond from the moment of Naiyah's birth and YaYa's first knowing gaze into her bright, but penetrating eyes. Big Sadie had become the guiding force in Naiyah's life as Lucky and Jade became more and more preoccupied with career success and other pursuits.

Work and travel put Big Sadie in contact with all kinds of things and all kinds of people—some good, some not so good. A deeply spiritual woman, Big Sadie wasn't fazed by the extravagant and sometimes depraved behaviors of the people, for whom she cooked and cleaned. She had an endless reservoir of love, continuously flowing even when her family or friends messed up or made terrible mistakes and bad choices. In fact, when circumstances looked otherwise unredeemable, Big Sadie remained faithfully optimistic. Years before Naiyah was born, her grandfather, Jesse Harland, a drunk, womanizer and hell raiser, was seen by everyone as having an unredeemable life, but not by Big Sadie—she loved him strong, so when his time had come, he died a respected man in the community after all.

Busy climbing the ladders of success, Lucky and Jade were remiss in passing on the spiritual teachings they received as children. But when she was home, Big Sadie took Naiyah and sometimes Nathan along with her to church. She taught them what it meant to be free in Jesus and how God works all things for the good of those who love Him. She told them constantly of God's love, of his mercy which she said was renewed each morning and how he loved them so much, he gave his own life so they didn't have to lose theirs. Big Sadie, strong in faith, taught Naiyah how to talk to God in prayer and from that, Naiyah learned what it meant to believe in Him. Big Sadie's home was filled with song and she could always be found singing or humming—old time gospel hymns, like "What a Friend We Have in Jesus" or "Blessed Assurance."

Pivotal shifts in the earth space that surrounded Naiyah began to happen the year Mr. Johnny died. They seemed slight at first, but in actuality they weren't. In fact, they signified her earth shattering, but

Naiyah didn't recognize it yet. It began on December 7, 1997, ironically, the same month and day of the bombing of Pearl Harbor, though that occurred fifty six years before. A junior in high school, Naiyah lost both her balance and her focus on that bone-chilling day, because it was the day her YaYa died. Almost immediately, Naiyah began feeling unmoored, as if she were an untethered balloon. She continued moving through life, but to an observant eye, it seemed her heart and soul had vacated her body the very moment YaYa transitioned. The death of Big Sadie Harland was a complete shock and totally unexpected. When she developed an acute case of pneumonia the week before, it was expected she'd pull through. However, she began to experience severe pulmonary complications, which quickly killed her.

Not long before YaYa's death, Naiyah's childhood dream about Mr. Johnny came true. Late one night, in the still hours before dawn, Mr. Johnny was hit by a train and died instantly when he was decapitated on impact. The next day, Naiyah overheard her parents discussing it over coffee in their sun-drenched kitchen. She remembered how full the moon had been in her dream. She felt the weight of fear gripping her once again and took off running the few blocks to YaYa's house, collapsing in an exhausted and tearful heap. She was inconsolable.

"Baby," YaYa said, lifting her to a chair, "what's the matter, Butterfly, why are you cryin' so hard?"

"Mr. Johnny's dead!!"

"Yes, baby. It was a terrible thing that happened to that man and no one knows why he was even on them train tracks."

"But YaYa, I saw him there. He was just sitting on the tracks waiting as though he knew the train was coming and would slice him clean in half." YaYa looked at her granddaughter with terror registering on her face. "What do you mean you saw him, what are you sayin'? Where were you, how did you see this, Naiyah?" she asked, her voice rising slightly.

"I saw it all in a dream. I dreamed it just the way it happened," Naiyah cried.

YaYa's mouth gaped open in awe. Cocking her head to the side, she removed her hand from Naiyah's arm and leaned back in her chair. "What did you say?"

"You heard me, YaYa. I saw the whole thing in a dream, but at the time, it didn't seem like a dream. I don't know why. I just know it felt real. And now look, it's happened, YaYa, and I'm scared, really scared," Naiyah sobbed before throwing herself into her grandmother's arms.

"Shh, hush now. Don't be scared, no need being afraid," YaYa said calmly as she stroked Naiyah's hair. "You know, baby, the Lord sometimes gives people the spiritual gift of sight. He does it to help His people, maybe bless them somehow—you understand what I'm sayin', to you Naiyah? You got the gift; I knew it the minute you were born. Now everybody's not gifted in the same way. The Lord may give one visions, another, the laying on of hands, and still another, the gift of faith. Don't be afraid," she said again. "In due time, He's gonna show you, watch and see," she said excitedly. Then she began to moan and pray, weep and pray some more. Naiyah couldn't understand what she was saying and moved to another chair, thinking the distance would help her hear better. But she still wasn't making any sense. But when YaYa finished, she told Naiyah very clearly, "Don't you run from the power of God. I believe He's gonna use you in a mighty way. Yes! Yes! Yes!" she said forcefully. "That's right, He's gonna use you sho' nuff."

However, Naiyah did run. She ran fast and hard. She didn't want to have visions. She didn't want to see or be used for anything God had in mind.

About this same time, Lucky started staying away from home many nights, openly taking up with a woman he met in Rio while on business, and Jade started nipping a little gin here and there to ease her pain. Nathan was even acting a little peculiar. Rather than hang with the boys his own age in their neighborhood, Nathan preferred to create and design outfits for Naiyah and Mani. Naiyah looked the other way; she didn't want to deal with her brother's problems, his *different* ways, she had her own to worry about.

Soon the shift in Naiyah's world took hold and she was on the move, ditching Mani and her other friends at Choice Ranch. She didn't have time for the things they used to do and started hanging with Danny West instead. Around town Danny, who, unbeknownst to Naiyah, was Mr. Johnny's son, was known as 'Strong' because he once got busted for strong-arm robbery, not to mention, he was also cut and chiseled hard as a rock from pumping iron every day in the high school gym. Strong and his crew terrorized his neighborhood stealing and dealing drugs. Despite this, Naiyah found herself seeking Strong out to drink wine and smoke weed with him and his boys. It made her feel good, made her feel numb. Most of all, it helped her cope with not having her YaYa.

The same winter her YaYa died, Naiyah had another dream vision similar to the one she had about Mr. Johnny. Because she was successful in numbing most of her thoughts and feelings of YaYa with the wine and drugs, the last thing on her mind, while she tossed and turned fit-fully as the dream unfolded with cinematic precision, was what her YaYa told her about visions and the power of God to use them for good.

In her vision, the heat from the blistering sun rained down on Nai-yah and Mani as they soaked up the liquid gold sunshine. Summer was Naiyah's favorite time of year. She loved the way her skin glistened a bronzy gold and the smell of the ocean made her smile as she and Mani stretched out on colorful beach towels. Now and then, they sat up to watch as their friends swam and played nearby. Then a loud scream and a shout for help echoed through the air. A sudden hush fell over the crowd like a heavy water-soaked blanket and a feeling of nausea and panic descended upon Naiyah. Mani jumped up and shouted for her brother Austen. Naiyah's eyes were glued on Mani's as she scanned one end of the beach and then the other. She called and called and called for him… but to no avail.

Then they heard a dreadful shriek as someone screamed, "HELP! He's going under!" Mani ran towards their screaming friends, but it was too late, Austen was gone. Naiyah turned and, with painful sorrow, watched her friend flailing and screaming from grief on the scorching sand.

The next morning, Naiyah woke exhausted and in a panic. Instead of going to school, and without YaYa to comfort her, she walked and walked, avoiding places where people might know her until she ran into one of Strong's boys. After tipping him a dollar for buying her a bottle of cheap wine from a nearby store, Naiyah went to the park where she sat and sipped all day from the brown paper bag. Blessed with an out-standing IQ, thank God, she never lost sight of the dream to go to Stanford or Vassar one day to study finance, like her Poppy, despite the obstacles looming before her.

1

To The Left—Slightly Off Course

Despite the fact that it had been a good while since they'd spoken, Naiyah missed Mani just as much as she missed her YaYa. She'd heard from Nathan that her best friend, who'd been more like her sister, was mad as hell that she'd blown off Austen's funeral and had the nerve to abandon her as well. Naiyah imagined Mani, who was no bigger than a minute with beautiful mocha colored skin and a short blonde natural, saying to Nathan, "I don't understand. How could she diss me like this? I thought we were girls." Naiyah could picture her, hands moving a mile a minute, criticizing her for ungirlfriend-like behavior. "Well," she'd say, "I'm pissed and nothing Naiyah says will ever change that." Naiyah feared confronting Mani, because she knew rejection, regardless of how slight, could bring intense pain. She wasn't ready to face that pain, if she forced Mani to go there, once she gathered the courage to call her. She thought about the tragic drowning of Austen and how it happened just the way she dreamt it. But she still missed Mani and knew she hurt her deeply when she was a no show at the funeral. So when high school finally ended and Naiyah moved across the country to Palo Alto, California to start her studies in International Finance at Stanford, she breathed a sigh of relief.

❧

Naiyah looked up at her new friend and roommate Faith, who had just come in from class, with a forced smile.

"Izzy, what's up with you girl?" Faith said to Naiyah. "You look like you've lost your best friend."

"Yeah, Faith," Naiyah sighed, "I feel like I have. I was just thinking about Mani, wishing I could hear her voice again."

"Why don't you call her," Faith replied "maybe she isn't angry anymore, maybe she's found it in her heart to forgive you."

Naiyah got up from the small sofa, making her way to the kitchenette of their small college efficiency and turned the flame on under the copper tea kettle. "Humph, fat chance. You weren't there when she lashed out at me and, honestly speaking, I can't say I blame her. We were so much more than just best friends, we were blood sisters. You know the kind when you prick your fingers and press them together? That's what we did. That's how close we were. We were cut buddies," she said laughing at the thought. "So close, I sometimes called her Cutty."

"Yeah, I know. My friend Maya and I were like that, always there for each other," Faith remembered fondly.

"Want some tea?" Naiyah asked just as the kettle began to whistle.

"Sure, give me some Red Zinger if there's any left."

Naiyah reached into the cabinet above the stove and pulled out the tea bags along with some fresh local honey. "Mani's given name, Imani, also means faith," Naiyah said, looking at her roommate. "It's Swahili, I believe. My grandmother always told me to have faith and to trust God. She talked about faith being some kind of supernatural gift, that it could move mountains. It was this faith, she said, that allowed Jesus to calm the raging sea. You'd think with my mountains and being surrounded by all these faith reminders, I'd have my faith thing down pat by now," Naiyah chuckled bitterly. "I want to talk to Mani so badly, to tell her that I'm pregnant," she said, gently rubbing her small, tight mound of belly hidden beneath an oversized shirt. "When her brother drowned, I was in a really bad place," she continued.

"Are you in a better place now?" Faith gingerly inquired, sipping her tea.

"No, not really," Naiyah replied sadly.

"So why now, where's this sense of urgency coming from?"

"I just miss her so much," Naiyah sighed. "Except for my YaYa, Mani was closer to me growing up than anyone else. She was closer than even my own Mum. She knew the rhythm of my heartbeat, but I let her down by not being there for her when her brother drowned. I should have been there for her. I should have helped her deal with her loss, her sorrow, but I just couldn't." Naiyah and Faith sat silently at the small island counter in the kitchen, sipping their tea, lost in their own private memories.

"When Austen died, a little less than two years after my YaYa, I started feeling like I was unraveling," Naiyah began again. "It seemed like wherever I stepped, the earth shifted. I started having frightening dreams that began to come true. The dreams got so bad and came so frequently, I couldn't trust anything, I didn't feel safe anymore."

"So, is that when you started drinking heavy?" Faith asked.

Naiyah looked at her questioningly, wondering how she knew about the drinking. It wasn't like she was all out in the open with it. *Either she's more perceptive than I thought or else I'm slipping and not being very discreet,* she thought.

"Well yeah, I guess," Naiyah replied hesitantly. "I started hanging with a guy named Strong and his crew; they were off center, far to the left. They were nothing like I was used to, nothing like the clique we hung with. Mani and I were the snobby intellectuals. Everyone admired us and thought we'd be the ones most likely to succeed. There was no way I could show them the side of me that was in the shadows, least of all my girl Mani. So I started drinking a little alcohol." Reflecting on the loss of her best friend made Naiyah's eyes fill with tears. Although she liked Faith, she couldn't betray her heart by releasing the floodgates, restraining a torrent of sorrow within her. Instead, Naiyah blinked as hard as she could, placed her mug on the counter and dabbed the corners of her eyes with a crumpled napkin before one tear dropped.

Faith got up from the counter to give Naiyah some privacy, but before disappearing into the bathroom, she said again, "I'd call her if I were you. What've you got to lose? One of you needs to start the ball rolling. Besides, you're going to need all the support you can get when the baby gets here. Have you thought about that? I certainly hope you're not just counting on Elijah."

Elijah was Naiyah's sometime boyfriend and the father of her unborn baby. Now composed, Naiyah picked up the tea kettle and poured more hot water into her mug. Before drinking, first she retrieved a hidden bottle of cognac from under the sink. She poured a little and then just a little more for good measure. It was times like these, when she felt lonely or stressed, that Naiyah pulled out one of her many journals and wrote herself back to a place of healing. In the single bedroom she and Faith shared, kept in a locked trunk in her closet, were Naiyah's journals. Moving aside the *Dear God, Dear Mother* and *Gratitude* journals, she came across the one titled *YaYa, wisdom from my ancestor.*

The bedroom Naiyah shared with Faith, upon entering, was unexpectedly elegant. The large window that stretched from one wall to the other was dressed with a makeshift window box covered in the richest gold-brocaded taffeta. The sheers, almost translucent, peeked through the most shocking and luxurious red paneled draperies. The large day bed they shared which converted into a trundle to sleep them comfortably was shrouded in a homemade sheer canopy that hinted subtly of romantic encounters. For added space they pushed the dressers together on the westernmost side of the room. On Naiyah's dresser stood a picture of her YaYa in a simple silver frame that highlighted her face and the long silver braid which was draped seductively over her shoulder. Displayed beside it was a wooden crucifix and a pair of ceramic praying hands. Naiyah took a large gulp of the cognac-laced herbal tea and then a deep breath. Once she exhaled, she began her journal entry.

November 5, 2002

My Beloved YaYa,

I miss you more today than I did at your passing. I don't know how that's possible, but instead of getting easier as time goes on, it gets harder and harder. I guess because I need you now more than ever. That's probably hard to believe, since I haven't written to you in this journal in quite some time. I'm having a baby, YaYa, and neither you nor Mani are here. It's been a struggle dealing with emptiness and the feeling of being alone. Both you and Mani left me to negotiate on my own, but I feel like I have no oars. I'm now a senior at Stanford, expecting to graduate in the spring. I've made some new friends. My roommate Faith is really pretty cool, but it isn't the same. After you died, YaYa, I had another one of those dreams just like the one I had about Mr. Johnny. Only, this time, I saw Mani's brother Austen drown while we were having an ordinary fun day at the beach. They pronounced him dead at the scene. Mani lost it and, because I wasn't able to cope, I stayed away from her. This was almost four years ago, YaYa, but to her, I'm still persona non grata. She's very angry and has not forgiven me. If you were alive, I know I could depend on you for guidance. But you aren't, so I'm not sure. I don't want Jade's advice because I don't trust it. Look at the mess she and Lucky have made of their marriage. No thanks! You're not going to want to know this and I'm so ashamed, but as I hinted earlier, I'm having a baby and it's out of wedlock. By the looks of things right now, I'm pretty certain we're not getting married. I hear you now, loud and clear, YaYa—telling me of God's will and plan; I know from your words of wisdom that sex outside of marriage isn't part of it. Yes, I knew better, if only I had listened, I wish I had. With you and Mani gone, I felt I needed something, perhaps something to make me feel strong and stable, like I was someone's priority. I thought sex, alcohol and drugs were the answer. Boy, was I ever wrong. Instead of making things better, I've made them worse. How I wish I could bury my head in your bosom, YaYa, and cry a river just like I did when I was little. Come, my beloved, give to me a reassuring touch. Let me know from heaven which road I should take. Thank you, YaYa, for always loving me, I love you, YaYa.

Your First and Only
Granddaughter Izzy

Just as Naiyah was finishing her journal entry, Faith emerged from the bathroom after washing her hair in a really long, hot shower.

"By the way," Faith said shaking the towel from her head, "what's Elijah saying anyway now that you know for sure you're havin' a baby?"

Naiyah said nothing for a few moments while Faith threw on a pair of sweats and a t-shirt and began towel drying her hair. "Damn Lijah, he can go to hell," responded Naiyah testily. After the calming peace of writing to her YaYa, the last thing she wanted to do was think about Mr. Elijah McCoy.

"Whoa! I didn't expect that response," Faith shot back. Then seeing that Naiyah was really upset, Faith moved closer. "Hold up, Izzy, what's going on?" she asked softly.

"Nothing," Naiyah replied.

"Don't tell me nothing, did Elijah say somethin' to you?" Faith asked angrily. "I heard the frustration in your voice the other day when you were talking to him."

"No, not really, he just wanted to know how I was so sure the baby was his."

"He asked you that?"

"As sure as I'm sitting here, he sure did."

"What did you say?"

"What could I say? I mean, he was calling my integrity into question. I may be a lot of things, but I'm not a liar and, besides, I didn't see a reason to try and offer any defense."

"Who else does he think you were with?"

"Faith, please, he knows I wasn't sleeping with anyone else."

"So, why did he ask you that?"

"I don't know, maybe because we only saw each other a few times over the summer. To make matters worse, he told me he's with someone else now."

"Oh God, ain't he a bow-wow," Faith said, starting to bark like a big dog.

"Faith, you know he's not a dog. There's a lot at stake for him right now." Naiyah got up to put her journal away. She hoped Faith would take the hint that she didn't want to talk about it. However, as usual, Faith kept right on talking. "Oh, so you won't defend your own reputation, but you'll defend his, what's up with that?" Faith asked, staring at Naiyah like she was some kind of new fool. "I don't think I'm defending him. He does have a lot on the line. He plans to start law school just as soon as he finishes his fellowship."

"So?" Faith shrugged and stared at her.

"So," Naiyah replied staring back, "he's getting on with his life nicely and my telling him I was pregnant with his child probably scared him."

"He wasn't scared when he laid down and did what grown folks do to get a baby, so please spare me, Izzy," she said.

Naiyah got up and left the room. She needed more tea. "It was hard enough dealing with Elijah, so don't you start on me too," she said shouting back over her shoulder.

"I won't start on you, but just remember, you're the one who has to deal with this situation and from where I'm sitting, you need to be starting with your health and that of your unborn child. You haven't had one prenatal visit since you dipped that stick three months ago, and drinkin' alcohol too, you think I don't know about that. But the kicker is, you're still snortin' cocaine." Naiyah looked across the room at Faith with wide-eyed amazement, like a deer caught in the headlights and wondered how in the world she knew about the coke. She thought she was being discreet. "I'm having more tea," Naiyah said slowly, "want some?"

"With or without the bourbon?" Faith replied.

"What's up Faith?" Naiyah was noticeably annoyed with a flushed look creeping up her face. "Are you spying on me?"

"No, I don't have to do that, because you, sweetheart, aren't as slick as you think. With as much as you drink, I can't believe you can still function, not to mention the harm you're doing to that innocent baby."

"So why didn't you say anything before now, and," she said smugly, "I happen to drink top-shelf cognac not rot-gut bourbon."

Faith rolled her eyes, ignoring Naiyah's stupid and inappropriate remark. "Look, I'm not trying to get in your business, especially since you function so well for an alcoholic in denial, but that unborn child is innocent and can't speak for itself. You need to get yourself together for that baby and it needs to be soon."

Naiyah flinched at Faith's words and began to feel uneasy. In so many words she had just been called a functioning alcoholic. What she thought was her secret had been exposed. Now, on top of everything else, she'd have to deal with her drinking and cocaine abuse out in the open. She wasn't ready for that. She poured more cognac from a near empty liter bottle of Remy Martin, but this time left the bottle on the counter and walked over to the sofa where Faith was sitting with her feet propped up on their glass-topped table, twisting her damp shoulder-length natural hair that gleamed with the color of rich henna.

Without looking at her, Faith said to Naiyah, "Honey, you know we're home girls and I care about you. We've been hangin' for almost four years and I sense you've been hurtin', runnin' and hidin' a long time now. Look at you in that great big ole shirt with your boney behind." Faith pointed accusingly at Naiyah's oversized Stanford t-shirt. "What are you tryin' to hide? You're barely showing."

"I don't know, perhaps I am a liar, thinking that if people can't see the baby growing, I can pretend it isn't there."

"That's ridiculous."

"I know it is, but fear and shame aren't rational, are they?" Naiyah said sarcastically.

"I'm not religious," Faith said, "but I hear my Mama say all the time, God hasn't given us a spirit of fear. I imagine if He hasn't given you fear, He hasn't given you a spirit of shame either."

"Hum," said Naiyah, "that sounds familiar."

"What do you mean?" Faith asked.

"Spirits of fear and shame, that sounds like something my YaYa would say whenever she talked about spiritual warfare. She said an enemy of our soul comes against us, planting accusations in our minds. If we're not strong enough to stand against him, we'll believe the lie and start living our lives defeated."

"I'm not very religious," Faith said again, "but that makes sense to me."

"Yeah, me too, it makes more sense to me now than when she first told me. I'll have to think about that some more later." Naiyah nestled into the small sofa and silently sipped her tea.

Faith cut her eyes at her. "I guess nothing we said resonated with you, did it?" Naiyah remained quiet, focusing instead on the amber liquid in her cup, and once more the absence and loss of YaYa enveloped her in an emotional blanket of despair, which unlike everything else, felt familiar. After a long silence, Naiyah finally said, "It's not as remarkable as you think," referring to Faith's earlier comment about her functioning under the influence. "If I hadn't gotten my major courses out of the way early on, taking anything heavier than the electives I have left, I'm not so sure I'd be graduating this spring."

"Do you have a plan yet?" Faith asked. Naiyah shook her head no. "Don't worry, if I know anything about you, it's that you've given this situation a lot of thought. Fear may hold you in its vise for a minute, but you're too smart and savvy to be knocked off course by something like this. Just know, girlfriend, I've got your back. I'm here for you whenever you need me."

Naiyah placed the teacup on the table and reached over and hugged Faith tight. Maybe she'd found another true friend after all.

II

Something's Not Right

"*Hi B.B.,*" D'yanna called out slipping her arms around Elijah's neck. B.B. was short for Baby Boy, the pet name she called him. Startled, Elijah removed D'yanna's arms. He wasn't in the mood for her today. "I didn't hear you come in," he said.

"I guess not, you were far away, deep in thought when I let myself in. Is everything all right?"

"Everything's cool, I'm just dealing with some news I got yesterday. It's about one of my friends and it's pretty heavy." He felt like a fraud but couldn't tell D'yanna about Naiyah, at least not before trying to make sense of it for himself.

"Do you want to talk about it?" D'yanna inquired softly.

"No, I can't," he said.

"Okay, then put your worries aside, because today's the day we go to Manhattan to shop for my ring, isn't it?" D'yanna smiled sweetly at Elijah. She couldn't wait to be his wife.

"Yes, sweetheart," he said as a huge smile spread across his smooth, dark, handsomely chiseled face. "Just let me tend to a few things and I'll be with you directly. I don't know why we have to go all the way to Manhattan to buy your ring," he said. "What's wrong with the jewelers right here in Brooklyn?" D'yanna watched Elijah, his long legs covering the space from the living room to his office down the hall in a few quick strides. *Hmm,* she thought, *I love how he be soundin' all lawyerish and such. He's gonna be one mean, off, the-chain-brotha, defendin' folks better'n' Johnnie Cochran ever could.'*

When Elijah returned, he interrupted her reverie, "Sweetheart, I love you," he said, planting a luscious kiss on her lips with just a sliver of tongue for added spice. "When you become my wife, everything you want in this world will be yours, nothing will be withheld from you—ever, if I have anything to do with it." D'yanna wrapped her arms around his broad shoulders and returned his kiss with a more passionate kiss of her own. Perspiration beads quickly formed over his top lip and forehead. "Baby please," he moaned.

"What, don't you like my kisses?" D'yanna asked innocently. She knew the effect she had on Elijah and she planned on reminding him of it every day.

"Oh yes, I do," he said taking a step backward, "but you're making me feel like Mt. Vesuvius. I'm coming to a fast boil," Elijah chuckled.

"And your point?" D'yanna asked, slowly moving her hips into his.

"Do you want to go shopping or shall we, um, let's just say put out the fire?"

"Why not both?" she replied seductively.

"Girl, you better watch yourself, you better be careful," Elijah said playfully while licking his lips and grabbing at her behind. She side-stepped him lithely, strutting her long, lean sexy legs over to a large chocolate leather club chair to sit down. She'd worn stilettos and a white jersey wrap dress that left little to the imagination. When she crossed her legs, Elijah glimpsed her inner thighs and felt the fire erupt like a bolt of lightning in his groin. An almost inaudible moan sailed into the air with his released breath. Without looking, he knew his lieutenant was standing at full attention. All he could manage was, "Girl, don't play with me."

"Mmmmm," she said purring like a kitten, "I can't wait to go to Manhattan and Tiffany's. When we get back, I intend to do a lot more than play with you."

Elijah stared at D'yanna for a long moment contemplating his next move. Finally, he decided. "We'll see, Dee, I do have quite a bit of work to do this weekend."

"I know, but you never had any trouble squeezing me in before," D'yanna pouted sexily.

Elijah's head began throbbing at the temples and he wondered if D'yanna could see their rapid movement. He so wanted to lay her down, place kisses all over her body and hear her impassioned screams for more, but he was too distracted from the phone call he received from Naiyah the day before to act and it extinguished any desire on his part.

"Okay then. Let's go" D'yanna said, standing up and readjusting her dress. *Damn, she's fine!* Elijah thought. At the same time, D'yanna began tugging him towards the door, the phone rang. "Hold up, sweetheart," he said, freeing himself from her grasp, "let me get that."

"Elijah. It's me," said a woman's voice over the phone.

"Hello Mother," he said as he perched on the arm of the club chair. "What?" Elijah exclaimed. "When—is he alright? No, its okay, let me adjust my schedule and I'll meet you over there in about thirty minutes."

Having heard Elijah's side of the conversation, D'yanna knew that Tiffany's would be put off for another day. She waited for him to hang up. "So?" she asked anxiously.

"My father's been taken to New York Methodist Hospital. He was having palpitations and his heartbeat was irregular. My mother said she wasn't taking any chances. I'm sorry, sweetheart, but I've got to go."

"Awwh Elijah, I had my heart set on this trip."

"Yes, but my father's in the hospital and my mother's alone and very upset. I have to go." Elijah grabbed his keys and wallet as he hurriedly walked towards the door.

D'yanna nearly ran to keep up with him.

"Was it a heart attack?" she asked.

"D'YANNA! Stop it, I don't know yet and it doesn't matter. I'll call you later when I get a minute and have something to report. Stop pouting, after all, we haven't even set the date yet and who's to say we were going to find something you liked today anyway." *Arrggh, she could be so frustrating at times,* he thought.

"Okay, alright already," she snapped, "but can we go tomorrow?"

"Dee, you know I don't do stores on Sunday. Chill, baby, Tiffany's isn't going anywhere and neither am I." Elijah kissed D'yanna on the cheek, walked her to her car and quickly took off for the hospital.

Elijah decided to take the subway rather than pulling his car from the garage and hassling with parking. Besides, parking in the city was a big headache. His intention was to have his mother drive him back later anyway so he thought it best to leave the driving to someone else while he focused on what to do, now that Naiyah was carrying his child. *Oh hell, sorry, Lord, but what am I going to do now?* He wondered. Elijah took the F train to Seventh Avenue and headed to the hospital on Sixth Street. "Mother," he said softly while taking the seat next to her, "I'm here."

Her eyes fluttered open as he reassuringly placed his hand on her arm. "Oh baby, I'm so glad you came right over. Your father really gave me a scare. He's comfortable now and the doctors don't think it was a heart attack but they're still running additional diagnostic tests."

"What are they doing?" he asked.

"They said they'd start with an angiography to look for any build-ups or blockages in his arteries."

"So what happened?" Elijah asked.

"Okay," Esther McCoy began, "he was reading the paper after breakfast while I was clearing away breakfast dishes and making up the menu for tonight's supper. The next thing I knew he was calling my name. Not real loud, but it sounded like he was straining, so I dropped what I was doing and rushed in. When I reached the living room, he was sitting on the edge of the sofa holding his chest and gasping for air all at the same time. Baby, I didn't know what to do, I couldn't remember one thing I learned in that CPR class, so I called the paramedics. I laid him down, prayed for the Lord to please help him and just held his hand till they came."

A few minutes later, a slight, handsome man approached them.

"Excuse me, Mrs. McCoy, I'm Dr. Mittros. I've examined your husband and he's resting comfortably now. He had another incident of constricting pain so we gave him a dose of percoset. We're hoping to do a stress echocardiogram, but at the moment he doesn't have the strength to get on the treadmill. So we may have to do an echocardiogram pharmacologically."

"Have you detected any plaque build-up or other blockages?" asked Elijah. "We haven't received the results from the screenings yet," the doctor answered.

"What if his arteries are blocked?" Elijah continued.

"We'd then do a coronary angioplasty to open them up," Dr. Mittros explained. Esther tightened her grip on Elijah's hand. Fear and uncertainty shone through her dark eyes. Fixing a steady gaze on Dr. Mittros, she asked, "Are you sure he's alright? Will he have to stay here over night?"

"Yes, Mrs. McCoy, let me assure you that, although your husband has experienced some trauma and may continue to experience some discomfort, the chest pain he reports is really quite common. However, it's a good thing you brought him right in. If his chest tightening and pain symptoms were left unchecked, he might very well have had a heart attack. As for him staying overnight, we're still not sure. As soon as we know more, we'll let you know." Both Esther and Elijah remained silent as they watched the doctor walk past the nurse's station, down a long, brightly lit corridor and disappear around a corner. After several moments of silence, Esther finally said, "I know your father's going to take his diet serious now and cut out all those heavily processed, high in cholesterol foods, he eats."

"Yeah, you think," responded Elijah, staring ahead absent-mindedly.

"Baby, is something on your mind?" Mrs. McCoy asked. Elijah continued staring straight ahead. "Eli," she said nudging him, "what's wrong, are things okay with you and D'yanna?"

"Oh yeah," he said brightening up some. "We were on our way to Tiffany's when I got your call."

"Umm, I'm sorry," she said. "Oh wait now, how on earth can you afford Tiffany's? You're not a member of the bar yet and it'll be at least two years before you have a JD in your hands."

"Mother, don't be gettin' all up in my Kool-Aid when you don't know the flava," he said bobbing his head from side to side. This brief jest lightened their mood and they both fell out laughing, but not for long. Esther knew her son like the back of her hand and she could tell something wasn't right.

III

Holla Back

"*Izzy,* girl where are you, with your scandalous self," Nathan laughed into the answering machine after Naiyah failed to pick up. "I'm just playing. Don't get all riled up or go ballistic on me. It's just been a minute since we talked and I miss you, Sis. I'm callin' 'cause I want to know if you'll be coming home for the Thanksgiving holiday, so holla back." As soon as Nathan hung up the phone, a knock came at the door. "Oh Chad, what's going on, Boo?" Nathan asked walking with an embellished feminine stride back to his design table. "Nothing much, just felt like looking at something or someone pretty today," Chad sighed.

"Oh, and I crossed your mind? I'm flattered," Nathan responded sarcastically.

Chad looked at Nathan, ignoring his smart remark, "You're pretty, aren't you?" he asked.

Nathan fluttered his eyelids coyly, "So they say," he chuckled.

"No, really Chad, what do you want, 'cause you and I both know you can't handle any of this," he said, raising his right hand with dramatic flair, sweeping it from head to toe, with a slight and fluid bend of the hips.

"Stop teasing, I'm not up for it today," Chad said in a whiny voice.

"Oh my, Boo, aren't we being testy? What's wrong, baby, did your boy toy stand you up for a girl again?"

"Go to hell," Chad said sucking his teeth with noticeable irritation.

"You go first," Nathan snorted.

Chad kicked back on Nathan's bed and leafed, without much interest, through the November issue of *Fashion* magazine. "Who's this model, Shalom Harlow?" he asked. "I don't think she's very pretty and she's way too thin," he said.

"Yes, perhaps, "Nathan replied, without turning around, "but look at the simply exquisite design of the coat she's wearing, which costs only a mere forty-five grand."

"Oh," Chad said, still not in the least bit impressed. "Why do you have the Canadian version," he wanted to know.

"Actually, that magazine is only published in Canada," Nathan replied.

"So, again, why do you have it?"

"Who knows, maybe one day I'll have a collection in the Toronto shows," Nathan ventured, more as a matter of fact.

"You know, Nathan," Chad said, now sitting up straight, "seriously, you're an odd character."

"Thanks, I couldn't agree more," he replied, taking no offense.

"No really, you're so girly, designing clothes, *and* the way you dress, so impeccable," he said.

"Wow," interrupted Nathan, "so the *man* has a vocabulary."

"But really Nathan," Chad said, still looking through the magazine, how is it you can be so girly actin' and not be homosexual or at least bi?"

Just as serious, Nathan said, "Now you're getting in my business, Chad, and *my* business is my business, and the way I live my life damn sure is my business, but like I said before, I do fashion, I don't experiment like that. Now, in case you hadn't noticed," he continued, "there's a certain flava in the fashion industry, especially here in Miami. So I'm just gettin' in wherever I can fit in," he added.

"Oh," Chad said, fixing his eyes on Nathan. "So you want people to think you got a little sugar 'cause maybe if they do, you might attract some notoriety. So, it's all just part of the business plan. Is that what you're sayin'?" he asked.

"Now I think you got it, Chad."

"That's one pitiful use of a stereotype, Nathan. And why would you want to act like something you're not?"

"Because I love fashion and soft frilly things, that's why. I love how clothes are designed with feminine constructs, my style's fierce, and to top it off, I'm a complete drama queen," he laughed. "What I'm not is gay, but as I said, I do want a successful career in this business so I'm doing whatever it takes to realize my dream."

Wading in deeper, Chad asked cautiously, "have you ever been with a guy?"

"You're getting pretty deep and personal, Chad, and it's all good, but no, I've never been with a guy, but I will say, I am a little curious," Nathan said smiling nervously. "Admittedly," he continued, without reservation, "the heat and smell of testosterone has been known to excite me once or twice."

"So then," Chad pressed, "do you fantasize about guys?"

"I said I'm curious, the thought has crossed my mind, but no, I don't have fantasies and no, I'm not asexual either, I don't let myself go there. My G-Ma was a strong Christian woman who was a huge influence in my and my sister Naiyah's lives. She made sure we knew about Jesus. The Bible says the lifestyle you refer to, is sinful and I'm not lookin' for hell, so I don't mess around," he laughed.

"I've had affairs with guys, but I'm no homosexual," Chad replied confidently. "I'm a good person with a good heart, I don't believe in all that hell and damnation stuff."

"That's your prerogative; I'm just sayin', my G-Ma taught me from the scriptures, I believe it—simple as that."

"So, what if your grandmother didn't tell you it was sinful, would you have crossed over and experimented by now?"

"Are you suggesting it's a lifestyle choice?" Nathan quickly replied.

"I guess the way I phrased it, you might think I'm sayin' that, but even though I chose to have my affairs, I don't think I'm on one side or the other of that argument. What do you think?" he asked.

"Really, Chad, I don't know," Nathan said, sighing heavily, now growing tired of the conversation. "I haven't given it much thought."

"Okay, one last question," Chad said, now standing with his chest all puffed up, as if he'd gained some leverage, "you said the Bible says homosexuality is sinful, but did JC really say it?" Chad asked, looking at Nathan, who now had a look of bewilderment plastered on his face.

IV

Lackluster Diamond

Nathan spoke into the cordless phone receiver, "Hi Mum," he said as he moved about the room tidying up.

"Nathaniel, honey, how nice of you to call," Jade said.

He stood up straight feeling himself cringe just a little inside at the sound of her voice coming from the other end of the line. *Nathaniel, what a nice name,* he thought, *it just don't work for me, too damn straight, um, rather, stiff—mental note, check yourself, Nathan, let's not have any Freudian slips.* "How're things, Mum, everything okay?" he asked.

"Well, I'm keeping myself busy if that's what you mean. I've got several projects going, orders for gowns for the upcoming Christmas and New Year's galas, and I've also taken on a few new tutoring assignments."

"So you are busy," he said listening intently for any sign that she might not be doing okay. "I called Izzy a few days ago, but I haven't heard back from her yet. Have you heard from her?"

"No, not lately, I've only spoken to her once since she returned to school, but she's been in touch with your father, so that's good. I think they've talked a few times."

"How is Poppy?"

"He's still a whoremonger and adulterer, so I guess *he's* fine."

"Mum," Nathan said feigning surprise. Though he'd heard it before, he still expected his mother to speak with a little more decorum, regardless of how she felt.

"Well, what do you want me to say?" she asked defensively.

"Maybe that you're sayin' a prayer for him or somethin', that negative vibe's going to kill you, you know, while he keeps right on about his business."

Jade grew silent and walked over to the chrome and glass liquor cart she kept in the kitchen. As Nathan chatted away, she picked up the bottle of Belvedere and poured herself a shot of straight vodka into a highball glass.

"Mum, are you smoking?"

She took a sip of the vodka, swallowing it along with the smoke from her cigarette. "Yes, I'm smoking."

"What else are you doing?"

"Nathaniel, you are my little darling, but I don't answer to you. In fact, last time I checked, I was still your mother."

"Sorry, Mum, I can't help worrying about you, especially now that you're all alone. I want you to be safe and happy, that's all," he said earnestly.

"It's coming, honey, go on now, don't worry about your Mama. I'm Jade Diamond and, like the brilliance my name implies, you'll see, I will shine again."

Changing the subject, Nathan asked, "Are you planning to make Thanksgiving dinner? I was hoping to come home, give you an enormous hug, catch up and maybe kick it with a few of my friends."

"You know what honey that sounds like a good idea," Jade said brightly. "I hadn't even given Thanksgiving a thought. So good, let's make it a plan. When were you planning to arrive?"

"Mum, you know I don't have any money," he said. "I need a plane ticket out there and back and was hoping you'd fly me into MacArthur and back to Miami International."

"What's your schedule looking like?" she asked with enthusiasm.

"I can come anytime Wednesday and stay till Sunday evening."

"Wonderful. I'll make the airline reservations and call you back with the details. Honey, this is really great, I'm looking forward to seeing you. We'll make this Thanksgiving special, you'll see," she said again.

"Okay, I'll keep trying to reach Izzy. It'll be great if she can come too."

"Yes, please. It would be nice to have both my children home together. That would please me immensely."

Nathan felt his mother's heart leap, imagined the smile on her face and couldn't help but smile himself.

Jade began to hum as she started making lists. She started first on the menu then the guest list. *This will really be good for me* she thought, *perhaps the genesis of my reinvention, who knows.* She busied herself for much of the morning making plans to celebrate.

"Hello, Turquoise? Hi," she said again, "it's Jade."

"My Sissy Jade, it can't be, girl, what's going on, where've you been?"

Her sister's rapid fire questions took Jade's breath away. Aqua or Qua, as she insisted on being called, always seemed to swallow up all the air because she talked so much.

"I've been here," Jade replied.

"Well, who knew, it seems like ages since we've heard anything from your side of the globe."

"It's been a little rough the last few years. You know the trouble Lemuel and I are having, but I didn't call to rehash all of that," she added quickly. "I just finished speaking to Nathaniel. He wants to come home for Thanksgiving and suggested I have Thanksgiving dinner here. I was hoping you hadn't already made your plans and that it's not too late to invite you and your family to come."

"That sounds fabulous, J. Let me check in and I'll call you back."

"How's Johann," Jade wanted to know.

"You know Jon, he's groovin'. We're doing splendid actually."

"And my darling niece?" Jade asked.

"Sequoia, my impressive young lady, is doing great. She's considering her options for college. UC Berkley would be a free ride for her since both her father and I teach there, but she has her own mind, so we'll see. Where's my girl Izzy? She hasn't called me lately."

"I don't know. I was just telling Nathaniel this morning that I hadn't heard from her since she went back to school."

"Really, is anything the matter?" Aqua asked, hopeful that nothing was.

"Not that I'm aware of," Jade said.

"Hmmm," she responded thoughtfully with one raised eyebrow.

"Aqua, I was hoping if you all could make it, that maybe you could check in with Naiyah and arrange somehow to bring her with you."

"Okay Sissy, this sounds good. I hope Jon is down for it. I'll make some phone calls and call you back. How long would you like us to stay?"

"As long as you'd like, I'd really enjoy having the company," Jade said. "Alright—okay, call me back. I love you, sweetheart, bye."

"Bye Sissy, I'm so glad you called."

"Me too," she said smiling.

Jade felt really warm inside for the first time in a long time. "Thank you, Lord" she said out loud, "I will live." It wasn't until she mouthed that tiny breath of a prayer that she realized her life had been placed on hold, probably since the moment Lemuel moved in with that woman.

She went to the refrigerator, rested her glass in the holder under the ice maker and effortlessly pushed the gleaming stainless steel button to dispense the cubes. Several cubes tumbled into her glass and the loud crashing immediately irritated her, setting her nerves on edge. She abruptly released the button and rushed back to the liquor cart to pour another drink.

"I need to calm my nerves," she told herself. "Okay ole girl, don't lose your momentum. You know how you do." She laughed, "Yeah, how I do." She reflected on how easily, of late, she seemed to lose focus. In what seemed like the space of only a few moments, Jade was coaxed into awareness by the ringing of her doorbell. She looked at her watch and noticed dusk had replaced the splendid sunshine of the morning.

"Oh heck," she whispered ignoring the ringing doorbell, "I've gone and slept through an entire day and have managed to be unprepared for my tutoring session," she said, now quite perturbed. "I'm getting too old for this nonsense." Next, the phone began to ring. "Hello," she managed weakly.

"Mrs. Harland," her student said, "I'm sitting in your driveway with my mom. We thought we'd try your phone, when you didn't answer the door."

"Oh honey, I'm so sorry. It seems I had the worst migraine today, worse than I've ever had. I took something earlier which must have knocked me out. Please apologize to your mother. Give me a few minutes to get myself together and I'll be down to let you in," she lied.

Getting down on all fours, she crawled into the kitchen to deposit the now empty glass into the dishwasher. She then crawled into the foyer hoping that her silhouette could not be seen as she mounted the stairs, still on all fours. "This is some real doodoo dang caca. What in heaven's name am I, Jade Diamond Harland, doing crawling around on a freakin' floor?" she whispered. *Girl, who you tellin'?* came a voice from inside her head. *You better handle it baby the voice continued, or else your business is going to be all out on Front Street.*

V

Going Home

"*Izzy,* someone by the name of Aqua called for you this afternoon. She said she was your aunt and wants you to call her back—it sounded kind of urgent," Faith called out to Naiyah when she heard her come in the room.

"Thanks, Faith, I'll call her in a bit." Naiyah wondered why all of a sudden her Aunt Turquoise was calling and why Nathan, whose call she still hadn't returned, had called as well. *I better call one of them soon,* she thought, *or they'll start worrying.* Noting the lateness of the hour, she thought aloud, "Qua won't mind me calling this late. Auntie Aqua, hey, it's Naiyah."

"Hey Butterfly, thanks for calling back right away. I spoke with your Mum and she seems a little uneasy. What's up, why haven't you called her? You were raised better and I know you know better."

"Auntie, it's senior year," she said. "I'm almost through and tryin' to keep a steady pace."

"Izzy, there's no excuse good enough, that's your Mum."

"Yes Ma'am, I know."

"Then act like it. You know it's been rough on her, especially now that you and Nathan are both away at school. I don't know what the issues are, but whatever they are, squash em, she's your family and could use your support, I'm sure," Aqua said.

Naiyah nodded her head as she sat in the darkened living room listening to classical music on KPSC 88.5 FM.

"Do you hear me talking to you, Izzy?"

"Yes Auntie, I hear you."

"Good! Anyway, when I spoke to your Mum yesterday, she and Nathan had just gotten off the phone with each other. He's going home for Thanksgiving and of course Jade's very excited."

Of course, Naiyah thought sarcastically. "That's nice," she said.

"Yes and she's invited us to come too, a mini vacation—family reunion, sort of thing."

"Out on Long Island in November, come on, Auntie, I don't think so."

"Well, we think it's a great idea and we're excited too. Uncle Jon, Sequoia and I've decided to go. We think it'll be fun. Your mom asked us to bring you with us, that's if you can get away."

Naiyah felt her heart stand still, sheer panic coursing through her. *Oh God, I'm not prepared to tell Mum about this baby.*

"NAIYAH," shouted Turquoise, "what's going on? Why do you keep withdrawing and going silent on me, and furthermore, why have you lost touch with your mother and brother?"

"Nothing Auntie, I'm cool. I told you its senior year, that's all."

"No baby girl, I get the sense it's much more than that. When would be a good time to pick you up for lunch tomorrow? I'm coming over there. I need to put my eyes on you, because something's not right."

"No Auntie, really, everything's good, I'm cool," Naiyah said a little too anxiously.

"Good, I'll see for myself tomorrow. Good night, Naiyah."

Turquoise hung up without giving Naiyah a chance to say anything else in protest. *Oh hell,* she thought, *what now?*

Bending down low to meet the table and the lines of coke she laid down before placing the call to Turquoise, Naiyah then snorted one up into her anxiously awaiting nostril. As she closed her eyes, easing back and resting her head on the sofa, she felt her breathing begin a slow return to its normal rhythm. "I'm sorry, little one, I really am. Lord knows I don't want to turn you over to unsuspecting adoptive parents with some lame birth defect," she whispered.

November 14, 2002

My Dear and Beloved YaYa,

It started because I wanted relief from my fear and pain, but now I need relief from the relief. That sounds absurd, downright crazy I know. My Aunt Aqua senses something is going on with me. She's coming to campus tomorrow to see for herself. When she sees me, she'll know immediately that I'm pregnant. I don't know what to do. I didn't expect to tell any of them so soon. YaYa, I feel your presence with me. Is it true that Jesus prays to the Father for us? Will you pray to Him and ask Him to pray for me? I believe if you were here, you'd say to me, 'Butterfly, consider all your options, count the cost, and then make whatever choice is right.' I think you'd also say to be sure that my yes is yes and my no is no, or more precisely, 'make my words few but truthful.' I'll have to tell them about the baby, of course, but there's no way I can tell them I'm using, they wouldn't understand. I've thought about raising this baby, but what a frightening prospect that is, especially the idea of doing it alone. Adoption is a good choice and I'm sure Elijah will be relieved; he's the baby's father. He's really a sweet man and responsible too, usually. You'd like him, I'm sure.

Well, my beloved, I've got to get ready to face the wrath of Qua. Lord help me!

I love you and miss you more, YaYa.

Your loving Granddaughter, Izzy

❦

Shuffling into the kitchen while wiping sleep away from her eyes, Faith looked at Naiyah, blinked hard and looked again. "What are you doing up? You don't have a class, I know, and I can't remember the last time I passed you at seven in the mornin'."

Frowning, Naiyah wrapped her hands around the coffee mug in front of her, trying to remove the slight chill in her fingers. "I've got trouble."

"What's the matter?" Faith asked.

"My Aunt Aqua is coming today to take me to lunch," Naiyah replied.

"She is?"

"Yeah, she is."

"Does she know about the baby?"

"Not yet."

"Is she cool?"

"Oh yeah, she's cool, the coolest, but no matter what, this isn't going to sit well with her, not at all."

"Oh," said Faith sleepily pouring herself a cup of coffee. "Will she trip the same way you think your mom's going to?"

"No, I don't think so. Mum will be upset mainly because of appearances, not the fact that I'm having a child out of wedlock. My Auntie, she'll be disappointed because of school, thinking it'll be a setback for me."

"Do you want me to come?" Faith asked taking the seat next to her.

"Could you?"

"I will if you want me to."

Thinking better of it, Naiyah said, "Thanks for offering, roomie, but I probably should do this in private so she's free to express her disappointment however she wants."

"Alright, honey, have it your way, but I'm here just like I said," Faith reassured her.

A few hours later, freshly showered and dressed, Naiyah answered the phone.

"Izzy, I'm downstairs," Turquoise said, speaking into the mouthpiece of her mobile phone. "Should I come up?"

"No Auntie, I'll be right down." Naiyah felt the heat of perspiration rise from her chest to meet her face and her stomach felt like little people were inside stomping around, tying things into tight little knots. She was nervous and didn't seem able to will her feet to move her to the door. *I don't want to do this,* she thought. Opening the door to Turquoise's shiny black, gold trimmed Pathfinder, she peered in. "Hi, Aunt Aqua," she said stepping onto the runner and heaving herself up onto the long seat. As she leaned over and kissed her aunt on the check, Turquoise turned and kissed her back on the lips.

"Where do you want to eat?"

"We can go to Ruby Tuesday's, if that's okay," Naiyah said as they navigated down her narrow street.

"That sounds fine to me." After a moment, Turquoise said, "How about Janoon East's instead, I haven't had good Indian food in a while, and you eat Indian, don't you Izzy?"

Reflexively, Naiyah covered her mouth the same way she would if she were about to throw up. Just the thought of smelling all the spices set her stomach to churning again. "That'll be nice," was all she could manage.

"How ya been doing?" Aqua asked. "I want you to know," she continued, "I was somewhat alarmed when Jade told me she hadn't heard from you in a minute. At least now I can report that you're well, even though you look a tad bit worn."

"I haven't been getting proper rest lately and, sad to say, I've been eating on the run, but like I told you last night, I'm fine."

"Ummm, eating on the run, girl, from the looks of you, it doesn't look like you're eating at all. Your face seems much thinner and your skin isn't as bright and vibrant as usual," she said glancing over at Naiyah and, without skipping a beat, asked, "How do I get to Janoon's from here? I go straight down campus to Palm Drive, right?"

After arriving at the restaurant, out the corner of her eye, Naiyah caught her aunt checking her out from head to toe as they waited for the hostess to show them to their table.

"It seems comfortable in here to me. Are you cold, Izzy?" Aqua asked.

"No Auntie, I'm comfortable," she replied.

"Why not take your coat off then?"

"I will, in a minute."

Okay Turquoise thought, *I'm going to leave that one alone. If she wants to sit up here with her coat on, so be it.* "Well anyway, Butterfly, whatcha gonna do after graduation?"

Naiyah let the question dangle in midair. "My YaYa always called me Butterfly," she said. "I miss her and feel so lost without her."

"Oh sweetheart, I'm sorry, I didn't mean to make you sad," she said staring at Naiyah from across the table.

"I am, Auntie Aqua, I am sad. Nobody in this whole wide world loved me like my YaYa loved me and no one understands me like she did. Every day I wake up, I hurt knowing she's not here."

"Baby, that's not good. Does Jade know what you're going through?" she asked raising her eyebrows with concern.

Raising a finger in the air, Naiyah said, "Wait, let me see, three things occupy Jade's world—Lucky, Nathan and vodka. No, four, and that's what anyone thinks of the world they spin in."

"Naiyah, that's not true and you know it," Aunt Aqua replied vehemently, though she silently agreed with Naiyah's assertion.

"It is true. With all due respect, Auntie, you don't know, you haven't been there."

"Is that what you're mad at your mom about?"

"I'm not mad, really, I just feel sorry for her. When Lucky checked out on her, she checked out on herself. And Nathan and alcohol are the drugs she anesthetizes herself with."

"What became yours?" Aunt Aqua asked ignoring the implication just made.

"My what?" Naiyah replied, puzzled by her aunt's question.

"Your drug? If what you say is true, then certainly you must feel abandoned by both your mom and grandmom. Feeling shut out and losing your grandmother, must have messed with your ability to cope as well. You must have needed something too," she said.

Without warning, the floodgates opened and the hurt Naiyah had successfully, or so she thought, covered in drugs, alcohol and sex for the last four years erupted and poured out like a waterfall.

Turquoise didn't move. She sensed that Naiyah was full and just let her be until she was spent.

"I can't go on," Naiyah said finally. "I'm tired, I can't go backwards and I don't know how to move forward."

Turquoise looked into Naiyah's eyes. "Let's start by going home for Thanksgiving."

"I can't."

"What do you mean you can't go home? Regardless of how you may feel, Naiyah, your mother loves you, so don't punish her for her short-comings. This could be a new beginning, not to mention how much there is to be thankful for."

"I'm pregnant," Naiyah blurted out.

Turquoise quickly waved over their passing waitress, "Please bring me a Jack Daniel's from the bar, straight up, no chaser." When the wait-ress had left, without words, Turquoise stood, moved over to her niece and cradled her head and neck in a long, loving embrace. Kissing her on the top of her head, she let go and stepped back. "You must go home" she said. "Now that we're past that, let's take this from the beginning."

As they ate, Naiyah poured her soul out to her aunt, telling her about the dreams and about Elijah. She left out the details of the drugs and alcohol.

"Do you love him?"

Naiyah palmed her head with her right hand, breathed in deeply and, with a whistle, released a long stream of air. "Elijah McCoy is every woman's dream, Auntie Aqua, but I don't have a clue how to love him."

"Does he love you?" she asked.

"No, he couldn't, he doesn't trust me." When a puzzled look crossed her aunt's face, Naiyah quickly said, "Oh no, it's not that he thinks I'm loose and easy, he says it's because I'm emotionally unstable."

"Oh, you know what, Izzy, this is one hot mess." Turquoise lifted her Jack Daniel's, gulped it down, sat back and just stared across the table at her niece. She was lost for words and brokenhearted from the disappointment and pain that was now torching her heart. Looking at her niece, Turquoise saw a light being extinguished. *Her Naiyah was* competitive in everything. It didn't matter if she was jumping in a horse show, checkmating someone in a chess match, out-stroking someone in a swimming competition, or tearing up the dance floor with the latest dance steps, Naiyah excelled. The Naiyah sitting across from her at this moment seemed like an absent, lifeless shell. *Where'd this chick come from?* she wondered. Finally, Turquoise spoke, "You not knowing how to love, that's ridiculous. Of course you know how to love. Naiyah, you're a sweet, loving girl. You always have been."

With her head lowered, Naiyah whispered, "I was Auntie, but now I feel soiled. In the years since my YaYa left me, I haven't gone to church, I don't pray much anymore and I've been in some really strange places."

"Naiyah, look at me! If you don't know or remember anything else— you need to know that Big Sadie is right there," Turquoise said reaching over and touching the place where Naiyah's heart rested. "Her spirit lives within you." Turquoise took a moment to exhale, dabbing at her eyes which were now full of unshed tears. It was too much for her to handle seeing her niece, who had always brought her great joy, in this state. "I'll get your ticket today, so when you get back to the apartment start getting your things together. Do you want me to prepare Jade? Let me know if you do."

VI

And Baby Makes Four

Hearing movement in the kitchen, Esther McCoy knew Elijah had let himself in with the in case of emergency key. *When left unchecked, folks will sure take liberties,* she thought. Dropping the crossword puzzle she was working on into her favorite Pier 1 woven basket at the foot of the sofa, Esther went in to greet her son. "Hey there, Mr. Eli," she said looking over his shoulder and, without hesitation, added "where's D'yanna?"

The deep creases appearing on her otherwise smooth cocoa brown forehead immediately told him he couldn't hedge much longer. "Mother," he said, moving towards her with the swift rhythmic precision of a West Point cadet, "how are things around here?" He punctuated the question by delivering a quick kiss to her cheek.

"Things are pretty much quiet, but we'll get to that. Now answer my question. We haven't seen or heard anything about D'yanna in a good little while. I don't think we've heard a peep out of you about her since your father's heart attack scare. So where is this woman you plan to take to Tiffany's and spend thousands of dollars on?"

Elijah walked swiftly through the door separating the kitchen from the large living and dining areas of the spacious Brooklyn brownstone, away from his mother's unrelenting questions. He left trailing, in his wake, the words, "Where's Pop?"

"He's resting," Esther said. "He went in after dinner, which was about an hour ago, to lie down."

Elijah looked at the clock on the mantel above the fireplace. "I lost track of time. I didn't realize it was already after seven."

"Have you had supper?"

"Not yet, I stayed late to finish some research and came straight here from downtown."

"Let me fix you a plate and we can chat while you eat."

"Mother, I don't feel like talking this evening," he said calmly.

"Elijah, I'm the Momma and I won't be put off," she said, only half joking. "You've been moping around here for weeks and we haven't seen your fiancée, soon-to-be fiancée or whatever she is in just as long, so don't tell me you don't feel like talkin'."

"Okay, Mother, you asked for it," he said. "I've got myself a situation, I'm not exactly sure how to handle," he continued.

Instinctively, Esther began to panic. But then she calmed down and took a deep breath. She knew her son to always be on point, never out of control or without an answer. "Baby, do you want me to go wake your father so we can have a family meeting?"

"No Mother, that won't be necessary. But thanks for listening. I do need to talk about this," he said.

"I'll get us a glass of wine and we can sit inside and talk," she said moving swiftly to the cabinet.

Elijah removed his plate from the table while his mother grabbed two wine goblets and an opened bottle of Pinot Noir. He loosened his thin red tie as he moved into the living room. Joining him there, Esther placed the goblets and the bottle on the coffee table. Elijah poured them each a glass of the strongly aromatic dark blackberry, oak-tinged wine, while his mother put on one of her favorite tranquility CD's. Immediately, the flute and harp chords began to soothe Elijah even before he took the first sip. He sank into the deep sofa while his mother sat across from him in a matching arm chair. He hadn't noticed before, but it now dawned on him that the furniture in this room was new. It was really plush and comfortable but seemed incongruous to the otherwise conservative and traditional tastes of his parents. Then as he relaxed more, he noticed a remarkable peaceful energy permeating the room. Clearing his throat and forming a triangular tent with his index fingers which were resting on his lips, he appeared to think for a moment before dropping his now clasped hands into his lap. "Mother," he said, "in about six months my world, I believe, is going to be turned upside down and completely altered."

Cautiously, she asked, "What does that mean?"

"I have done a very foolish thing."

"Go on," she said taking a sip of her wine, though in her heart she wasn't sure she wanted him to continue.

"I casually dated a young lady at Stanford, who I was very fond of, but it didn't become serious even though we were pretty exclusive throughout her freshman year. After that, it was more off, than on, up until D'yanna and I got back together permanently. It seems that she's now with child."

"No, Elijah! No, please tell me it's not yours," Esther gasped.

"I wish I could, Mother, but she says it is and I don't have any reason not to believe her."

"Oh Lord," she wailed, "This can't be happening, not now." Something seemed to mysteriously come over Esther and she calmed down almost immediately. *Panicking isn't going to help the situation*, she thought, realizing what her son needed right then was consolation and support not condemnation or regret. "Baby, I'm sorry, that response was purely a reflex and not at all helpful, I'm truly sorry. When did you find this out?" she asked softly.

"The day before Pop went to the hospital. The timing, as insensitive as this may sound, couldn't have been better."

"Oh?"

"Yes, it's bought me some time, even if I haven't utilized it well," he quipped.

"Time for what?" his mother wanted to know.

"To try and figure things out—redirect, refocus, plan…"

"I thought you already had a great plan."

"My professional career plans, sure, but I'm talking about my personal goals." He thought for a minute then added, "I don't think I'm fully committed to the personal success path I'm on."

"Does this have anything to do with D'yanna?"

"Indirectly, I guess it does," he continued. "She's one terrific woman. She's smart, focused and spirited—not to mention gorgeous, but sometimes her independence seems to get in the way."

"So what about this Stanford girl?" Esther said, slowly putting her glass down.

"She's beautiful, she's funny…" he said as his voice started to trail off.

"And?" Esther pressed.

"Mother, with her, it can get so complicated. You know me, I'm easy, no drama. At times her emotions don't seem stable and she can be very indecisive. One minute she's high and positive, the next low and negative."

"She sounds more than emotionally unbalanced to me. She sounds crazy."

"She's really not crazy, she's brilliant. But something happened along the way that's caused her to distrust the world. I think it has something to do with her grandmother's death a few years ago."

"So what does she want from you?"

"I don't know, we really haven't had an opportunity to talk. When she called to tell me, I was no good for the rest of the day, and I couldn't say much over the phone. Since then, I've been trying to process this on my own and at the same time trying to avoid D'yanna."

"Are you telling me that she doesn't know?"

"I didn't know what to say, how to tell her," he said hanging his head.

"Oh, I get it, that's what you meant about buying time. You're not even sure about marrying D'yanna anymore, are you?"

Hearing his mother say it out loud, Elijah realized that he wasn't. Esther noticed the look on his face. It seemed like the light just came on for him and she knew he was uncertain.

"If the baby comes and you know without a doubt it's yours, then what?" she asked.

"I don't know, but what I know for sure is that I wouldn't want another man raising my child."

"Then that's where you start," Esther said, "and what about the mother?"

"That, I *really* don't know," he laughed. "In a perfect world, I'd want for us all to be together, but as you and I both know, there's nothing perfect about the world."

"What about getting it right with God?" she asked directly.

"Yes, definitely, that goes without saying; of course I want to clear my heart before the Lord," he said.

✻

"Hello, oh hi, Lijah," Naiyah said surprised and slightly annoyed that it took him this long to get back to her. "And to what do I owe this honor?" she asked, speaking sarcastically into her cell phone.

"Let's not, okay, Naiyah?" Elijah retorted.

"My bad, I should have known this was business and not a social call."

"Naiyah, girl, be easy. I don't want to argue." When no rebuttal came, Elijah continued, "That was a heavy bomb you dropped on me a few days ago."

"Then you know how it felt when it hit me," Naiyah shot back.

Uneasily, Elijah fidgeted with and adjusted some already organized papers on his desk. His focus had only been on himself and he knew it. He hadn't put himself in Naiyah's shoes. *Man,* he thought *she must be frightened, with still having school to finish.* "I apologize, Ny, I was only thinking of myself. I'm ready to talk now, I think. I mean, umm, if that's okay with you."

"Yes, it's okay. There's so much to talk about," she said. "I'll be in New York over the Thanksgiving break. Would that be a convenient time?"

"I'll make it convenient," he answered. "Do you remember me telling you that I have an aunt that lives out on the Island near your family somewhere?"

"Oh yeah, cool—perhaps I can come to see you there, or better yet, you can come to me so I can use you as a human shield when I tell my mom and dad."

Elijah laughed nervously. "So when do you arrive?" he asked.

"I fly in late Wednesday with my auntie, uncle and cousin."

"Let's talk at the beginning of the week and make plans to get together Friday," he said, taking control.

"Thanks Lijah," she said, now a little more playful, "I'd really like that."

Hedging slightly he said, "Me too, Ny, I've missed talking to you."

Naiyah smiled to herself. She didn't want to admit she'd missed him too. So instead she said, "Talk to you next week, enjoy your day," before lightly flipping her phone off.

VII

Catching Up With Izzy

"*Naiyah Isabella Harland,* where in the heck have you been?"

"Whoa, back up, Nathan, give me a chance to explain, or at least say something in my defense."

"*H to the naw, sister* girl. I'm too through with you," he said feigning outrageous upset.

"What if I told you how much I love you and how sorry I am, my sweetheart of a baby brotha," Naiyah teased. It felt good to play and tease after so much crying and carrying on.

"Well," he said, "I just might accept that. Dang Sis, what took you so long to call me back and whatcha up to anyhow?" he asked.

"Nathan, I'm over my head with stuff, but I can't go there right now. I'm comin' home for Thanksgiving though," Naiyah said hoping that would make him happy.

"Are you really, Iz? This is going to be really fabulous. I get the feeling that Jade is going to outdo herself this year, especially since she hasn't done much holiday celebrating in the last few years."

"Did I just hear you call our mother Jade, since when? You must be trippin', Nathan."

"You know better," he said. "Jade Diamond is hundreds of miles away and that's the only way I'd call Mum by her name, otherwise she'd knock my head off if she heard me."

"Yeah," Naiyah laughed. "Wait, here she goes, *Nathaniel, what did you call me, boy? Do I look like one of your nappy headed cronies? Boy, if you ever disrespect me again, you nappy-headed natural-born cuss, I'll knock you so far into next week that it'll be a long time coming before even the good Lord gets the news.*"

"Stop, Iz," Nathan said, laughing so hard he was crying.

"What, what did you say, boy?"

"Stop, Iz," he said again, "before I pee myself."

It took them both a minute to recover from mocking their mother. Naiyah was still laughing when Nathan broke in, "Izzy, what's the 411?" he wanted to know.

"It'll keep, love. I just wanted to tell you myself that I'm coming."

"It's tough all over for everybody, Naiyah, just remember that," Nathan said turning serious. "You're not the only one dealing with stuff."

"I'm sorry, Nathan," she replied, hearing an echo of Elijah's words in her head, "I've been selfish but I'm trying to do better."

"What are you bringing for the head when you come?" he asked her.

"What are you talking about?"

"Don't play stupid, Iz. Let's just say I know you be kickin' it with Danny West, aka. Strong."

"You don't know anything, Nathan."

"Yeah, right," he said dropping the subject. "I wonder if Mani's coming home too?" he added.

Naiyah's pulse quickened. "Have you seen or heard from her lately?"

"I saw her at the end of the summer, we hung out together at Club Atlantic."

"Did she ask about me?"

"No," he said.

Naiyah's heart sank and before long she ended the call. "I can't wait to see you, Nate, love ya. Bye."

VIII

And You're Here—Why?

Just as she reached the landing, Jade noticed Lucky coming up the walkway. She dashed into the powder room facing the stairs and took a quick peek in the pewter framed mirror. Combing through her coal-black straight hair with her fingers, she wondered what in the world he was doing there. Still, she couldn't deny that his very presence caused warm sensations to pulse through her. She was now acutely aware that her delicate Venus Flower was throbbing so intensely that it was both deafening and startling. Sitting on the edge of the toilet, she pressed her legs together hoping the sensation would wash over her before he rang the doorbell. *If he rings the door bell,* she thought, remembering he still had a key. "I'm being ridiculous," she breathed, "acting like a school-girl having my first crush."

"Excuse me," she said coldly upon entering the kitchen where Lucky had let himself in and was now browsing through the mail neatly stacked in a tray on the computer desk. "I prefer that you ring the bell when you drop by unannounced," she said with annoyance. "And furthermore, why are you here?"

"Hold up now, Baby J," he said turning to face his wife. "I'm expecting mail to be delivered here for me, besides, I wanted to see how you were."

"I'm fine," she said ignoring his notice that mail would be coming for him there. After all, technically, this was still his house.

"You're lookin' great, what's different?"

"Nothing, just the fact I'm in peace heaven having the house all to myself." He laughed, "Yeah, I imagine that's pretty tight."

"What do you want, Lemuel, and where's your pretty young thing?"

"Come on now, J," he said coolly, "we don't have to go there."

"You're in my house, so I can go any damn where I please."

"Our house," he whispered. "Jade," he said more assertively, "this barrier between us is really chilly—brrrrrr." He gave a mock shiver. "It's been up a good while now, do we really have to continue like this?"

She moved past him, creating a comfortable distance.

Lucky continued, "You know what this is about, you knew when you married me that I would have some monogamy challenges. But you also know that it's *you* I love and always will."

She couldn't respond. She'd heard this "It's you I love" speech many times before but believed his intentions, when he said it, had nothing at all to do with her, but rather his words were released only to soothe his own conscience and assuage his guilt. With resignation, she said, "Of course, Lemuel, you love me, but because I'm not a toe-tapping, rump-shaking, lust-provoking interloper, you're unable to honor the commitment you made to me and our children."

"I've provided for you," he said raising his voice.

"I salute you, Lemuel, now if you're finished here, please leave."

"J, wait—I never meant to hurt you. I didn't marry you under false pretenses, you know. I really thought I was ready to settle down, that fast living was out of my system." He made a move towards her.

She drew back quickly, "Too little, too late, Mr. Harland, I don't cry for you any more," she said and left the room.

Stunned by her frosty dismissal, Lucky stood there; he managed to find the computer chair nearby and sat, though he could have collapsed from the weakness he now felt in his legs. The gravity of the encounter caused his shoulders to slump, belying his 6'2", 200 pound, muscularly tight frame. He sat motionless for a moment and then ran his fingers through his thick curly hair. *She's right,* he thought. *What a fool I've been all these years. I chased the four inch heel, the skirt and the tail and thought it was life. I had the Word, a weapon for offensive and defensive battle. I should have drunk from my own fountain, forgetting not the wife of my youth.* He sighed a deep sigh of regret. Rising, he said out loud, "Big Sadie, I messed up and I don't think I can fix this one." Meanwhile, Jade eased into the Jacuzzi tub, with the jets going full throttle. She hoped Lucky had gone. She'd rather he not hear any moan of pleasure that might escape her pressed lips as the vibration from the water massaged and tickled her all over.

IX

Get Ready, Company's Coming

"*I better* get a move on, four days and it'll be Thanksgiving," Jade said to herself as she sat polishing the sterling silver flatware when the phone rang. "Hello, Jade?"

"Hello?"

"Jade, don't act like you don't know who this is."

"Well, who is it?"

"Girl, pleeez, quit playin'."

"Nooo," Jade squealed, "this can't be who I think it is."

"Yeah girl, it's Willie, your one and only."

"Wilhelmina Alexander, I have missed you so much, Lord knows."

"I've missed you more," Wilhelmina exclaimed.

"Where are you?" Jade asked excitedly. It had been years since she had spoken to her long-time friend and college roommate.

"I'm staying uptown in Harlem on 110th Street at the moment. I'm not sure for how long though."

"Oh really, so when did you leave Atlanta?"

"About a year or so ago," Wilhelmina said.

"What brought you back here to New York?"

"The wear and tear on my already broke-down behind, runnin' up here almost every weekend to check on my mother, who had a stroke a while back," she sighed.

"Where is she now?" Jade asked sincerely. Mrs. Alexander had always seemed so strong and vibrant.

"She's at home still. My brother and I, believe it or not, have been holding it down, trying to keep it together."

Taking the opportunity Willie provided, Jade smiled to herself and said, "Oh yeah, how's Ronnel doing anyway?"

"Girl, he's good, we're all good. It's just hard some days dealing with Mother. She's lost her verbal communication skills but, besides that, it's okay. But Ronny, girl, I'm so proud of my fine-ass brother."

"Willie, shut your mouth."

"Oh, sorry Jade, I almost forgot that you were always Miss Priss," she said with a snort.

"Don't start, Willie. Did you say your mother's in a nursing home?"

"Oh no, weren't you listening? I said she's home. Ronny and I were taking turns coming in on the weekends while private duty nurses cared for her around the clock during the week."

"Oh, I'm sorry. That must be really hard."

"It is, but by the grace of God, she's still with us. Like I said, she's not communicating verbally, but she's alert and knows what's going on."

"Oh," Jade said thoughtfully. There was a brief silence between them when Jade broke in, "What are your plans for Thanksgiving?"

"None that I know of, maybe I'll pick up a small turkey breast and throw something together."

"Why not come here and celebrate with us? Naiyah and Nathan are coming home from school and Turquoise and her family are coming in from California."

"That sounds like a mighty good plan. If Mother's up for the ride out to Long Island, would it be okay to bring her along too?" Wilhelmina inquired.

"Absolutely, plan to stay overnight even, if you like. That is, if you think your mother would be comfortable."

"Can I bring my brother too?"

"Well, of course, but isn't Ronny married?"

"Not anymore," Wilhelmina said.

"What happened?" Jade wanted to know.

"Long story, let's save it to gossip about when I see you on Thursday."

"Girl, I can't wait."

"Me neither," Willie said, "we'll get my brother to make the martinis."

Loosening up some, Jade laughed and said, "Aw shoot, sookie, sookie now." They both laughed, excitedly buoyed by the prospect of seeing each other after so many years.

"Girl, I always knew you had some ghetto hidden somewhere deep within," Willie laughed.

"You don't know the half, honey," Jade said hanging up the phone.

Wow, thought Jade, *Ronnel Alexander, it's been a long time since I've seen him.* She took a break from the chores, and this time poured some gin with a splash of tonic into a glass and allowed herself to remember some of the good times they shared when he visited them in Atlanta, when she and Willie attended Clark University, later renamed Clark Atlanta University when the two schools merged. *Unh, unh, unh, he sure was fine,* she thought, feeling herself getting warm, *I dare not wonder how things might have turned out had we let our flirtations and brief sexcapades turn serious.* "Ummm," she moaned licking the cool drink from the top of her lip, "what if he does come," she wondered out loud.

X

Pick Up the Phone—
What's the Number?

"*Okay,* that's it. Elijah, pick up the freakin' phone! I'm trying to respect your wishes and give you some space, but you're not being fair. I don't have a clue what's going on here." When there was still no answer, she said, "Elijah, if you don't call me back this evening, I'm coming over there. You owe me an explanation!" D'yanna shouted. "We're getting married or have you forgotten?"

Elijah nestled deeper into the luxurious leather club chair, feeling somewhat insulated and protected while staring at the phone, listening to D'yanna's rant through the answering machine. He turned his thoughts to the upcoming holiday and seeing Naiyah again. He thought about the first time he saw her on the campus of Stanford University. As they did every year, he and his fraternity brothers stood outside the student activities center checking out all the incoming freshmen, the girls in particular. Across the quad strolled a pair of the most beautiful, long, shapely, honey-bronze legs that he'd ever seen. He wasn't the first to notice them, but *he was* the first to say, "Back off, brothers, I saw 'em first." He remembered how they laughed at him—but he was dead serious. He allowed his eyes to wander slowly up those legs to behold a body, (yes body) and face equally as magnificent. He was captivated by what he saw: a megawatt smile and a mane of coal black waves flowing down the middle of an otherwise straight back, with the slightest inward curve above her athletic behind. All Elijah could say was—"Oooooh." He sprinted over to the small group of girls, and using his best *for com-*

pany manners and gentlemanly demeanor, introduced himself. When he got to Naiyah, he held onto her hand a few seconds longer than he had the others. His dark eyes bore into hers. He wanted desperately to send the message that he was interested. "I'm Elijah McCoy," he said, squeezing her hand a little firmer. "That's a strong pair of legs you have there, do you run track?"

"Not really," she said assertively. "I jog and ride horses."

He was impressed, but revealed nothing. "Hope to see you around campus," he said. "Afternoon, ladies and welcome to Stanford." When he reached the fellas across the quad, they all clamored to find out about Naiyah. "Sorry guys, I didn't get the digits, but she's mine and that's my first and my last warning to you." They all laughed again.

D'yanna was still ranting to and through the answering machine. "Why do I have that dang thing" he wondered out loud. "I need to get voice mail."

In the meantime, while she got ready for the trip home, Naiyah breathed, "YaYa, I feel his lips on me, they're soft and sweet and his touch is gentle. I love him. He's going places," she mused. "Now here I sit—stuck. Even when I get my degree this coming May, I'll still be stuck. Stuck with a baby and a habit." *Just a habit* the voice within said. *Remember you're giving the baby away.*

XI

And It's Only Thanksgiving Eve

Jade stood anxiously at baggage claim #4, watching and waiting for Nathan to appear. She couldn't believe the time had passed so quickly and tomorrow was Thanksgiving. She tried to contain her excitement, but she couldn't. It had been awhile since she'd entertained and she hadn't seen her son in three months. Seeing Wilhelmina again and Ronnel also sent positive vibrations through her. Excited, yes, indeed, she was excited. Passing the time chit-chatting with other waiting family and friends, Jade didn't notice Nathan sneaking up behind her. A blood-curdling scream escaped her lips after he covered both her eyes with his hands and whispered loudly, "MUM! See, I knew you weren't livin' right," he said laughing.

"Boy, come over here and give me a proper hug and some sugar before I knock the living daylights out of you for scaring me so badly."

Nathan wrapped his arms around his mother's waist and squeezed her tight. He wanted to pour into her the love he'd been holding since August. "Ummmm," Jade sighed, "I have really missed you, son."

Nathan smiled at her as they waited for his checked luggage to come down the chute. "What are we going to do today?" he asked struggling to pull his suitcase from the belt.

"Nathaniel, my Lord, you're only here for the weekend. What in heaven's name is in there?"

"Mum, really—do you have to ask? You should know by now, I'm not one for traveling light. One never knows what opportunities might present themselves. And you know my motto: keep a case, just in case.

There's one thing that will never be said of me and that is that I was not prepared." She laughed and hugged him again. "Boy, you are one for the books. Let's stop for lunch and then head on home. Aunt Turquoise, Uncle Johann, Sequoia and Naiyah get in later tonight."

"Are they flying into MacArthur too?"

"No, not this time," she said. "I don't know why, but they decided to fly into La Guardia instead. Once they pick up the rental, it'll be about seven or so before they get to our house."

"Good, that'll give us time to catch up and me a chance to nap."

"Nathaniel, your hair has really grown since I last saw you."

"Um-huh, do you like the braids?" he asked shaking his head from side to side, giving her the full effect of their length.

"I do, but they make you look too girly."

He looked at her but didn't say anything.

❧

Naiyah watched the lights flickering from the houses and stores as her Uncle Johann pointed the car east and sped quickly through the small county towns. She wasn't sure how fast he was driving, though it felt like they were a speeding bullet and she imagined they were going at least a hundred. Her thoughts muted the chatter between Uncle Jon and Auntie Aqua while seventeen-year-old Sequoia slept peacefully, completely oblivious. She did catch her uncle's reminiscence, however, when he said, "It's gonna be some real good eatin' and a good ole time at Jade's tomorrow. Lucky always said Jade was good at a lot of things and cookin' was definitely one of 'em."

Aqua laughed, "Yeah, it's gonna be great."

Later that evening after everyone was settled and fed, "Jade, honey," Turquoise said to her sister, "why don't we girls go into the smoking room and have us a little powwow?"

"Me too, Mommy?" Sequoia wanted to know.

"Of course you too, you're one of us, aren't you?"

"Have at it then," said Johann, "see if we care." Nudging Nathan, "Come on, man, let me hear you get down on that piano while I relax with a glass of that fine Remy I saw on your mother's liquor cart."

Johann joined Nathan in the formal living room. The elegant baby grand was even more beautiful than he remembered. Nathan had begun to play a jazzy rendition of an old Funkadelic song that Jon remembered well. He began tapping his feet. Next, he was up groovin' to the beat.

63

"Man, you don't know nothing bout that thang there," he said pumping and twirlin' and making deep zig-zaggy impressions on Jade's freshly shampooed and vacuumed carpet.

"Whatcha mean, Uncle Jon," Nathan taunted back. "Let's just say that's why I'm not constricted or butt twisted—I dance," he laughed, not missing one stroke on the ivories.

"Man, go head young blood, whatcha know about it?" Johann asked in his well-honed 60's street voice.

"Unc, please, we all got constrictions and George Clinton and Funkadelic set us free to dance right on out of 'em." Swinging his long braids, he laughed "Some get it, some don't."

"You got that right," Johann said taking a gulp of the smooth cognac as he sat down to accompany Nathan by playing the melody to "One Nation Under A Groove."

❀

The smoking room was a small enclosure added to the solarium which was right off the kitchen. It was really a small den or oversized closet, a space Jade made comfortable with a couple of Queen Anne chairs, a large ottoman, a TV pillow and a few plants. Lucky hated cigarettes and the fact that she smoked. So when the sunroom was added, she designed this space out of love and consideration for him. She often wondered why she continued relegating herself to this area when he no longer stayed at home. And just as often, she repressed the not so subconscious thoughts that she wanted him to come back and believed that one day he would.

Sitting on the oversized, overstuffed TV pillow at her mother's feet, Sequoia stared up at her, "Mommy, I wish you'd give up those stinkin' cigarettes once and for all, and you too, Auntie Jade," she said, looking from one to the other. She scrunched up her nose and rolled her eyes. Neither of the sisters commented.

"Naiyah," Jade inquired, "how's the school year coming? It's such a monumental year and I was hoping to be more involved."

"Sorry, Mum, I should have kept in touch more, but class work and activities really have me overwhelmed," Naiyah lied convincingly.

Aqua cleared her throat, trying to make eye contact with her niece, who in turn felt the blaze of her eyes and avoided them.

"You *must* be overwhelmed," continued Jade, "seems like you're neglecting your healthy eating habits, you don't look as lean and toned as usual."

Aqua cleared her throat again, but this time remarked, "Yeah Izzy, you do look a little paunchy."

Naiyah stood at the door the whole time they were in the smoking room just in case a hasty retreat was needed. Though small framed, she was built. Her legs were long, tight and muscular. It was evident she was into weight training despite the slight hint of diminished muscle tone in her arms, yet no question girlfriend was cut and well defined. By now she'd learned how to position herself to disguise her steadily growing belly mound.

"Auntie Aqua, as the ever so observant one, I knew we could count on you. Paunchy," she said clenching her strong jaw, "that's a good word, but pregnant is even better." As she turned to leave, she said over her shoulder, "If y'all will excuse me, I have to go pee, which is something pregnant women do quite often." A hush fell over the room but the energy was palpable. A disturbing vibration rippled through the small space and shock, fear and disbelief all seemed to reverberate off the walls, echoing... PREGNANT, PREGNANT ... she said PREGNANT, in the now thickened air.

"Just wait one New York minute here. I didn't hear what I think I heard. Did my baby just say she's having a baby?" Jade asked, raising her already elevated voice.

Sequoia lowered her head and began brushing imaginary lint from her mother's bejeweled Capezio slippers.

"Turquoise," Jade shouted, "did you know about this?"

"Welllll," Turquoise hedged.

"Well hell, did you know?"

"Don't be lookin' at me, Jade, with those accusatory eyes."

"Am I looking at you?"

"Yes."

"Then speak," she demanded.

Hearing raised voices above the piano, Nathan said, "What do you think is going on in there?"

"Go on and find out, nephew, you know you'd rather be in there with them hens anyhow."

Nathan wondered what exactly his uncle meant by that but didn't ask. "Come on, uncle, let's go see."

"Naw man, I'm good right here where I am," Uncle Jon said while continuing to pluck at the piano keys.

As he walked through the door, Nathan heard his aunt saying, "She wanted to tell you herself, J, in person, not over the phone."

"Tell who what in person?" he asked.

Looking up, Sequoia said, "Izzy's going to have a baby."

"Hush, honey," her mother said. "Nathan, go back inside with Uncle Jon and take Sequoia with you. Give your Mum and me a moment."

"Yes Ma'am."

"Jade honey, I know this is another hard one and it probably won't get easier for a long time, but it will get easier, you'll see."

"You should have told me, Qua."

"I wanted too Sissy, I really did, but it was Izzy's call, not mine."

"What's there to celebrate now," lamented Jade. "It feels more like a wake than a Thanksgiving celebration. I'm so mad, I could kick Naiyah's behind from one end of this house to the other."

"Quit the drama," Turquoise said looking critically at her baby sis.

"I'm serious, I'm mad and disappointed. I feel like she let me down."

"Do you think you're the only one, how do you think Izzy's feeling?" Turquoise asked.

"She should feel like a fool and, by the way, whose seed is it anyway?" Looking sadly at her sister, Turquoise shook her head and walked out. Once in the kitchen, she added some ice to a glass and poured herself a drink from the bottle of Remy left on the counter by Jon. She added a splash of coke and breezed into the living room to join her husband, daughter and nephew, hoping that by giving Jade and Izzy their privacy, the healing process might begin.

When Naiyah returned from the bathroom, Jade was alone. "Come in and close the door," she said sternly.

"Mum——" Naiyah began.

Jade held up her hand, "Shut your mouth, you've said enough, I'm speaking now."

Obediently, Naiyah positioned the chair vacated by her aunt to face her mother and sat down slowly. She began a nonverbal dialogue by matching Jade's posture and body language. For a brief moment, they stared unflinchingly into one another's eyes.

Jade was searching for the reasons of her failure, Naiyah for compassion and understanding. What they found were dark wells of nothingness which they reflected back to one another like mirrors.

"Mum——"

"Naiyah, didn't I tell you to shut your mouth? When you should have been talking, which from the looks of things now, was about four months ago, there was nary a peep out of you. Why didn't you protect yourself?" Jade shouted indignantly.

Naiyah didn't respond.

"Who's going to want to marry you now?" Jade continued. "What about school, grad school? What were you thinking? How could you have treated your virtue so casually?" Jade continued assaulting Naiyah with question after question, hurtful statement after hurtful statement. Naiyah took the blows as direct hits to her heart. She caved into the chair from the weight of them and the deep internal wounds created from the assault nearly arrested her heart completely.

She was screaming inside, *Stop judging me! Stop trying to put me in a box! Listen to me! Know me! Trust me! Guide me! Love me! I'm hurting!* The screaming was so loud Naiyah thought her head would explode.

After some time, a knock on the door came. "Can I come in" Turquoise asked.

"Naiyah, I just don't believe this," continued her mother, "you're too smart to be so damn stupid."

Again, a cascade of tears flowed from Naiyah. She ran from the room, through the kitchen and up the long stairs to her bedroom, blinded by her tears.

"Sis, you need to be easy," Turquoise said gently, taking Jade by the hand. "This is a delicate situation and emotionally draining on Izzy, I'm sure."

Jade, now spent, lay sprawled out on the chair. She looked at her sister through moist eyes and said, "Easy, Turquoise? How am I supposed to do that? We placed a lot of our hopes and dreams on what we knew Naiyah could achieve, especially Big Sadie. She's probably turning over in her grave by now. Our expectations for her were so high."

"That's part of the problem, Jade. I'm sure getting pregnant wasn't Izzy's plan. Besides, it isn't about your expectations for her or Big Sadie's either for that matter. It's about how she's going to negotiate and execute her own expectations, what she learns from her mistakes and how she self-corrects."

Jade began to weep softly. "How can this be happening? First, Lemuel took off to be with another woman and now, Naiyah's going to interrupt her education to have a bastard child."

Turquoise looked at her sister in horror.

"Oh, so it's like that, is it, Jade? You're the victim of your husband and daughter's imperfections, huh? What's the matter, they didn't stay within the designated lines you prescribed? Get real, Jade."

"Why are you being so harsh towards me?" she cried.

"Because you need to wake up and, besides, weren't you just being pretty harsh towards Izzy? You seem to be up on a mighty high horse actin' like you have selective amnesia, or did you really forget that Nai-yah wasn't the first baby your womb held?"

"Now wait a minute, Turquoise, that's downright cruel. We weren't to bring that up ever again and you know it."

"Yes, I know—I remember. No one can hear us *and* this conversation *is* only between us, but obviously you need to be reminded that you yourself haven't always been Ms. Perfect. What do you think Izzy would say if she knew?" When there had been a long silence, Turquoise continued, "I thought so. Now, little girl, wipe those tears from your eyes. We're going to get through this. We Diamond women come from good strong stock, you know. It's going to be okay. Pull yourself together now, Jade, and put on your happy face. We got us some celebratin' to do. You're going to be a YaYa yourself," she said smiling as she hugged her baby sister. "And we're celebrating life this Thanksgiving." Then she pulled Jade to her feet.

Jade took a deep breath and blew her nose. "Girl, Izzy was right about one thing, we sure can count on you. You always know how to get right to the heart of the matter. Thank you, Qua, I really love you and I'm so glad you came. Do you think I should call Mom?"

"Don't even think about it. Mom and Dad planned and waited a long time for their trip to Morocco. Don't you dare spoil it with this news, it can wait till they get back. Besides, y'all need to do some sortin' out first."

Jade exhaled and wiped her eyes. She moved outside the smoking room to the solarium where she composed herself amidst the beauty and life of her many plants. When Jade came into the kitchen, Turquoise was busy looking to see what more needed to be done in preparation for the next day's feast. "Oh Sissy," she said gaily, "you have really been workin' it out up in here. There's enough food to feed an army."

Jade pushed her hands up through her sister's curly spiraled hair, "Qua, you're so bohemian."

"Yes, and isn't it grand?" she laughed.

"A YaYa, Qua—, puleeze, I'm only forty-seven and so not ready, on any level."

"Well, honey, from the looks and sounds of things—you better be gettin' ready."

"Poppy," Naiyah cried into the phone receiver.

"Hey, Princess," he said, lighting up from inside out. After realizing that Naiyah was sobbing, he pulled his car off to the side of the road and brought it to a halt. "Baby girl, what's the matter, where are you?"

"Poppy," she said sniffling and hiccupping, "I just had a real bad blowout scene with Mum."

"What for?" he asked, his forehead creasing involuntarily. "I told her something she didn't want to hear and now she's very upset with me."

"Oh, is that all," he said relieved, "you'll work it out. You know how your mother is."

"No, I don't think so, this isn't going to smooth over anytime soon," Naiyah said. "Can you please come over here?"

"Naiyah, baby, I'll see you before you leave, and besides, you know your mother doesn't want me there ruining her holiday."

"Poppy, I need you to come over here—PLEASE!"

"Sweetheart, I'm on my way to meet some of the guys. We've been planning this boy's night for a long time. You know the long hours I put in, I need this break."

"Poppy, you have to come. If not tonight, please say you'll come tomorrow."

"Naiyah, have you lost your mind? You know that's definitely out of the question. Your mother will kill me for comin' and Analise will kill me for goin'. Is that what you want, a dead Poppy?" he laughed.

By now, Naiyah had calmed down. The calm and non-threatening reassurance in her father's voice made her relax. "Poppy, I just want to see you. I need to see you …please?"

"Alright, alright, I'll be there," he said. "If not later tonight, then tomorrow."

"Thanks, I'll see you then, smooches Poppy."

"Girl, you're so silly." Lucky moved his eye-poppin' red Lexus SC430 back onto the highway, wondering what Naiyah could have said to upset her mother so much that she would bring tears to their baby girl's eyes.

XII

What do You Mean by That?

"*Hi, it's me*, Naiyah."

"Hey, Ms. Stanford U, you out here on Strong Island for the Thanksgiving break, huh?" Strong asked.

She ignored the colloquialism, which originated from Long Island Hip-Hoppers and their perception of how they were livin' now that so many had blown up in the rap music business.

"What' up, shorty?" he asked.

"I'm a bit tense, can I come over your way for a minute? I need a little something for my head," she said quickly.

"Ny, you can't keep sampling my product, there's no return on my investment, if you know what I'm sayin'."

"I know what ya sayin', Strong," she said in an exasperated tone. "Like I was saying, I need to set my head straight. The jump off with my Mum didn't go too smooth, I just need a little sumpin' sumpin' to calm my nerves, that's all."

"How you gettin' over here?" he asked, easing up a little.

"I was hoping you'd come pick me up and bring me back. My Mum's hotter than a hornet's nest right now, so I know she's not giving up her car and I dare not ask my auntie or uncle for the keys to the rental."

"Okay Ny, I'm comin'. I'm leavin' right now—so be ready."

"I'll be out front waiting," she said with relief. Naiyah took time to get herself together. She washed her face, reapplied her mascara and lip gloss. Just as she was walking to the end of the driveway, she spotted Strong's

Mercedes ML 500 coming up the street. "I'm glad he was cool and didn't trip when I told him we couldn't be more than friends. He's good people no matter how he makes a living. People do what they do to make it through, I guess," she said to the night breeze, laughing that her words rhymed, but quickly becoming somber, knowing how true it really was. "Hey, Danny Boy," she said sweetly, leaning in to brush his cheek with her lips. "I'm so glad you came, it was gettin' real hot up in there."

"Ny, you know how you be kickin' gas on things, you musta done somethin' to set your moms off."

Naiyah rolled her eyes and looked straight ahead as Strong maneuvered the SUV onto Highway 27 and headed it in the direction of the small town of Bridgehampton.

"How long you home for?" Strong asked once they were settled in at his apartment. "Damn girl, it sho was nice to hear your voice, I didn't know you was comin'," he said trying to sound matter of fact.

"How would you know unless I told you," she said, thinking, *how stupid.* "It's not like we travel in the same circles, even though my brother Nathan did mention your name to me a few weeks ago, which I thought was odd." Nervously, Strong asked, "What made your baby brother ask about me, I don't kick it with him?"

"Right, I know," she said looking across the room at him, "I wondered the same thing myself. He acted like he knew you and I were down for a minute."

"What do you mean by that?" Strong asked while pouring Cristal into two champagne flutes for him and Naiyah.

"He asked if I was bringing anything home for the head, then said he knew about us being more than friends," she answered admiring the elegant flutes and the rapidly rolling bubbles, on the table before them.

"Huh, gimme a break, Ny, Nathan's lame. He don't know nothing. He just needs to do what he do and leave me to look after my business like I do."

"And what would that be, Strong?"

"What?"

"His business, your business—whatever?"

"Hey, Ny, don't go gettin' all tight with me, yo. I'm just sayin'——"

"Sayin'?"

"Yeah, sayin', don't make me go there," he said sounding irritated.

"Look, Strong, I came here to get away from the drama for a minute, but you seem to be taking me somewhere way in left field. If you have something to say about my brother, don't be a punk, Strong Man, just say it."

"It's just," he said stammering, "Nathan don't know nothing, 'bout my enterprise, so he best keep his mouth shut. I don't go, round tellin' folk how he be turning up and fanning his tail all around town."

Naiyah froze for a moment. It felt like a vise grip was tightening both her heart and lungs all at once. She seemed to momentarily lose both her sight and hearing. And now she was livid—the cocaine rush she had, had dissipated quickly into thin air. *Oh, no he didn't, Danny West just outed my brother,* she thought. *But worse, he said it like he was intimately sure of what he spoke. 'WHOA! (push pause—click) Is Nathan gay and is Danny on the low?* Naiyah wondered. In an instant, time stood still, she couldn't breathe, yet managed to ride the wave of nausea threatening to overtake her. Her thoughts formed an irrational kaleidoscope in her mind——

Strong, intimate with me and intimate with Nathan? Naiyah couldn't believe it. *STRONG, not strong but... weak—gay even—oh my God, a deviant maybe, WHAT, WHAT, WHAT!!!* Thoughts crashed with pounding force in her head.

"Naiyah, what's wrong with you? You lookin' wild and crazy in your eyes, girl," Strong said, all the while trying to backpedal and do damage control as fast as he could, not wanting Naiyah to think he knew anything about Nathan's suspected proclivities. "You didn't take what I just said seriously, did you, Ny? Girl, please, that was just a figure of speech. I don't know nothin', 'bout your brother 'cept, that he be walkin' around all swishy, that's all."

Naiyah guessed the color had left her face only because it now felt like her blood vessels were contracting. There were still three lines of coke perfectly aligned on the table. She reached down and quickly inhaled them. *I'm not going to jeopardize what I came here for over some stupid remark from Strong,* she thought, though she couldn't deny that hearing someone say out loud they noticed Nathan's strong feminine side made her feel uncomfortable. She shrugged, *maybe he's just a metro sexual,* she thought.

XIII

I Can Say I'm Sorry

When Naiyah returned home, she found Jade and Aqua still up, talking, sipping, and preparing for the celebration.

"Naiyah, sweetie, please come in here," Jade said when she heard the door open and then noticed her moving through the wide foyer towards the stairs.

Don't come messin' with me, Jade, she said to herself, *I'm not trying to lose this high.* "Yes Mum?" she answered.

"Come into the kitchen, I have something to say to you." Jade swallowed hard, steadying herself as she moved towards her daughter. She'd had a few gin and tonics over the course of the evening. "Sweetheart, first let me apologize," she said. "I can't tell you how ashamed I am about the way I spoke to you earlier. I'm so sorry, Naiyah, please forgive me."

Naiyah looked at her mother in disbelief, thinking, *She never says she's sorry.*

"Aunt Turquoise helped me see how I was making things worse, not better, with all the hurtful things I said. I was angry and afraid, but one thing I know is that I don't want for you to go through this alone. You, Naiyah," she said, gently cupping Naiyah's face with her hands and staring intently into her eyes, "are my baby girl and I love you more than you'll ever know. We're going to get through this together, one day at a time," she added with sincerity.

Naiyah exhaled and kissed her mother's cheek. All she could say was "Thank you." She turned to her auntie and told her "I love you" then said good-night to each of them and left the room.

Closing the bedroom door behind her, Naiyah sat down at her vanity and stared at her image in the mirror for a very long time. She now had the courage to examine her reflection. Before now, the disappointment she'd felt with herself over decisions she'd made caused her tremendous discomfort. Her thoughts, feelings and actions were so compartmentalized that she'd become fragmented without realizing it. She exhaled again, thinking aloud, "Maybe I should call Poppy and tell him he doesn't have to come after all," but then thought better of it and called Faith instead.

"Izzy, this better be good," Faith said wiping sleep from her eyes. "Have you lost your mind? It's twelve o'clock midnight."

"I know, love; I just couldn't wait to talk to you."

"What's up, how are things going?" Faith asked, now fully awake.

"You're not going to believe this but my Mum took it down a thousand and is being easy."

"What, you're kidding?" Faith remarked now perking up.

"Well, not at first, it took her a minute," Naiyah continued. "Girl, I mean she could have killed me when I said I was pregnant. You would have been proud of me, Faith. I dropped the news like a bomb and then walked out the room."

"You didn't?"

"I did. I didn't know what else to do. Auntie Aqua kept goading me into telling. Girl, she said I was paunchy." Faith lost it and was near hysterics when Naiyah cut in, "Okay, but let me finish."

"No, wait, paunchy, Iz?"

"Yeah, but wait—I said that's a good word but pregnant is better. There was dead silence. You hear me—absolute stillness. I said, 'Excuse me, I have to go pee like pregnant women often do.' When I got back, Mum was ready with both barrels cocked and loaded," she said, pushing her thumb down to her outstretched index finger as though it was the hammer to a loaded pistol.

"Oh my goodness, honey, then what?" Faith asked excitedly.

"She tore into me, that's what," Naiyah said. "You should've seen the Native American fire come blazing out of her."

"Ouch," Faith said, "are you okay?"

"Yeah, the worst is over. I called my father, just talking to him made it better and I went to visit my friend Danny for a while."

"Danny, do you mean that character you call Strong?"

"Please don't start, roommate, I've had enough battles for one night."

"Naiyah, really, what's your problem?" Faith scolded. "Don't you care anything about the innocent life growing inside of you? What if you change your mind, what if Elijah fights for custody? Have you given any thought to the damage you might be doing?"

"Faith, I got this covered, love. It's okay, really it is."

"You're fooling yourself, Iz. I hope your Thanksgiving is a happy one. See you when you get back to Stanford," she said dismissively. "One last thing, Izzy, I know I've said this many times before but I love you and I'm here for you no matter what."

"Happy Thanksgiving to you too, Faith, I love you back." Naiyah snapped her cell phone shut and stared again at her reflection in the mirror. However, this time she rubbed her belly gently and wondered what it was going to be like seeing Elijah on Friday.

November 28, 2002

Dearest YaYa,

It's very early in the morning on Thanksgiving Day. I'm home for the holiday; I came with Aunt Turquoise and her family, at Mum's insistence. So far, I've gotten over one hurdle and I'm facing one or two more before this weekend is over. I don't have to tell you how things went with Mum. That was hard enough. Tomorrow I have to muster up the courage to tell Poppy and Friday I'll see Elijah for the first time since this all happened. My friend and roommate Faith keeps getting on my case. She seems to think I might keep this baby or maybe Elijah might. I don't see that happening but, as you would say, "God works in mysterious ways." Who knows, beloved YaYa, I guess anything can happen. I've been thinking about your friend, God-mommy Inez. Maybe I'll get a chance to see her while I'm home. She's really been on my heart. I hope she's okay. I love you, YaYa.

Your Granddaughter
Naiyah Isabella
"Izzy"

Quietly opening the door and peering in after her knocks went un-answered, Sequoia whispered, "Izzy, can I come in?"

"What time is it?" she asked with a muffled voice from having her head buried under the bed covers.

"Good morning, cousin, rise and shine," Sequoia said brightly.

Naiyah pulled the covers from over her head and stared at Sequoia. "Are you for real? It's not even eight o'clock yet."

"Oh, I know, but I'm just so excited. Today's Thanksgiving and our families are all here together."

"You know what, you're right," Naiyah said pushing herself up, resting her back against the headboard of her four-poster, lace canopied bed. "Today is going to be outstanding, I feel it too."

"Yeah, too bad NaNa and Paps can't be here," Sequoia said.

"Humph, Naiyah snorted, can't say they'd agree with you. Given the choice, I think they'd still choose to be in Morocco," she chuckled.

Sequoia frowned, "Me too, I guess." They both fell into spontaneous laughter just as Jade and Turquoise came knocking at the door. "Good morning, sweet peas," Jade sang entering with a tray of herbal teas, scones and jam, her sister following with a handful of festive cloth napkins.

"Good morning, sweet peas," Turquoise echoed. "We thought you young ladies were up, so we came with some lite fare before breakfast and perhaps even a time of prayer to start off this glorious day."

Naiyah and Jade exchanged a questioning glance before Jade scooted into bed next to her, putting her arms around Naiyah and drawing her close. Turquoise retrieved the bench from the vanity and pulled it closer. "Honey, isn't this simply wonderful," she said to Sequoia who was nestled cozily at the foot of the bed.

"It is, Mother. I feel blessed and happy today. Before you and Auntie Jade came in, I was about to tell Izzy that despite the situation as it seems right now, I'm really happy for her."

"Sequoia, that's so sweet—you're going to make me cry," Naiyah said.

Jade hugged Naiyah tighter, "I'm not going that far yet, but I feel deep down that we're going to work through this and it'll all turn out for the best."

"Family has to stick together and, as a family, we're going to get through it," Turquoise said, "now let's pray." After they bowed heads, she began, *"Father, this wonderful day you have made, graciously and lovingly you have given it unto us and we thank you. Let our hearts be glad and may your peace, protection and blessing of favor be upon us. Help us to love on our family members this Thanksgiving day as you have loved on us, for the sake of your son, Amen."*

"That was beautiful," Jade said, "thank you, Qua. This house hasn't had a blessing like that since Big Sadie passed away, I don't think."

"Well then, you'll just have to get back into the habit of blessing it, now won't you, the way you were raised to do," she said looking at Jade.

Naiyah looked up at her mother whose eyes softened as they met hers.

XIV

This is the Way We Do

"*What* y'all got smelling so good up in here?" Jon asked as he lovingly wrapped his arms around his wife's waist, kissing her lightly at the nape of her neck.

"Watch it, baby," Turquoise cooed, "don't go startin' trouble."

"I starts nothing I can't finish," he chuckled. "Good mornin', sister-in-law, how did you sleep?" he asked as he moved to the customized marble-topped island where a carafe of fresh brewed coffee was waiting.

"Actually, Jon, I slept quite well, how about you?"

"Girl please, after that delicious dinner and cocktail and my beautiful wife snuggled up next to me, what do you think?" They all laughed as Johann put down his coffee mug and gave Jade a warm hug. "Happy Thanksgiving, sister-in-law," he said. "I hope a special blessing comes your way today."

"Thank you, baby, you're so sweet, that's why you're my favorite brother-in-law."

"Oh, is that right? It's not because I'm your only brother-in-law?" he teased. Jade knitted her thick, perfectly shaped brows together, looking coquettishly at Johann, "Oh, are you my only brother-in-law?" she said teasing him back. "Go on inside now and make yourself comfortable, breakfast will be finished in a moment."

"Great," he said moving into the dining room with the latest issue of *Newsweek* in hand.

Just then the phone rang and Naiyah picked up the extension in the upstairs hallway. "Good morning, Harland residence, Happy Thanksgiving," she said.

"Hi, Naiyah, it's me, Ms. Wilhelmina. Happy Thanksgiving to you, baby. You sound wonderful. How are you?"

"Hi, Ms. Willie, I've been better, but I'm happy to be home for the holiday."

"Oh, and I know your mom's thrilled you're there."

"Not so sure about that," Naiyah mumbled to herself.

"Sweetheart, is your mom available?"

"I believe she's in the kitchen. Let me get her for you."

"Okay, I'll hold on."

"Mum," Naiyah shouted from the top of the stairs, "Ms. Willie's on the phone."

Jade walked to the bottom of the stairs. "Naiyah, lower your voice, are you trying to wake up everybody in the house?"

A few moments later, Nathan emerged rubbing the sleep from his eyes. "Dang, sis, what's with all the noise, it's disturbing, you know? I was trying to get the last few winks of my beauty rest."

Looking Nathan up and down and trying not to remember her reaction to what Strong said the night before, nonetheless, she felt a brief surge of disgusting bile reach her throat but quickly disguised her revulsion for the sake of her baby brother whom, she loved deeply and unconditionally. Instead Naiyah hugged Nathan and placed a delicate kiss on his forehead. After the exchange of a few pleasantries, she rested against the beautiful teak wood banister. "I went over to Danny's last night," she said casually.

"Yeah, I wondered where you ran out of here to. So, what was going on over there?"

Naiyah, now hypersensitive, noticed that Nathan had grown quiet and seemed to be avoiding eye contact with her. "Not much, I went lookin' for a safe haven to wait out the storm."

"Who else was there?" he asked in a whisper.

"No one, just us. By the way, I didn't know that you and Danny go clubbing together."

"Clubbing?" he repeated nervously. "What makes you say that?"

"Oh, just some remark he made."

Pretty certain he didn't want to know, Nathan's curiosity got the better of him and he pressed on, "What did he say?"

"Something about you fanning your tail or turning up your tail all over town. I took that to mean you guys were hitting the dance clubs. Isn't that what it means?" she asked nonchalantly.

"I don't know what that fool is talkin' about," Nathan said sucking his teeth. "He's ridiculous."

"Hmmm," she said shaking her head, an unspoken question hanging in the air. "Now that I woke you up, you should go down for breakfast, I think it's ready."

"Are you comin'?" he asked.

"In a minute, oh yeah love," Naiyah said kissing him again. "Happy Thanksgiving."

"Wow, Iz, today's the big day, I hope Mum has a great time."

"Me too. I think she will. I think we all will because the day has already started off well. I'll see you downstairs," she said turning to leave.

"Who's calling me?" Naiyah wondered, feeling the vibration of her cell phone in the pocket of her flannel PJ's. "D'yanna?" she said out loud, not recognizing the name or the phone number. Scanning her memory bank and coming up short, she flipped open the phone.

"Who is this?" asked the voice on the other end of the line.

With no cause for concern or alarm, "This is Naiyah, who are you trying to reach?"

"Naiyah who?" the caller pressed.

A prickly warm sensation began to radiate up and down Naiyah's neck and she felt her palms grow moist. "Okay Miss, you most certainly have the wrong number and I don't have time for this."

"Wait, hold on a minute," D'yanna said, in a less threatening tone. "Do you know Elijah McCoy?"

"Who wants to know?" Naiyah said cautiously, now sitting at the phone station in the upstairs hallway.

"Well, my name is D'yanna James and I'm engaged to be married to Elijah. I'm calling this number because I saw it in Elijah's outgoing call log as belonging to a woman whose name I didn't recognize, but now know is yours. So back to my first question, who are you?"

"Look, I don't know you, I'm not trying to know you, and if you want or need to know who I am, I suggest you go ask your fiancé." Naiyah snapped the phone shut and sat on the red and gold, velvet cushioned phone bench in a state of confusion, hurt and anger all jumbled up together. "He didn't tell me he was engaged. How could he withhold such an important piece of information?" she breathed.

Nathan came out of the hallway bathroom. "Sis, are you alright?" he asked seeing that the expression on her face was now all jacked up.

"Yeah, I'm cool, but when you go downstairs can you please ask Auntie Aqua to come up?"

"Sure," he said bounding down the stairs two at a time.

"Hey, everybody, good morning—Happy Thanksgiving" Nathan said, pouring a cup of coffee and simultaneously taking inventory of the breakfast foods on the serving counter and their delightful aromas. He sashayed over to his mother who was walking in from the dining room.

"Hi, baby" she said joyfully. "Good morning. Everyone's inside, get something to eat and go join them."

He piled his plate high with egg, turkey sausage and cheese casserole, melon and a whole cranberry bagel.

"Nathan!" Sequoia shouted incredulously as he sat down beside her. "Where are you going to put all that food?"

"Yeah, nephew, with your little narrow behind, you don't have any place to put it," Uncle Jon added.

"Don't worry about it," he joked. "I didn't ask for any opinion or commentary," he said reaching for the Smuckers black currant fruit spread for his bagel. Changing the subject, he asked, "Did everyone sleep well? I sure did." Then he stuffed his mouth with a forkful of egg casserole.

"Nathan, you know better than to talk with your mouth full," Jade said walking in at that moment with a pitcher of fresh carrot juice. "Where's Naiyah?"

"In her room, she'll be down in a few minutes. Auntie Aqua, Izzy wants you to come upstairs, I almost forgot," he said.

Jade and Turquoise looked at each other, wondering what that was all about. "Okay, you all excuse me. I'll be right back," Turquoise said.

"It's open," Naiyah said when Turquoise knocked on the door.

"Nathan said you wanted me to come up, what's the matter?"

"Auntie, you're not going to believe this. I just got a call from some chick saying she's Elijah's fiancée. What in the hell am I supposed to do with that?"

"Watch your mouth, Izzy. No matter what, you're still a lady. Anyway, how does she know about you?"

"She snooped through his cell phone," she replied.

"Okay, you knew he was in a relationship, so that shouldn't surprise you."

"But," she protested, "he never said anything about marrying her. The last time we were together I knew we were having goodbye sex, and he said he wanted to try and make it work with his longtime girlfriend from high school. I had no idea it was that serious."

Turquoise sat down next to Naiyah. "So how do you feel about it?"

"I'm angry."

"Why?"

"Well, for one, I was caught off guard."

"And?"

"I'm hurt."

"Why?"

"Auntie Aqua, you aren't helping."

"Why?"

"Because you keep asking why, that's why."

"Naiyah, I think you need to get in touch with your feelings, and I'm just trying to help you do it, that's all."

She took a deep breath and exhaled, "I'm hurt because I decided I wanted Lijah for myself. I started to hope this baby I'm carrying would change me or change him, and that somehow we might become a family. I guess I'm angry because now my hopes are dashed and I'm really mad because he didn't tell me."

"Sweetheart, I understand why you're hurt, but do you really have a right to be angry? He told you he was with someone. At the time, he didn't owe you anything more."

"Why would you say that?"

"First of all, sweetheart, you and Elijah hadn't seen or spoken to each other in three months before you called and hit him with that bombshell. Give the man some credit; he is processing a whole lot here. Yes, you're carrying a baby, but whose decision was that? It was yours and yours alone, wasn't it?"

"Okay, you got me there, but I'm still mad."

"It's your prerogative to be mad, but being mad won't help your situation any, and that toxic energy is only going to hurt the baby. I hope you won't use this as an opportunity to inflict more hurt and misunderstanding. Instead, why don't you let it be a catalyst to a meaningful dialogue when you see each other tomorrow?"

"I don't know about that. I may not want to see him after all."

"Naiyah, don't be silly," Turquoise chided. "Now that I have your attention, let me play the devil's advocate." She watched Naiyah stiffen and shift uneasily. "I asked you this before, but I'll ask again, do you love this man? The day we had lunch at Junoon East's, you said you didn't have a clue how to love him. What's changed, what do you have to offer him now in the way of a sustaining love? And don't say the baby because that won't cut it. Get real and serious with yourself, Izzy, and when you see Elijah, be mature, lay it out plain and simple—everything,—and let the chips fall where they may. Believe me, it's the only way to move forward. I'm heading back downstairs, today's a day of celebration and I want to go get my party started, so come on down."

"I'll be right there," Naiyah said uneasily.

"Oh, and one last thing, Izzy," Turquoise said, "when we get back to Cali, I want to get you into a prenatal fitness program, maybe yoga or something."

"Yes ma'am" she replied with reservation.

❦

"Oh no, she didn't," D'yanna said to the air and walls surrounding her as she paced the floors of her apartment, now overcome with anxiety and rage. All she'd been getting from Elijah lately was some cock-and-bull about a time-consuming project he's working on. What made matters worse, was her finding the name and number of a woman she didn't know in his phone log. The other day at his apartment, one of the few times Elijah now allowed her over, she noticed his cell phone on the counter. When he left the room, she quickly peeped at both the incoming and outgoing calls made. Seeing a Naiyah Harland in the queue, she quickly jotted down the number. Something in her gut told her this was going to be trouble. But being the firecracker she was, she also knew she was going to nip it in the bud immediately. *If this woman, whoever she is, thinks she can just click me off, she sure has another think coming. Something ain't right,* she continued in deep thought, *and Elijah has a whole lot of explaining to do; he must really not know who I am.*

"Good morning, Ms. Esther," D'yanna said restraining her anger, "is Elijah there yet?"

"Hello Dee, and a Happy Thanksgiving to you too," Esther said shaking her head. "Elijah isn't here yet but he called and said he was on his way. You're coming too, aren't you?" she asked.

"That was the plan, but I haven't spoken to Elijah in a couple of days, so I don't know if there's been a change in plans and he just failed to inform me or not," she said gritting her teeth.

"Elijah wouldn't do that, D'yanna," his mother said in his defense.

83

"He's been actin' real strange lately, Ms. Esther, so I'm not putting anything past him."

"Well, okay then, honey, that's between y'all. When he arrives, I'll tell him to call you, but I'm lookin' forward to seeing you."

"Me too, Ms. Esther, it's been awhile, talk to you later, bye. OOOOH!!!" she fumed, kicking off her slippers and then stretching out heavily across the bed. She was so full she wanted to burst into tears but her anger wouldn't let her.

"Good morning, Uncle," Naiyah said walking over and hugging him around the neck. "You're the only one I haven't seen yet, did you sleep well?"

"Yes Lawd, I did. How 'bout you?" he asked turning to offer her a kiss.

"Yes," she said simply. "Mum, besides this carrot juice, what other juice is there?"

"We have some pineapple, orange and grapefruit but, by far, the carrot would be much better for you."

All eyes were on Naiyah, knowing fully the implications of Jade's words. "You're so right; I think I'll have some," she replied.

"Nathan, honey, get the phone on your way into the kitchen," Jade commanded as he headed in for his second helping.

"Hello, it's Nathan, talk at me."

"Boyfriend, what's going on?" Mani asked demurely.

"Mani!" he screamed. "Girl, are you in town?"

"I am," she said.

"You better not be playing with me and you better be getting yourself over here sometime today."

"I don't know, Nate, is Izzy there?"

"Yes," he said lowering his voice, "and she's going through a lot right now. She needs a friend, Mani."

"I don't know" she repeated.

"Listen," he said, "I stayed out of it before, trying to give you time and space for healing and putting things back together, but now it's time. You and Naiyah need to talk and patch up this rift between you. You two are sisters. Maybe not by blood, but in every other way that matters."

"We'll see," Mani said. "Now, may I speak with your mom?"

"I'm not playin', Mani, I'm dead serious."

"Okay, okay, I'll see you later, now put Ms. Jade on."

A short while later, after putting the phone back in its receiver, Jade sauntered into the dining room. "That was refreshing," Jade said, more for Naiyah's benefit, though her comment was directed at Nathan.

"You mean Mani's phone call?"

"Yes, she's such a delightful young lady."

"Izzy, isn't that your best friend?" Sequoia inquired.

"We were best friends, but I'm not so sure anymore."

"Oh, I'm sorry, what happened?"

"It's a long story, cousin."

"Jade, honey, when will Willie and Ronnel be getting here?" Turquoise asked.

"Somewhere around three," Jade replied.

"Are they bringing their mother?"

"No, she's going to stay at home after all. The nurse is coming and will stay until Mrs. Alexander goes to bed."

"Yeah, that's probably best."

"Um-hum. Okay kiddos, let's get a move on," Jade said hurrying everyone to finish a breakfast which had now turned into brunch.

"Jade, is Lucky going to make it over?" Johann asked.

She stared at him as though he'd lost his very mind. "You're kidding, right?"

"Actually," Naiyah said, getting up from the table, "Poppy is going to stop by. I called him last night and asked him to come."

"You didn't say anything about this last night," Jade said evenly, "and I think you should call and tell him not to come after all."

"Mum, he's coming to see about me... and Nathan," she added. "Chill, he's not bringing Analise with him."

Jade let her back down slightly, "Still, we're having a family celebration today. Laughing and joking, having fun. Where does Lemuel fit in that?"

"He's our father and still very much your husband," Naiyah said sharply.

"Enough already you all, it's a good thing he's coming by. I can't wait to see my brother-in-law. It's been a long time," Johann interjected trying to put a stop to the sparring.

Turquoise kissed him long and hard on the mouth then added, "You're so right baby, I can't wait to see him either. Now Jade, scoot, let's get in the kitchen and get busy 'cause before you know it, company will be here."

Once they'd left the room, Naiyah went over to Uncle Jon and put her arms around his waist. "Thank you, Uncle, for being the voice of reason, sometimes my mother can be so unreasonable."

"Ssssh," he said drawing her head to his chest, "try to see this from her perspective, baby girl. Husband or not, as far as she's concerned, he's still estranged with someone strange. It shouldn't be hard for you to understand why she doesn't want him here. He wounded her deeply, but at the same time," now holding Naiyah at arm's length, "I can also see why you need him right now."

Sequoia got up as well. She walked over to them, "I want in on the love," she said, surrounding them both with her outstretched arms.

Leading the way out of the room, "Come, Sequoi," Naiyah said, "let's go get ready."

XV

Old Friends

"*Girl,* look at you," Jade said opening the door for her friend Wilhelmina. "Fabulous doesn't even begin to describe how you're lookin'."

"Girl, quit," she said, grinning with embarrassment.

"I'm serious, Willie, you look gorgeous, like you're growing young."

"Jade, honey," Wilhelmina laughed, "it's just been too long since we've seen one another, come over here and give me a hug."

Walking into the huge foyer, Turquoise took one look at Wilhelmina and said, "She ain't lying, girl, you're workin' it."

"Ah, hello," Ronnel interjected, frantically waving his hand and looking all good and delicious warmed by a scrumptious grey cashmere trench coat. "In case no one noticed, I'm standing here, ladies," he said. When he moved out from behind his sister, though he stood a statuesque six feet, three inches tall, Jade gasped, as though, she really hadn't seen him standing there and her breath had been taken away at the same time. He was *GQ*—smooth as he reached out to greet her. As he leaned in to kiss her cheek, an electric charge fired. Jade wondered if it was friction from the Persian rug beneath their feet or from underneath her Diane Von Furstenberg wrap dress.

"Jade, thanks for letting me crash your holiday dinner party. I was thrilled when Willie told me it was okay with you if I came." Just then, without warning, he glided his tongue out, lightly licking at the corners of his mouth. He wasn't being seductive. This was a mindless habit, and it was his way, Jade remembered. Yet there was something intensely erotic about this benign gesture.

"I'm glad you could come," Jade said, brushing her cheek against his and feeling yet another spark.

"And if it isn't drop-dead gorgeous, don't-hurt-em Qua," Ronnel continued as he extended his hand to Turquoise.

"Ssssh, Ronny, that was back in the day. My husband's inside, don't let him hear you say that," she laughed.

"Come on inside," Jade said, "so we can introduce you to Qua's husband Jon, and our children are also inside. Jon will get you a drink and please help yourself to the hors d'oeuvres. I have to run upstairs for a minute, I'll be right, back" Jade said hurrying off.

"Sissy," Aqua called out to Jade, walking into her bedroom without knocking. "Are you alright," she asked after finding her in the master bathroom sitting and gripping the sides of the Jacuzzi tub. "What's up?"

"That man put the F-I-N-E in fine," Jade whispered loudly.

"No doubt," Qua said in agreement, "and time has certainly seasoned him to perfection, did you see him?"

"Puleeze, why do you think I'm up here holding onto this tub?" Jade asked. "I wasn't expecting these crazy feelings. I was actually turned on, especially when boyfriend started licking his lips."

"Yeah, all of that," Turquoise said dismissively. "But isn't it ironic how just last night we were speaking indirectly of his and your past?"

"Qua, don't."

"Okay," she said, "but I hope seeing him will help you better deal with your own daughter's situation. What do you think Lucky's going to say if Ronnel's still here when he comes?"

"What do you mean, he doesn't know about Ronnel and me."

"But still, it's some other man in his house, you know how territorial men can be."

"Are you saying he might feel threatened?" Jade asked.

"He might. Wouldn't you if the shoe were on the other foot?" Turquoise responded.

Ignoring the question, Jade said, "Good if he does. He needs to feel more than threatened with his selfish, unfaithful ass."

"Come on, Sissy, let's go get our party on," Turquoise said taking Jade by the hand.

※

"Them gals put a serious Stomp Johnson on that meal," Johann said patting his belly.

"You got that right," Ronnel answered. "They put a whole lot more than their feet in it, for sure. That's what I call a real down-home-cooked meal," he continued.

"What in the world is a Stomp Johnson, uncle?" Naiyah wanted to know.

"Just like Mr. Alexander here implied, that be old school, Izzy. You ever hear about someone gettin' a pistol whupping?"

She nodded.

"Well, it's the same concept," he laughed.

"Unc, you're so crazy," Naiyah said. "What I want to know is, what do your African American Lit students think about you and your style of talking."

"Let's not go there," he said, turning his attention back to the conversation he was having with Ronnel. Naiyah left them to themselves, pleased that they were hitting it off so well.

Ronnel took a liking to Johann. He could tell he was a throwback, keep-it real kinda brotha, unlike most of the dudes in suits he knew. He chuckled to himself because he was one of those suit-wearing dudes. Sometimes he grew very weary of that whole corporate thing, but lately he was wearier of living his life alone. He hadn't been an unfaithful husband yet his wife, when he was married, said he was. She said his work was his mistress and she wouldn't put up with it any longer. So she had her own indiscretion that ended up being a painfully cruel chapter in their lives. He had to admit, as the Chief Information Officer at American Express, he was required to work long hours and many weekends, so he understood how she could feel that way. In the end, their marriage didn't survive the pressure. One consolation, as it turned out, was that they never conceived a child together. This weighed heavily on him though, especially since, somewhere in this world, he later learned, was a child he helped create yet was given no say in the decision to place it for adoption. It had been more than twenty years since he suffered that loss, but the pain of it still remained lodged deep within his heart. His marriage was a casualty of the war waged inside him from the pain of losing his right to be a father. There was enough bad press about absent black fathers or the image of black men as being nothing more than baby-makin', unsupportive, irresponsible boys. It made him sick just thinking about it.

Upon walking in from the smoking room, Willie was met by an alarming look plastered on Ronnel's face. Sitting down beside him she asked, "Honey, is something wrong?"

"I'm okay," he said flatly. "I just had a memory I wasn't expecting."

She covered his hand with hers. "Oh honey, I didn't think... it never occurred to me."

"It's okay, Will, it didn't occur to me either," he said. "But maybe this'll bring about some much needed closure. Believe it or not," he whispered, "I really thought this was settled, that I was good, but I now know I'm not." He sat up and shook his head while his sister soothingly rubbed his back.

After eating his fill, Nathan was now ready to get the party started. He had brought some of his music home with him and slid KeKe Wyatt into the CD changer. By now, everyone was relaxing in the lower level family room while Keke crooned on...

...Baby, I been thinkin' how you been actin' strange. I remember how you used to love. ...You used to love, but you don't love no more ...You used to care, but you don't care no more ...That's alright, that's okay, grab your keys and be on your way... I guess you thought I'd keep lettin' you walk on me like the floor... Like, I'd let you keep bringing dirt inside my door... Grab a bus, ride a train, a plane, doesn't matter, just be on your way ...Grab your shirt, shoes, pants and drawers and get up outta here...

"Who's that?" Jade asked, "Turn that up, that soul sista is hittin' it. Come on, Willie, dance with me, like old times." Jade was getting her groove on. She had paced herself well, sipping only champagne with strawberries all day. Now she was ready to get loose. "Jon, mix me up something good," she yelled.

"Wait," Willie said, "don't go hard, J.D., let Ronny make us those apple martinis. Qua, what about you honey," she asked.

"Count me in," Turquoise said while getting her own groove on.

"Willie, I haven't been called J.D. since Clark," Jade laughed.

"And you should be glad," Naiyah shot in. "I saw that seventies blaxploitation flick, 'JD's Revenge' with Glynn Turman."

"I remember that movie. You're right, Naiyah, that brotha was crazy," Ronnel said. Turning to Jade, he added, "She's right, I wouldn't answer to it either," and chuckled.

Jade reached out to Ronnel in a reflexive gesture. He met her extended hand and took it into his own. For a moment, their eyes met.

He continued gazing upon her while she lowered her eyes and let go of his grasp.

"Nathaniel, baby, what else do you have over there?" she quickly asked.

Ronnel was accustomed to awkward moments, but he didn't want Jade to feel uncomfortable. He quickly turned to Johann, hoping that no one witnessed the exchange between he and Jade. "Man," he said, "come on in the kitchen and help me hook up these martinis, and Qua, come show me where Jade keeps her aprons."

"Aprons, man, what's up with that?" Johann laughed, poking Ronnel teasingly in the chest.

"You see me, don't you and I've been checkin' you out too, so we both know, we don't mess around in our clothes" he said, winking at Jon.

"Go 'head, man," Johann teased.

XVI

Letting Go

"Doorbell," Willie tiredly called out from the leather recliner she'd plopped into after dancing with Jade.

When Nathan opened the door, he was greeted by Mani and her parents. No sooner had he kissed Mani and welcomed Mr. and Mrs. Davis the doorbell rang again. This time a few of the college students his mother taught were stopping over to say hello.

"Leyan, Kalu, how wonderful to see you, let me take your coats," Jade said to Mani's mother and father as she turned to hug Mani. "I'm so glad you came, and if it isn't some of my favorite students from Adelphi, what a pleasant surprise," she said.

"Mum, I'd like to speak to Mani for a minute. Do you mind showing our guests inside?" Nathan asked.

Jade ushered the Davises along with her students, into the family room and introduced them around.

Nathan led Mani into the kitchen. He continued talking as he picked and nibbled at the white meat of the turkey left out on a platter. "I'm really glad you came and I know Izzy will be beside herself when she sees you."

"Nathan, I already told you, I'm not so sure about this. Why do you think I dragged my mom and dad over here with me? I still don't think I'm ready to face Naiyah. When I was at my lowest, she flaked on me, that isn't easy to forgive or forget. She was my girl, my sis. How could she?"

Nathan looked Mani squarely in the eyes. "We've already been through this. How could she, we don't know, and it's really beside the point. I never said this to you before, Mani, because I love you so much and didn't want to hurt you, but I think you've been a bit selfish too. We lost our grandmother, you know. G-Ma was Naiyah's life's breath almost. Did you ever stop to consider that or have you only been able to feel your own pain? If so, then maybe you don't deserve Izzy's friendship and maybe she doesn't deserve yours."

"That's cold, Nathan."

"So is the world we live in, now what. Come on, Mani, you know we got nothing but love for each other, and if we can't take the high road and forgive, what in the world can we expect from the people who don't have love for us?"

Mani put her arms around Nathan's neck and whispered, "I hear you and you're right. Thank you, sweetheart, for caring."

Walking in, Naiyah nervously said, "Hi Mani, it's nice to see you."

"Hello, Naiyah," she responded.

"Nathan, do you mind excusing us, I'd like to speak to Mani alone," Naiyah said patting Nathan's shoulder reassuringly. "Come with me into the solarium," she said leading the way. It had been several years since the two friends had been this close to one another and, suffice it to say, they were feeling a little nervous.

"Mani," Naiyah began, "I know it took a lot of courage for you to come today. Thank you. I've really missed you and I'm sorry for the role I played in this."

"Naiyah, I know I was wrong to stop speaking…but I wanted you to feel my pain," Mani said.

"Mon, you have no idea to what depth I felt your pain. The tears you cried, I cried. The emptiness you felt without Austen, I felt too. The guilt you felt, I feel every day because I wasn't able to save him or help you. The isolation you sometimes feel without your baby brother, I feel it too without my YaYa, without you, and now in the distance trying to encroach upon my relationship with my own baby brother."

"Oh Izzy, I have prayed for this moment for a long time. I wasn't sure we'd ever make it back to one another. I was being stubborn. Please say you'll forgive me," Mani cried.

The two friends reached out to each other and freed themselves in the baptism of each other's cleansing tears. They cried and kissed each other's cheeks, hugged and held onto one another for dear life. They would never again let the other go. They'd learned that when you hurt, you hurt. They also learned that pride destroys.

"Mani, it seems like a lifetime ago that we drifted from one another. I have missed you more than I can say. I don't know what it's like to lose a limb and still have a residual achy feeling after the loss, but the way I've felt without you must feel just like that."

"Nathan is a good brother, Izzy," Mani replied. "He didn't let up."

"Really, I didn't know."

"He was probably protecting you, but he always reminded me ever so gently," Mani laughed remembering their earlier conversation, "that our friendship was way too important to throw away."

"Baby B, you go, boy," Naiyah said of Nathan. "That reminds me how I have to support him too."

"Is there something up with Nathan?" Mani asked, looking quizzically at Naiyah.

"Oh no," Naiyah said quickly, "I'm just sayin'."

"How about we rejoin the celebration?" Mani said finally.

"Mani, wait, there's one more thing I want to share with you." Naiyah's tone sounded urgent so Mani sat back down.

"Okay, Izzy, after all this, I doubt there's anything we can't shoulder together."

She took a deep breath. "Okay, here goes. I'm going to have a baby, Mon."

Mani didn't move. She drifted off for a brief moment, wondering what being hit by an avalanche must feel like. She then fully understood what Nathan had spoken of earlier. She let herself go there. *This must feel like an onslaught of fecal gravity to Izzy,* she thought. "Baby," she said finally, "is this okay, are we happy?"

Naiyah laughed, "Let's just say Mum is having more cocktails than usual." They both laughed.

"So, who is he?" Mani wanted to know.

"His name's Elijah and it's a bit of a story. He's coming out from Brooklyn tomorrow and we're supposed to talk face to face for the first time in almost four months."

"How long has he known?"

"About three weeks."

"Let me do the math, so you're almost four months pregnant and he just found out recently?"

"Um, something like that."

"How's Mr. Lucky handling this?" Mani asked.

"You would ask, wouldn't you? Poppy doesn't know yet. I just told Mum last night because Auntie Aqua forced me to."

"What, were you thinking that you weren't going to tell her?"

All of a sudden, Naiyah didn't like Mani's tone. *Was she trying to get all self righteous on me?* she wondered to herself.

"Ny, baby, I'm not judging, really, I'm just gathering the facts. I want to help. Come here, girl, and let me hug you." The two friends stayed locked in that embrace for a long comfortable while. When they finally joined their families, they found them all freestyling to J. Lo. Naiyah grunted to herself, "Humph, *love don't cost a thing* alright."

XVII

God-Mommy Remembers YaYa

Lucky knew better than to not ring the doorbell this time. He'd received Jade's message loud and clear the last time he was there. As a matter of fact, whenever he thought of it, he still felt a bit overcome. He stood there, both nervous and annoyed, waiting for someone to come let him into his own home where he could hear the music and laughter coming from inside. "Sounds like they got themselves a party going on in there," he said, his words sailing through the chilly night air on the wings of frost escaping his mouth as he continued standing...and ringing. Jade finally answered the door.

"Lemuel, good you could stop by, Naiyah mentioned this morning that you might come." Lucky followed Jade into the house, wondering all the while what was up, and thinking about Naiyah's phone call from the night before. When Jade turned to take his coat, he saw instantly that there was a radiant glow about her. She seemed bright and happy *and* she looked spectacular in the dress she was wearing, which clung nicely to each of her soft curves. Just as he was about to tell her how nice she looked, Ronnel walked in with a martini in his hand.

"JD," he said with laughter in his voice, "here's the martini you ordered." As he passed it to her, he reached out to shake Lucky's hand, "And you must be Lucky. I'm Ronnel, Willie Alexander's brother. Nice to finally meet you, man."

Lucky stood stunned for a moment, "Oh, good to meet you," he stammered, "welcome to our home."

Both Jade and Ronnel looked at him curiously but only Ronnel saw his reply for what it really was: an alpha male move to establish his territory.

All kinds of thoughts began dancing through Lucky's head. He wondered if this dude Ronnel was the reason for Naiyah's call or, worse, for the glow he was now witnessing on the face of his beautiful wife, the one he'd foolishly deserted for a Brazilian sex toy. As he followed Jade and Ronnel down to the family room, he silently sized Ronnel up. *This brother is rockin' Hugo Boss and damn if he ain't smellin' good too,* he thought to himself.

Johann got up with outstretched arms when he saw Lucky. "Brother-in-law," he said, "how good it is to see you. Man, you're lookin' good."

Turquoise joined them, planting a kiss on Lucky's cheek and hugging him tight. "It's been too long," she said with a tone in her voice that implied he needed to make this right.

"What's happenin' everybody," Lucky said, freeing himself from Aqua's embrace and walking over to greet Willie. "It's great to see you, Wilhelmina," he said. "So glad you could make it. We'll have to catch up before you leave." Lucky glanced past Willie to Ronnel, "I don't remember meeting your brother before," he said pointedly. Willie ignored Lucky's remark and brushed his cheek with her lips. "Baby, you are still a hottie after all these years," she said.

"Go on, girl, no, you're the one," Lucky teased. "How long are you and your brother in town for?" Lucky asked.

"Oh, we're pullin' out a little later. Ronnel and I both live in the city. We just came to celebrate the holiday with my girl Jade. As for my brother, you probably just don't remember him. When he came to Atlanta to visit, you weren't around, and besides, he wasn't heavy into the party scene."

Now more than a little suspicious, Lucky needed time to clear his head. "Excuse me for a minute, Willie, I want to say hello to the Davises and catch up with my little princess," Lucky said before making his way to the other side of the family room. "Leyan, Kalu, how are you?" he asked. While they continued in animated conversation, Jade stewed, waiting for an opportunity to yank Lucky away from her company. After all, it was her party.

Before Lucky could tell another tall tale, Jade walked over and lightly touched Lucky's arm to get his attention. "Excuse us, please, I just want to speak to Lemuel before he gets too comfortable. Lem, come upstairs with me for a minute, please."

Lucky wasn't sure what this was about, but he was praying that he wasn't in trouble. In the meantime, the phone rang. Naiyah got up to take it in the kitchen. As she passed her father on his way out with Jade, she asked him, "Can we talk when you're finished?"

"Yes, Princess, of course, that's why I'm here."

Naiyah picked up the phone, feeling a sense of satisfaction that things were really going quite well in spite of everything that had led up to this Thanksgiving Day celebration. "Hello, this is the Harland residence, Naiyah speaking."

"Naiyah, baby, it's me, Ms. Inez."

"God-mommy! God-mommy! Oh my God. I was thinking of you just the other night while writing in my journal to my YaYa."

Inez Jones couldn't get a word in edgewise but it was just fine with her. She was energized by Naiyah's excitement. At that moment, it came back to her why her best friend, Sadie Harland, sometimes called her granddaughter Butterfly. Inez and Sadie worked for many years in a lot of the same neighborhoods as domestics until Sadie got the big idea that she "wasn't workin' for white folks no more." Inez remembered their conversation like it was yesterday, "I done learned and done more than enough cleanin', cookin', tendin' children and travelin' to be able to strike out and do something on my own," Sadie had said. Despite her misuse of the English language at times, Big Sadie was well read and never once missed the evening news. Inez just listened politely until one day her friend announced, "I'm an entrepreneur, Nez." Inez had no idea what her friend was talking about. Big Sadie had finally stopped talkin' and started doin'. And after planning and saving for several years, she was finally ready to go into business for herself. She was a one woman corporation hiring herself out as a personal chef, caterer and nanny. She even charged her clients service fees just like the big businesses did. She was the receptionist; scheduler and customer service rep all rolled into one, yet no one was the wiser. Eventually, Sadie actually did hire an answering service in order to have, as she said, "a more professional enterprise."

Lulled back to their conversation by Naiyah's incessant chattering, Inez said, "Naiyah, I took a chance you'd be home for the holiday. I think of you often and wonder how you're doing. Your grandmother would want me to keep an eye on you."

"Oh God-mommy Inez, hearing your voice sounds so sweet to me right now. When I listen close, I hear my YaYa singing to me, with gentleness and genuine love and care. I'm coming to see you before I leave to go back to Stanford, okay?"

"Baby, I wouldn't have it any other way," Inez replied.

"God-mommy, did you have dinner today?"

"Yes baby, I made myself a little somethin'."

"No, I mean dinner, a real Thanksgiving meal?"

"Well no, I didn't have that kind of dinner."

"My Poppy's here now, so when he leaves I'll fix you a plate and send it over."

"You don't have to do that, Naiyah. Don't put your father out of his way."

"It's no problem. I'm going to send you everything, enough to last a couple of days. Mum and Auntie Aqua made so much food we have to practically give it away," she laughed. "I'll see you soon. I love you God-mommy."

"I love you too, Naiyah. You be good," Inez said smiling broadly.

XVIII

I'm to Blame?

When they reached the master bedroom and before Lucky could close the door behind him, Jade had already started. "What do you mean, 'welcome to our home'? What kind of game are you playing?"

Lucky had made himself comfortable on the chaise lounge by now.

"Jade, let me lay this out for you nice and slow-like, so in the future there'll be no mistake and no room for misunderstanding," Lucky said casually. "Whatever you think or don't think about me, let's be very clear about one thing. This *is* my home. My name's on the deed and I pay the mortgage. And that fact I'll make known to whoever I decide needs to know."

"And so you thought Ronnel Alexander needed to know?"

"You damn right, just in case ole boy wanted to get some crazy ideas."

"Don't be ridiculous, Lemuel."

"And don't you be so naïve. I don't know that brotha and I'm not giving him the benefit of the doubt."

"What do you think? That because it's your home, he'll be afraid to speak to me now, or visit me, or for that matter, sleep with me in this big ole bed right here?" Jade gushed angrily.

"Jade, don't push me."

"You don't have any right coming in here, trying to assert authority over what I do!"

"Jade, for the last time, I gave you proper respect under the circumstances, but you're not going to tell me how to conduct myself in my home. It's bad enough I stood in the cold tonight ringing the doorbell when I have a key in my pocket."

"Do I have a key to where you stay?" she asked, staring a hole through him.

"Now who's being ridiculous," he countered, staring back just as hard. But as he looked at her, he felt himself start to submit. He was captivated by her. *What was I thinking* he asked himself. *This is one gorgeous, classy lady standing before me.* Hardly able to contain himself, he took her all in and at once beheld her flawless skin, the color of a chai tea latte but more translucent, if that were possible, and a perfectly sculpted nose and dainty, pouty lips. He imagined covering them with his own, tasting their sweetness. He felt himself becoming aroused, only half listening now to the babble coming from her delicate mouth. He moved his eyes discreetly downward, visualizing her round pretty breasts beneath her Diane Von Furstenberg dress. He remembered how, whenever he massaged them or gently tugged on them with his mouth, he had excited her so. *She opened up with sweet love to me like a beautiful flower,* he thought. He wanted her desperately, not for the sake of lust but for the sake of all the years of love shared between them—for the life they had. He followed his impulse and moved quickly across the room. Jade seemed startled but he didn't care.

"I'm sorry, but I have to." He began licking her lips, tasting the sweet apple puckers from the martini she had earlier. He licked some more and, before she had time to resist, he'd maneuvered her down onto the bed and began kissing her deeply. As he started moving in a slow, rhythmic grind, Jade found herself moving with him slowly. Tentatively at first, then finally she found his rhythm and locked in.

"Jade, let me—please," Lucky pleaded huskily, no longer in control.

"No, I can't…I won't. You made your choice, Lemuel, live with it," she said, pushing up on his well-defined chest.

At first he didn't move. He needed this moment of closeness. She'd been his first love, his only love. He missed her and, surprisingly, he had to admit he needed her. He felt somewhat foolish now knowing he just played himself, exposing a piece of himself he wasn't comfortable exposing. Nonetheless, he couldn't help it when he found himself saying to her, "When I tell you I love you, I mean that with all my heart." He reached for her again. "Please Jade, please baby, let me kiss you or at least hold you," he pleaded.

She stood up, smoothed her dress and started towards the bedroom door. Without turning around she said softly, "I waited a long time

for this moment and I'll be damned, but all I feel is benign contempt."
Then she gently pulled the door closed. Lucky sat for a long while as
his pulse returned to normal. There in the dimly-lit room, silhouetted
by the light of the moon, was the reality shining in like truth, that both
he—and love—really didn't live here anymore.

"It has to be the full moon," Jade thought fleetingly as she entered
the bathroom in the upstairs hallway to freshen herself up before going back downstairs. "Everyone seems to be acting a little strange this
weekend or is it me?" she wondered aloud. Looking at her reflection in
the mirror reminded her of something else she wanted to say to Lemuel
while she had the chance. When she reentered her bedroom, she found
him laying back on the bed staring at the ceiling.

"And one more thing, Lemuel, while you've been off dishonoring
our family, your daughter's been out searching for love in the arms
of men."

He sat up like a shot. "What are you saying, Jade?"

"Naiyah's pregnant and I blame you," she said sharply.

"Me?"

"Yes, damn it, you."

"Pregnant? When? Who? How far along is she?"

"I just found out about it last night. She'll get around to telling you
too, I'm sure."

Then he realized this was it, the reason for the phone call, for the
tears.

"What do you mean, I'm to blame?"

"You abandoned her, you fool," Jade snapped.

"That's crazy and you know it."

"Humph" was all she uttered as she turned on her heels and walked out.

XIX

D'yanna's Drama

"*Thanks again* for having me, Ms. Esther. Everything was delicious," D'yanna said as she pulled on her lambskin suede coat.

"Anytime, baby. It was good you could make it after all."

At the door, D'yanna hugged Ms. Esther. "Hope to see you again sometime soon. Goodnight, Mr. McCoy," she said, hoping he heard her from the living room where he'd gone to watch TV before turning in.

"Let's go, D'yanna, so I can take you home," Elijah said brusquely.

"No sweetheart," she whispered seductively, "tonight I want to go back to your place."

"Baby, tonight's not good," he said with a little less edge. "Didn't I tell you I was going out to Long Island tomorrow? I need to go home to rest up, I'm leaving early in the morning."

"Elijah, sweetheart, you know I won't be in the way," D'yanna said innocently. "Anyway, how about I drive out to Long Island with you? That'll be fun, don't you think?" she asked displaying a toothy smile.

Yeah, Elijah thought. *About as much fun as a trip to the dentist.* Instead he said, "Sure it would, but next time, okay, Dee? I've already got this trip planned. I'm running out to see my aunt and I'll be back to the city before you know it."

D'yanna was undeterred. "That's okay, I don't mind," she said still smiling, "besides, we could stop at Tanger outlets on the way home and get an early start on our Christmas shopping."

Esther McCoy could see where this was going but didn't want to see her son squirm or hear him tell a lie he felt pushed into. Nor did she want to witness any horrific scene between him and D'yanna if the truth came spilling out right there in her kitchen.

"Baby," she said to Elijah, "I'm really happy you came and spent the holiday with us, I love you so much. Now, I hate to see you go but how about you and Dee continue this discussion on your drive home while I go inside to see about my husband." She kissed Elijah on the cheek. He turned to kiss her back, looking at her with pleading eyes.

Esther, determined not to get involved, knew all too well how it was to end up on the clean-up committee just by asking the right question at the wrong time, the wrong question at the right time or, for that matter, simply stating the obvious. She also knew this was for Elijah to deal with himself, seeing as he hadn't asked her advice directly or indirectly. She also knew bailing him out wasn't the solution to his problem.

"Goodnight, children," she said, now a bit more forcefully. "Have a pleasant evening. Dinner was really nice, see you later," and closed the door behind them.

"Why don't you want me to go along with you tomorrow?" D'yanna whined.

"It's not that I don't want you to," he lied. "It just wasn't planned, that's all."

"I haven't spent any quality time with you in a while and the drive will give us a chance to talk more about our married life together. I'm really excited about that, aren't you, Elijah?"

He was at a loss for words and being stopped by the many lights on Atlantic Avenue wasn't helping any. Finally, without looking at her, he said absently, "Yes, of course I'm excited about marriage."

D'yanna caught what he said, not knowing if he said what he meant or if she was just being paranoid and reading more into his words than was intended.

"Why did you say that?" she asked.

"Say what?"

"That you're excited about marriage."

"You asked the question and I answered you, are you trying to start something Dee?"

"No," she said calmly, "I asked if you were excited about *our* marriage."

"D'yanna, are you trying to start something just because I said I'm going on with my trip out to Long Island as planned?"

"No, Elijah, I'm not starting anything because of that but it's about to be on all up and through here if this trip has anything to do with a skank named Naiyah."

"A who named what?" Elijah snapped, refusing to take his eyes off the road.

"Don't play with me, I know about this Naiyah chick and you need to be about fillin' in the blanks real quick or you won't be taking that drive you're so fired up about either."

"What are you talking about?" he said bristling from her obvious invasion of his privacy. *She is straight trippin',* Elijah thought anxiously. *But how does she know about Naiyah?* "You know just what I'm talking about, D'yanna hissed. Then just as quickly as she'd gotten angry, she became eerily calm. "So, as I was sayin' before, I'm going with you to your apartment. I'm gonna make myself comfortable and hear what you have to say. For too long, Mr. McCoy, I let you do it your way and you should thank me for it, but quite frankly, I'm done now—through. Do you hear me!" she shouted. "You're going to explain to me what's going on."

"You're right," Elijah agreed, "I am. But not tonight." Elijah steered the car left onto Washington Avenue bringing it to an abrupt halt on the corner of DeKalb. After turning on the hazard lights, he turned to D'yanna and said, "I'm sorry, but I can't do this tonight. I don't expect you to understand, but there's no more I have to say on the matter, case closed."

She looked at him in utter disbelief. In all their years together she'd never known him to act like such a jerk. "This isn't over," she said quickly exiting his car before slamming the door with such force that the windows should have shattered.

Elijah watched her walk to the gate leading to her apartment building, looking stiff and rigid like a zombie. He knew he was in big trouble.

XX

Lucky, the Don

After downing a straight shot of cognac, Naiyah was caught somewhat off guard when she heard her father's footsteps behind her. Startled, she quickly set her glass down on the counter. "Poppy," she said turning to face him and finding a look etched across his face she couldn't discern. Putting her arms around his neck she whispered in his ear, "Thanks for coming. I knew you wouldn't let me down."

Lucky stepped back and removed her arms from around his neck. "Funny, that's not what your mother thinks," he said bitterly.

"What?" Naiyah asked, puzzled by his remark. *Where had all the good vibes from earlier gone to?*

"She seems to think I let you down," he said wearily. "Go get your coat, Naiyah. We're going for a drive."

While Naiyah went for her wrap, Lucky went back to the family room where everyone seemed to be having a really good time laughing, talking and dancing. He felt left out, a feeling he wasn't used to. *Jade is the center of attention tonight, full of laughter and animation,* he thought. It had been a long time since Lucky noticed another man admiring his wife, yet that was exactly what this Ronnel Alexander was doing. He was looking at Jade in a way Lucky didn't appreciate. But Jade was right. What right did he have to feel one way or the other about it?

"Excuse me," he said, "it's been so good seeing you all. I'm taking Izzy out for a little while. Jon, my man" he said walking over and grabbing Johann's right hand and then leaning into his right shoulder in the universal brotha hug. "How about we go for a drink and parlez for a minute when I drop Izzy back off?"

"Oh yeah, that'll be sweet. I'll be right here waitin'" Johann said.

Lucky shook Ronnel's hand, "Good to meet you" he said flatly and turned to kiss Willie on the cheek. "It's been really nice seeing you again. Keep in touch with Jade this time, you hear?"

"I will, Lucky, don't worry. And let me say to you that, after all these years, it's been good seeing you too," she said giving him a warm hug.

"Sister-in-law, I'll see you later," he said blowing Turquoise a kiss.

Just then Izzy walked into the room. "I'm ready, Poppy," she said locking her arm through his.

"Goodnight everybody," he said again turning with Naiyah to leave.

As they were passing Mani, Naiyah let go of Lucky and hugged her tight. "I love you, Mani. I'll see you tomorrow, okay?"

"Yes, sweetheart, I'm looking forward to it. Good night and good luck," she whispered.

"Oh yeah," Naiyah remembered, "I bagged up some food for my God-mommy. Is there any way you and your folks can drop it off on your way home?" she asked hopefully.

"Of course. Go on now. We'd be delighted to drop it off to her."

In the car moments later, Lucky drove silently not knowing what to say to his baby girl. All the while, Jade's harsh words played over and over again in his head, "You're to blame." His own voice, which he didn't want to confront, was playing over and over in his head as well, telling him what a selfish SOB he was, making it impossible for him not to feel responsible. He had left Jade and his children and for no good reason. How ironic that a working vacation in Rio de Janeiro with his best friend six years ago would cause him to betray every good thing he knew and loved. Not to mention how he might as well have pissed on all the sacrifices Big Sadie had made to raise him well and provide for him. "Naiyah, you had me really worried last night," he said finally.

"I didn't mean to upset you, Poppy, but Mum wouldn't listen to anything I had to say."

"Naiyah, your mother told me what the discussion was all about and I'm tellin' you right now, I'm more upset than she is. We're going to talk this thing out, you and me, but first let's take a drive to the ocean. I need the sound of the breaking waves to clear my head. After that, let's go talk somewhere. Starbucks, okay with you?" he asked.

Naiyah nodded but didn't respond. She was angry now knowing that her Mum had let the proverbial cat out of the bag. *How could she. It wasn't her place,* she thought angrily. Nestling deeper into the soft leather seats of her father's Lexus sports coupe, Naiyah seethed as she thought about how the conversation with her father was now going to go since she was without the benefit of telling him about the pregnancy herself.

Lucky pulled a CD from the console. Soon, the smooth sound of Paul Hardcastle quieted Naiyah's racing thoughts as they silently headed towards the ocean waves.

"I made some butt-ugly mistakes," Lucky said looking across the Starbucks table at his daughter an hour later. "I let my ego get the best of me."

"Poppy," Naiyah interrupted.

"Wait, Naiyah, let me finish. I messed up, I didn't do the right thing. Your mother didn't deserve any of the crap I put her through, and you and Nathan didn't deserve it either. I didn't think I was being neglectful," he said, "since I never stopped providing for you all, but I understand clearly now that it *was* neglect."

"Why weren't we enough?" Naiyah asked softly, assuming the posture of the innocent young girl she was the day her father walked out on them.

"Baby girl, don't you ever think you weren't enough. It was me who wasn't enough," Lucky said dropping his head into his hands.

With the effects of the cognac now wearing off, Naiyah said soberly, "It'll be a long way back, Poppy, because everything is all messed up. I mean everything," she added, stabbing at the table pointedly with her finger.

Lucky looked up, "What's that supposed to mean, Naiyah?"

"Don't tell me you can't see," she said.

"See what?" he inquired.

"I don't know how everything got so whacked and I'm not sayin' it's your fault, but since you haven't noticed, let me inform you. Your wife's drinking on the regular, your daughter's pregnant and your son...well, I don't even know what to say about him except that I think he's confused."

"Confused? Confused about what?" Lucky asked.

"How sad," Naiyah said shaking her head in amazement. "You really don't have a clue, do you?" Lucky just looked at her blankly. "Poppy, I think Nathan might be experimenting sexually."

"Oh, hell naw," Lucky said in a raised voice. "Are you tellin' me that my son is sleeping with dudes?"

"I don't know for sure," Naiyah said taking a sip of her now luke-warm espresso. "But I heard something on the street recently that makes me suspicious."

Lucky slumped back in the chair, unable to speak, unable to even collect his thoughts.

Naiyah continued, "So now you have it and, like I said, I don't know who's to blame, maybe no one is, maybe it just is what it is, but your leaving was devastating to each one of us."

"Naiyah," Lucky said, "when I met Analise in Rio, she caught my eye. She was hot and sexy and I'm ashamed to say I wanted her in a lust-ful way. I'm more ashamed to say that I got exactly what I asked for——"

Naiyah held her hand up. "Please, Poppy, spare me, I'm not inter-ested in hearing about your sexcapades," she said quite seriously.

Lucky blinked quickly. He was really losing it. *Sex-talkin' with my daughter and worst of all—sex with Analise?!* "So, what about the baby?" he asked, rapidly changing the subject to the real reason they were sit-ting in Starbucks on Thanksgiving night.

"Life is a miracle, Poppy, that much I know. And this life," she said touching her belly, "is now very much a part of me. God created it and I know I want to raise my child," she continued as a bright smile flashed across her face.

"How do you plan to do that?" Are you sayin' you're done with school?"

"I don't know, I haven't figured that part out yet. Of course I want to pursue my master's degree" she said.

"What about dude?" Lucky asked sarcastically.

"You mean Elijah?" Naiyah responded.

"Is that his name?"

"Yes, that's his name," Naiyah sighed. "I don't know. We haven't talked in a while. We're supposed to get together tomorrow."

"So he's from around here?" Lucky asked. Lucky's brain quickly scanned all the neighborhood guys but he couldn't remember anyone named Elijah.

"Yes," she said. "He graduated from Stanford last year and he's now in a fellowship program at NYU. He plans to go to law school in Boston next year," Naiyah said proudly. "He and his family live in Brooklyn."

"Where is this meeting supposed to take place?"

"He's coming out here to his aunt's house. She lives somewhere near us."

"I want to meet him," Lucky said, fixing his eyes on Naiyah.

"That might not be a good idea, Poppy," she replied. "I've only talked to him twice since August and meeting my folks might just be too much for him."

"Is he your man or what?" he wanted to know, eyes still steadily fixed on her.

"Not exactly," she said looking away.

"Explain that to me."

"As a matter of fact, we were just seeing each other casually," she said.

"So, you just gave it up to him," Lucky asked directly, pulling no punches.

"There was a little more to it than that," she said returning her gaze to him.

"Just make sure when he gets to town you call me," he said with finality.

Later, after dropping Naiyah off, Lucky took Johann to Jettison's, a local club where the celebrities and ballers hung out when they came to town. This club, with its strobe lights, pulsating music and beautiful people, wasn't one you just walked into, you had to be "somebody" or known by "somebody," otherwise you could forget about getting in. Because Analise's face and body were a knockout thanks to Premier Omega Fitness Club's facials, body wraps and Pilates classes, she'd skillfully maneuvered herself into the Long Island celebrity circles of Diddy, Russell Simmons, Donatella Versace and many others. Being able to get into Jettison's because of this beautiful woman was a perk Lucky had come to enjoy. He also liked being invited to Diddy's white party every Labor Day or going to one of Russell Simmons' many fundraisers. Indeed, another reason for his strong attraction to this beautiful Brazilian sex kitten was that she knew how to connect and was very much connected. Sitting across from Jon, Lucky asked, "Man, what am I going to do? Between my wife and my mistress, I got one hot mess on my hands."

"Go easy on yourself, Lucky," Johann said. "You had it all, or so you thought, so naturally you wanted it all. But as you can see now, it was just an illusion. And since you can see more clearly, the good news is, you can fix it, but it's going to take some real humility on your part."

"Man," Lucky lamented, "Analise put some moves on me I never heard of, never knew existed. She came with some tricks that made me absolutely lose my mind; so much so, I left a helluva good woman and my beautiful bright kids. I was the playa, but man, did I ever get played. I don't know what I was thinking. Now I got a freak on my hands, who only wants to look good and spend my money. She was smooth, man, had me believin' for the longest time that I was the great Don Dada."

"Go 'head, man," Johann countered. "You know nothing good ever comes out of infidelity—nothing."

"Yeah, I shoulda known that from watching my own skirt-chasin' Papa, that ol' Jesse Harland was some teacher," Lucky said stroking his clean-shaven chin.

Johann nodded his head and stared into his glass meditating on what he wanted to say to his brother-in-law. Finally he said, "You know, Lucky, I love you like you were my own brother, but I gotta tell you, man, I'm really disappointed. I sure as hell don't want to make you feel any worse after what you just shared about why you left your family, but what happened to the honorable Lucky I once knew, where's he?"

Inexplicably, Lucky began to feel the burden of the last several years, especially the day Jade walked out of the kitchen leaving him sitting there feeling a sense of dismissal, and then the dam finally released and he broke down right there in Jettison's, sitting across from his brother-in-law and friend.

Johann calmly said, "Its okay, man, just let it out." Johann could see people watching them quizzically but he didn't care, Lucky was family. "Let it part like a river around a rock," he said metaphorically.

"Jade was my best friend," Lucky sobbed miserably. "She was the only one I ever trusted with my heart. When I didn't have her, I had no where safe to go to hide my fears, my confusion, or even my dreams. When there was no Jade lookin' out for me, all I could do was stuff it all down. Act like everything was fine. The mistake I made was stuffing it in a soul-murdering hole of illicit sex and make believe. You're right," Lucky said, finally drying his tears and scratching his head, "an illusion. That's what my life has become. A deception of my own creation, just because I refused to control my impulses. How insane," he moaned out loud.

By the time Johann reached the guest bedroom back at Jade's, it was way past twilight. Turquoise was sound asleep, snoring ever so lightly. He wanted to wake her but knew she needed her rest more than she needed to hear about his conversation with Lucky. It had been a long time since Johann had hung out all night in a disco lounge. In fact, he couldn't even remember the last time he was in one. Although the club was nice enough, he'd outgrown that kind of stuff. He'd rather dance up a storm with his wife in their living room. Although it was late, Johann was anxious to take a nice hot shower and remove the club's grit and grime. While the water pulsed firmly on his shoulders, he shuddered thinking about Lucky's situation. He'd never cheated on Turquoise after all these years and didn't understand how Lucky could throw away everything like that. Johann offered a prayer of thanksgiving that he himself had never acted on impulse. He was grateful that love always won and that love really was "stronger than pride," and he realized that Sadé had never lied when she sang that song.

Qua reached for him when he came to bed. "Is everything okay?" she asked.

"Yeah baby, everything's going to be just fine. Lucky knows he's out of order and I believe he's really sorry."

"He should be, the fool."

"Let's not judge, that's for God to do. All we can do is pray," Johann said.

"Thankfully, nothing's too hard for God," she replied.

Johann pulled his wife close. "Sweetheart, you mean everything in the world to me and I love you so much," he said, holding her tight.

There, bathed by the moonlight streaming into the room and kissing them tenderly, Johann and Turquoise made righteous love with the very same passion they had some twenty years before.

Spent and basking in the afterglow, Aqua said, "I hope this kind of love finds its way back to this house."

"I do too," Jon said sleepily as he curled into his wife's warm back and drifted off to sleep.

XXI

Following Where the Trail Leads

"*Hey Kirk*, this is D'yanna," she said to Elijah's good friend and running partner.

"Oh hey, Dee, what're you doing callin' me so early?" he asked sleepily.

"Sorry if I woke you, but Elijah's on his way to visit his Aunt Lydia in Southampton and I can't reach him on his cell. It's really important I get a message to him. Can you give me his aunt's address or phone number?"

"Yeah sure, but how come you just didn't call and ask his mother?"

"Duh, for the very reason you stated. It's way too early to call Ms. Esther's house."

Kirk chuckled, "Hold on. Let me get it for you."

D'yanna smiled to herself, thinking it was almost too easy. "Thanks Kirk, I owe you one. Talk to you later."

"Yeah Dee, talk to you later," he said.

"Hey girl, it's D'yanna," she said to her long-time best girlfriend Nadira. "Put your riding clothes on. We're going on a road trip."

"Hold on, heifer, I'm not going anywhere," Nadira said. She was not in the mood for D'yanna's antics today. "Today's my day of well deserved R&R."

"Come on Nadira," D'yanna pleaded. "I need you to ride with me."

"Dee, I'm not going. I just told you what I'm doing today and no, I don't even want to know where you're going."

"Oh please, please, please! Come on, girl, get your lazy bones up and take this ride with me out to Long Island."

"I know you're crazy now, I'm not taking that long, boring drive."

"Come on, Dira, please. How about all the times I did some crazy ass s#@* with you, just because you asked me to and whenever you asked me to," she pleaded.

"Listen, witch, I told you—I'm not going."

"Even if I buy you something at Tanger Outlets?" D'yanna said slyly. "How about those Via Spiga shoes you've been drooling over for months?"

"You don't play fair, do you, Dee?" Nadira asked quickly, sitting up in bed, finger-combing through her luxurious, freshly weaved golden mane. "Damn you, Dee, I don't want to get up. I was out partying until really late, I'm tired."

"I don't want to hear it, I'll be over to get you in about an hour and you better be ready," D'yanna said.

"Why are we going way the hell out there anyway?" Nadira wanted to know.

"I'll fill you in on the drive out, but just let me say, it's serious. Thanks, girl, for havin' my back. You're a true friend," D'yanna said as she hung up. *Good, that didn't take a lot of persuasion either,* she thought. *That Nadira, she's my girl, I love her, and she always has my back.* D'yanna smiled to herself. "Okay, so what do I need——" she muttered as she scurried around her apartment. "I'll need to take a camera, my running shoes and, oh yeah, just in case, a pair of binoculars." Finding everything she needed, D'yanna packed her bag and left the apartment, but not before casting a backwards glance to the photo of her and Elijah on her coffee table. Somehow she knew things would never be the same after today.

"So what's this about?" asked Nadira as she slipped into the passenger seat of D'yanna's Honda Del Sol, adjusting her oversized sunglasses and trying hard, but faking the fabulous.

"Put a lid on it, just let me get onto the Brooklyn-Queens Expressway and I'll let it rip," she said.

"This better be awfully damn good," Nadira responded.

As she settled in for the long ride to Long Island, pulling a bottle of Fiji water from her bag, Nadira closed her eyes and took two large gulps. As they approached the entry ramp to the BQE, she turned to D'yanna. "Okay, let's have it. You said this was serious. What's so serious that we're out here in the mix like some fools on Black Friday? Good gracious, Dee, have you lost your mind or are we stalking somebody?" she said, staring at D'yanna like she really believed she had lost her mind.

D'yanna gave her friend a quick sideways glance. "Okay, since you've been so patient, here it is. I have reason to believe Elijah's cheatin' on me and I'm going out to Long Island to see for myself and confront him if I have to."

"Oh Lord," Nadira said, sitting up and looking over at her friend. "What gave you that idea?"

"Come on, Dira, I've been tellin' you for weeks now that Elijah's been actin' funny. He doesn't want me over at his apartment, and it's hard to get up with him on the phone."

"Did you ask him what's up with his strange behavior?"

"I've tried, but every time I bring it up, he shuts me down. Yesterday I called a phone number I found in his phone log. The name Naiyah was next to it. You know me, I'm not about to let things go. So when I called the number, this Naiyah chick told me to go ask Elijah who she was and hung up on me."

Nadira snapped her neck in D'yanna's direction. "Oh no she didn't!" she exclaimed through clenched teeth.

D'yanna smiled to herself. Nadira was the perfect friend to have if a beat—down was called for. Nadira had whupped many a butt of those who were fooled by her handsome face and polite demeanor.

"I asked Elijah to tell me what was going on but first I told him I'd like to drive out to Long Island with him today. He didn't have anything to say and then told me in so many words he didn't want me going with him."

"Oh, hell yeah, this is serious," Nadira said with jaws tight. "Girl, if we catch him with somebody else, it's gonna be over for the both of them, I promise you," Nadira continued.

D'yanna wasn't surprised; she knew her girl would feel the same way she did. They may have graduated from Howard, but they were still Brownsville Brooklyn girls at heart and could scrap with the best of them.

"Okay, so what are we going to do, what's the plan?" Nadira asked.

"I think we should play it by ear. I thought we'd go by his Aunt Lydia's first and see what we can find out there then we'll wait and see." D'yanna gripped the steering wheel tightly as she maneuvered the car off the BQE onto the Long Island Expressway heading east. By now, she'd worked up a simmering rage and was nearly out of control. Elijah's behavior was puzzling and out of character for him. Besides that, his attitude towards her had turned downright mean and she felt she didn't deserve it. D'yanna wondered who this Mr. Hyde was that snatched and took over the mind and body of her man? How could they have gone from planning their wedding and being on their way to Tiffany's to this? She became even more incensed as she fingered her naked ring finger with her right hand. "Oooh, how could he?" she shouted.

"Calm down, Dee," Nadira comforted, "it's going to be okay. When we see Elijah, he'll explain everything, and who knows, maybe he's even planning some kind of engagement surprise for you."

The thought of that made D'yanna smile finally. "Maybe you're right, Dira, maybe I'm letting my imagination get the best of me, maybe I'm blowing things out of proportion. I hope so," she said. "I mean really, Elijah is my Baby Boy and I'm not letting him go anywhere, not without a serious knock-down, drag-out fight anyhow," she said, the smile quickly disappearing.

"I know that's right," Nadira said pulling a cigarette from her bag.

"Unh, unh, Dira, you know I don't allow cigarette smokin' in my car."

"Well, you're allowing it today after you made me get up and take this ride with you. I know you're not gonna give me heat about my cigarette."

"I don't care about all that," D'yanna said, "I can't let you smoke in here."

"Watch me," Nadira said, rolling down the passenger window and lighting up a Newport. "Dee, I always give you respect and you know it, but come on, you got to give me a break here. I need my nicotine fix after all this. I promise I won't drop one ash and I'll keep the window down till I'm done," she said hoping D'yanna would get off her case. Nadira turned the radio on to Hot 97. D'yanna glanced at her friend who was about to rock her seat right off the track. She couldn't help joining in though, pounding the steering wheel to the beat of Usher's "Good Ol' Ghetto" from his latest 8701 album while the boogie demon took complete control of Nadira's soul, rockin' rollin' and dippin' her like she was still in the nightclub.

※

"You were dazzling last night, Mum, so full of life" Naiyah said joining her mother in the kitchen where they sat in the breakfast nook recounting their blessings from the day and night before.

"Thank you, sweetheart, it was a Thanksgiving I'll never forget," Jade said. "It reminded me of how important family and friends really are, and beyond that I feel like a new thing began between you and me. I'm so happy, Naiyah. You know we've lost so much time with each other. I'm ashamed but so grateful. Qua helped me see myself this week in a very real way. Her presence is such a balm. My heart is open and tender this morning," Jade continued, "and I'm prepared to put the past behind us and do everything in my power to repair and restore our relationship." Jade's eyes shone with tears and hope as she reached over to hold her beloved daughter.

"It's not all your fault, Mum. Instead of helping you to understand me better, I hid behind Poppy and YaYa. It was easier. I shut you out and I'm sorry." Naiyah sadly apologized before hugging her mother back with a force she never had before.

"I told your father last night that it was his fault you're pregnant, but I'm just as guilty as he is," Jade admitted. "I was also absent and unavailable. But all that changes today, I need my daughter and I love you, Naiyah," Jade said planting a kiss on Naiyah's smooth cheek.

"I love you too, Mum," Naiyah said. *This was truly the best Thanksgiving ever,* she thought happily. And thank you too, YaYa, she murmured to herself before returning her mother's kiss.

Naiyah then began to cry tears of joy and release in hearing her Mum's comforting words. Words she'd longed to hear for a very long time.

"I was envious of your relationship with your father," Jade admitted.

"I fully understand Mum, just as I envied the close relationship you and Nathan have."

At that moment, they both felt a release of tension.

"I heard some of that," Aqua said, walking into the kitchen. "Good morning, sweethearts," she said cheerfully as she sat down to join them. "This is so huge. If only y'all just made it a goal to understand and to be understood, even when it hurts, I guarantee you'll keep moving forward. Even when you don't know what you're feeling, keep talking; eventually you'll get to it."

Jade got up and made her sister a cup of fresh brewed coffee. "I know that's right," she said, "and with a baby on the way, we've got to iron out these wrinkles and get back on track."

"Not to change the subject, but what are we doing today, sis," Aqua asked "Lucky's got something planned for Jon, so it looks like it's just me and you."

"Yeah," said Izzy, "cause Sequoia and Nathan are going out shopping with Mani after she drops me off at Elijah's Aunt Lydia's house."

"Well, I thought we could go for a brief workout or perhaps a Pilates class at the fitness club and finish up with facials or a massage or something," Jade said. "I don't know what the crowd is like at this time of the day since I'm usually there much later, but I can at least call ahead and schedule our spa treatments. I think I'll have a European facial, a body wrap, and finish with a soothing hot stone massage. How about you, Qua, what will you have?"

"What you're havin' sounds wonderful, schedule me for the same," Aqua said while pulling a bright yellow banana from the bunch sitting in the fruit tray on the counter.

"Mum, so as not to have any more surprises, Poppy wants to meet Elijah and I think he's expecting me to bring him back here later. I hope you're okay with that," Naiyah said half expecting an explosion.

"Not really, you know I'm not particularly fond of the idea of Lemuel coming by, but under the circumstances, I guess it makes the most sense for him to meet him here."

Naiyah poured herself another cup of coffee "I'm going to take this upstairs and finish it while I'm getting dressed."

"Sweetheart, go easy on the caffeine," Turquoise said to her.

"Okay, I will, Auntie Aqua. You two have yourselves a relaxin' time today," she said leaving.

"One more thing, Izzy," Aqua interrupted. "Don't forget what I said to you yesterday. Be honest with Elijah and give him a chance to man up."

❧

"Hey baby," Lydia McCoy said greeting Elijah at the door.

"Aunt Lydia, it's so good to see you."

"Nephew, if you aren't a sight for sore eyes," she said.

"Go on, Aunt Lydia," he blushed.

"Let me get a good look," she said eyeing him from head to toe. "Boy, if you weren't my nephew, I don't know, I just might have to jump you," she continued, squeezing him tight. They both laughed not noticing Elijah's cousin Pinky coming down the back stairs.

"Ma!" Pinky yelled. "You so nasty and what you're sayin' is against the law," she added with mock indignation.

"Oh girl, hush your mouth. I can kid my nephew if I want to."

"Uh-huh, you sure can, but if Aunt Esther heard you talkin' 'bout turnin' her son out, your old behind would be lookin' for somebody to pick it up off the floor."

"Pinky, all you talk about is brawling," Elijah laughed.

"Boy, hush before I'm tempted to jump you my own self," Pinky laughed. "So what brings you way out here anyway?"

"I'm meeting a friend of mine from Stanford. Besides, it was a perfect opportunity to come see about my people," he said.

"Yeah, it's been a minute," she said, "and ever since Daddy died, we hardly ever get over to Brooklyn anymore."

"I know and y'all know that's not cool," Elijah said. "My Daddy misses his brother just like y'all miss him, but daddy misses y'all too. You need to go see him. He was in the hospital recently, you know."

"What?!! Really?!! What was wrong?" Aunt Lydia exclaimed.

"He's okay now," Elijah said reassuringly. "He thought he was having a heart attack but it was just a very severe case of angina."

"Oh, thank God he's okay," she said.

Elijah turned from his aunt back to his cousin. "So Pinky, are you still breaking all the fella's hearts and clubbin' every weekend?" he asked.

"No E, I settled down, man. I ain't tryin' to live that fast life no more. I got a decent job and thinkin' 'bout going back to school. In the meantime, I'm just stayin' here helpin' Mama out the best I can. So who'd you say you were meetin' out here?"

"A young lady I dated off and on at Stanford."

"A young lady," Pinky said staring blankly at Elijah. "Hold up. What about that Dee chick you dated all through high school? I thought y'all were gettin' married."

"It's a long story and yes, as of right now, D'yanna and I are getting married," he said.

"Yeah, so when did you get ole girl from Stanford pregnant?" Aunt Lydia said knowingly.

"Did I say anything about a pregnancy?" Elijah retorted.

"You didn't have to!" Aunt Lydia and Pinky exclaimed in unison.

"Get out of my business you two. I swear I love y'all but y'all are nosy as all get out." Changing the subject, Elijah asked, "Where's a nice place you can have a good lunch and a private conversation?"

"Well, if you want atmosphere and real good food, take her to 75 Main. It's a really popular restaurant," Pinky said. "Lots of people go there and I hear the food is off the chain."

"Elijah, baby, it's always nice when we hear from your side of the family and seeing you today makes for a damn good ending to the Thanksgiving holiday, but I'm still curious about this young lady from Stanford."

Nodding in agreement with her mother, Pinky said, "Me too. Is that why D'yanna didn't come with you?"

"Okay y'all since you won't leave me alone, I'll tell you this. Her name is Naiyah and, like I said before, we went to school together. I met her the year she came in as a freshman and I was a sophomore. Her family lives right here in Southampton and, let me be truthful, y'all, she's one beautiful woman, and I confess I loved her even though she broke my heart. She doesn't know it, she has no idea how I felt, and meeting her today makes me really anxious because I think she's about to break my heart again," he sighed.

"Wow, darn Elijah, sounds like you had it bad. But why do you think she's going to break your heart again?" Pinky asked.

"Like Aunt Lydia already guessed, she is pregnant and I don't know what that means for us. And before you ask, no, D'yanna doesn't know yet, I'm trying to sort it all out before I tell her," he replied.

"What'd your Mama say?" Aunt Lydia wanted to know. She offered Elijah a drink while popping the cap off a cold bottle of Killian Red Ale.

"Ma, come on, it's not even noon," Pinky said pointing to the bottle in her mother's hand.

"Pinky, what does the time of day have to do with anything?" Lydia asked.

Pinky waved her hand in the air ignoring her mother's question. "Finish tellin' us," she said to Elijah.

"We're going to talk, that's all. I'm sure nothing will be settled."

"So then it's definite she's keeping the baby?" Pinky asked.

A puzzled look spread across Elijah's face, a question of whether she'd keep the baby or not had never crossed his mind. His moral compass hadn't registered any alternative direction.

"Hey honey, I see you made it in to work on time." Wilhelmina usually waited until 10:00 to call Ronnel at work. He was definitely not a morning person. But today was different, Jade wasn't in the picture before.

"No doubt," Ronnel said lightly. Wilhelmina sat at her desk admiring a picture of her brother taken recently at their mother's house. She noticed how tight his honey bronzed skin was, looked at his shimmering eyes and flawlessly shaved head and still couldn't help thinking how deliciously handsome he was. It made her smile even though he was her brother, especially when she remembered how all the girls tried to be friends with her just to get next to him.

"So Willie, what's up?" he asked impatiently.

"Oh, I was just checkin' in to see how you were after last night and to ask if you had a good time."

"Yeah, I did. Thanks, I had a really nice time. I like Jade's brother-in-law, Jon. He's really together and I couldn't help but notice how skillfully and diplomatically he handled things when Lucky came. That was cool."

"I agree," Willie said. "The situation could have gotten somewhat uncomfortable. Lucky doesn't know anything about you and Jade's history though, does he?" she inquired.

Ronnel loved his sister but sometimes she was just too much—especially early in the morning.

"No, I didn't mean it like that. I wasn't even thinkin' that Lucky thought anything about Jade and me. I meant that Jon might've felt pressed with Lucky being his old friend and brother-in-law and his just meeting me and we clicked too. I can see us becoming friends, Jon and me."

"Oh, I see. I didn't think about that. Anyway, what do you think?" Willie continued, slowly sipping her morning cup of coffee.

"Think about what?" Ronnel said puzzled.

"Our girl Jade. She still got it going on, doesn't she?"

"Where are you going with this, Willie?" he asked slightly annoyed. "Jade's a married woman with some obvious issues."

"Yeah, that's true. But have you considered the remote possibility that you and she might have another chance?"

"Chance at what, more dishonesty?" he said, feeling a sense of frustration creeping in. "Don't take me there, Willie, if it weren't for you, I never would have known the reason Jade went to study abroad that year was to have my child and give it away. To make matters worse, she never told me about it. Willie, please," Ronnel said with marked annoyance. "I realized yesterday how much that wound still hurts."

"So then, if nothing else, maybe now's the chance to deal with it," Wilhelmina said. "But tell me the truth, aren't you still attracted to her?"

"I have to confess," he said, "I've already played out all the what-if scenarios—what if Jade had taken me seriously, what if she didn't think she was better than me, or what if she had confided in me about the baby and accepted the offer of marriage I would have made to her. Yeah, sis, I've played the what-if tape to death."

"But baby, from the looks of things, Jade isn't feelin' Lucky" she interrupted hopefully, "I can only imagine how it must have devastated her when he took up with that Brazilian woman."

"I guess," Ronnel said resolutely, "something like that would devastate anybody."

"Um-hum. That's why, my brother, I'm tryin' to tell you to strike while the fire's hot or iron, however that saying goes," she said.

"I don't know, Willie; really, I have to figure out first what to do with my hurt. Truthfully, I don't even know where to put it," he said softly, his voice tinged with pain. "Before I can deal with Jade on any level, I have to deal with that."

Wilhelmina didn't say anything, but she understood fully.

❦

"Got it!" Nathan yelled as he sashayed through the foyer in response to the doorbell chimes echoing throughout the large, wide open entry way.

"Good morning, sweetheart," Mani said moving in to brush his cheek with a feather light kiss. "I hope everyone's ready," she said. "I'm anxious to drop Izzy off and get to the outlets early."

"We're ready, but come inside real quick, Sequoia and Izzy are in the kitchen with Mum and Aunt Aqua. Come say hello," he said.

"Of course, lead the way, cutie, and you can just quit with the runway walk," she said shoving Nathan affectionately in the back.

"If you don't know, you better ask somebody," he chuckled.

"Hi all," Mani said in greeting. "How's everybody after that fabulous party last night? It was a really nice time, Ms. Jade."

"Thanks, Mani," she said. "It was nice and I'm happy that your mom and dad came too. It was just like old times."

"Yeah," she said, "the love energy was definitely off the hook. It really felt good." Turning to Aqua, Mani said, "Mornin', Ms. Turquoise."

"Oh no, Ms. Mani, you know we've been family a mighty long time, don't go changin' up on me," she said with a smile.

"Yes Ma'am—, Auntie Aqua," she said.

"Now, that's better." Turning to Sequoia, Qua said, "And don't you even think about going buck wild with the MC Platinum."

"Auntie," Nathan said giving Qua a sideways glance, "why'd you even waste your breath? Especially since you know I'm going on this trip. We're going to blow that mall up! You might even want to call and get your line of credit increased," he laughed excitedly.

"Boy, you haven't had a but whuppin' in a good while, I know, but let me warn you, just be sure the check you write, your but can pay for. In other words, you don't want to try me," she laughed swatting at Nathan as he whisked past her.

"Okay, okay, okay," he said raising both hands in mock surrender. "We hear you, Auntie Aqua, you made your point."

✽

Naiyah stood nervously on the porch waiting for someone in Elijah's Aunt Lydia's house to answer her knock at the door. She began to feel little knots of tension forming in her stomach remembering that day not long ago when her Aunt Aqua came to take her to lunch, the day she broke the news of the pregnancy to her. "Whew," she said out loud, "this is gonna be hard."

A few moments later, the door opened. A cute, petite, brown-skinned woman was waving her inside. "Hey, what's up, you must be Naiyah. Come on in, my cousin Elijah's expecting you, I'm Pinky," she said opening the door wide into their modest living room. Naiyah nodded and stepped in, standing just inside the doorway.

"Come in," Pinky said again. "Don't be shy, Elijah's in the kitchen with Mama. Let me introduce you to her."

"Oh sure, of course," Naiyah said, relieved that Pinky was being friendly. Up until now, Naiyah never had a reason to come into this neighborhood and had heard how rough the girls were here. Just the thought of them made her feel afraid, *but* she thought *this Pinky seemed different.* When they came into the kitchen, Elijah stood up. He put his arms around Naiyah and hugged her warmly. "It's good to see you," he said, "you're lookin' good," he continued noticing that despite being pregnant she seemed a little thin.

"Enough already," Pinky interrupted, "let me introduce her to Mama. Ma, this here is Naiyah, Elijah's friend," and turning back to Naiyah, she said, "and this is Mama, Elijah's Aunt Lydia McCoy. You can call her Ms. Lydia."

"Hello, Ms. Lydia, it's very nice to meet you."

"My pleasure," Aunt Lydia replied.

"We're going to get going," Elijah said. "Aunt Lydia, Pinky, I'll call before I go back to Brooklyn and try to stop back by. Don't forget what I said about going to visit my father."

"Come get us and take us over there, you know we're not drivin' in the city," Pinky said with a wave of her hand.

"I love y'all," he said waving to them from the door, "call you later."

"Nice meeting you both," Naiyah said politely. Once outside, she directed Elijah to Mani's car in order to introduce him to her, Nathan and Sequoia. None of them noticed the Honda Del Sol parked at the corner.

"Lijah," Naiyah said, "I want you to meet my best friend Imani, who we all call Mani, that's Nathan, my brother and my cousin Sequoia's in the back." They all said their hello's while D'yanna and Nadira watched from a safe distance. Mani, Nathan and Sequoia hopped out of the car to have a less encumbered conversation with Naiyah and Elijah before they went on their way and Naiyah and Elijah went on theirs.

Nadira asked, "Are those people Elijah's relatives too?"

"I'm not sure," D'yanna said, "but I seriously doubt it. One thing I do know, though, is that I'm about to find out."

"You damn straight we're going to find out, we didn't drive all this way for nothing and, I'll tell you the truth, it looks awfully suspicious to me," Nadira said.

"Thanks again, Mani, for the ride," Naiyah said. "We're going by my God-mommy's for a minute, and after that I think Lijah's taking me for lunch somewhere. We'll see you back at the house later. Nathan, you and Sequoia will do well to remember what Auntie Aqua told y'all," she said laughing. It was feeling really good to Naiyah to be in Elijah's company again. She didn't know why, but it just seemed right. She also felt safe, sheltered by the sheer physicality of his presence.

D'yanna watched as he escorted Naiyah to his car and, being the gentleman he was, took hold of her arm to help her inside. Nadira lit another cigarette and this time D'yanna didn't protest at all.

"That girl's really pretty, Dee, and you can tell from that fur-collared leather swing coat she's wearing that she got some style and class about herself."

"So what's your point, Dira?"

"No point, I'm just makin' an observation, that's all."

D'yanna didn't know how she planned to use the pictures she was taking, but that didn't stop her from clicking away. "These pictures might come in handy," she said absent-mindedly to her friend.

Nadira didn't respond, she was too focused on watching what was happening out on the street. She made a mental note of Mani's Toyota Corolla, the license plate number and the direction it headed in when she pulled off.

Once they'd gotten good and comfortable in the car, Elijah turned to face Naiyah. "I couldn't wait for this day to come. I really wanted to see you," he said.

Naiyah's heart warmed and she smiled sweetly. "I have to admit, Lijah, I couldn't wait either, but let me tell you, I'm really nervous, there's so much to talk about. I just hope the friendship we have stays intact once we're finished discussing what needs to be discussed."

"It will," he said with an air of certainty, "and Naiyah, before we go one step further, please forgive my stupidity for implying that the baby you're carrying could be someone else's. I know the kind of woman you are, and I'm really sorry."

Naiyah nodded her head but remained silent as they headed towards Inez's house.

✤

"Naiyah, baby, you're even prettier than I remember," Inez Jones said, moving aside to allow Naiyah and Elijah entrance into her home.

"God-mommy, you'd say that no matter what I looked like," Naiyah teased.

"Maybe so," Elijah added, "but what she said is sho nuff the truth. Hello, Ms. Jones, I'm Elijah, a friend of Naiyah's," he said extending his hand to her. "I've heard so much about you."

"How you doing, baby?" she asked him. "I must admit though, this is the first time I'm hearing about you, I'm sorry to say."

"That's okay, Ma'am, I've always been one of Naiyah's best-kept secrets," he responded smiling brightly.

"Naiyah, you sent over so much food I had enough to put in the freezer for at least another week," she said.

"Good, I'm glad," Naiyah said removing her coat, "because we really had more than enough."

"So baby, how is everything?"

125

Her eyes misting up a little, Naiyah replied, "I don't know God-mommy, things aren't going exactly according to plan and you of all people must know how much I miss my YaYa."

"Yes baby, I know, *and you should know,* I'm here to help you in any way I can, to give you whatever you need. Why do you think Big Sadie appointed me your unofficial God-mother? She knew there'd come a time when you'd need someone older and wiser to help you through things when your mother and father might not understand or be available. That's what I'm here for."

Elijah kept silent, not wanting to intrude on this moment between the two women.

Cutting straight to the chase, God-mommy Inez continued, "Naiyah, baby, how's your walk with the Lord? I'm askin' you directly only because I know you know Jesus. If I don't know anything else, I know Sadie Harland didn't leave this earth without introducing you to Him. That much I know," she said fervently shaking her head up and down as though that would make her point. Embarrassed by the question and more ashamed to have to answer in front of Elijah, Naiyah said, "You're right about that God-mommy, I know all about Jesus but, He and I, we haven't been cool like that in a good little while."

"He's your salvation and the answer to your every need," Inez said calmly. "When you decide you want a personal relationship with Him, when this hard cold world really gets to be too much for you, you call me, you hear. But let me tell you this, you can call on the name of Jesus anytime. You can call Him right now and He'll be faithful to meet you just where you are. It don't matter where you been or what you've done. Okay baby, you understand me?"

"Yes, God-mommy, I understand, I know," Naiyah said. "Though I may not be walking right at the moment, I believe God's trying to get my attention. My Aunt Aqua prayed a beautiful prayer of thanksgiving at our house yesterday. I was really moved by it. I felt reassured, but in spite of all that, I can't stop to listen right now," she said turning her eyes away from Inez.

"Baby, I know you heard this all before, but it's true, tomorrow isn't promised. Don't go presuming upon God's benevolence thinking you have all the time in the world to get it right. What about that beautiful girl, Aaliyah? She was doin' it, blowin' up like you youngstas like to say. She didn't expect to leave this world so soon, I'm sure. I'm not sayin' she didn't know the Lord, I'm just sayin' life can come to an end in a blink of an eye. Why gamble with your life?"

"Ms. Jones, I want to thank you for speaking honestly to Naiyah, I'm hearing you too, I'm listening," Elijah said. "My mother says the same thing to me all the time."

Somewhat surprised, Naiyah looked at Elijah before directing her attention back to her God-mother and said, "Yeah, but tell me this, what I want to know is what do you know about Aaliyah," she laughed, "what's going on up in this camp when no one's around?" she asked, still laughing, casting a lighter mood over the room. They all laughed but Naiyah and Elijah were convicted in their hearts by what Inez Jones had just said, knowing that their bringing a baby into a precarious situation outside of marriage couldn't be pleasing in God's eyes. Yet, they remained silent and unrepentant.

Elijah thought about how he loved being in the soft warm embrace of his fiancée D'yanna. She rocked his world and oh, how he loved it, but at that moment, he asked himself, *But don't I love God more?*

"So Elijah, tell me, how did you come to meet my God-daughter?" Inez asked, placing a cup of hot herbal tea in front of him.

Naiyah interrupted, "I'll tell you the whole story another time, God-mommy. After a few more sips of this delicious tea, we really have to be going. Elijah's going back to Brooklyn later this evening and we've got some other stops to make."

"Oh, I'm sorry, I didn't mean to hold you up."

"Not at all," Elijah said. "I'm really enjoying myself and I can tell you're a very special lady. I'm glad Naiyah has you."

"You're sweet and quite a gentleman, I know Big Sadie would have loved you. She would, you know," she said turning to Naiyah.

"Yes I know, she certainly would, God-mommy."

"Elijah, don't be a stranger now, come on back anytime you want."

"Yes Ma'am, thank you, I will."

"Thanks for everything," Naiyah said, "I'll stop back by before I leave on Sunday."

"Okay baby, I love you," Inez said squeezing Naiyah tight.

"I love you back," Naiyah said kissing Inez lightly on her weathered cheek.

XXII

A Rare Pearl and an Oasis

"*Lijah,* do you mind if we take a drive to the ocean before heading to the restaurant?" Naiyah asked once they were back in the car.

"No Sweetheart, I mean, Ny, but why do you want to go to the ocean? It's 40 degrees outside."

"I love the ocean. It's one of the few places I go to purge and restore. As a matter of fact, I went last night with Poppy, which helped me realize just how much I need to keep going there. When I was younger, I went all the time, I'd toss all my troubles in the ocean and imagine them riding away on the rough waves. Then I'd watch the sand sweep across the dunes knowing its grit was what gave the pearl its beauty. I fantasized secretly of becoming the rare and mysterious one, the Tahitian——"

"Rare and mysterious, that's for sure," Elijah smiled "but why'd you stop coming?" he asked once they'd settled themselves on a firm piece of driftwood.

"Fear of its power, especially after it claimed the life of Mani's brother Austen four or five years ago. The power source I feared was far greater than this ocean though, in fact, it moved the ocean," she said flatly.

Missing the underlying meaning in her last statement, Elijah expressed compassion, "I'm really sorry, Naiyah."

"No, it's okay. I don't talk about it much, but it was a really hard time. As a matter of fact, Mani and I were estranged for a very long time after that."

"I'm really sorry," he said again.

"Thanks, Lijah, your understanding and support mean a lot to me."

They sat in silence watching the breaking waves for what seemed like a very long time before she turned and said to him, "Come, walk with me."

"I don't know, Ny. My shoes aren't exactly beach-walkin' shoes."

"Come on, man, are you a sissy or what?" she teased. "It's really not that cold, so take them off then," she said.

With great reluctance, Elijah pulled off his black leather Tommy Bahama loafers and agreed to walk with her.

"You know, Lijah, you should loosen up some, you're so serious about everything and it makes you seem so much older than you are."

"*Really now,* we'll see who's so serious after I toss your behind into the Atlantic Ocean."

"Oh no you don't," she replied as she took off running playfully towards the water's edge.

Still following them, D'yanna and Nadira pulled up just in time to see this light-hearted play between Elijah and Naiyah.

"Well," said Nadira, "they do indeed, look a little too playful to be family."

"Exactly," D'yanna said, "that's what my gut has been tellin' me all along. Somethin' ain't right here."

"What do you want to do now?" Nadira wanted to know. "You don't want to confront them just yet, do you?"

"No I don't, I want to see if anything more incriminating unfolds first."

"If it turns out to be true that Elijah is cheatin', I'm gonna have a real hard time believin' it," Nadira said, "I mean really, he's one of the good ones."

D'yanna sat somewhat paralyzed, her thoughts rapidly colliding into one another so fast that she couldn't grasp any tangible thread, yet she knew it was too early to play her cards. She needed more information. And though it was killing her, she knew she had to patiently wait and allow Elijah enough rope to hang himself with. *But what if he does hang himself with it?* she wondered. *What will it mean for us? I love that man and I need him in my life, how can I let him go even if he is cheatin'?* Then her own voice of reasoning came to goad her, *Quit whining, Dee, stop actin' like some weak woman with no freakin' self-respect. Elijah ain't the last man on earth with a big stick and he sure as hell won't be the last Circuit Court Judge or whatever he's trying to be. You can meet another one. But that big happy willy stick is mine,* D'yanna protested as the battle continued to rage within her.

"Well," interrupted Nadira, as if reading her friend's mind, "if this *is* what it looks like, Dee, what are you gonna do about it?"

Fueled both with fear and anger, D'yanna replied, "I'll cut his thing off and give it to that trick he's skippin' around out there on the beach with."

Surprised by what was coming from her own mouth, Nadira asked, "Would forgiving him be an option, D'yanna?"

"Puleeze, when have you known an African-American woman or any African-American for that matter to forgive somebody for taking their piece and sharing it with somebody else? You know we don't do that and, sad to say, it's probably one of the major reasons many of our families are all broke down and broke apart."

"Maybe," Nadira said softly letting her guard down a little and her abrasive demeanor soften ever so slightly. "My mama forgave my daddy and I'm glad she did," she said staring out the window at the crystal blue water.

"Dira, I didn't know, I'm sorry."

"That's alright, it's not like we broadcast it," she laughed. "We kept that thing in house, you know what I'm sayin'? Except for Mama's pastor and a few other church folk, no one knew. Can you remember back when my daddy was sellin' hair care products and doing a lot of travelin'? He met a woman in one of those salons, and they took up together. Long story short, she tried to break my mama and daddy up, but you know Mama, church lady or not, she wasn't havin' any of it."

Intrigued, D'yanna wanted to know what happened, how Nadira's mother handled her father's betrayal.

"At first she didn't do anything."

"What do you mean?"

"Just what I said, she sat tight, waited patiently and did nothing," Nadira replied.

"How do you know?" D'yanna pressed, leaning in close so as not to miss one word of this juicy revelation.

"Well," Nadira answered, "you know how close Mama and I are, and being that I was in high school at the time, I guess she felt she could confide in me. That's how I knew."

"Really, how come you never said anything?" D'yanna wanted to know.

"Come on, Dee, be for real. First, I was embarrassed by what Mama was dealin' with and I was so mad at Daddy, I could've killed him. It was best for me not to talk about it. Besides, a lot of people cheat but they're not all out in the open with it, talkin' about it like it's an ordinary everyday conversation. Let's face it, it's really the worst kind of betrayal and violates everyone involved in one way or another."

D'yanna focused her attention on Elijah and Naiyah's backs since they'd returned to the piece of driftwood they were sitting on earlier. "Look at them," she said to Nadira, "do you really think forgiving him is possible?"

"I didn't say it'd be easy," Nadira said, rubbing D'yanna's shoulder soothingly.

"Look how close she is to him. Forgive him humph, all I'm thinkin' is how much I want to choke the mess out of both of them."

"Maybe you should ask yourself why you want to be married to Elijah, then you'll know if it's even worth it."

"Good point, now finish tellin' me about your mama."

Pulling another bottle of water from her bag and almost downing it in one long gulp, Nadira continued. "Girl," she said, "My Mama stepped it up. She wasn't about to let no hairdresser take her good man, you hear me," Nadira said proudly. They both laughed at how silly that sounded.

"First, she went to prayin' and fastin'. I even think she did some chantin.'"

"You lying," D'yanna said with eyes wide with amazement.

"Yeah, I'm lying about the chantin' part, but seriously though, she didn't argue or try to reason with that fool, she just kept on about her business."

"Then what?"

"She beat him at his own game, that's what. She cut her hair into a cute sassy style, bought some new figure-flattering clothes and started going out at night."

"Dira, don't tell me your mama cheated too?" D'yanna shouted still wide eyed.

"No, no, no, nothing like that. She went to the movies or the library or just over to a girlfriend's house. She wanted to make him think there might be somebody else."

"Oh, that was a slick move."

"Yeah, it was and it taught me some good lessons. *One,* how to run game and *two,* don't shut down your feminine wiles after you get a husband and some kids. A man wants to be captivated by a woman's beauty, having all his senses stimulated by what he sees—all the time—he needs it!" she said.

D'yanna wondered if Elijah was being captivated by the woman he was sitting next to now. She sat up straight, trying to conjure up an alluring air. She thought *that maybe she needed to step up her game.*

"Dira, what will I do if there's no game to run on Elijah, what if he wants to be with her?" she asked painfully, pointing at Naiyah and Elijah who were sitting quite close to one another.

Elijah pulled Naiyah close to him, shielding her from the chilly November air that was heavy with the fragrance of sea salt and seaweed. "Ny," he said staring out at the ocean, "I'm excited about the baby, about becoming a father."

"Lijah, I never thought I'd get pregnant. I'm afraid," she said.

"You don't have to go through this alone," he said. "Don't worry, I got you."

"I don't know, I'm not ready to raise a baby. I don't think I can."

"What are you saying, Naiyah," he asked, somewhat alarmed.

"I'm planning to put the baby up for adoption," she said while looking out at the rolling waves.

"Oh no, not my baby you're not."

Naiyah was stunned. She thought the choice was only hers to make. She hadn't counted on Elijah wanting a say in the matter. She mistakenly thought this talk was really just about him giving her financial support, the fact that she just told her father the night before that she wanted to raise this little miracle didn't matter. *I'm so confused, I don't know what I really want,* she thought just as Elijah began.

"No, I don't think so, my baby's not being adopted by anyone. I'll raise it myself if I have to," he said angrily.

"Lijah, baby please, don't be upset with me, I was just trying to make this easy on everyone."

"No," he shouted, his dark, smooth-as-silk skin turning ashy with fear. "Hell no, Niayah! You're not making anything easy. You're just being plain selfish, like always. It's only ever about you. Did you really think I'd be cool with this?"

"Lijah," she said, reaching for him, trying to sound assertive, though inside she was trembling. She'd never seen him this angry before and his sudden outburst frightened her. He pulled away. "Don't touch me, Naiyah. You just told me that you plan to give my child away to strangers and you want to touch me, are you crazy?"

"Please, Elijah, don't. What did you think I'd do?" she asked, bewildered by his reaction. "You're about to be married, for God's sake, and I have grad school ahead of me. It's not like we're a couple, not like we're here to plan what color we'll paint the nursery or what we're going to bring our precious darling baby home from the hospital in," she taunted.

"If I could hit a woman, Naiyah, I'd be catchin' a case right now 'cause I'd box you good," he said getting up and moving swiftly towards the water. Naiyah followed him while D'yanna and Nadira looked on.

"Lijah," she said gently slipping her arm through his, "if there was any way I could, I certainly would want to keep this child."

They stopped walking and once again stood staring at the water, allowing the rolling waves to bring calm to their volatile situation.

Softening a bit, Elijah said without looking at her, "Ny, you know I care deeply for you," he began. "I wanted to fall deeply in love with you from the very first moment I laid eyes on you but you made sure I didn't get too close."

"Is that what you think?" she asked softly.

"Yes."

"It's not true," she said, tears rising to the surface. "I needed to hear that you felt something for me, but you never said a word."

"How could I, you were always running away anytime I tried to be intimate or move our relationship to the next level?"

"I was dealing with some difficult issues, Lijah," she said earnestly, "I still am."

"Naiyah, you said you needed to hear something from me, well here goes, I love you, girl. I've loved you for a long time."

"What about——" she began, turning towards him, but before she could finish her question, he grabbed her and began kissing her as though she were the oasis he desperately needed to soothe a parched and withering heart. He kissed her deeply, trying, it seemed, to pull life water from her, letting the love he'd held deep within flow between them. Naiyah's passion was also ignited and she dared not let Elijah think she didn't appreciate this moment. She kissed him back, licking his lips, forcing her tongue deep inside his mouth, exploring him. They were now completely oblivious to everything and everyone around them.

"Oooh," he said huskily, pulling back to gaze into her beautiful eyes. "I want so badly to lay you down right here and make righteous love to you. Give you everything I've held inside all this time." Saying these words to Naiyah felt right, unlike when he said them to D'yanna in the heat of the moment.

Naiyah whispered, "Sssh. Please don't talk, just keep kissing me." She felt him grow hard for her and moved her hand down to caress his massive bulge. "Umm," Naiyah moaned. "You feel so good. It's been so long. I wish I could feel all of you," Naiyah breathed as they continued kissing passionately.

"I wish *you were* feeling me too," Elijah moaned, remembering how good she felt the last time they were together, the hours they spent making their baby.

"Are you still mad?" she asked timidly, suddenly shy and feeling more exposed with him than she ever had before.

"After a kiss like that, no sweetheart, I'm not mad," Elijah grinned while he adjusted himself comfortably.

Nadira saw Elijah grab for Naiyah and knew instinctively he would kiss her, so she quickly engaged D'yanna in conversation, hoping to distract her long enough that she wouldn't see it. Luckily, D'yanna didn't. *Whew, that was quick thinking.*

⚘

"I expected this to be simple," Naiyah said, "and now you've gone and made it complicated."

"Me!" Elijah exclaimed, laughing and feeling lighter and happier than he had in months. "Don't you think you're twisting things just a little?"

"No, I don't think so. After that little episode, we're worse off now than when we started. So what now, Mr. McCoy?" Naiyah asked, smiling up at him.

"Let's finish this over that lunch I promised you," he said kissing the tip of her nose. "Girl, I could eat you up," he said seriously.

She just looked at him. She felt the same way. As they made their way back to the car kicking sand from their feet, they both glanced longingly back at the ocean before making their way through the path on the dune.

⚘

"How much longer, Dee?" Nadira asked.

"Not much, I just want to see what they'll do next."

"Okay, but let's move the car and get in position before they come," Nadira said. "We don't want them seeing us now after all we've done to stay under cover."

"I'll move and park between some cars down there aways. That way we can pull out behind them," D'yanna replied, alternately wagging her finger at the windshield and starting the engine. Shortly afterwards, Elijah and Naiyah drove past and D'yanna maneuvered her car

134

out and began following them once again. She followed them to the main street of the village and found a parking spot a safe distance from where Elijah parked.

He went around to open the door for Naiyah and D'yanna almost lost it when she saw him take her hand in his. "What kind of freakin' ill mess is this?!!" she exclaimed. "Oh, H-to-the-NO!"

"Calm down, calm down, Dee, we got to see this thing through."

"Ooooh, Dira, girrrl I'm tellin' you, I'm-a bout to explode up in here. I'm madder than two somebodies. He's been playin' me all this time and what in the hell for?"

"Dee! Get a hold of yourself, come on, girl, seeing isn't always believing, you still don't know what's going on. You haven't heard one word of their conversation, just hold on," Nadira said trying hard to take control of the situation and keep herself calm at the same time.

"Dira, I think you're crazier than Elijah right now, quit with the Pollyanna bull crap."

"Whatever, Dee," Nadira rolled her eyes. "One thing I know is that you're not going to get very far if you provoke a confrontation, so just chill, see what happens and then we'll make a plan."

D'yanna relaxed a little despite the fact that she was boiling hot and out of control inside.

Once inside the restaurant, Elijah and Naiyah sat quietly, alone with their own thoughts as they feigned perusal of the seasonal lunch menu. Now with nothing else to distract them, they'd have to seriously get down to the business at hand. Elijah, however, was feeling relieved, though he wished it hadn't taken all this. He knew he needed rescuing from the mistake he had been about to make. Despite his strong affection for D'yanna, deep down he knew he didn't love her in the way a husband should love a wife. He felt disgusted with himself, realizing in his heart that he deceitfully charmed her into accepting his marriage proposal, but worse still, was that he had no clue what compelled him to do it in the first place. The longer he pondered the question, the surer he was that in his ridiculous attempt at not displeasing God, by pursuing sanctioned sex, not Holy Matrimony, he must have displeased God all the more. He continued to sit while looking across the table at Naiyah with a silent prayer on his heart, *God forgive me and show me what to do to make this all right and how might I make Naiyah my wife and make a family with her and our baby.*

"Lijah, I'll be right back," Naiyah interrupted, "I've got to run to the restroom."

"Before you go, did you decide what you want?"

"Just order me a lobster salad sandwich and small caesar salad. I'll also have a blackberry mojito."

Elijah watched her head for the ladies lounge and thought, *She must be out of her mind—a blackberry mojito, I don't think so.*

When she reached the restroom, Naiyah pulled out the last of the cocaine she'd gotten from Strong. She peed first and then proceeded to snort the coke through a tiny straw out of a tiny metal pill container she carried in the navy, patent leather Quincy Hobo bag she had just bought at J. Crew before leaving Cali. When she was done, she leaned back and took a very deep, cleansing breath, letting it out slowly. She lingered in that spot, daydreaming about the kiss with Elijah and wondering if it could really be possible? She was excited, yet she couldn't imagine this turn of events. It was hard to take in. *But now what? Certainly Elijah hasn't fully counted the cost of all he's putting at risk. That D'yanna James expects to become his wife and, from the gritty sound of her voice, she sure as heck isn't just going to go away,* Naiyah thought remembering the phone call of yesterday. *Elijah's going to have a serious fight on his hands if he tries to end their engagement,* Naiyah mused. Naiyah got the very strong sense that D'yanna was heavily invested in becoming Mrs. Elijah McCoy and would have a lot to lose if Elijah became a father, and he himself would surely be put to the test having to deal with an unstable baby mama. Bowing her head, Naiyah breathed out her YaYa's name, drawing back her grandmother's spirit for strength. Before returning to the table, she examined her reflection in the mirror, moving in close to see if any reassuring answers could be found in the penetrating eyes staring back at her.

Rejoining Elijah at the table, Naiyah found at her seat a glass of water with lemon and a small glass of milk. She sat down slowly eyeing Elijah, *Negro, puleeze, you've got to be kidding me.* Feeling those very same penetrating eyes on him, Elijah refused to look up from his Blackberry phone, he was now toying with. Naiyah thought *she should say something,* but decided to let it go. He didn't need to know how desperately she wanted that alcohol, not now anyway. Elijah reached across the table and took Naiyah's hands into his, "Ny, sweetheart, you don't know how relieved I am right now. I know our situation is less than ideal but I'm feeling like there's so much possibility. I believe we'll come to an understanding."

Just then, both Elijah and Naiyah heard a ding from their cell phones, alerting them of an incoming message.

Excusing themselves, they each went to retrieve their message, completely oblivious to any coincidence. D'yanna and Nadira, now standing at the front of the restaurant watching the two of them, had each sent simultaneous text messages. The message sent by D'yanna to Elijah read: "I don't know what you think you're doing with that trick you're with, but baby you're about to wish you never met this mad witch here. Look up and look in my eyes. I'm standing in front of you." As Elijah finished reading, he slowly looked up to have his eyes meet those of an angry Dee. Naiyah was finishing a text from Nadira which read: "I don't know what you're doing in a restaurant with my girlfriend's fiancé but if you want to remain a pretty young lady, you better just walk away—get ghost **NOW**."

D'yanna and Nadira stared at Elijah, making certain he understood they knew what was up. After a brief moment, they each flipped him the bird and walked away.

XXIII

Fit to be... or Fixin' to be...

Jade took Qua by the hand and led her to the juice bar. "I feel like a wet noodle," she said jokingly.

"I know that's right," Aqua said, "that was a really great Pilates class, I'm glad you suggested it."

"May I take your order," the fresh-faced young man asked.

"We'll each have a raspberry protein smoothie," Jade replied.

After paying for their order, they went to find a table while they waited for their smoothies. Looking over her sister's shoulder, Jade couldn't believe her eyes. There was Analise standing across the room near the spa entrance, carrying on a conversation with a handsome young eight-pack with buns of steel.

"Excuse me, Qua," she said handing Turquoise the receipt, "when they call our number, go get the drinks, will you?" Jade left the table and Qua turned to see where she was headed. When Jade reached the two who were engaged in what seemed like a very intimate conversation, Qua couldn't help but wonder who they were. She watched as the woman, who was an extraordinary beauty, began to back up as Jade approached and the young man seemed to politely walk off just as their order number was being called. "Dang" Qua said to herself aloud.

Returning to the table, Aqua put the smoothies down and walked over to stand at her sister's side.

"Turquoise," Jade said with forced politeness, "this is Analise, the woman Lemuel's been sleeping with."

Qua resisted the natural urge to extend her hand. "Hello," she said curtly.

"She was just saying she didn't want any trouble," Jade continued.

"No trouble, it's a bit late for that, isn't it, after all, isn't she the one that started the trouble?" Qua asked, looking at Analise pointedly.

"Wait Qua, hold on," Jade said with a flick of her wrist, "this is a beautiful thing. Let me assure Ms. Analise of one thing I know for sure she doesn't ever have to worry about, and that's any trouble from me." Staring coldly and unflinchingly at Analise, Jade continued, "Quite the contrary, I'm overjoyed that you're able to give Lem what he says he wants, but don't get it twisted sister," she snarled with the slightest hint of threat. "Make no mistake. If I wanted Lemuel home, it wouldn't take much to get him there. He made that quite clear to me last night," she said triumphantly. "Good seeing you," Jade said before turning to walk away with unmistakable poise and confidence.

"Later," Qua said simply.

Back at the table, Qua said, "Sissy, you surprised me. I didn't know you had it in you."

"Yeah, me neither. I've just come to realize that I'm tired of wasting time, and letting this thing between Lemuel and her consume me is definitely what I call a waste of time."

"Right on, Sissy, that's my girl. You can't make people do the right thing and you can't go making yourself sick over it," Turquoise said sipping her drink.

"You sound like you're happy that I'm choosing to move on," Jade said.

"No, I'm not happy at all. What I want is for you and Lucky to find your way back to each other, but right now I don't think either of you are in a healthy place and that concerns me. Besides, I want to see you get free, baby. You don't need this weight, that's all."

"Qua, you know, I haven't done much of anything for myself lately. Something as simple as a day at the health club has made a huge difference. My head actually feels clearer," Jade said.

"Outstanding! Now drink up so we can go top the day off with our hot stone massages. I'm enjoying being here at the club too, it's state of the art," Qua said hurriedly grabbing her bag.

"It is, and can you believe I stopped coming here because of her? Not any more though." Jade looked back and saw that Analise had made her way back over to the young man. At first she wondered what that was all about, and then, shaking her head, she realized it didn't matter anyway. *That's Lemuel's problem not mine.* Putting her arm around her sister's shoulder, they walked leisurely to the waiting area in the spa's lounge to be called for their massage treatments.

༘

"Who was that?" young eight-pack asked.

"No one important, just a woman I met in the past," Analise replied. "Now, as I was saying, sweetness, you sure know how to tantalize all of my senses. Being with you last night set me completely on fire especially since you seem to have found all of my hot spots."

He moved closer to her and whispered, "How about I continue my exploration tonight after some hot and sweaty bumping and grinding on the dance floor at Jettison's?"

"You're such a tiger," she purred, "but I like how you just get right down to it. I'll call you later, sweetness, and tell you when and where. I can't wait to have more of you. You're so delicious," she said brushing up against him as she sauntered off.

༘

Naiyah drew her attention from her cell phone and looked up without displaying any reaction. She scanned the restaurant dining area looking for anything amiss. She remembered Auntie Aqua telling her yesterday that "she was still a lady," so she didn't want to jump up and make a scene. She knew how to open up a can of whup ass and get busy if she had to, but Auntie Aqua was right, she was a lady and not a tramp. Measuring her words as she sat back, she said to Elijah, "I don't want to alarm you, but I just got a text from a friend of your fiancée. She threatened me." Still looking discreetly about, she continued, "She must be in this restaurant somewhere, do you see her?"

"Who do you mean? Nadira?" he asked feigning surprise, knowing full well it was Nadira.

"I don't know, her name didn't come up, only the number," she said holding the phone up for him to see.

"How did she get your number?"

"Well, this may surprise you big time, but your fiancée called me yesterday."

140

He began to wring his hands and wipe at his forehead, "Did she say how she got your number?"

"No, but I can say this. She definitely wasn't the most pleasant person I've talked to lately."

Worry lines creased deeply into the dark skin of his smooth forehead and frown lines etched prominently at the corners of his mouth while he searched his memory bank looking for a glimmer of truth in how D'yanna may have come to possess Naiyah's number. He still hadn't put one and one together from D'yanna mentioning Naiyah's name on their drive from his mother's house.

Drawing his attention back to the conversation, Naiyah said, "She asked me a lot of questions about you and told me that she was your fiancée. You know that came as a shock, especially since you didn't tell me yourself."

"Fiancée" hadn't registered with him when she said it the first time. Ever since he received the phone call several weeks ago about the pregnancy, Elijah had put such a chasm of emotional distance between himself and D'yanna that he no longer recognized her as that.

"Let's forget about that, we have this baby's future to discuss and that trumps any discussion about my fiancée or her friend."

"Wait," Naiyah said, "no it doesn't. It's all the same ball of wax. How can we discuss the baby and not discuss the woman you're going to marry, who, mind you, will have some influence in my baby's upbringing."

"Naiyah, listen to me," he said getting up to take the seat next to hers. Staring intently into her eyes, "I want you and our baby, I don't want D'yanna."

Naiyah's eyes widened with hopeful surprise but with realistic caution she asked, "How can you say that, Lijah?"

"Because I'm speaking straight from the heart, that's how. What do you say, Ny?" he asked. "Please say you believe we have a chance. I want you, I want our baby, I love you. I want to make you my priority. Isn't that really what you meant when you said earlier that you needed to hear something from me? That's it, I want you and our child to be my priority. That's what I've been feeling ever since you called me."

Naiyah sat stunned by Elijah's words. She didn't know what to say.

※

"Are you cool, Dee?" Nadira asked, seeing the tears forming in her friend's eyes, sensing the hurt emanating from her as she shrugged her shoulders, mumbling an almost inaudible "ummmm" in reply.

D'yanna was now drained. Nonetheless, with her energy obviously low, she managed a simple, "Let's just go shopping."

Nadira didn't respond. She wasn't really prepared for what they'd witnessed, and with the mood now somber, not knowing how to comfort her friend, she just rode in silence.

D'yanna wondered what was happening, who the woman with Elijah was and why she was there. She had her ideas of what she thought was going on. *Perhaps he met her at the school of law during his fellowship; she might be a clerk he became interested in, maybe that interest turned to something more serious.* Still, without hearing it directly from him, even though she let him know what she thought in the restaurant, she was still left with wild thoughts running all up and through her mind, 30,000 per second, making her very tired. *I got what I wanted,* she told herself. *What you go looking for, you'll find,* she sighed, *but can I handle the truth now that it seems to be staring me in the face?*

Nadira kept silent. By the time they'd driven the thirty minutes to the outlet mall, D'yanna had become a little more animated. "I just remembered, Dira, I've got the credit card Elijah gave me. He added me to his account a while back, just in case. I haven't used it, didn't want to compromise my independence. But to hell with independence today, he's about to get a little payback and it's just the beginning. Yeah, we're going to Barney's, Jones of New York and Kate Spade's instead of Saks off Fifth Avenue," she laughed viciously.

Nadira was having a challenge of conscience since she knew this wasn't right, but she was also feeling hurt and anger for her girl. *Elijah does need to pay for what he's doing,* she thought, *and this will only be the beginning if he truly has stepped out on her.* "D'yanna," she said turning to face her, "I still say we should have all the facts before launching into all-out war."

"Dira, yours is the voice of reason, I know."

"Let me finish," she said, "I told you about my mama's strategy, it was cool and it suited her just fine. I agree that manipulating the situation to your intended end is sweet, and that getting a brother's attention sometimes requires drastic measures, but I think if you're still planning to marry Elijah, you need to be wise in the moves you make."

As the two walked towards one of the mall entrances, Nadira spotted the trio she saw earlier leaving Elijah's Aunt Lydia's house in the Toyota Corolla. "Dee," she said hunching her, "watch this." She stepped up the pace and D'yanna hurried along to keep up. Nadira bumped into Nathan, who was walking on the outside as they passed.

"Oh, I'm so sorry," she said apologetically, "I was so busy talking, I didn't even see you."

"It's cool, no harm, no foul," Nathan responded with edgy Miami urban flavor. Mani and Sequoia had continued walking, but when one of them noticed that Nathan was still engaged in conversation with the woman who bumped him, they turned and walked back. Nadira was saying to him as they approached, "That's a bad saddlebag you're sportin' there, my brother."

"Yeah thanks," he said, stroking the beautiful leather bag hanging from his shoulder, "my sister gave it to me as a gift; she brought it back with her from California."

"The leather looks like its smooth and soft like butter, do you mind if I touch it," Nadira asked.

"Sure, go ahead," he said holding the bag out to her.

"She has damn good taste, the leather looks like Tuscanella, is it?" Nadira asked.

"As a matter of fact, it is. Thanks for the compliment, my sister does have good taste, actually, it's superb. She's about to have a baby soon though, so she'll be rocking and styling maternity gear," he laughed.

Mani, standing closest to Nathan, kicked his foot, signaling to him he was talking too much. "We've got to be going, Nate," she said pulling him away from Nadira. "You ladies have fun shopping." Out of D'yanna and Nadira's earshot, Mani socked Nathan in the arm. "Are you crazy. You don't go telling folk's business like that, you don't know those people."

"Come on, Mani, we'll never see them again, what's the big deal?" he asked.

"I'm just saying it's not polite to tell someone else's business like that and I know you know about six degrees of separation. You saw that movie, didn't you? For all you know, they might know someone we know or someone Izzy knows and, before you know it, we'll hear about them or see them again."

"Take it down, Mon, it's not that serious," Nathan joked.

XXIV

D'yanna Gets a Word

"*I'll catch* up to you, Dira," D'yanna said, "let me make a quick phone call."

"Okay, honey, I'll go check out the directory and meet up with you in Nordstrom's. I'm sure they have those Amanda 3's or Yvonne's by Via Spiga that I want. I haven't forgotten your bribe, I mean promise," she kidded.

"Okay, I'll be over as soon as I'm done." D'yanna took a seat on an empty bench and scrolled her contacts list for the number she wanted.

"It's four o'clock in the afternoon, I wonder who's calling?" Esther said dropping her crocheting into the basket at her feet after being jarred by the ringing telephone. "Lord have mercy," she lamented as the basket tumbled over and several skeins of yarn began to unravel. "Oh no you don't, devil," she warned, "this peace of mind you didn't give to me and you surely won't be taking it away." She took a deep breath, "Hello, God be with you, this is the McCoy residence. How may I help you?"

"Ms. Esther, this is D'yanna."

"Hi baby, what's wrong, you don't sound so good."

"Ms. Esther, why didn't you tell me that Elijah's going to have a baby with someone else? I told you how distant he'd become, but you didn't say one word," D'yanna said accusingly.

"Now wait a minute, Dee. It wasn't my place to say anything. Elijah had to find his own time in his own way," she countered.

"Yes, you're right, I'm sorry. I can't be upset with you. It was up to Elijah to say something. Now he and I both know the truth," she said bitterly.

Esther could hear the bitterness in D'yanna's voice. She liked D'yanna but had heard about her fighting days. "D'yanna, I hope you won't be hasty because what's happened in Elijah's life had nothing to do with how he feels about you. These kinds of mistakes happen."

"Yes, Ma'am, I know. Thanks, Ms. Esther. Goodbye." D'yanna clutched her phone to her chest and ran to the nearest restroom. Once secure behind the bathroom stall, D'yanna wept hot, bitter tears. *What did I do wrong*, she wondered, *I gave him everything, great sex, attention, partnership, whatever he wanted, but it still wasn't enough. This is crazy as hell, but I'll be damned if he's gonna kick me to the curb. He promised me a life and I'm going to have it*, D'yanna thought with new resolve. *I'm gonna keep my man. I don't know who the trick is but she's not gettin' him*, she said firmly to herself before heading out to catch up with Nadira.

As soon as she hung up with D'yanna, the phong rang again. "God be with you, how may I help you?" Esther McCoy answered cheerily.

"Mother?" Elijah called. "Mother?" he called again.

"Elijah, calm down! Where are you?" Esther tried to still the rising panic in her body. She'd never heard her son so panicked.

"Mother," he said for the third time, "D'yanna followed me and Naiyah."

"What do you mean she followed you?" she asked, slowly easing herself into her chair.

"She showed up here at the restaurant where Naiyah and I are having lunch."

"How'd she know where you'd be? Did you tell her last night when you told her about the baby?" Esther inquired, beginning to panic all over again.

"I haven't told her yet," he said.

Esther's heart raced and she felt the panic she'd been trying to keep at bay sweep over her. "Elijah," she said in a measured tone, "Dee just called a few minutes ago and asked me why *I hadn't told her* about the baby. She sounded like she already knew. Who could have told her?" she asked, raising her voice.

"I don't know, Mother," Elijah said incredulously. "It wasn't me and I'm sure it wasn't Naiyah even though Dee managed somehow to get her number and call her too," he said, his voice matching the panic he heard in his mother's.

"Well, son, it sounds like this is going to get ugly. Even if you do still marry Dee, you're going to have a lot to deal with. Call me when you get home," she said a little more calmly.

"I will, but maybe I'll just come over. It may not be safe to go back to my apartment," he said, laughing nervously. Elijah knew too well how D'yanna could go off. "Just joking, I'll call you later. I love you," he said before hanging up the phone. When Elijah returned to their table, Naiyah was sipping on what looked like an alcoholic beverage. His look informed her that he wasn't happy but he didn't say anything.

Let her have it, he thought, *what was going so well has now become quite stressful.* Which reminded him, he still had to face her parents, Oh brother, he groaned silently.

XXV

Nathan and Strong, Get It On

"*Mani,* drop me off at Strong's house," Nathan said as they were leaving the outlet mall.

"Why would you want to go there?" she asked curiously.

"I have some old business that needs to be dealt with," he said sharply, without going into detail.

"Humph, I can't imagine anyone wanting to deal with him about anything. Isn't he dangerous?" Mani asked.

"No, that's just his press report, don't believe the hype."

"If you say so," she said unconvinced.

Strong's SUV was parked in his driveway when they arrived, but Mani waited until he opened the door for Nathan before driving off.

Sequoia, who'd been quiet for most of the drive back, watched Nathan enter the house and remarked casually, "That seems really strange. What business could Nathan possibly have with that man?"

"I wonder too," Mani said before quickly changing the subject, although in her mind she suspected that Nathan and Strong were a lot closer than they needed to be. Mani and Sequoia then talked about all the wonderful finds they discovered at the mall.

"Nathan, my man, what's up?" Strong smiled. "I won't lie and say I'm surprised to see you, but I am surprised to see you this early. You usually make your move over this way under the cover of darkness," he laughed. Despite his reputation for being a bad boy, Danny West was a nice-looking young man. The meticulous way he groomed himself gave the impression that his mama must have really loved him. He was wearing a wife-beater t-shirt and dark jeans hanging low off his 6-foot athletic frame. His turned down smile and hazel eyes lit up the chestnut glow of his face. Nathan could see the ripples beneath his shirt and almost lost his breath and his mind staring at those big guns resting on Strong's biceps. Strong strolled into the living room where a football game played silently on his large screen television.

"So, Nate, holler at me, man. What brings you way over here?" he asked while tightening his belt and adjusting his pants just a little lower so they rode nicely on the curve of his behind.

Nathan couldn't stand Danny sometimes, and Strong knew the effect he had on him, so he always took a moment to remind him of it.

"Have you lost your mind, you signifying SOB! What's up with trying to make my sister think I'm out there," Nathan hissed.

"She don't need any help from me, man, all she got to do is open her eyes," he said evenly. "Let the gas out, man. Chill, I didn't say nothing to Ny."

"You're lying!" Nathan shouted, his braids moving from side to side with each jerk of his head. "You said something. Why else would she think I'm hanging out with you all around town?"

"Well, what of it, Nate? If I did say something, what do you think you're going to do to Strong?" he asked, flexing his chest with both hands on his hips as if to say 'I dare you to jump bad.'

Nathan was no match for Danny and they both knew it. But he couldn't completely back down either. "Listen, man," Nathan said a little calmer, "I'm just sayin', I don't need my sister or anyone else thinking I'm a homo or sissy or anything of that nature when I'm not."

"Man, you're delusional but it's not me you need to convince."

"What do you mean by that?"

"Nate, how is it that you've only shown up here on the nights me and the boys are kickin' it on the oral orgy tip, gettin' our high and freak on?" Strong asked.

"Oh mercy," Nathan sighed. "Coincidence, pure coincidence. You know I come over here only to get a little weed or a snort, nothing else."

"Well maybe, but I'll be the first to say you're not very convincing when you say no to the dudes after they ask if you want to get down. Sounds wimpy to me and, I'll tell you another thing, I believe if the right offer came along, you'd be givin' and takin' it like the rest of us."

"That's a horrible thing to say, especially when it's not true," Nathan whined unconvincingly, slowly sinking into the couch.

"Whatever, man, whatever you say. It don't matter to me what you do. I'm down with it."

"You like being with men," Nathan pressed with caution.

"It's just oral sex, Nathan, that's all. What man you know don't want his jimmy warmed?" Strong laughed.

"Maybe, but not by another man."

"It's a phase, Nate, it's not that serious, dude. If any of us had a serious girl or wife, we wouldn't be doing this s*@#."

"I don't get it, it doesn't make sense."

Strong pulled hard on a freshly packed Black and Mild cigar and passed it over to Nathan. He left the room and returned with two champagne glasses and a bottle of chilled Cris. "So," he said sitting down close to Nathan, "how 'bout I show you how good it feels to rock and roll?"

Nathan didn't move nor did Strong advance farther. Instead Strong poured the sparkling bubbly into the glasses. After taking a sip, he leaned over and kissed Nathan on the mouth, slowly at first, and then a little more aggressively. Then he straddled his legs opposite Nathan's and tried to pry the zipper to Nathan's slacks open. When he did, he was met with a hard slap to the face and a strong shove with a strength Nathan didn't realize he had. Nathan hollered, "Man, are you crazy?!" Wiping furiously like a wild man to remove the taste of Strong from his lips, Nathan ranted, "I told you, you damn fool, I don't do men. If you ever touch me again like that, you'll regret it like you've never regretted anything in your life!"

Strong was stunned. This reaction was a first. Whenever he surprised a dude with a kiss to the mouth it usually aroused his passion and moving on to the next level was automatic. "Look, Nathan, I'm sorry, man. I really thought you wanted it too. Don't mention this to Naiyah, aw-ight?"

"I told you I wasn't about that, why didn't you believe me, why didn't you take me at my word?" Nathan asked straightening out his clothes.

"You just look and act like you might."

"Strong, that's some judgmental bulls*@#. Do you look and act like you might? Or perhaps I should ask my sister about that?" Nathan threatened.

"Don't mention this to Naiyah. I'm begging you," Strong pleaded. This was a first too. He'd never had to beg for anything.

"And why not, why should I do anything you ask me to? I was just about to be violated by you," Nathan shouted.

"I'm not a taker, Nate. I wouldn't have done anything against your will, for real, man."

"Yeah right, what I need to know is if you've ever done my sister, 'cause if you have, she needs to know about your scandalous activities."

"No, we only kissed a few times."

"Ill," Nathan spat, "you're not right. Just how many women have been put at risk because of your selfish, whorish behavior?"

"Listen, man, I'm not going to say this again, it's just oral sex."

"Yeah right, Strong, just oral sex." With a newfound sense of power and awareness, Nathan said, "Take me home."

Turning to walk down the hall to the bathroom, Nathan's thoughts were racing a mile a minute. *Why did Strong think he could have sex with me?* He wondered. After muffling a scream into a clean facecloth retrieved from the linen closet, Nathan said 'How many times do I have to say it; I AM NOT GAY! I AM NOT GAY! Regaining his composure, Nathan thought, *it's got to be paranoia, especially with all the D.L. stuff. It's really made things cloudy and people of every persuasion seem to be hunting for gay and bi men under every rock, nook and cranny,* he thought sadly. Nathan had never cared what people thought about him before. In fact, he was used to being mistaken for gay. But this episode with Strong had really shaken him. What if he'd been raped? Nathan returned the facecloth to the towel rack and checked himself in the mirror. For the first time in a very long time, he didn't like what he saw.

✼

"Hello, Mani? It's Nathan. Can you come pick me up please?" he pleaded, deciding he wanted to spend as little time as possible in Strong's company.

"I'm having a cup of tea with your Mom, Auntie and Sequoia," she said. "Do you need me to come right away?"

"Yes Mani, please hurry. And do me a favor, come alone, okay?"

"Okay, baby. I'm on my way, give me about fifteen or twenty minutes."

"I'll be lookin' out for you," he said before hanging up quickly. Nathan returned to the living room where he found Strong mouthing the words to an Eric Sermon CD. He stared at him for a long moment before sitting in the reclining chair next to the sofa.

"This is a mind-blower for real. Who knew?" Nathan said, "I thought you were just frontin' for your boys. I didn't think you got down like

150

that, Strong. What a joke, I'm more man than you are," Nathan laughed cruelly. "Wow."

"Just keep it to yourself," Strong said again.

"Sorry, man, no disrespect, but I can't do that. My sister's ignorant and naïve to your ways, you could have hurt her, damaged her for life. I can't keep that kind of information from her. Besides, she's pregnant now and you're still hurting her by giving her drugs. Man, your conscience must be seared. Something serious must have happened to make you so callous and unfeeling."

"Don't try psychoanalyzin' me, man, there ain't nothing wrong with me. I'm rollin' and livin' how I want to, and what you say don't matter to me. I'm not hurtin' nobody. Naiyah's my girl, I wouldn't hurt her." Nathan stared at him in disbelief. "Don't give me that look," he said glancing sideways at Nathan.

"I can't help it, man, *I'm, I'm* disgusted," he stammered. "It was one thing when I thought it was just your crew, who I barely know, but I know you and I didn't expect you to flip the script on me like this," he said shaking his head.

Just then he heard Mani pull up and blow her horn.

"Thank goodness, she's finally here," he said almost to himself.

"So you don't want a ride from me?" Strong asked, genuinely surprised.

"Naw man, just let me get an ounce of weed 'cause I won't be coming back over here for a long time. Here," Nathan said dropping twenty dollar bills onto the table. Shaking his head, he looked at Strong one last time, "You're sick, man. You need some help."

"Hear me when I tell you, Nathan, everybody needs a little love and don't you forget it," Strong said snidely.

Nathan practically ran to Imani's car and hopped in. "Don't say anything, just drive, please, I don't need anything right now but an ear and a glass of wine."

Mani kept her eyes on the road and drove to a nearby neighborhood pub where she and Nathan could talk uninterrupted.

"Dish," she said once they were seated in a corner near the restrooms far away from the rowdy Friday, late afternoon, lunch crowd.

"I can't believe what just happened to me."

"C'mon, quit with all the suspense. What happened?" she asked while leaning forward conspiratorially.

"Strong came on to me. That freakin' dude actually put his lips on me."

Mani gasped, "Get the freak outta here! You're lying, Strong kissed you?!!" she spat with shock and disgust.

"Yes, Strong," he replied with the same measure of disgust and proceeded to tell Mani everything that had happened. Nathan had had suspicions about Strong for a while because of the number of times he went over to his house for weed or coke and witnessed blatant sexual foreplay between some of the men there, but Strong didn't participate so Nathan never suspected he got down like that, *not really.*

"You're really freaked out, aren't you?" Imani asked gently.

"You damn right I am! That dude putting his mouth on me was revolting." Nathan took a large gulp of the Riesling that was placed before him earlier and again began rubbing furiously at his mouth, trying to wipe away the remnants of that horrible moment.

"Well," Mani said slowly, "he probably thought you were an easy mark."

"Mani," he said raising his voice, "how many ways do I have to say I'm not gay? Have I had sophomoric crushes on guys or been attracted to guys, sure, many men have, but that doesn't make me gay or easy because I'm not," he said in a loud whisper.

"C'mon, Nate, look at you. You're so sweet and fine that both women and men alike would sex you if they could. Strong was just the one to decide he was going to assert himself, and if you took the bait well, woo hoo for him."

"You're no help," he said downing the last of his drink. "Let's go," he added then broke into a smile at Mani's complement. "You know what? You're right. I'm just too irresistible!" Nathan joked before they both doubled over with laughter.

"How about asking your Uncle Jon for some advice? He's really in tune with what's happening out there, don't you think?"

Nathan stared at Mani, thinking she could be hopelessly naïve at times. "That's the most ridiculously absurd thing I've heard in a helluva long time," he said making a goofy face at her. "But you know, I just might, the idea is so crazy that it might just work. C'mon, girl, let's go see what drama's unfolding back at the house because you know there's gonna be some," he chuckled. "I'll bet it's all the way live by now."

XXVI

Gathering at Jades, Again

Opening the front door, Naiyah called out, "Hey, where's everybody?" before leading Elijah into the brightly-lit foyer. When she turned around after hanging their coats in the closet, Sequoia walked in to greet them. "Hey cousin, what's up?"

Naiyah asked, "Where's Mum?"

"She and Mommy are in the kitchen fixin' supper and Uncle Lucky and Dad are in the living room."

"Poppy's here already?" Naiyah asked smiling easily.

"Yes, but he hasn't been here long," she said folding her arms in front of her. "What's the temperature—hot, warm or cold?" Naiyah wanted to know. "Cool, everything's cool. Mommy and Auntie Jade are chillin' after a nice spa day and Dad and Uncle Lucky are having cocktails."

"Where's Nathan?" she asked, looking around.

"Well, um," Sequoia awkwardly stammered, not knowing why, just a gut feeling that told her dropping Nathan off at that guy's house wasn't cool. "Mani went to pick him up," she said finally.

Naiyah raised one eyebrow and looked quizzically at her cousin, "from where?"

"I don't know," Sequoia hedged, "we dropped him off at someone's house after we got back from the mall. Mani went back to get him a little while ago. So," Sequoia continued, "did the two of you have a good afternoon?"

"Mostly," Elijah cut in. "Actually," he said more thoughtfully, "we did, we had a really great day."

Naiyah squeezed his hand, looking into his eyes with unmistakable affection. They had both, decidedly so, put the unsettling messages from D'yanna and Nadira out of their minds.

"I celebrate you," Sequoia said affectionately with a maturity that belied her tender age of seventeen years.

"Girl, hush your mouth, sounding like Auntie Aqua's Mini-Me."

Sequoia blushed leading the way back into the kitchen.

"Okay baby, straighten up. It's lights-camera-action time. We're about to be on," Naiyah said, turning to Elijah and kissing him lightly on the cheek.

"Lead the way, I'm down for anything and everything," he said nervously.

"Hello, everyone," Naiyah said again as the three of them walked into the kitchen where Jade and Aqua were sitting around the island counter chit-chatting in giggles and whispers like best friends still in high school. "Mum, Aunt Turquoise, I want you to meet Elijah McCoy."

Jade stared at him for several moments before a bright and genuine smile spread across her face. The young man standing before her, she thought, appeared to be very self-assured and in control. She had no doubt he could hold his own with Lemuel. She was also taken in by the dark, gleaming richness of his skin, the sharply sculpted features and long lean body.

"Welcome to our home, Elijah, it's a pleasure to meet you," Jade said while extending her hand to him and shaking his with a firm grip, trusting he'd get the message that she was about serious business.

"Hi, Elijah," said Turquoise. "My niece calls me Auntie Aqua but you can call me Ms. Aqua for now." Always the one out in front, she continued with a not so subtle interrogation. "So, Elijah, where are your people from?"

"I'm sorry, Ms. Aqua, do you mean where they're from originally or where they're from now?" he responded in a puzzled tone.

"Both," she said with an unblinking stare.

"Well, my mother and father were both born and raised in Jacksonville, Florida. My daddy followed his brother here when he was in his early twenties and my mother came soon after. We now live in the Red Hook section of Brooklyn, Ma'am."

Naiyah touched Elijah gently on the arm, "I'll be right back, I'm going inside to let Poppy know you're here. Don't worry," she laughed when she saw the nervousness on his face. "You'll be safe with them. Sequoia, make sure Mum and Auntie Aqua don't scare him away," she directed. Naiyah walked into the formal living room where Lucky and Uncle Jon were listening to jazz, sipping cocktails and talking about the state of world affairs after 9/11 and this crazy new Patriot Act that let people in the Bush Administration do whatever they wanted, including legalizing the outright denial of people's constitutional rights.

"Hey, Princess," Lucky said brushing past Naiyah, "excuse me for just a minute, I've got an incoming call I need to take." Lucky left the room and stepped into the foyer. Naiyah stared after him quizzically before turning her attention back to the situation at hand.

"Hey, Izzy," Uncle Jon said. "You lookin' quite ripe there, girl. Things must have gone well with the young man, huh?" he asked smiling at her.

"All in all Uncle Jon, things did go well," she said sitting down on the sofa beside him. Before she could continue, Lucky returned with an anxious look on his face.

"That was Analise," Lucky said, not looking Naiyah or Jon in the eyes. "I've got to run home for a minute. I'll be back shortly," Lucky said grabbing his keys and making a hasty turn towards the front door.

"Poppy, Elijah's in the kitchen," Naiyah said quickly, hoping to detain him.

"Good, I'll go in and meet him and when I get back, we can talk."

"Well alright, but don't take long. He has to drive back to the city tonight," she said.

❦

When they reached the house, Nathan ran upstairs to freshen up and change his clothes while Mani proceeded to the kitchen.

"Where's Nathan?" Naiyah asked as Mani moved comfortably through the kitchen just as she'd done so many times before.

"Upstairs to change or something," she said vaguely, grabbing an apple out of the bowl.

"What for?" Naiyah wanted to know.

"He didn't say," she said, avoiding Naiyah's stare and moving discreetly over to Sequoia who was sitting in the breakfast nook talking on her cell to her boyfriend back home.

"No, I miss you more," Sequoia cooed, fluttering her eyelids involuntarily when Mani interrupted.

"Go ask your dad to check in on Nathan," she whispered.

"I'll call you right back," Sequoia said hanging up.

Just then Jade and Turquoise came back in from the smoking room. "I don't believe it, don't tell me you're finally off the phone with that boy," Turquoise said.

"Oh Mommy quit, you act like you don't remember what it's like being in love for the first time."

"Sequoi, honey puleeze, I not only remember what it's like being in love for the first time, I know what it's like being in love for all time," she laughed, twirling her outstretched arms in the air.

"Oh, here we go," she said, "she's about to lecture us on successful love affairs. Don't start without me, I'll be right back," Sequoia said playfully to her mother.

"Girl, I'm not thinking about you," Aqua said as her daughter brushed by. "She can be such a smarty-pants sometimes, but I must admit, I'm very happy with the young man she's dating."

"Oh. Really?" Jade replied.

"Yes I am. They have an innocent and sweet romance going. It's nice to watch young love that hasn't yet been jaded or tainted by age," she said, her face beaming brightly.

"I think I remember," Jade laughed lightly.

Sequoia walked into the living room where her father and Elijah were getting to know one another, "Elijah, will you excuse us? I really need my dad for a minute." Pushing her father out into the foyer towards the stairs, Sequoia said, "I think Nathan needs to see you, he's in his room."

"Alright, baby, I'll go see what he wants and you go on back and keep Izzy's friend company. We don't want him gettin' nervous in there all by himself," he laughed.

"Unh-unh. He better come on back in the kitchen where the action is," Sequoia joked before going to save Elijah from himself.

Johann looked at his daughter and shook his head as he headed up to Nathan's room.

He knocked once and walked in. Nathan had taken a quick shower and was standing inside his large, completely organized walk-in closet. Thanks to all of Lucky's hard-earned money, Jade had every closet in the house professionally done by the world-renowned California Closets company. And the impeccable results were worth it. There were racks for slacks and shirts, shelves for sweaters, and cubbies for socks and shoes. Hearing his bedroom door open, Nathan walked out wearing a purple, grey and white striped oxford shirt and blended black wool slacks. Seeing his Uncle Jon, he visibly relaxed before sitting down at his desk to slip on his Cole Hahn black leather loafers.

"Nephew," Johann said, "what's up, man?" Johann sat down on the edge of Nathan's bed. From the look on Nathan's face, he knew it was going to be serious.

"I don't know how else to put this," Nathan started. "So I'm just going to ask you this question point blank." Nathan looked up from his shoes to stare Johann in the face.

"Uncle Jon, do you think I'm gay?"

Johann sat motionless wondering why he was being asked, but at the same time pondering what would be the most diplomatic response. Finally, he said, "I don't know, nephew, you didn't say you were, but I will say this. Gay, I doubt it, but flamboyant as hell, oh yeah," he chuckled. "So," he continued "out with it, why are you asking anyway?"

"Wait a minute, Uncle. Let me be clear. Say for instance I'm a stranger on the street. Are you honestly saying your only thought in passing me would be that I'm outrageously bold and dashing and not, 'that cat's queer' or something?" Nathan pressed.

Johann stroked his thin shadow of a beard and thought for a minute, "Well now, Nathan, with that being the scenario, in all honesty maybe I would."

Nathan was crushed. He put his head down on the desk in mock surrender.

"Nathan," Johann said a little sternly, "what's going on, what's this all about?" Lifting his head slowly, Nathan looked at his uncle. "I was hit on by a dude today and it knocked me completely off my square, I didn't see it coming and now I question how I'm representing myself out in the world."

"Naw man, unh-unh don't even go there. You know who you are. Don't go letting someone else's problem become your problem. You got to have your own strong constitution, man. Express yourself however you want. That's one of the things I admire about you nephew, that you're free to express yourself, and that's a good thing."

Nathan felt a sense of relief, "Thanks, Uncle Jon, that helped."

"Okay good, but you better not tell me anything other than you knocked that joker out."

"Unc, you woulda been proud of me for real. I did and it was so swift and sweet, I surprised myself. I cold-cocked him good," Nathan grinned.

Johann fell out laughing watching the instant replay Nathan was demonstrating. "C'mon now, we better get back downstairs before the women folk start worryin'. But one last thing, nephew, just be who you are man, as long as you're okay with it. That's your constitution, young blood. The values and laws that govern you, you write that script, so go on ahead, man, be yourself."

❦

"Well, it's about time," Turquoise said when Johann and Nathan walked in, laughing heartily. "We thought we'd have to start without you two."

"My bad, baby, I'm sorry," Johann said kissing her cheek, "I was catching up with my nephew, I guess we just forgot all about the time."

Naiyah and Elijah were now in the family room, talking and listening to music, while Mani and Sequoia finished up setting the table.

"Is Lucky back yet?" Johann asked moving towards the living room.

"Not yet," Turquoise said. "As soon as Jade gets off the phone, we'll be sitting down to eat."

"I'll go clean up then," he said, "be right back."

"Nathan, honey, you look good. I love the hook up, especially the shirt—perfect choice," she said, giving her head-to-toe inspection and a final stamp of approval.

"Thanks, Auntie," he said nodding his head and discreetly winking at Mani. "After dinner, all I want to do is put my feet up somewhere and breathe" said Jade rejoining everyone in the kitchen.

"Who was that on the phone?" Nathan wanted to know. He ignored the look on her face which he recognized as the "why you all up in my business" look. "Mum," he said again asserting himself from the favored position he had with her, the one he acquired and came to enjoy not long after his father left them.

"If you must know, it was Ms. Wilhelmina."

"Oh," Turquoise interjected, "did they have a nice time last night?"

"She said they had a ball. I'm so glad we reconnected," Jade said.

"Yeah, it'll be good for you. You should spend more time with your friends," Turquoise said.

"She's right, Ms. Jade, my ma was so happy to see you yesterday," Mani told her. "She said she missed visiting with you and plans to invite you to one of her club meetings real soon."

"That'll be nice," Jade said. "Nathan, go down and call your sister and Elijah for dinner."

"So what about Mr. Alexander," he asked her before leaving, "he had a ball too, I suppose?"

Turquoise looked from Jade to Nathan. "He sure acted like he had a good time," she said knitting her brows, "especially after those slammin' martinis we had."

"He asked Willie to ask me if he could call me sometime," Jade giggled in spite of herself.

"He did?" Turquoise smiled. "I hope you had the good sense to say yes."

"Aqua, honey, I'm not interested in taking up conversation with any man. In fact, that's the last thing I want to do," she said honestly.

"Just be open, Sissy, that's all I'm sayin'. It might be fun and you could use some fun in your life," Turquoise smiled mischievously.

"We'll see, now let's get the food on the table."

"Uncle Jon," Naiyah said coming into the dining room with Elijah and Nathan. "Poppy called and said he's handling something but he'll be back as soon as he's done. He also said something about the men going out to a neutral place to talk, you included, Nathan," she said turning to her brother.

This surprised Nathan but made him happy none-the-less. *This might mean getting to know Poppy better, perhaps on a more adult level,* he thought.

XXVII

Lucky Strokes Analise Reassuringly

Walking into their condo and dropping his keys on the kitchen counter, Lucky yelled for Analise, "Woman, what's wrong?! What's gotten into you?! What are you talking about?!" he asked, confused by the tone of her urgent phone call. Analise appeared out of the bedroom where she'd been seething most of the afternoon.

"Do you think I'm going to just let you leave me after all we've been through!" she yelled. "After I went against everything my Mãe and Pai taught me. Coming to this country and setting up housekeeping and a marriage bed with you. Oh no, Meu Marido! I won't let you get away with it," she said angrily. Lucky reached out to grab her as she stormed by him. He loved when she was all angry and feisty like this.

"I don't know what you're talking about, my darling Bonita, come tell Poppy what's wrong and stop calling me your husband, you know better," he teased pulling Analise onto his lap before plopping down on the plush love seat. "Tell me what's got you all fired up," he asked, noticing how she worked the mess out of the sexy cat suit she had on. The thought racing through his mind was how he wanted the delicious Buceta. He wanted to play here, kitty-kitty and lick it all over once he had it in his grasp. "Come, Buceta," he teased, but Analise wasn't in the mood for games, though he was exciting her with the way he called for her kitty. She felt her kitty slowly awaken, hunch and stretch out fully elongated.

"Come, Buceta," he pleaded sexily.

Analise was upset but she couldn't stop the kitty, it had a mind of its own.

Before she knew it, Kitty was in his face, ready to be stroked. Kitty purred, moving up and down his leg while he caressed her gently, then licking his fingers, he began exploring, looking for the openings he knew were hidden within Kitty's furry mound. Kitty purred louder and louder and he probed and stroked her kitty just the way she liked it. Or so he thought. Lucky was completely in the dark concerning this new thing heating up between Analise and the young man she was seen huddled in a corner with at the gym by Jade and Turquoise. He didn't know that she'd become just as bored and tired of him as he'd become of her. The only difference was that Analise was doing something about it, but Lucky, unable to kick the Mack Daddy Don thing back into high gear, didn't quite know what to do in this situation.

"Are you ready to tell me, now that I've calmed you down, why I had to rush home? I was about to be introduced to this young fellow of Naiyah's when you called," he said, releasing a deep sigh and running his hand over his head in exasperation.

"That's just it. You've been spending too much time over at Jade's," Analise pouted.

"Are you kidding me?" he asked incredulously, looking at her with complete disbelief. "Is that what this is about?" She didn't look at him. "Is it, Analise?" he demanded, now looking at her like she was stupid. "You think because I went over to see my children at the home I provide for them and their mother, it means I'm trying to end what we have?"

"I know you've never stopped loving your wife. You've made that quite clear and it makes me wonder if that's the reason our sexual chemistry isn't full of fire and popping, the way it was when we first met?" Analise said painfully.

Lucky pulled up his pants, and after pulling himself together sat back on the love seat and looked at Analise. "Sweetheart, we've been together a long time" he said rubbing her tenderly on her back. "And after a while, it's natural for physical intimacy to take on a slower rhythm. It's unrealistic to think there'll always be fireworks."

Analise looked at him like he was an alien or something. "No," she said slowly, "I don't agree. We're not having fireworks because your old butt is tired and lazy."

"Old!" Lucky shouted indignantly. "Girl, please, I'm not even fifty, who are you calling old?" he snapped angrily, rising up.

"Old or not, who cares," Analise snapped back. "When we first met, it was quite clear you wanted wild hot sex every chance you got. That's the way you wanted it and that's the way you got it. Now, you're trying to turn our thing into the same old tired routine you had with Jade."

"Leave my wife out of this, Analise. My family is off limits," he said jumping up threateningly from the loveseat.

"Your wife!" she screamed.

"Yeah, damn it, my wife."

"Your wife?!" she shouted again, not believing her ears. "So that's it. You are planning to go back to her."

"Analise, sweetheart, I don't know where this is going and, quite frankly, I'm tired of it. Even if I did want to go back to Jade, and I'm not saying I do, she wouldn't have me," he said very directly, but in a quieter tone.

Analise looked at him, her face slightly distorted from the sharp pain she felt in her chest. It was as if someone was stabbing her with the point of a very sharp knife. "No, you're right, you're not saying you do, but your actions betray your words," she said softly. She got up from the loveseat, quietly readjusting the cat suit that just moments before had drove them to lustful distraction and then went to the bedroom they shared. She steeled her emotions, refusing to cry, though, at the moment, she was suffering crippling emotional pain.

"Lise," Lucky called out. "I'll be back later." He closed the door of their condo behind him, but not before adding, "I love you."

XXVIII

It's the Men's Turn Now

Elijah wasn't the least bit nervous around Naiyah's family. In the short time he'd spent with the men, Uncle Jon and Nathan, he knew he liked them and felt getting to know them better would be easy. He wasn't so sure about Mr. Harland, but from their brief introduction, he got the feeling he was cool too, regardless of the fierce protective cover he placed around his Princess Naiyah, as he called her. They were all ready to go when Lucky returned. Since it was getting late, Elijah called his aunt, letting her know he might have to spend the night. He didn't want to drive back to Brooklyn too late.

"Jon, my man," Lucky said, "You'll have to drive. Everyone can't fit in my car."

"No, not in that selfish vanity ride," Johann laughed.

"I can drive, if there's a problem," Elijah offered.

"It's okay. I got this," Johann said. "So where're we going? I hope not back to Jettison's."

"What? You've got to be kidding me. You didn't like that spot?" Lucky asked, opening the door to the crisp night air.

"Don't get me wrong, it was cool, just a little too fast for my taste."

"What's that supposed to mean, Uncle Jon?" Nathan wanted to know.

"Just that I'm not into loud, hip-hop club music, the younger crowd or the skimpy outfits the women had on."

Nathan looked at Elijah who knew better than to weigh in on this one.

"Oh, alright chump, we'll go someplace nice for the old, old heads."

"Lucky, don't make me bust a lump on your head, man," Johann laughed. "I might be a lot of things, but I'm nobody's chump," Johann said, opening the car door. He eased the rented Mazda 626 onto the roadway as Lucky navigated them towards Tierra Dunes, a laid-back lounge with a piano bar. To get there, they passed the sign pointing to B. Smith's restaurant at Long Wharf. "Whoa, B. Smith's, how long has that been there?" Johann inquired.

"About a year or two, but it's closed now, for the season. I think it opens up again in May. You know, she and her husband have a home in Sag Harbor Hills," Lucky said.

"Yeah," Johann replied, "I think I remember reading something about that. Damn," he said, "what black celebrity doesn't have a home in the Hills?"

Nathan piped up from the back seat, "I know that's right—all of 'em, every last one. Dad," he continued, "have you been to their house?"

"Not yet," Lucky replied, "but believe me, Analise is working on it. She met B. at the farmer's market this past summer, so my bet is, it won't be long." When they finally reached the spot and were walking inside, Elijah thought to himself, *how unusual this was, here he was supposed to be explaining his intentions to the father of the young woman full with his child, but instead he felt like he was just hangin' out with the boys.*

"You, my man, come sit over here," Lucky said motioning Elijah over to the seat next to him. "I want to be sure if I have to jack you up, I won't have to reach all the way across the table," he joked.

"And let me sit on the other side of him," Johann bellowed in laughter, "We need to lock the brother in, just in case."

"I should have known what I was feeling was a false sense of security," Elijah replied laughing also.

Nathan said, "Take it easy, man. Don't be nervous now. Look, you're swallowing so hard it looks like your Adam's apple is break dancing," he laughed.

Elijah threw his hands in the air, "Okay, gentlemen, you caught me with it, so I got to get it."

"Oh, he got jokes, I like that," Lucky said turning to the young cocktail waitress who had just appeared at their table.

"What can I get for you fine men?" she asked seductively with eyes fixed unashamedly on Elijah's mouth.

Lucky looked from her to him "Excuse me, Miss, but that one there is completely unavailable, trust me, while I, on the other hand, just might be up for the taking," he said with a poker face.

"Humm," she replied looking him up and down, "with all due respect, sir, I'll take that into consideration, but I'm willing to bet you'd enjoy my mother's company so much more." She smiled flirtatiously, "So what will you gentlemen be having this evening?"

Johann said, "I'll have a Hennessey VOP with a twist of lemon and a coke chaser on the side, the old head you just so graciously put in his place will have the same and, for the two young men accompanying us, they'll give you their own order."

Nathan looked at Lucky, who nodded, before ordering himself a Peartini.

"And you, sir," she asked Elijah, while standing very close to him. As she leaned forward, he sensed a gravitational pull surrounding the energy field of her beguiling and erotically scented D cups which were now directly in front of him, nearly scraping his forehead. Both Lucky and Johann turned their heads in an effort to conceal their suppressed hysterics.

"Club soda and lemon," he said turning away from her.

"Keep it tight, gentlemen, I'll be right back," she said strutting off.

"Girlfriend was bound and determined to get your attention, Elijah," Nathan said.

"That's the truth. There was sure no lack of tryin' there," Johann added.

The remark gave Lucky the start needed to broach the subject they came there to discuss. "That's right, from what I hear you're quite popular with the ladies, isn't that right, Elijah?"

"I wouldn't go so far as to say that, Mr. Harland."

"But you do have a woman you're engaged to and my daughter, who you've gotten pregnant" he said.

Okay, Elijah thought, *now that feels like the sting of a surprise left-hand jab.* "Yes sir, that's right," he said.

"So how is it my Naiyah's pregnant? And what's your plan for seeing to it she's not hurt in this process *and* that the innocent child is properly supported and cared for?" he hammered.

"I really can't answer that, sir."

Lucky stiffened and stared at Elijah. "Naw man, absolutely not, that answer is completely unacceptable. We're talking about my daughter, my baby. You need to come better than that" he said deepening his already bass voice.

"I know you expect me to, Mr. Harland, but for real, sir, all I can tell you is what my position is, I can't speak for your daughter. If it were up to me, I'd break it off with my fiancée in a heartbeat, suffer the consequences and make it work with Naiyah. I've already expressed this to her, but she doesn't know if she wants to keep the baby."

"What?!" Lucky exclaimed, looking at Elijah with obvious confusion.

"Yes sir, she's considering putting the baby up for adoption."

"I didn't know that," Johann said, taking a sip of his drink.

Nathan's ears perked up, but he didn't say anything. Instead he looked from Elijah to Lucky and back again.

Elijah continued, "Sir, I love your daughter but I didn't pursue her when I had the chance because I thought she wasn't that interested. I found out today, I was wrong. I'm a responsible man and want to make this right if I can. I don't want to put my child in the position to be raised by someone else. Still, sir, with no disrespect, I don't believe Naiyah's ready for a commitment, she seems to be working through some serious issues."

Getting in Elijah's face, Lucky asked angrily, "What are you talking about?"

"I don't know, I can't put my finger on it, sir, but she seems deeply hurt and troubled by something. She's about to have a baby, but still she had a strong drink of alcohol at lunch, and I think something's seriously wrong with that. I don't know if it's delayed grief from the death of her grandmother or the weight of having a long separation from her friend, I'm just sayin' there's something going on way below the surface." Elijah shrugged, looking Lucky square in the eye. "I don't know, Mr. Harland, but trust me, I'm going through it with her, sir, I promise you."

Lucky sat back, now it was his turn to be silent. He reflected on the conversation he had with Naiyah the night before and wondered how much of this *was* his fault, which made him bow his heart in agreement with the words of blame Jade had hurled at him. "If Naiyah wasn't ready for a commitment, then how did she manage to get pregnant? Didn't you practice safe sex?" he asked in an accusatory tone.

"Mr. Harland, I already feel bad enough about this. I'm ashamed to say I convinced her to be with me despite the fact I didn't have condoms. I was at Stanford getting the things I left in storage, I saw Naiyah and my heart just melted, even though I was about to be officially engaged to my girl. It felt comfortable being in her company again, and not knowing when or if I'd see her again, I pressed her. She wasn't on the pill and at the time she wasn't seeing anyone. So, yes, sir" he said, head lowered, "I'm to blame. It's my fault and like I said, I take full responsibility."

"Whew," Lucky exhaled scratching his head. "This is really too much information," he added before taking a much needed sip of his drink. "Listen," he continued, we all make mistakes but making a mistake doesn't have to ruin our entire lives. I believe you're a man of integrity, Elijah, so I'm just gonna let you handle your business and stay out of it. But whatever I can do to help, just let me know and I will. I'll be sure to tell Naiyah the same."

"Thank you, sir, I really appreciate that."

"Now," Lucky said, turning his attention to Nathan, "I need to address something with my son here and y'all excuse me if it gets too personal. Nathan, what's this I'm hearing about you being sexually confused?" Nathan's head jerked involuntarily and, when he'd steadied himself, he looked at Johann who made hand gestures indicating he didn't know where this was coming from.

"Dad," Nathan said, his voice squeaking to a high pitch. "Do you really think this is the time and place for this discussion?"

"Why not, we're all family here, at least we are now," he said slapping Elijah on the shoulder. "I don't know what confused means but what I do know is that it better not mean gay 'cause, if it does, let me be the first to tell you when they find your behind, they'll be picking you up with sponges and tweezers." Nathan gasped. "Seriously man, they'll know it's you, but I'll be damned if they'll be able to recognize you."

Nathan's eyes grew wide but he was speechless and quite afraid. His father was sounding violent right about now and Nathan didn't have a frame of reference to draw from. He didn't know his father to be violent. Stern, yes. Sometimes callous even, but never violent. Lucky was a lover, not a fighter.

Johann interjected, "Man, take it down a notch, Lucky. What's gotten into you?"

"Aw shoot, I'm sorry, son, I don't know." Lucky looked at Nathan. "I'm really sorry," he said again. "I heard about this sexual confusion thing and got this crazy visual in my head, it messed me up, seriously," he said to Johann. Nate, baby, you know there's no way I'd knock you to smithereens, I mean hurt you," he laughed, trying to lighten the mood. Elijah sat stunned. He didn't know what to think, but the thought crossed his mind that, *if he proceeded in his pursuit of Naiyah, there'd be a whole family worth of drama to contend with*. Elijah made a mental note to sit and really think on this when he had time to himself. He realized he needed to ask himself the hard questions, the most important one being if he'd really be able to deal with Naiyah and her family's high-brow dysfunction?

Nathan was now beside himself. How could his father be so vicious and insensitive? He became so angry he started to cry. "If I am what you think I am, so freakin' what!" he shouted at Lucky. "Who are you to comment on my lifestyle, gay or otherwise. What gives you the right?" he snapped. "I'd be low down and dirty if I said anything about you and *your* adulterous lifestyle, now wouldn't I?" he asked venomously. "If you really want to know about my lifestyle as you call it, you should have used some tact and you should have given me some respect by approaching me in private."

"Son?" Lucky started, "I——"

Nathan threw up the infamous hand, letting his father know he was no longer listening.

"Son," Lucky said again, "please, Nathan, can we start over? I'm sorry. Can't you please forgive me?" he asked, looking embarrassed. "I understand I was wrong and out of line, please, baby," he said in trademarked, cool Lucky style.

"Man, you're so out of touch," Johann said to Lucky.

"That's easy for you to say, Jon, this is my son we're talking about. I don't know a man alive, at least not a real man, who could handle something like this, not with finesse anyhow."

"That's bull and you know it. If you care about someone's feelings and don't want to hurt them, you figure out how to discuss difficult issues so everyone keeps their dignity. You don't disregard someone's humanity, dang man!" Johann continued. "You attacked Nathan something fierce right then."

"I said I was sorry, what more can I do?" Lucky pleaded.

"It's not what you said, Dad, it's how you said it. What if it was my lifestyle? Do you think with the attitude you displayed, I'd tell you? No, I wouldn't and that's why, I'll bet, people don't tell. It's not safe and where's the help in that?" he asked, looking at Lucky with convicting eyes.

"But it's not natural, Nathan," Lucky countered.

"That may be, but it's still an individual's choice who they choose, isn't it?"

Johann let the two go at it without interruption. He was hoping they would get down to hearing one another and agree to be accepting no matter what the outcome.

"Nathan, you know the Bible teaches against it."

Nathan lowered his head and measured his words, "But I suppose it teaches leaving your family for an adulterous affair is okay? I'm not gay, Dad," he continued, "but if I were, I believe Jesus, who G-Ma taught me is Lord of all, would still expect you to love me. It's not for you to try and change or judge me, no matter what you think my issues are. Only God can work in a man's heart to conform or change him to His will. But who's to say God hasn't allowed this lifestyle. Maybe it's a test to see if the self-righteous can truly love as He loves."

Lucky looked at Nathan with newfound admiration. "I respect that, son, and admire you for the way you presented your defense for a person's right to choose even when it's unpopular, especially since it's not even your own personal choice. You showed me just how judgmental I am—thank you, and I mean that. I see I have a lot to learn about sensitivity and demonstrating love that's truly unconditional," he said contritely.

"Aw man, it's cool. You're human and we accept you. Besides, we know you can be a damn fool sometimes," Johann said. "We just want you to evolve but until then we'll keep putting up with you," he laughed and extended a fist bump to Lucky to show that they were still cool.

"Boy, this day has taken everything out of me," Lucky said, "I'm drained. I can't take one more thing. Call that cocktail waitress back over here, I need another drink." Then, no sooner had the words escaped his mouth, Lucky caught the silhouette of two people dancing slowly to the piano man's music. He looked harder into the smoky mist and saw that it was Analise hugged up close to some young cat he didn't know. Nathan and Johann's backs were turned from her and Elijah didn't know her, so only he saw. Lucky watched without saying anything for a very long time. Analise and her friend had met up together shortly after her encounter with Lucky. After being with him earlier and getting herself all warmed up. Analise drove over to the young man's house for round two. Lucky's teasing was just a prelude to what she'd come to enjoy and expect with this young hottie. He was great at giving her deep, pounding sex. Because he was in such outstanding shape, he could go the distance, which is something Analise desired her sex play to be. Not only was he an ardent and sensual lover, discovering all of her secret hot spots, he was also fixated on pleasing her orally which blew her mind beyond anything she'd experienced with Lucky. As the young man whispered into Analise's ear, she giggled excitedly enjoying their public foreplay. Lucky watched all of this and was by now stoked to the max.

Ain't this some fragganagle bull. This wench is playing me, he thought. He slowly sipped his Hennessey trying to watch Analise discreetly while adding something to the conversation at the table every now and then so as not to alert the guys to what was going on. Nathan was satisfied that he'd gotten some respect from his father. *Finally,* he thought. With a sense of relief, he engaged Elijah in conversation. "Man, I wouldn't want to be in your shoes. What's your fiancée going to say once you tell her about my sister?"

"I don't want to think about it, but I'll say this, I have every reason to believe she might kill me," he laughed uneasily and only half jokingly.

"What? She's gangsta like that?" Nathan asked laughing.

"Let's just say she's nothing to play with."

"Well, just hold that pit bull down cause I'm not about to let anyone do harm to my sister. Besides, Izzy's a lady. She don't get down like that if she doesn't have to. But she can scrap if she has to, don't let that Stanford education fool you."

"Nephew, please, Izzy won't stoop to that level," Johann said. "She's part Diamond girl and street fighting is what common folks do. Diamond girls aren't common."

"Don't worry, I can handle D'yanna," Elijah said.

"Make sure you do," Lucky said. "Nothing better happen to my Princess, that's for sure." After that, Lucky stood up. "Excuse me, gentlemen, I'll be right back. I think I see someone I know across the room." The three men at the table continued talking as Lucky walked over to the table where Analise and her friend were now sitting hugged up pretty close.

"Lucky!" Analise exclaimed, surprised to see him standing there.

"Be quiet! Don't say another word," he hissed at her. "So I guess the head-banging I gave you at home earlier wasn't enough for you, huh? You needed another stroking to be satisfied?" He turned to the young man and without another breath said, "I hope you can afford her, my man, 'cause you just bought her. She's yours lock, stock and barrel." He turned and walked back to the table and tried now to hurry everyone along. He was so ready to get the heck out of there. Lucky was reeling inside and he felt like he was trapped in an imploding building. "I didn't realize how tired I really am," he said. "Do you guys mind going back to Jade's now? After all, Izzy did ask me not to keep Elijah out too long," he said trying to remain calm.

"That's cool, I'm down for going back to relax," Johann said. "Are you coming in, Lucky? There's still plenty of leftovers."

"Naw, I think I'm going to call it a night. I need to lay my head down." Nathan stood and reached out and hugged his father. "I love you, Dad, and I'm glad we had the chance to talk."

"Me too, Nate, I love you too, son. Listen, maybe we can get together before you leave, just you and me," he said. "I'd like to hear how school's going and see some of those cool designs I've been hearing all about."

"Really?!! That'd be great!" Nathan exclaimed. "I'm leaving Sunday evening but maybe we can have breakfast in the morning before Mum takes me to the airport."

"Deal," Lucky replied embracing Nathan again. "I messed up, Nate, big time, and I really want it to be better between us. Elijah, it was a pleasure meeting you, regardless of the circumstances that brought us together. I believe you'll do the right thing where my daughter and grandchild are concerned and I look forward to seeing you again," he said, massaging his tight neck muscles.

"Thanks, Mr. Harland," Elijah said breathing a deep sigh of relief.

Once they reached Jade's, Lucky said goodnight before driving off. Johann, Nathan and Elijah joined the women in the family room. Naiyah was so anxious to hear how things went between her father and Elijah that she dragged him off to the living room to hear all about it.

"So, how did it go?" she asked breathlessly.

"Your father's cool, Ny, I like him. Bottom line, he recognizes I'm here for you and that I'm going to do the right thing no matter what you decide."

"Did you tell him everything?"

"Everything," Elijah said simply.

"Including the adoption," she pressed.

"Everything," he said again without elaborating.

"Poppy's going to think I've lost it. I told him I saw this child as a miracle from God and that I really wanted to raise it."

"Sweetheart, look, there's no question this is a very emotional time. I don't think it's unusual for you to vacillate between wanting to keep the baby and wanting to give it up, considering the fact you're still in school with no job. But like I said, I'm here now and want to support you in every way that I can."

Naiyah turned from Elijah and wiped at the tears rolling down her cheek. She was overcome with emotion. She understood clearly now that she didn't have to do this alone. She had her whole family behind her, including Elijah. She felt an immediate sense of relief and realized that on this amazing Thanksgiving holiday weekend she had a lot to be truly thankful for.

"Sweetheart, don't cry," Elijah said drawing Naiyah to him. "I want you and this child. God is giving us a chance to be a family, to restore what's broken. It won't be easy, not at all, but if we turn to the Lord for help and guidance, I believe we'll succeed."

Elijah took Naiyah's hands into his and prayed a simple prayer. *"My Lord, we come with humble hearts to your throne of grace, asking you to forgive us so that nothing is standing between us, this prayer and you. We pray, Lord, that you will see us and provide wisdom and guidance by your spirit. We pray for the unborn child we conceived together and pray for your blessing. Help Naiyah and me to partner with you, so that we might live victorious lives in Christ. Amen."*

Naiyah sat back. "Thanks," she said, "I like that you've got a spiritual thing going on, Lijah, I really do. I guess I didn't know how deep you were."

He smiled, "I may act a fool sometimes," he laughed, "but my mother didn't raise *no heathen*. I'm about to head back over to my Aunt Lydia's and leave for Brooklyn in the morning. I'll have to tell D'yanna the truth when I get there," he sighed. "In the meantime, I want you to think long and hard about the offer I'm making you and one last thing, Ny, you need to lay off that alcohol, it's too dangerous for our developing baby and you don't need it either." He kissed her on the cheek. "I got to go, sweetheart, do you mind getting my coat?"

Naiyah met Nathan in the foyer on her way to the closet. "Izzy, I want to talk to you for a minute," he said.

"Sure, go in the living room, Elijah's about to leave, we can talk in there." Walking over to him and shaking his hand, Nathan said to Elijah, "I'll see you soon. It was nice meeting you."

"Yeah man, it was good for me too," he said. "Not to worry. You'll be seeing me sooner than you think, I'm sure of it. By the way, Nathan, you made your father proud tonight. You really held your own and left me with a new appreciation of people who seem different. Thanks again," he said easily.

Surprised by Elijah's last remark, Nathan took his hand and shook it firmly, "Be easy, man. Peace out."

Elijah buttoned his coat while walking with Naiyah to the door. "Depending on how things go, I'll call you tomorrow or Sunday, remember I'm with you all the way, baby," he said turning to leave.

Nathan was playing the piano when Naiyah returned. She sat down beside him and listened for a moment to the soft melody before asking, "So what's up, B?" Nathan kept playing without looking up and after a brief moment he stopped and turned to her, "I probably shouldn't say this, sis, 'cause it's none of my business, but you're not to see Strong anymore," he said.

"What, where's this coming from?" she asked defensively. "He's just a friend, Nathan. And I like hanging out with him sometimes. He's edgy and there's something about that, that appeals to me. I'm not sleeping with him, if that's what this is about," she said enjoying the music.

"He's off limits, Iz. The dude's dangerous," Nathan said without looking at her. "How do you know?"

"I don't need to go there, Izzy. Just stay away from him, and for the record," he said, shifting gears, "Dad knows I'm not confused."

She put her head down. She didn't expect her words to get back to her so soon. Nathan put a finger under her chin and lifted her face to him. "Sis, it's all good, I'm your brother, I know you love me and want no harm to come to me, I feel the same about you. You know this, so let's just leave it at that. And another thing, we've got to do better about staying in touch."

"It's mostly my fault, Nathan, with all that's been going on, I've had a hard time coping and I admit my relationships have suffered," she said softly.

"I understand that, but that's not all there is to it. Let's face it, Iz, we let Mum's and Dad's stuff come between us. You have to agree we took sides."

She nodded, "I'm afraid you're right."

"That's all behind us now, Izzy and so is Strong," he said again, making sure he'd made himself very clear.

"Need I remind you that I'm the elder here," she said.

"Doesn't matter," he teased, "because right about now I'm the wiser." They both laughed and fell easily into each other's warm embrace.

"So Nathan, did you meet anyone, while you were out shopping?" Naiyah teased.

Nathan ran through his day quickly and couldn't think of anyone he'd been introduced to and so replied, "Not that I remember."

"Hum," she said, shaking her head, "I had this really strong feeling earlier that you had a conversation with a stranger and they paid you a compliment of some kind."

"Oh wait," he said "you won't believe this, but you're right. We did run into two women when we were leaving the outlet mall and one of them complimented me on the messenger bag you gave me."

"Did you happen to mention where you got it from?"

"I did. I told her my sister, with impeccable taste, brought it back from Cali."

Naiyah smiled, but knew in her heart that the two women who talked to Nathan were D'yanna and her friend Nadira. She also knew that they were going to be real trouble.

XXIX

Freely Stepping Towards the Sun

Naiyah rose early the next day and got out of the house before anyone else was awake. She grabbed the keys to Jade's new, brilliant silver SL 550 MB Roadster and headed for Starbucks, leaving the Mercedes station wagon in the driveway, thinking her mother wouldn't mind now that they had a chance to settle some of their differences. Once there, she ordered a Caramel Macchiato Grande and a raspberry scone. Naiyah was humming to herself because today she woke with a greater sense of purpose and determination. She realized that she had lived so much of her short life focused on herself and her own needs. Now, there was the baby to consider and Naiyah knew she had to face and rid herself of some things that no longer served her, like being spoiled and self-centered, the selfish behaviors that paid off well. They got her the attention she desperately craved; *but those are the attitudes of immature, dangerously narcissistic children, not productive, healthy living adults, time for me to grow up,* she thought. With order in hand, she returned to the car and drove to the beach, but not the one she and Elijah went to the day before. She watched the waves roll gently and began to hum some more as she thought long and hard about what becoming a mother really meant and how altered her life would become if she made that choice. She warmed her hands on the coffee cup and caressed it in a way that gave her comfort. She meditated on the conversations she engaged in over the holiday weekend and smiled to herself. She was genuinely happy again for the first time in a long time because she now knew that, in a crisis, her family would come through, which gave her hope that they would also find ways to be fully functioning as a family when there wasn't the threat of crisis. She was overjoyed and feeling very hopeful especially since Mani, too, was back securely in her life. It was now 8AM; she called her mother so she wouldn't worry. "Mum, I have your car; I got up and out early, wanted to have a quiet cup of coffee and to swing by God-mommy's house, so I could see her again before going back to school. I hope it's okay, I'll be back soon."

"Yes, sweetheart," Jade said groggily since she was still asleep when the phone rang, "we'll be here, it's going to be a lazy day today. Give my love to Ms. Inez, sweetheart, see you when you get back." Not completely out of it, Jade asked, "You did take the wagon right?"

"No Mum, I didn't, I couldn't resist, I had to push your new whip just once."

"Bye, Naiyah," Jade said, sounding slightly irritated despite hanging up with a smile on her face. She turned over, intent on sleeping at least one more hour.

Naiyah continued watching the rolling waves, contemplating motherhood and the possibility of becoming a wife as well. Just as quickly, she had the sobering thought once again that this D'yanna chick was not going to give up without a fight. *But,* Naiyah thought, *I'm not either. If Lijah's serious, I'm going to fight just as hard, somehow, if God is willing, my baby will have its Mom and Dad, and will be raised in a good and loving home* After a while, Naiyah put the car in reverse and turned to go back down the lane to the highway. "Well good morning, Butterfly Princess, you're up bright and early today. What brings you over so early?" inquired Inez Jones.

"I said I'd be back before I left and, besides, I wanted to talk with you." "Come in out of the cold then, can I get you something, have you had breakfast yet?"

"Yes Ma'am, I'm fine, but please don't let me stop you from getting yours. I'll come into the kitchen and keep you company, we can talk there, if you don't mind," Naiyah said.

Inez busied herself fixing coffee and a poached egg with toast. When she was done, she sat at the table across from Naiyah, but before eating or saying anything more, she bowed her head and said a blessing over her food. When she looked, up, Naiyah's head was also bowed. "It's good to see you give honor to God in prayer, baby, so tell your God-mommy what's up."

"Mom Inez, you know me well enough to know I don't usually ask for advice. Charge it to my ego or false sense of pride in that I think I've got all the answers, but today I'm finding myself at a crossroads of sorts and am not really certain how to handle the situation. I was hoping I could get some spiritual direction from you, as the God-sent stand in for my YaYa."

"This sounds serious," Inez said, placing her fork onto the plate, moving it off to the side along with her coffee mug. "So tell me precious, what's troubling you?"

"There's so much, I don't even know where to start, but anyway——"

"Before you get started, would you like to move into the sitting room where we'll be more comfortable?"

"Yes, Ma'am, that would be better." Naiyah followed her into the next room which was as resplendent with the morning sun as the kitchen. She noted the many family pictures displayed on the credenza, including several of her YaYa and even some recent ones of her and Nathan. God-mommy Inez was a widow like YaYa had been, with two grown children who lived in the Midwest. She didn't get to see them or her five grandchildren very often, so instead she filled her heart and home with the love, joy and tears of those she came to know and who needed her right there in their small community. "I don't know where to start," Naiyah said again, "so much has happened since my YaYa died."

"Just say it, baby," Inez coaxed, "it's okay, whatever you tell me stays with me unless you tell me otherwise. You're safe here."

"The man I introduced you to yesterday," Naiyah began, "I'm carrying his child, but he's engaged to someone else, and they were engaged before he knew anything about the baby. He says he loves me and now wants to break it off with her and make a family with me. He seems sincere and I believe him, but I don't know if I'm ready to have a child."

Inez listened intently, nodding her head every now and then. "Go on baby, take your time," she added, seeing Naiyah's eyes begin to water.

Naiyah tightly gripped the arms of the chair she was sitting in before saying, "I'm dealing with so many issues on so many levels right now, God-mommy, that I don't know what to address first."

"Honey, wait," Inez interjected, "you need a cup of tea, I'll be right back." While she was out of the room, Naiyah took several cleansing breaths to calm down and reached for the box of tissues on the end table beside her and dabbed at the corners of her eyes. She thought about Elijah and imagined the two of them pushing their baby on a swing at the most lusciously green park, with everything a child needed to make playtime special.

Inez always had a kettle of water simmering on the stove, so it didn't take her long to rejoin Naiyah in the sitting room. "Okay, precious," she said, setting the cup down on the table next to Naiyah, "that should do it, go on now, continue."

"So in a nutshell, I'm trying to figure out what to do. Do I keep the baby and raise it myself, do I accept Elijah's offer and deal with the wrath I know inevitably will come from his fiancée, who'll then be a woman scorned? Besides all the questions I have, I feel so much stress and anxiety over so many other things."

"Like what?" Inez asked, trying to keep up with everything Naiyah was saying at the same time, suspending any and all judgment.

"Well for one, the bickering between my parents, the fact that I was on the outs with my friend Mani for a really long time and I'm also worrying constantly about my brother."

"Baby, may I——" Inez inquired, her way of getting permission to comment. "Please, God-mommy, I really need clarity, another perspective so to speak."

"Baby, you aren't responsible for your mother and father's problems and I doubt you're responsible for what might be going on with Nathan. You didn't cause the separation between your parents and you can't mediate their fights, they've got to work that out themselves. But since you're an adult, I think you should think about establishing some boundaries, but the most important thing is, you need to first start taking care of yourself and your baby. It won't be easy, I know, it's going to take a lot of work," she said.

"What do you mean?" Naiyah asked.

"You're not a child any more, Naiyah; you decide what does and doesn't happen between you and your parents. It comes from the heart, the place inside that says, this is me, this is what works. You understand me?"

"Yes Ma'am," Naiyah said nodding.

"It sounds like you and Mani worked things out, thank God," Inez continued, "that's a blessing and, as for Nathan, stop worrying and start trusting."

"Trusting?" she asked, raising an eyebrow.

"Yes trusting, what I want more than anything right now is for you to learn to trust God and believe He sent His son so you can have peace and live free."

"Peace, I can surely use some of that," she laughed, *"and protection too,"* she added.

"Jesus offers everything you need that pertains to life and godliness, all you need is to receive it with an open heart," Inez said.

Naiyah's spirit yearned for this free offering, but the residue from six years of parochial school and her Mum's religious teachings somehow kept her from accepting it. Despite YaYa's influence, Naiyah believed she had too many vices that needed to be handled before she was ready for the Lord to take over.

When Naiyah didn't respond, Inez realized the timing still wasn't right, so she offered a silent prayer that the Lord would answer hers and the many of Big Sadie's before her, that Naiyah would soon come to know Jesus, turn her life over to Him and trust that He came only to save her, heal her and give her His righteousness. "So tell me, what else is going on with your brother?" Inez asked.

Naiyah took several sips of her tea and, before answering, she took a deep breath. When she'd finished, she had told God-mommy all about her suspicions of Nathan's sexual confusion and her own substance abuse.

"Baby, let's not focus on Nathan, okay, it's not about him. You have a serious problem and I'm tellin' you straight out, stop drinking and taking those drugs. You're only going to hurt that baby if you don't, then down the road, you'll have a mountain of regret to try and get out from under. If you decide to give the baby up, have you thought of the grief you might be heaping on those unsuspecting people?" she asked. "I want to encourage your heart baby, really I do, but seems like to me, what you're doing is careless and downright selfish. Your child's well-being oughta come first," Inez said sternly. "I know your troubles look mighty big to you, that you just want to hide from them. But we don't know how God's going to work, whether that young man will make you an honest woman or not, but if it works out, wouldn't you want the child to be healthy?" Inez asked, getting up for a Kleenex to wipe tears from her own eyes.

"Yes, God-mommy, I would. Everything you've said today, I've already been told by my Auntie, my roommate Faith and even Elijah."

"And as for Nathan," Inez continued, "first and foremost, love him just the way he is, and we'll pray the Lord works it out."

Inez took a Bible off a nearby shelf and opened it to the book of John, chapter 3 and read verse 16 to Naiyah, *"For God so loved the world, that he gave his only begotten Son, that whosoever believeth in him should not perish, but have everlasting life,"* she said, closing the book.

"Thank you, God-mommy, I feel a lot better now," Naiyah said, taking another deep breath and releasing it with a smile.

"I'm glad baby," Inez replied, "seek God to help you and your baby and keep me posted on how you're doing, let me know how things work out with you and Elijah."

Naiyah reached over and hugged her tightly, before letting go, she planted a kiss on her cheek and said again, "I love you so much."

Inez smiled and helped Naiyah into her coat "I love you too, Butterfly, be good and be sure to think about what I said."

"I will, most definitely," she said, "bye, God-mommy." Naiyah was humming again by the time she reached the car, so many thoughts were racing through her mind but they were of a positive vibration which elevated her in spirit even more. As she drove towards home, she began an awkward dialogue with God, hoping to connect with the God her YaYa knew, the same one, God-mommy Inez had just referred to. "Lord, it's Naiyah, it's been a long time I know. I think you know how complicated and messed up I've made things in my life but it wasn't intentional; well okay, I confess, it was intentional." She eased on hesitantly, "L-Looord, thank you, I'm grateful, very grateful for my YaYa and God-mommy Inez's guidance. Because of them I'm on the right path, they got me started, but I guess now I have to go the rest of the way on my own." Naiyah was emotionally full and overcome by the gravity of her situation, yet radiating from the love vibe experienced all weekend with family and friends.

As her visibility diminished, she realized she was being blinded by her tears but managed to pull off safely to the side of the road. She sat still for a few moments, trying to collect herself. "Lord," she said again, "I've heard about your love and the blood, I realize my need to be washed in it. I've come to the knowledge, rather, I accept the fact I've sinned and I desperately want to be forgiven. I don't want to live my life like I've been living it. I want to be cleansed and made new. I don't want the drugs or alcohol. I need your supernatural strength to overcome myself, I need to change, I want to be present for my baby." With that said, she knew in her heart that she had made her choice. She would finish school, be a devoted mommy and, if Elijah would have her, a devoted wife. She sat back and smiled brightly, bathed in the warmth of the hopeful feelings she had earlier.

XXX

Always Count the Cost

Jade sat alone at the kitchen nook contemplatively looking out into the grayness of the late morning, wondering to herself what next, and attempting to stimulate good self-talk about what living her best life really meant and what it would look like. As was her custom she taped, "Oprah" every day and especially loved it when it was Iyanla's or Dr. Phil's day. She knew what *their* best lives looked like, but this weekend had inspired her to define her own and she decided now was the time to craft the roadmap to get her there.

Startled out of her contemplative solitude by the jangling of the ringing phone nearby, Jade jumped before answering it, sending her teacup sailing across the table and stopping just in the nick of time before it had a chance to shatter to the floor. "Hello" Jade said slightly flustered.

"Jade, hi, it's Leyan, is this a bad time?"

"Oh hey, girl, no it's fine," she said wiping up the small pool of English breakfast tea from the table.

"We had a blast at your house Thursday night, I just wanted to call and thank you personally. Kalu and I really enjoyed ourselves."

"It was good to see you both also. Let's keep in touch; it's been much too long. By the way, my Sister and I don't have anything special planned today, why not come over and visit with us, unless you've got other plans."

"No, I'd love to, it'll give me a chance to tell you about the women's group I'm involved with and maybe you'll decide to join us sometime."

"Alright then, good, we'll see you later on today." Jade placed the cordless phone on the table and tried to find her way back to the contemplative thoughts she was engaged in before Leyan's call. She reflected on the conversation she had with Naiyah in the smoking room the night they arrived, shuddering at the thought of her unguarded reaction. Yet she couldn't help the sense of pride she felt knowing that Naiyah seemed to be facing her situation head on, that she wasn't running away the way she had when she found herself in the very same situation at about the same age Naiyah is now. Jade wondered what Ronnel would have done if she'd been honest with him and whether or not she would have been happy being his wife if things had turned out like that.' She formed Ronnel's image in her mind and smiled broadly, remembering how gentle he was with her, the tokens of affection he bestowed upon her, including the prized state championship track and field medallion he won for completing the 3200 meter run in 10:10 and the lyrics to the first love song he'd ever written that he passionately played on his bass guitar. But no, Ronnel had been a simple, unassuming disciplined young man. He didn't have anywhere near the same electric, charismatic, lady-killin' vibe that Lemuel Harland had. The minute Lucky noticed her and expressed his ardor, Jade knew that, whatever it took, she was going on the fast ride with him. He was the prize and she knew if she beat out all the campus sweethearts vying for his attention, the sky was going to be the limit. That's what she wanted, the house, the cars, the jewels, and travel she envisioned life with Lemuel would ultimately bring. With Ronnel, though he was gorgeous, she got the sense life with him would be ho-hum and predictable. "Jade Diamond," she remembered telling herself, "deserved better than that." But she thought ruefully, *I should have counted the cost. If I'd known that competing with women to get him in the beginning, would mean competing with them to keep him in the end, I could have saved myself time and a whole lot of freakin' heartache.* The absurdity of the whole thing amused Jade so, that she just started laughing uncontrollably.

XXXI

Nathan and Strong Get It On...II

Nathan was looking forward to going out dancing on his last night home with some of his high school buddies, but first he had to settle some business. He navigated the family wagon down highway 27, and feeling his nerves dancing wildly, he massaged his naked neck as he drove along. Still uncertain about why he was going or what he'd say, he steadied his hands on the steering wheel and continued on.

"What's up, dude," Strong asked, opening the door and stepping aside to allow Nathan sufficient room to enter. "What brings you over here? I wasn't expectin' to see you, *son.*"

Nathan's only response was to keep moving until he reached the living room where he sat in a lone chair away from the sofa where Strong had assaulted him the day before. "This really isn't a social call," he said.

"Oh, my bad," Strong replied lighting up a black and mild, "aw-ight then, state your business."

Nathan put his index finger to his mouth and thought for a minute. "You know, Danny, I couldn't help thinking about how you violated me yesterday but more so, how it didn't phase you. I wondered how that could be."

"Nathan, I already done told you, man, it ain't no thing, don't come over here startin' up with me again, go on now wit yo stuff."

"Let me finish," Nathan commanded. "Maybe it's nothing to you, but it might be life or death to someone else." Strong drew a long toke from the slim cigar, while kicking a crossed leg nervously back and forth. "There was a man once who lived near our neighborhood, everyone liked him, he was handy, but he did evil things to young children, which I don't think anyone knew." Strong continued swinging his leg. He had no idea what Nathan was about to say but it didn't stop him from feeling uncomfortable. "This man," Nathan continued, "used to call out, 'Hey, pretty boy,' whenever I passed by. I wasn't afraid of him because he was always so nice to us, he would give us chicklet gum and sometimes marbles."

Danny remembered how his father John West chewed chicklets all the time when he lived at home with them before his mother kicked his drunk ass out of the house all those many years before. Now he kept silent with eyes downcast while he listened.

"One day he said to me, 'Hey, pretty boy,' I'm going over to the nature trail, come ride with me. I loved to watch the fish in the pond whenever I went there with my Mum, so I hopped into his truck feeling the nice spring breeze spraying my face as we drove along. I think he told me the name of every flower and plant we passed, but as we neared the edge of the reserve he pushed me to the ground and tried to stick his penis in my mouth. When he couldn't pry it open, he stuck it between my legs and started humping furiously. Ever since then, I've been fearful and unsure of my sexual gender preference, until I started doing soul discovery work with a therapist in Miami."

"What you tellin' me for," Strong asked with an edge to his voice.

"Danny, I never wanted to be with a man sexually but there was something about male masculinity that attracted me. I didn't understand why. Since I always wanted a wife and children, I was confused, but I'm not anymore. I'm telling you because I need to forgive you from my heart for what you did to me yesterday and to encourage you to find out the truth of why you're turned on by dudes."

Strong's leg slowed down a bit and he lifted his eyes slowly to meet Nathan's. He tried to maintain his hard edge, but Nathan had touched a sensitive nerve. "No one's ever taken the time to care before," he said, "thanks, man. I hear you and I will do something to figure this out, I promise you."

"Be easy," Nathan said, "I'm out." Strong didn't get up to see Nathan to the door; instead, he sat silently, deep in thought. He wondered why it took his mother so long to toss his father out of the house. He wondered if she knew how often Johnny West, her husband, was putting his penis between Danny's legs and humping him like a dog in heat before she'd had enough of his drunkenness and parted company with him for good, not long before his tragic and lonely death. How ironic it was that Naiyah had dreamed of Mr. Johnny's death so many years before, given the pivotal impact he had on both his son and her brother's lives. Had she shared the dream with YaYa at the time, would it have made a difference to Strong or Nathan?

XXXII

She Still Wants Him, Dira, Don't be Mad

It had been a few days since Nadira had talked to D'yanna, so she decided to check in with her. "What's up, girl, haven't heard from you, is everything okay?"

D'yanna's voice was so muffled, it sounded like she had several pillows over her head, which concerned her friend.

"Dee, have you heard from Elijah?"

"No," she finally managed, "he changed the lock on the door to his apartment and he's not returning my calls," D'yanna said.

"What about his mother, have you heard from her?"

"She lies and says she doesn't know where he is," she said flatly.

"Well, it's obvious he's dodging you."

"Yeah, I know, Nadira."

"Did you go to his office?"

"Dira, I don't have the energy it takes to chase that fool all around this city."

"I feel you," Nadira said, "how about lunch, you wanna get together?"

"Not today, I'm depressed and I just want my life back."

"Listen, I'll be over after work today to cheer you up. You're not going out like this, you're going to get your but up and get on with it. See you later."

❀

"Elijah," Nadira shouted as soon as he answered, "what in the hell is wrong with you?"

"Hold up."

"No, you hold up, my girl is all messed up over this bulls*#@ and all you have to say is 'hold up.' You must be out of your ever-loving mind if you think it's going down like this."

"Nadira, calm down—please."

Nadira took a deep breath. She was so mad at Elijah for what he was putting her friend through that she couldn't help herself from going off.

"Alright," she said, "but she's really messed up over this and she doesn't deserve it."

"It's complicated, Dira."

"I don't give a damn; you owe her an explanation or something. How can you leave her hanging like this? You must really be a fool."

"I'm sorry, I never meant for this to happen. I feel really bad and I didn't know how to face D'yanna," he said.

"Well, running away is surely not the solution. And you're planning to be a lawyer, you sure as hell couldn't represent me," she snapped.

"I deserved that," he said. "Is she okay though?"

"Hell no, she's not okay—call her," she said slamming her phone shut.

※

"How come you're not at work today?"

D'yanna spat into the telephone, "Elijah, don't be stupid."

He stood up from his desk and walked over to the window with the view over-looking Washington Square, still not believing his good fortune in having landed a fellowship at NYU before even beginning his law studies at the graduate level, and with a very hefty stipend on top of that. He was looking at a very bright future but knew he had to get it right before moving forward—he didn't want the bad karma.

"What do you want, Elijah," D'yanna interrupted, "or did you just call to torture me some more with your silence?"

"Will you meet me later this evening?" he asked simply.

D'yanna came out from under the covers and sat up in bed. "Where?" she asked hopefully.

"Junior's Restaurant," he said noticing a painful throbbing in his temples again.

"I'm not coming down to Times Square," she fumed.

"No, I should be getting back to Brooklyn around seven, can you meet me at Junior's on Flatbush Ave?"

"I'll be there by seven-thirty," she said and hung up.

By the time Nadira arrived later that afternoon, D'yanna had gotten up and gone out. She hit the Avenue and ran into her favorite salon for a quick wash, blow dry and curl. Before leaving the salon, she also had her nails and toes done.

"You don't look anything like you sounded this morning," Nadira said dropping her Windsor coach bag on the coffee table.

"It doesn't take much," D'yanna said beaming. "Elijah called, I'm meeting him at Junior's later."

"Is that the best he can do, treat you to some big ass hamburgers and fattening cheesecake?"

"I'm not stressin' over that."

"Humph," Nadira snorted, "you oughta."

"Honey, I've had enough rain on my parade, and like Angie Stone says, *"my sunshine has come, and I'm all cried out. There's no more rain in this cloud,"* "I'm alright," D'yanna sang.

"Humph," Nadira said again, "and all it took was for that black ass Negro to call and invite you to a cheesecake restaurant? You said it right when you said it didn't take much. But don't get me wrong, Dee, I'm not trippin', I'm glad he called, I just wouldn't get my hopes up so high if I were you."

D'yanna ignored her friend's comments. "Dira girl, I don't know what I'd do without you, you've always been there."

"And it's fortunate for you you'll never have to find out, but I'll tell you this much, Dee, I'm not going to be more angry over this s*#@ than you are; you best believe that," she said, grabbing her bag. "Have fun, D'yanna, I'll check you out later," she said, walking out the door.

Elijah was standing at the entryway rubbing his hands back and forth when D'yanna arrived. "Thanks for coming," he said awkwardly.

Dee didn't respond; she was as anxious as he seemed to be.

"Let me get that," he said, taking her coat.

"Okay," she said finally, "I didn't come here for nothing, what do you have me all messed up and entangled in, Elijah, and don't leave anything out," she snapped. D'yanna thought, *with the way this fool's been actin', this may be the only chance I've got to get to the bottom of this madness.*

"Sweetheart," he said, and having called her that for some time, it still seemed natural to him, "this is really difficult and most of it, it seems, you've already figured out."

She wasn't about to help him, instead she remained silent, staring unblinkingly at him, hoping he was uncomfortable as hell. She remembered the last thing Nadira had said and felt the heat of her anger begin to rise from the back of her neck.

"I don't know what to say, I feel ashamed and really sorry for what I've done to you. I loved you, D'yanna."

At that, she put her hands up to her mouth realizing she was holding her breath and feeling the beginnings of a serious pain in her stomach.

"I came home from Stanford," he continued now looking her straight in the eye, "with the intention of giving you my heart forever."

She was thinking how much agony he must be in, having to tell her about the baby. She also thought they could weather this storm together. It wouldn't be easy, but she would do it.

"But my heart wasn't mine to give, it belonged to someone else." "Aaaaaahhhhhh," howled D'yanna trying to ease the pain from the sledge hammer blow that just struck her in the chest. "Aaaaaahhhhhh," she howled again, shaking her head furiously from side to side feeling like a caged animal trying desperately to find a way out. "What are you saying, how could you," she said with a venomous hiss.

He reached over to restrain her by forcibly holding her shoulders, not caring what the onlookers were thinking. "I didn't mean to hurt you, I swear. I couldn't have known things would turn out the way they did, but the woman who's going to have my child also has my heart." Elijah released his grip on D'yanna's shoulders.

"Has your heart, has your heart," she hissed again. "I don't understand this. The last time we had any meaningful conversation we were about to go shopping for an engagement ring for me. But now you say there's a woman who has your heart and your baby. What's wrong with this picture, Elijah?" "Dee, I don't think you'll be any angrier or disappointed with me than you are right now, so I'll spare you the details and just ask you to forgive me. I hope somewhere down the line we can be friends again."

"So that's it? This is all there is? We've dated on and off for the last four years, a year ago you promised to love me forever and asked me to be your wife, but tonight you say it's over, just like that, no further explanation!" "There's nothing else to say, D'yanna, I don't love you like that and I don't want to hurt you any more than I have already."

She laughed as she slid her stocking foot out of her shoe and found her way to his crotch. "You sound like you've bumped you head, B.B., but I know it's just because you haven't had any of my delicious cookies in a while. How 'bout that, how 'bout you come over to my place and let's work this out?"

"I can't, Dee, I've got to move on. I've got a baby coming."

"I get that, Elijah, I know there's a baby coming and I plan to be the best step mother to it that I can possibly be."

Elijah couldn't believe what he was hearing. He grabbed her foot and pushed it away. "D'yanna," he said with noticeable irritation, "nothing can change what's happening, certainly not sex. I'm telling you the truth tonight so we can both be free to start over and be happy."

"Do I look happy, Elijah, do I sound happy? You promised me and now you're expecting me to just say okay, you made a mistake, go have a nice life? I don't think so."

"D'yanna, I'm not going to be with you," he said, his head now hurting. "That might ever be, Mr. McCoy, but I promise you, you won't be happy without me. I will see to it that you and your precious Naiyah Harland are never happy."

"Don't threaten me and you better stay far away from Naiyah or you'll be sorry. Don't make me, Dee," he said putting more than enough money on the table to cover the bill. He then headed for the door, leaving her sitting alone. Before he got a good six feet from her, she quickly retrieved her shoe and sent it sailing through the air to whack him good and hard upside his bald head. Elijah turned on instinct with hands clenched into fists and nostrils flaring. He looked at D'yanna and knew he deserved worse for what he was doing to her but he couldn't turn back now, not when he was so close to the family he dreamed of with Naiyah.

XXXIII

Elijah Blues

"**Sweetheart,** I'm glad you're safely back at school. I just met with D'yanna and told her about us and the baby."

"How'd she take it?" Naiyah asked sitting comfortably on the sofa flipping through the latest issue of *In Style* magazine, looking forward to the day she'd get her shape and fashionista groove back.

"You don't want to know. Get some rest." he said, "I'll call you tomorrow." "Wow, wow-wee—this is heavy," Elijah said while pressing the speed dial number to his friend Kirk's phone. "Hey man, I need to talk."

"Cool," Kirk said, "I was wonderin' what was up since you haven't been around the way in weeks. Anyway man, what's up, how was your holiday?"

"Not over the phone," Elijah replied "can you meet me at the sports bar? I need some objectivity and a good strong drink." There was a long pause before Elijah continued, "I've just left D'yanna and she's completely devastated."

Kirk did an involuntary backwards mental flip to the morning a few weeks ago when D'yanna called and asked for Elijah's Aunt Lydia's number. "Damn," he said, "give me twenty minutes, bro, I'll be there.

XXXIV

Letting It Go, Moving On

Jade peeked out the side window of the downstairs entryway door, happy to finally see the sun after what seemed like weeks of snow, rain and frigid temperatures, which brought to mind that spring was soon on the way along with a new baby. She wondered aloud how much planning Naiyah had done to make way for this baby she decided to keep. "Naiyah knows we're all behind her but beyond that, I wonder what the plan is." Jade was dealing with enough ambiguity in her own life without having the added stress of worrying about Naiyah's decisions. On the one hand, she was over the moon that she and Ronnel were now seeing each other pretty regularly. She was having more fun than she remembered having in quite some time. She was feeling young and alive again. It felt good, yet at the same time she was feeling bad for Lemuel. It wasn't clear what happened, but all of a sudden Lem and Analise were having what seemed like serious problems, so bad that he asked her to move out. Jade heard through the grapevine that Analise had moved in with one of her girlfriends. Jade didn't want to interfere but she was moved to compassion nonetheless over what she knew Lemuel had to be going through. Though she worried about him, she wasn't about to let it interfere with her life or slow her down.

"Good morning, Ms. Inez."

"Jade, honey is that you?"

"Yes Ma'am," Jade said walking into the formal living room to bask in the glorious sun rays that were streaming in with powerful brightness and warmth.

"How are you, baby, is anything the matter," Inez asked, worry creeping up uninvitingly.

"Oh no, not at all, everything's great," Jade said, "I was just wondering if Naiyah's been in touch with you lately?"

"No, not lately, I was hoping she'd call soon after she got back to school but she hasn't called yet."

"There's no excuse, I know, but you know how these young kids are Ms. Inez."

"Yes Lord, I sure do."

"Well," Jade pressed, "I know this isn't my place, but I was wondering if you'd consider providing unofficial foster care to Naiyah's baby when it comes."

Ms. Inez did a turn around move stopping short of a holy dance, not wanting to assume anything, though, she asked hopefully, "So she decided to keep the child?"

"Oh, so you don't know. She called the family together before she went back to school and told us she made the decision to keep it. She's not sure how things are going to turn out, but after speaking with you, she said she got the courage to believe the Lord would work it out."

Elated, all Ms. Inez could say was "Are you serious?" Once it sank in, Inez Jones came to the sobering realization that, at her age, she wasn't up to the task of caring for an infant. As much as her heart yearned to help out, she knew she had to decline. "Jade, honey, I'm more than honored over your askin' me, but I can't handle no little baby, no chile, not at my age I can't," she said staring out the window of her kitchen wondering who she could call on at her church to help out. "But if you want, I can ask around at my church. There must be some young family serving the Lord there who'd be willing to care for the baby for a little while."

"If you get any leads, Ms. Inez, please let me know. I'm trying to do what I can so Naiyah can complete her studies before taking on full time motherhood."

"But she's graduating right around the time she delivers, isn't she?"

"Yes Ma'am, but we'd like for her to obtain her masters degree right away, it'll be better for her and the baby."

"I see. What about her young man."

"What do you mean," Jade asked.

"Oh nothing, except I was wonderin' where he fits in all this."

Jade didn't know herself where Elijah fit, Naiyah hadn't said much about it.

"Thanks Ms. Inez, I've got to run now. Call me," she said again.

"Alright baby, you be good now."

Jade sat back and again felt the warmth of the morning sun caress her face. Outside the window, she could see the bronze wind spinner with a bright yellow sun in the center twirling gently. She sighed contentedly and thought to herself that the sun does indeed bring life. As she began to regenerate her life, Jade found herself indulging less in the destructive drinking she'd been doing, and the sharing with Leyan and the women in her group was a tremendous help in reminding her, who she was, independent of her estranged husband and children. She began to realize how much she needed to let go. Let it all go, the past, the pain of Lemuel's rejection, control of her now grown children's lives, and her own insecurity and doubt. It had come, she remembered, that day at the health club and her chance encounter with Analise. There was something at her core that awakened, alerting her that she was deeply blocked on an emotional level. She knew then, though she didn't express it fully to Aqua, that she had to do something or she'd die or, worse, suffer severe emotional retardation. She had to change but the very thought of it frightened her.

XXXV

...I Wish I Could, But I Just Can't

Jade stood with great reluctance, knowing it was getting late and she had a mid-afternoon class to teach. Gathering herself to leave, with outstretched arms she turned in a slow, circular motion breathing in deeply the bliss and peace she'd found in her living room sanctuary. She was experiencing in the moment a sense of light heartedness which wouldn't be contained, and warmth erupted from deep within and established itself firmly in a warm glowing smile across her face. "Mine must be the busiest phone around," she thought aloud while walking into the kitchen to retrieve the cordless. Quickly glancing at the caller ID, 'Intentional International Diversification,' "What does he want?" she asked, feeling an abrupt reentry to reality. "Jade, it's Lucky," she felt the pause of his breath, "I wouldn't ask if it wasn't important" he said.

"What is it?" she asked impatiently, feeling frustrated, knowing her bliss had just flown out the window.

"Don't be so cold, I need to talk to you. Can I come over this evening?"

"What's this about?" she wanted to know.

"It's about Analise and me."

"I don't have anything to do with that and I'm certainly not interested in hearing about the two of you."

"Please J, hear me out, all I want is for you to listen, please," he pleaded, rocking gently in his large, leather executive chair.

"Does this have anything to do with your split from Analise?" she asked him, thinking for a moment how he must be feeling and, against her better judgment, agreed. "I'll call you when I get home," she said, "and don't think for a minute you're going to hang around all night dumping that stuff on me."

"Okay," he said quickly, "I'll see you tonight, thanks, J."

In a split second, before she'd hung the phone up good, Jade's heart started beating fast and she felt a big lump in her throat. She knew better than to spend time alone with Lemuel especially now when he was obviously very vulnerable. *And so am I,* she thought. *How could I be so foolish, maybe I should call Ronnel, he'll know what I should do.* She walked to the window seat in the breakfast nook and stared out at the crystal blue sky. *I'm wide open, so how can I allow myself to be alone with him,* she asked herself. Dismissing her reservations, Jade went to the master bedroom suite and busied herself with getting ready to go to campus. She chose an Adrienne Vittadini black knit sweater to wear over black slacks with a cute pair of Bandolino low-cut, black boots. Once in the car, heading towards Interstate 495, the Long Island Expressway, Jade spoke a voice command and her car phone began ringing without hesitation. "Hello, it's Mrs. Ayers, may I help you?"

"Hi, honey, it's your little sis, what's up?"

"Oh hey, Sissy girl, what are you doing calling me at this time of the day?" Turquoise asked.

"I'm heading to school for a lecture, but I wanted to run something by you first," she said.

"Cool, alright go ahead, I've got a few minutes."

"Lemuel called and said there's trouble in paradise and asked if he could come over and talk about it."

"Are you okay with that?"

"No, but it seems that since Thanksgiving weekend, things have been a little less strained between us."

"Alright then, so what's the problem?"

"*Well you know, Qua,* I'm beginning to feel sorry for him, but I don't want him to read anything more into it, besides, I'm afraid he might be tempted if he comes over here."

"Tempted by what?"

"I don't know, I mean, he's a man *and* I suspect he's not getting any if Analise isn't there."

"Honey look, don't worry about that, that one's not yours."

"I know," Jade said, about to approach the exit ramp for Adelphi, "but he sounded so lost when he called."

Turquoise took a deep breath focusing on the painting by Chagall of 'I and My Village' hung nicely on her office wall, "I don't have anything against Lucky, he's my brother-in-law, he'll always be my brother-in-law, but Sissy, you don't owe him anything, he cheated on you," she said without any sign of malice. When Jade didn't respond, Turquoise continued, "This is your time, Sissy; write your script however you want."

Finally, Jade said, "You're right again. I'm about to pull into my parking spot, sis, I'll have to get back with you later."

"Okay Sweetie, keep me posted. Oh, Jade, have you been meeting with Leyan and her women's group?" Turquoise asked.

"Yes, Aqua, I am and I'm gaining some really good spiritual and personal insights, I'll tell you about it next time. Love you, Qua, Ciao."

"I love you back, be good now."

Jade grabbed her bag and, while securing her car, thought, *I'm strong enough to resist anything Lemuel comes with, because to do anything else would be down right foolish indeed.* She sighed.

XXXVI

Stress Leads to Fatigue, Get a Grip

It seemed that for weeks D'yanna could barely raise her head up off the pillow when morning came, and she found today to be no different. After Elijah walked out of Junior's Restaurant leaving her to hobble in embarrassment over to where her shoe landed, she went home and drank an entire bottle of Kendall Jackson Chardonnay. Since she wasn't sleeping well anyway, she knew it was more than the morning-after wine headache or the consistent tension headache that was dogging her ever since Elijah started actin' foul. Other than that, she didn't know why she was constantly so fatigued and fuzzy headed. She called out sick again from work and chuckled a bit while wondering what to do when she finally ran out of excuses. She shrugged and thought, *No time for that now, I've got to pay a visit to Mr. Going To Be a Baby Daddy McCoy, and maybe get a referral to see a doctor later this afternoon.*

When D'yanna reached Elijah's office, she found the door open and walked in without knocking. Startled by her entrance, Elijah quickly stood up and without thinking placed his hands firmly on his hips. "Why are you here, D'yanna, everything that needed to be said was said last night."

Ignoring him, she walked over and got right in his face, "Okay Elijah," she said, "so you didn't bump your head and I guess I'm really supposed to believe you're serious about leaving me for this Naiyah chick."

"She's having my baby, Dee, and truly, I'm sorry this happened, but I love her, I told you that."

D'yanna was now really mad, "What about me!" she shouted.

"Dee, this is a place of business, you can't come in here disrupting things."

"I don't give a damn!" she shouted louder. "What about me?" she asked again. "What about you," he snapped, "we're over Dee, I can't make it any clearer than that."

The last thread popped and try as she might, D'yanna was now completely out of control. She littered his office with the papers she began flinging from his desk, then started screaming obscenities and clawing at him at the same time.

Elijah tried to restrain her but it was no use.

She began shouting, "Elijah McCoy is a cheater."

Elijah rushed to close the door of his office but it was too late, someone had already called security. "Excuse me, Mr. McCoy, is everything alright in here?" the officer, who was now standing in the doorway, asked. Elijah turned to D'yanna with a look of impatient disgust and, turning back to the guard said, "No sir, please remove this woman from the premises, she doesn't have permission to be here."

D'yanna, now restrained by the officer, kept trying to strike and claw at Elijah while shouting, "Why, Elijah, why? I love you, don't do this, please."

When her pathetic attempts to change his mind didn't cause him to relent, the flame of her anger rekindled to a raging fire. "You cheater," she yelled, "I'm going to make you regret this for the rest of your natural born days."

"Sir, remove her," Elijah said with dismissive finality.

Outside his office, people were gathering, buzzing with curiosity and speculation as to what was going on. Elijah quietly closed the door. When he returned to his desk he sat motionless, looking over the flood of papers littered about the floor. In a soft whisper, he prayed, *"Jesus, what do I do now? How can I forgive myself for the hurt I've caused? I didn't mean it, but wouldn't it be worse for me to betray the love I have for Naiyah and the precious life growing in her womb?"*

XXXVII

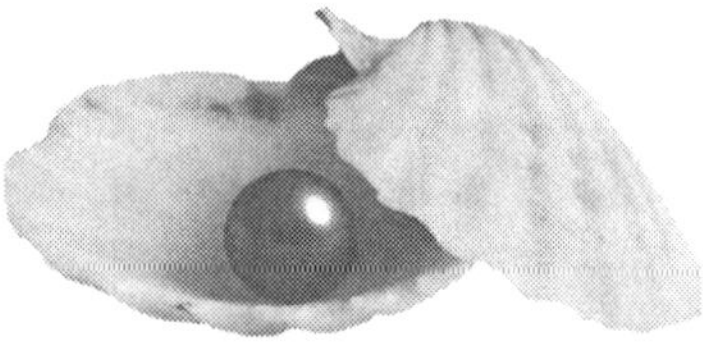

Could You Walk Away

Naiyah noticed that while in her morning class, she missed a call from Lijah. *I'll call him after lunch,* she thought, *I'm already late for my lunch date with Faith.* "Izzy, over here," Faith called when she spotted Naiyah coming into the student center. While looking over the menu of the vendor, specializing in organic fare, Faith remarked, "In a few short months, girlfriend, all of this will be behind us."

"Can you believe it?" Naiyah asked, picking up a taster's sample of humus.

"No, it's like a dream, but I bet it's sometimes overwhelming for you," Faith added.

"Yeah, a little, but what makes it bearable, is that Lijah and I are doing it together."

"I can tell," Faith said. "I'm so happy for you, Izzy, ever since Elijah came onboard over Thanksgiving break, I've seen so many positive changes in you, what a beautiful thing," she said smiling.

"Well, that, plus the fact I'm trying to have a more meaningful relationship with the Lord. I plan to sacrifice everything so my baby and I can live and live well," she said, suggesting her trust was in God, not man.

Faith smiled as the waitress approached them for their order.

"Wait, WAIT, Elijah, slow down, she did what?" Naiyah asked when Elijah finally connected with her. She spoke loudly, attempting to drown out his hurried account of the day's events and the unexpected visit from D'yanna. "Oh baby, are you alright?" she asked, deep concern lacing each word.

He laughed "I don't know what I was thinking, Ny, I actually thought she was just going to go away."

"Yeah right, do you hear yourself," she asked, "c'mon, Elijah, seriously, in D'yanna's defense, girlfriend was just about to marry a fine black honey drop, the man of her dreams no doubt, with an enviable future in law; who in their right mind walks away from that?"

Elijah rolled his chair out from his desk staring once more at the litter of paper, while a groan left his lips. "Sweetheart," he said, "I hope you're up for the challenges we're surely going to face with her."

"No, more to the point, Mr. McCoy, are you ready? I'm sure we'll have a lot more challenges then just the wrath of hurricane Dee," she laughed.

He stood up. "I'm ready, I've counted the cost, and I'll do whatever it takes to secure our future."

A veil of guilt and uncertainty descended upon and engulfed Naiyah. "Yes baby," she said, "it's going to be uphill for sure, but I'm ready too."

"One more thing, Ny, when will you be back in New York, do you know?" he asked. "I'd like for you to meet my mother and father before the baby gets here and, since we've agreed to be together," he laughed, "I think we should consummate the deal, don't you," he said smiling to himself, the thought of joining together with Naiyah and his baby in physical oneness stimulated joy and excitement within him.

"Li, you're so nasty, besides the law, all you think about is gettin' some."

"That's not true," he said unconvincingly.

"But seriously though," she continued, "I know I have to meet your parents, but I have to be honest, I'm really dreading it, after all, I doubt that your mother's feeling me right now."

"Don't worry, my mother is very open-minded and she only wants what's best for me and that would be you, sweetheart," he said, this time quite convincingly.

"I love you, Lijah," she said sweetly, "and I'm sorry it took all this for me to finally tell you."

Elijah nodded his head and smiled.

"I've got to go to the library, sweetie, I'll talk to you soon, and in the meantime go somewhere and have some fun and cool off. Oh yeah, Lijah, another thing, It might not always seem like it, but I'm a lady and soon to be the mother of your child."

"Why are you telling me that?" he asked, confused by the statement. "C'mon, *'seal the deal,'* I hope you see the act of making love to me as more than a cold clinical exercise," she teased.

"You got me," he laughed, "but for sure, little shorty, I know you're a lady and all girl too. I love you, Ny, be safe going out alone, you hear."

XXXVIII

Jade's Song

When Ronnel came back into Jade's life, he brought with him romance and tenderness. His sensitivity sparked her femininity and drew out her sensual womanly passion, which made her feel fully alive and satisfied with herself, so much so, she'd even taken to romancing herself again. She remembered back when she and Lucky were still together and still deeply in love, he had flowers sent to her every week. On date nights, she surprised him with gourmet dinners, soft glowing candlelight and delectable, eye-pleasing lingerie. She sometimes used wildly seductive props she'd get from Frederick's of Hollywood. When their intimate encounters cooled, Jade thought it was because they were getting older and everyday life was becoming more demanding. She didn't realize that natural life progression could threaten her marriage, and now she wondered, *if Lucky was bored with me, did I unwittingly send him into her arms?*

When he left her and the children, she still had the flowers delivered despite the beautiful plants and blossoms in her own solarium. She'd come to love being greeted by a large beautiful bouquet sitting prominently on the foyer table when she walked in her front door. Ronnel's presence was a reminder of what she was missing, so she vowed, no matter who or what was in her life, this essential piece would never be taken from her again. "I'm a beautiful, vibrant woman" she said out loud, "and I won't give pieces of myself away and surely won't let anyone take pieces from me either, I don't care what they come with." She chuckled. "If I don't sound just like Aqua," she laughed. This new sense of self was an important breakthrough for Jade, because not long after Lucky left, she stopped the flower deliveries, she stopped filling her home with soft glowing candlelight, and grew tired of fixing gourmet meals for herself when the children were away. Instead, more and more she'd have one, then two and maybe three cocktails while lounging on the chaise in the master suite, thumbing mindlessly through celebrity or house décor magazines. But even before Ronnel, she knew she was in a rut and wasn't sure how to get out, but worse, she lacked the energy and motivation. Now things seemed to be turning around, especially after recently spending time with her sister and her sister's family and learning she was about to be a grandmother. Jade looked back over the last several weeks and recognized she was depending on the beauty around her and not a drink to get herself up and going.

Cleaning up after enjoying a delicious piece of blackened swordfish and grilled vegetables she prepared for dinner, Jade grew anxious knowing Lucky was stopping by soon. She looked around her warm kitchen with the soft low lighting and hoped he wouldn't get the wrong idea, then just as quickly, *so what if he does, that's on him. Life's short; I've got to do me*, she thought, remembering her earlier conversation with Turquoise. Just then Jade heard the chimes of the doorbell. She put the last dish into the dishwasher, removed her apron, adjusted her belt and ran her hands down her legs to smooth out any wrinkles in her slacks. She was relieved that Lucky respected her wishes by no longer letting himself in with the key he kept, and which he was entitled to. She took a deep breath and released it just as she opened the door to Lucky and the bitter cold from the January night. "Hey Lemuel," she said easily, "let me take your coat." Handing it to her, he greeted her with an innocuous light kiss on the cheek, "Thanks, J."

She led him into the kitchen, ignoring the gesture.

"Wow lady," he said, looking around, feeling the warm rhythmic vibe flowing through the space, "you really have things nice in here, something feels different, like new life's generating everywhere."

"I'm glad you noticed, that's exactly what I'm creating in the atmosphere and in myself—new life. I'm not sure though, if I'm regenerating or reinventing, only time will tell," she giggled, not able to help herself.

"That's good, that's what time it is—time for change," he said, taking a seat at the island counter. Jade stood in front of him. "Can I get you a cup of tea, a glass of wine or anything before we get to what brought you over?"

"Sure, tea would be nice. Do you mind if we talk in the living room?" he asked.

"Not at all, go inside, I'll be right there."

Lucky looked around the room, taking in the soft beauty, comfort and family photos, including one of his beloved mother, Big Sadie. A lump formed in his throat, as what he'd given up was becoming more and more apparent, especially when he was last here, but even then, he had not felt his pain and the depth of his loss as acutely as he felt now. *What can I say to her,* he wondered, pushing tears and emotion back into that soul-murdering hole he so candidly told Johann about the night they went to Jettison's.

"So," Jade said entering the room with a tray filled with an assortment of herbal teas, slices of zucchini bread, butter and jams. She noticed he'd taken the same seat she'd chosen earlier that day, the one facing the rising east sun. "So," she said again, settling in comfortably on the matching sofa opposite him, "your tone sounded rather urgent this afternoon, what's going on?"

"You already know Lise and I are split up, right?"

"Yes, I heard."

"Do you know why?" he asked.

"No, but I imagine one of you were unfaithful."

"I saw her with another man and found out later she'd been sleeping around with him for quite awhile."

Jade put her finger to her mouth for a moment, and finally she said "That must have hurt you badly, not to mention the blow to your super-sized manly ego, but what I don't understand is why you want to talk to me about it."

"Because I believe you're still my friend, that's why. Even if we didn't get the love and devotion thing right, I believe with all my heart that our friendship is still intact. And how you handled, with dignity and grace, the mess I put you through, I know you must have a word of wisdom for me."

"Oh, so you want to flatter me now?"

"No, no," he said shaking his head, "I've always had mad respect for both your heart and mind, you stood out, Jade, you were miles above all the other women. I trusted you and I still do."

"Well, I'm sorry to disappoint you, I really am, but I don't have anything to offer."

Lucky felt his heart sink while his hands rose involuntarily, forming the prayer position, to meet his lips. He stared at her but she looked away. "Jade, I could have forgiven Analise and part of me has, but the real reason I made her leave is because I recognize and acknowledge my foolish mistakes." When Jade looked up, Lucky was on his knees in front of her. "I'm sorry, Jade, I'm so sorry, please let me come home. I'll do anything you want me to. I love you—I want to come back, please." Jade searched his eyes and found deep sorrow and repentance. She felt his pain deeply, but found her own need to find herself and live fully, even greater. Placing his face within her hands, she gently kissed his wanting lips and more feverishly forced his mouth open to receive her tongue of fire. She kissed him deeply and passionately, cradling and rubbing his head in an earnest desire to baptize and purify him in the cleansing whiteness of forgiveness. She drank in his tears, now mixed with her own, and felt a righteous kind of oneness with him.

"I love you too, Lemuel," she said while he remained knelt before her, "and you're right, we're always going to be friends, but I can't take you back, not now anyway." He looked up at her, his eyes pleading and hopeful. "If I took you back, it would have to be on my terms. It can't be like it was and right now, I have to be honest, I'm not fully aware myself what my terms are." Lucky got up slowly, not feeling any regret or less of a man, instead he felt hopeful possibility.

Once Lucky had gone, Jade cleared their teacups and finished cleaning up in the kitchen before going upstairs for a hot bath. Afterwards, she spent a good while moisturizing her skin with ginger soufflé from Origins until her skin glistened and smelled good enough to eat. Jade moved towards the ringing phone in the master suite after first being startled by it. "Oh, it's Willie," she said smiling. "Hey girl, what are you doing calling me so late?"

"Sorry, Jade, I didn't realize how late it was, I just wanted to talk to you. So what's going on?" Wilhelmina asked.

"Not much, but girl, that ex of mine is relentless."

"What do you mean, what's he done now?"

"He's trying everything to get me to take him back."

"You're joking," Wilhelmina laughed, "what about Ms. Chiquita Banana?"

"Well, the word is, she stepped out on him."

Willie couldn't contain herself and nearly choked on the vitamin water she was about to swallow. "What! You're not telling me the Don got played."

"Umm-hum, he sure did."

"Wow, oh well, such is life. Did you tell him that you've been seeing my brother?"

"No, I certainly didn't, that would be cruel and I don't think he needs to know that just yet."

"Are you considering his request?" she asked slowly.

"I don't know, I haven't thought about it really."

"Does Ronnel know?"

"No and don't you say anything either."

"Jade, I'm not going to keep secrets."

Jade felt herself get defensive. "It's not a secret, Willie, it's my business to share with whomever I please, and in case you forgot, Lemuel *is* still my husband."

"Oh, excuse me. I didn't know it was like that."

"It's not like that or like anything else, Wilhelmina," Jade said, feeling herself getting heated, "and tell me, why are we at each other, come on now. You didn't call to start a fight with me, did you?"

"You're right, this is crazy—so when was the last time you spoke to Ronnie?" Wilhelmina wanted to know.

"We spoke last night; we have theater tickets for this weekend."

"How nice, did he ask you yet to join him at the Grand Del Mar Spa Resort in San Diego?"

"The Grand Del Mar, you've got to be kidding me? That place is pretty swanky."

"You know about the Del Mar?"

"Yes, but only what I've read in one of my spa finder magazines, but what's this about Ronnel asking me to go with him?" Jade asked with keen interest. "He wants to surprise you with a trip there; he's going on business next month and thought you might enjoy it. I thought he already asked you, so when he does, don't let on that I told you."

"I'm not keeping secrets, Wilhelmina," Jade teased.

"Touché," she said recognizing what was being mirrored back at her. "How're the kids doing, are things going well with Izzy's pregnancy?"

"The last I heard things were okay although she's been complaining lately that the baby kicks furiously at times, other times she doesn't notice movement for days."

"That doesn't sound good."

"I don't know," Jade replied, "but I told her to be sure to mention it to the doctor the next time she goes. At the start of the pregnancy, she wasn't going to the doctor regularly, but now that Qua is on it, she makes sure she gets there and that she takes her prenatal vitamins. She's even got her going to a prenatal yoga class."

"Oh good, so anyway, start packing your bags for a scrumptious spa weekend in fabulous, sunny San Diego. Ronnel will probably bring it up when you two get together over the weekend."

"I don't know, girl, it sounds really tempting, but I don't know if I'm ready for an away weekend with a man."

"Jade, quit playing and get in the game. Good night, sweetie," Wilhelmina said.

Jade hung the phone up and stretched her naked body out on the chaise. The warmth of the master suite made the cold temperatures outside seem really far away, especially as she allowed her mind to transport her to a massage table at the luxurious wellness salon at the Grand Del Mar. Pulling the chenille throw up to her shoulders, she smiled contentedly, thinking about resting in the gentle embrace of Ronnel's arms. She also thought about Lucky, but the thought was quickly overshadowed when she found his face transposed by Ronnel's, as she pictured herself being kissed sweetly by him. Jade drifted off to sleep in the sweet embrace of Ronnel and a vision of tender love.

XXXIX

Seeing the Baby Alone

"*That* would be great," Naiyah said walking into their apartment, waving to Faith who was reading a book on the sofa. "I can't wait. I love you, sweetie, see you soon, okay, I will, bye," she said snapping her phone shut. Taking off her wrap after dropping her books down on the counter, "Hi, honey," she said turning back to Faith. "How was your day?"

"Brutal."

"Sorry to hear that, what's up?"

"Chemistry class as usual, but I can't duck it, I've got to go through it," she said sighing, "what's going on, you seem excited."

"I am, that was Mani, and she's coming for a visit during spring break."

"That's great, I'd love to meet her."

"Of course, you'll be here won't you?" Naiyah asked.

"I'm planning to be, so Izzy, how're you feeling? It won't be long now."

"I know, right. I feel pretty good especially since the baby calmed down some."

"Did you bring your concerns to your doctor's attention yet?"

"I mentioned it and she did a sonogram, but nothing abnormal or irregular showed up, so maybe it's just something I'm eating or drinking that's not agreeing."

Faith looked at Naiyah with a curious expression. She hadn't seen her take a drink lately and hadn't seen any evidence of alcohol in the apartment, so she thought it best not to say what she was thinking.

Instead she hoped the baby was alright, but felt strongly that the fetus may have been affected by the heavy drinking Naiyah had done during her first trimester. Faith put down her book and the two chatted awhile about Mani's upcoming visit and the rapidly approaching delivery. Naiyah was expecting, when her family came for graduation, that her mother would stay over afterwards to wait for the baby, who was due to come the following week. "Honey, I'm so happy that things are working out between you and your mother, a girl always needs her Momma."

Naiyah sat opposite Faith with her legs folded. "It's a beautiful thing and truly a blessing. It's scary though, you know."

"What do you mean by scary?"

"I feel like I'm getting to know my mother for the first time actually. I want the kind of intimacy with her that I shared with my YaYa, but it feels awkward sometimes."

"That's a normal feeling, given the circumstances," Faith said reassuringly, "and the beauty of this is that you get to deepen your relationship with your mother while building something special with your own child."

"You're right and I'm really excited. I believe soon after graduation I'll get to finish my master's program and, the sweetest of all, I'll have a beautiful baby with a wonderful man who loves me, who knew?" Naiyah beamed reaching over, clasping Faith's hands knowingly. "I'm going in for a shower, love, then write a little in my journal and off to slumber land."

"Pleasant dreams," Faith said returning to the book she was reading.

❧

January 30, 2003—Thursday

My Beloved YaYa,

I'm holding on, it's not easy but I believe you're holding me in your heart and sitting at Jesus' feet asking him to be merciful to your foolish granddaughter. God-mommy Inez has been an amazing blessing. She gives me words of wisdom and a lot of love and encouragement. I'm thankful for that. But I'm worried; my baby seems very frantic at times. I don't want to say violent, but that's how it feels. After visiting with God-mommy, I've been trying very hard to surrender the drinking and the drugs. I'm not dulling my pain nearly as much, hardly at all. Things are going unbelievably well. Everything is great, Mum and I are getting it together, Nathan and I are too, and best of all, the man I love wants to marry me and make a family. I couldn't be happier. I'm praying again, YaYa. I don't know if God is hearing me, but I hope so. I'm praying for my unborn child, I want him or her to be happy and well. I love you with all I have and I pray someday I'll see you again.

Love, Izzy

Naiyah reached up for the light on the dresser to turn it off, but paused to gaze longingly at the picture of her YaYa, and she then dropped her swelling body heavily onto the bed, punching at the pillows for the right fluffiness, thankful for Faith's generosity in letting her have the top trundle now that she was growing in her pregnancy. She was confident her dreams would indeed be pleasant as she drifted off to sleep with Elijah and their baby on her mind. But her sleep soon turned fitful as she felt herself subconsciously wrestling against something heavily ominous.

🌱

Naiyah dressed the young toddler in a light jacket, looking every now and then out the window at the sparkling cloudless sky. "I can't wait to get out into the sunshine, sweetheart," she said to the fidgety baby, "and I can't wait to see Daddy either." They were on their way to Brooklyn by train to see Lijah, who was taking a break from law school to come visit with his mother, father, Naiyah and their baby. Naiyah was content with the way things were going, despite the fact she was still snorting a little cocaine from time to time. Elijah assured her they'd be married the following year, once he finished his degree and sat for the bar. Scribbling a note for her poppy, she and the baby headed out. At Jamaica station where they changed trains, Naiyah turned to a group of teen girls. "I've got to run to the bathroom, would you please keep an eye on my baby?" she asked. The girls nodded and Naiyah ran for the washroom to do a few snorts before the train came. Meanwhile, the young girls' train pulled up and they left the baby sitting alone in its stroller. In her sleep, Naiyah began to toss and turn. She heard an audible voice but couldn't discern where it came from—she listened again, this time closely and heard a voice say: "Surrender to me, just as a helpless baby would, and when you have surrendered, follow and never leave me."

While she tossed and turned, Naiyah must have screamed out, because Faith was now shaking her. "Honey, what's wrong, what's wrong, what are you shouting about?" Naiyah was trembling and sobbing. She grabbed Faith around the neck and held her tightly. "What's wrong?" Faith whispered gently in her ear.

Through her jagged sobs, Naiyah revealed, "I saw my baby alone on a train platform, I left the baby," she cried.

"Izzy, it was a dream, look honey, it's fine, everything's fine." Naiyah settled down a little but continued to hold onto Faith. She wanted to believe her roommate, yet wondered would God let this happen to her child. What if she did leave her baby unattended on a busy train station platform? Could she do such an irresponsible thing just to satisfy a drug craving?

XXXX

Ronnel is Inspired

Ronnel and Jade walked arm in arm down neon-lit Broadway, occasionally jostled by the throng of theater goers leaving the theaters just as they were. Yet they were in no hurry. They breathed the night air as they strolled towards the restaurant where they were to have dinner. "I enjoyed that," after a brief pause, "I really enjoyed that." Jade said. "The acting was superb. Charles Dutton was absolutely splendid as Levee."

"I thought so too," Ronnel replied, "I've seen several stage renditions of 'Ma Rainey's Black Bottom,' but this was the best yet."

"I agree, thanks again for asking me."

"Baby please, it was my pleasure. I love going to the theater, though not particularly by myself. It's nice having you to go with. I've chosen a special place for dinner, but it's a surprise," he said. Jade smiled and snuggled closer to him, feeling the warmth of his breath on her face.

"Oh," she said, once they'd been seated, "Chez Josephine's, I've heard so much about this place."

"But you haven't been here before," Ronnel interjected hopefully.

"That's right, I haven't, and I can't wait to see the menu."

Smiling to himself, Ronnel lowered his eyes. He was pleased, believing he scored both with the choice of stage play and dining experience. "Baby, have whatever you like, I want this to be a night to remember. "How about a cocktail?" he continued. Jade considered the offer but decided to pass; instead, she ordered Perrier with a twist of lime and didn't

213

react when Ronnel asked for a scotch on the rocks, but quickly teased, "That should warm you up."

"So why did you choose Chez Josephine's?" Jade inquired.

"You inspired me, of course."

"Oh," Jade said, "why is that?"

"Because you have the same scintillating sex appeal and sensuality the legendary Josephine Baker had, so I thought it befitting to bring you to the restaurant her sons own as their tribute to her." Jade looked squarely at Ronnel, unable to contain a heated blush from spreading over her face while at the same time offering a low purring growl in a near perfect Eartha Kitt voice "Well, thank you, darling." Blushing a bit himself, Ronnel smiled again as he perused the menu.

"The colors here are so rich and vibrant, almost electrifying" Jade said.

"Yes and so in keeping with the whole theatrical ambience of it's time, I love coming here," he said.

"I already adore it myself especially knowing that I inspire this much excitement and drama in you, and the piano player is absolutely delightful." Ronnel lifted Jade's hand to his lips and kissed it lightly, "Honey," he said, "you have always been exciting and alluring to me. I'm thrilled just being in your company again." Jade was about to speak when their waiter appeared for their dinner order. He turned to Jade on cue after Ronnel nodded in her direction, "What will Madam be having this evening?" Jade was tickled, "For starters I'll have the Maine Lobster Bisque soup, and for my entrée I'll have Lobster Cassoulet with shrimp."

"Man, that sounds good," Ronnel said to the waiter.

"Yes sir, it's one of our signature dishes and what can we entice you with this evening?"

"There are so many great choices of course, but I've decided on the Roasted Breast of Long Island Duck à l'Orange since I haven't tried it before."

"Anything to start with, sir" he asked poised to scribble it down.

"How about the crispy blue point oysters" he questioned rhetorically with eyebrows raised.

"Superb choice," the waiter said gathering up their menus, "I'll be right back with your appetizers." Jade amused herself looking around at the paintings on the wall, the interesting banana tree near the piano and what looked like Josephine's plumes sitting prominently on the bar. "There's quite a bit of provocative art work here," she said finally, "especially those nude paintings of Josephine."

"Yes, but you have to admit, the work is very artful and tastefully done." Before she could reply, Ronnel said, "Baby, I've been wondering how your schedule looks over the next few weeks and if you can take anytime off?" "Time, like what?" she inquired.

"Like a week or so."

"This sounds intriguing," she feigned, "what's up?"

"American Express is participating in a new information technology security symposium in San Diego and I've been asked to be a presenter."

"Wow, that sounds fascinating."

"Not really, I do this kind of thing all the time," he said as though it was really no big deal, "but what I'm asking, is if you can join me, I'd really love that."

"You want me to go with you for a week to San Diego, I don't know," she began.

"Hold on, baby, I'm not asking you for anything, all I want is to treat you to a relaxing, stress-free get away."

Jade's head screamed no, but her heart won and she excitedly said, "yes, yes, yes, I'd so love to go with you."

"That, my dear, makes me very happy," Ronnel said, "we have a lot of catching up to do." After a delightful dinner and good conversation, Ronnel drove Jade to the commuter rail station where she'd left her car. As they drove she found it much harder to resist his ardent advances, his charm was irresistible and he was most persuasive. When he rested his hand on her thigh, she felt powerful electricity and remembered the spark he ignited in her on Thanksgiving Day.

"Are you sure you don't want me to turn around and drive us back into the city to my condo, I could make it very much worth your while? Tomorrow's Saturday so we can stay in all day. I'll fix mimosas and serve you breakfast in bed," he said flicking his tongue rapidly through slightly parted lips. Jade had her hand on the door handle while at the same time being completely mesmerized both by what he was saying and doing. "Man puhleez," she nearly shouted, "What's wrong with you, tempting and teasing me unmercifully like this?"

He laughed, "You can't fault a man for trying," and believe me, I'm going to try. I'm too old for games, I know what I want and I'm not about to waste time by not going right for it."

"Maybe," she said, "but I need you to slow your roll, remember, I haven't dated anyone except my husband in almost twenty years, so at least let me regain an understanding of the playing field, Mr. Too

Old For Games." They both laughed as Ronnel reached over and held her in a loving embrace, even though the reference to her husband had struck a cautious chord in him. "Don't go yet," he said, moving Jade's hand away from the door handle "smoke a cigarette, talk to me some more, anything..."

"I guess you didn't notice but I'm trying to give up cigarettes and besides, I'm sure you don't allow smoking in this car. I'd love to stay awhile longer, but have you forgotten I still have a little bit of a drive ahead of me, so my dear, I need to be getting on the road and heading on home."

"Call me when you get there, let me know you got home safely." Jade opened the door and swung one leg out. Ronnel reached for her again, "I hope you get reacquainted with the playing field and the ground's level by the time we leave for California."

Jade looked back, "Me too," she said closing the door.

The next morning, Jade decided to go to the health club not caring whether she ran into Analise or not, but first she wanted to call Naiyah while she was on her mind. "Good morning, Ny, it's your Momma."

"Oh hey, Mummy, what's up, you do know it's only 8:00 here, right?" "Sweetheart, I'm sorry, I wasn't thinking, you were on my mind, I just wanted to check in with you, see how things are going."

"Besides the kicking and indigestion, things are going pretty well," she said. Naiyah wanted to tell her mother about the latest dream, but decided against it; instead she made small talk and asked Jade about her plans for the day. She started telling her about the time she's been spending with Ronnel and before she knew it, she was gushing like a schoolgirl.

Naiyah listened quietly feeling herself stiffen a little. "Mum, I'm happy for you, you deserve joy and happiness but my heart and hope is with my Poppy, you know that."

"Naiyah, I'm just dating for heaven's sake."

"I know and I respect that, but let me speak my mind too okay, so anyway," Naiyah continued conspiratorially, "do you get butterflies when he's around?"

"Yes, it's amazing; I didn't think I would ever feel this way again."

"I understand, I'm so there."

"What do you mean?" Jade asked her.

"I'm glad for the chance to share this with you, what I mean is, this thing with Elijah and being pregnant. I feel so different, Mum. I feel free to love him, to receive his love and to let the love flow. I understand when you say amazing, it really is," Naiyah gushed.

"Sweetheart, we're coming into our own, you and me," Jade said, "I believe great things are going to come out of our difficulties."

"I don't know why, but I feel it too, I'm very hopeful," Naiyah replied.

Jade put her arm over her shoulder and gave herself a squeeze shaking her head gently up and down. "Naiyah, baby, take care until we get there for graduation and keep in touch."

"Yes Mum, I will, be good to yourself," she added.

Jade smiled and hung up the phone, Naiyah laid back down, pulling the covers up, unable to keep herself from smiling, and she was really happy for her mother and hoped she would indeed find love again.

XXXXI

Preparing the McCoy's

"*Mother,*" Elijah said when she picked up.

"Hi baby, what's going on? We haven't heard from you in a while."

"It's been hectic," he said.

"Yeah, I imagine it has been. Is everything okay though?"

"I think the worst is over. D'yanna came to the office the other day and wreaked havoc all over the place but I think it's settled, I think she gets it, finally. Whether or not she can get over it completely and be happy for me," he continued, "remains to be seen."

"That's a tough pill to swallow, son," Esther said gently, "but it is what it is."

"You're right, but the reason I'm calling is to ask when we might be able to arrange a meeting between you, Dad and Naiyah and ask if you would go to California with me when the baby comes in a few months."

Esther's eyes lit up, the idea of her first grandchild hadn't registered with her yet, but by Elijah's simple question, it suddenly became real. "Well," she said finally, "I hadn't considered that before now. Let me talk to your father and see if we can work it out, it *would* be nice to meet this Naiyah before she gives birth."

"I agree," he said, "but I'm not really sure how it can be arranged. Her girlfriend's going out to visit her for spring break, so she's not coming home.

I don't know when else she can get back to the east coast before graduation and the delivery. Maybe in the meantime you and Dad can meet her parents, Jade and Lucky."

"Lucky," snapped Esther, "what kind of name is that for a grown man?" Elijah laughed, "I don't know, I think he's always been called that, but if it makes you feel any better, his real name is Lemuel and he's quite a successful business-man."

"What kind of business?"

"He's a financial investments executive."

"That sounds mighty impressive and it also sounds like this Naiyah and her family are hoity-toity, high maintenance folks."

"They're not good ol' ghetto by any means, they're regular, but believe me when I tell you, they have ghetto passes just like the rest of us," he laughed, but his humor was lost on Esther.

"Maybe we can get a ticket and fly her out just for the weekend," Esther thought out loud.

"That's a good idea, although I'm not sure she should be flying so close to her due date."

"Eli, honey, she's not due for another three months, she should be able to mange a five-hour flight, I know women who worked labor intensive jobs right up to their due dates, so an easy flight shouldn't hurt her."

"Alright," he said, "you should know."

"Son," she said, "your father and I support your decision and we're behind you one hundred percent. We think you're doing the right thing, even though our hearts go out to D'yanna. When the time is right, I'm going to reach out to her, so she knows, regardless of how things turned out, we still love her."

"Thank you, Mother," he said, "I appreciate that and I'm sure she will too."

"Okay baby, keep us posted and let us know when we get to meet the in-laws," she laughed.

"Will do, tell Dad I love him."

"What about me?"

He puckered up his lips and made a loud smooching sound into the receiver. "It goes without saying, but I'm giving you my kisses anyway to be sure. I love you, Mother, see ya soon—bye."

"Bye baby," Esther replied placing the phone back in its cradle. She sat back and continued listening to Shinji Ishihara's arrangement and felt herself immersed in "Aqua Blue." I really love this, Lord, the music soothes my soul and keeps me in the center where I belong. Thank you, she breathed.

XXXXII

Leaving on a Jet Plane

"*I thought* this day would never come," Jade said turning to Ronnel as they walked down the jet way to their waiting plane. "Me neither," he said smiling back at her.

"I'm looking forward to an enjoyable time," she continued. After picking up the rental car and arriving at the resort, Jade was nearly breathless, taking in all the beauty surrounding them. This is fabulous, it's everything I expected." Ronnel handed the keys to the valet as the bellman began loading their bags onto the luggage cart. Once they reached their suite, Jade was somewhat surprised to see they had connecting yet separate rooms. Ronnel smiled, noticing the puzzled look on her face. "Don't be alarmed, baby," he said, "I told you I wasn't here to take anything from you; my only desire is to give you whatever you need from me." It had been such a long time since a man had given her anything but hell, that Jade was having difficulty settling into the comfort of this space. "Relax baby, and just receive it." Ronnel embraced Jade in a tender hug and she melted into him allowing herself, for the moment, to feel safely cared for. With her head buried into the strength of his chest, she whispered, "Thank you."

He kissed the top of her head, "I'm meeting up with some of the VP's later for a round or two of golf, how about we unpack and get settled? While I'm gone, why don't you spend the afternoon at the spa and later we'll get together for a great dinner."

"Excellent idea," she said. While Jade explored the resort, Ronnel played golf and prepared for his presentation the next day. The vista was amazing; Jade was taken in by the lush grounds and the calming waters. She couldn't wait to experience the spa, after all that was the reason people really came here. While she waited in the common area to be called for her treatments, she reached into her bag for her cell phone and called Turquoise. "Qua, this place is absolutely magnificent, you and Jon have to come here sometime."

"Oh good, you arrived safely. How long are you lovebirds planning to stay?"

"We're here until Saturday, I can't believe how really spectacular it all is."

"So you're feeling comfortable, no reservations?"

"I am," Jade said, noticing a therapist coming into the room, "I think I'm about to be called for my body wrap, sweetheart, talk to you later."

"Have fun," Qua said, hanging up. She looked at Jade's smiling face in the picture on her desk and said, "Please, Lord, let her find joy and happiness again."

Jade tipped her girl well, saying, "I'll be back tomorrow for a full body massage, I'll ask for you." Once back at their suite, Jade saw that Ronnel hadn't returned, so she drew herself a scrumptious bubble bath and took a relaxing soak. After a day of pampering and the long flight, she took off the luxurious bathrobe provided by the resort and laid down on the queen bed for a quick cat nap.

Hours later, Ronnel came in startled by the darkness. "Where is Jade," he wondered. He turned on a soft light and started calling out for her. He tried the door to her room, and when he found it unlocked, he peeked in. "Jade," he whispered. When he went over to her, she still didn't stir. He was moved by the dainty sounds escaping her lips, noting that even her snores were delicate and ladylike. He wanted to resist this tempting sight, but as hard as he tried he couldn't, he moved closer. "Jade," he whispered again. He sat on the bed near her, leaning over, he moved her hair to the side and kissed the nape of her neck. She stirred slightly. He blew on her ears lightly and then began to nibble them ever so gently.

"Umm," she said softly, and then said nothing more. He kissed her more deliberately, grateful that he had showered before leaving the club house. He was surprised when she turned over and her perky, yet full breasts stood yearning towards him. Trying to position himself so as not to put his full weight on her, he began kissing her slowly.

Jade desired his affection and kissed him in return. She remembered briefly the kiss she recently shared with Lucky and knew this was not that kind of kiss. This was a kiss of true sexual desire, yet intimate wanting. She didn't want to rush, nor did she want him to rush. "Ronnie," she said breathlessly, "I'm feeling the electrifying heat between us but I don't think I'm ready."

"Sssh, we don't have to; let's just experience the closeness." Though she didn't stop kissing him, she began to feel conflicted. She knew on so many levels how wrong it would be, to enter into communion with him in this way. *For God's sake, he's not my husband,* she silently screamed, *but if it's my husband I'm waiting for, I may be waiting forever,* she silently moaned.

"Jade, where are you?" Ronnel asked, interrupting her inner reverie and conflict.

"I'm here sweetheart," she said, "waiting for you, at this moment, wanting you more than anything, but I'm not ready."

"I know, baby," he offered generously, "I'm not either," he said finally, "when we do, it's got to be on a greater plane than just the physical." He kissed the top of her delicate pointy nose, "Come on baby girl, get your lazy bones up and let's go get dinner."

Over the next couple of days, Jade lounged poolside and took long walks to the ocean below while Ronnel worked. She was happy that they spent their days doing their own thing; it gave them something to talk about when they got together in the evenings. Jade was enjoying the afterglow of another full body massage; she was completely limp and relaxed as she browsed through the latest issue of 'O Magazine.' She liked the Aha moments and celebrity interviews best. She looked down at her vibrating cell phone. *Naiyah,* she thought, *I hope nothing's wrong.* "Hey sweetheart, what's up?"

"I'm just calling to see how your trip's going."

"Oh, Izzy, everything is magnificent. I'm relaxing and the spa treatments are just what the doctor ordered."

"Oh good, is Mr. Alexander having a good time too?"

"He's working mostly, but he's gotten to play several rounds of golf since we arrived. He likes that a lot. How are you?" Jade asked. "Is the baby getting ready for his or her introduction to the world?"

"Yes Mum, things are well, you know Mani's coming in a few weeks for spring break."

"That'll be good for you," Jade said.

"Yes, and then I'll be flying to New York to meet Lijah's parents; I'm hoping you'll go with me."

"Of course I will sweetheart, you know that."

"Mum, on the serious tip, are you and Mr. Alexander knockin' boots?"

"Izzy, I'm ashamed of you," Jade laughed.

"I'm serious."

"Why are you trying to get all up in my business, Miss?"

"Because, you don't know how things go down anymore, Miss," she said teasingly, "take it from someone about to have a baby before getting a husband."

"Izzy, are you suggesting I'd be foolish enough to give my stuff away without protecting myself?"

"Would you, are you protected?"

"Well, no I'm not, if you must know. Your Poppy's been gone for several years, what do I need protection for?"

"Mum," Naiyah shouted incredulously, "are you at a romantic resort with a fine ass man, you once had feelings for? And in case you haven't heard STD's are on the rise, especially HIV for African American women your age and older. Does he have protection?" Naiyah pressed.

"You know this conversation should be going a little differently."

"I know," Naiyah laughed, "just be careful Mummy, you don't want to be caught up like me at your age and remember, a woman with her own condoms, is grown, sexy and cool."

"That's beside the point; I could have gotten busy with this man, without thinking and been totally unprotected, good looking out, daughter."

They both laughed, Jade's was more a shudder.

"One more thing, Mum, if you have a moment of weakness and I'll bet you will before you get on that plane to go home, call Mrs. Davis, she can pray you through."

"Pray me through?" Jade asked rolling her eyes up towards the bright sky, "what are talking about?"

"In case you still don't get it, prayer really does change things."

"I get it, Izzy, I know. I'm glad you called, sweetheart, I'll talk to you when I get home."

"Mum," Naiyah said, "I love you, have fun, but be careful, okay."

Jade slid her phone shut, grabbed her sun hat, bag and towel and dashed up to the suite. She threw on a halter sun dress over her bathing suit, her golden tanned skin radiating. Before going back downstairs she called to have the car brought around. "Yes, directly," said a pleasant voice on the other end *'mmmmm he sounds delicious'* she thought. "Good afternoon, Mrs. Alexander," the young piece of eye candy said, greeting Jade with the rental car keys in hand. She was preoccupied trying to stop herself from drooling at the tender young thing, speaking to her, that she didn't even bother to correct him. "Thank you, doll," she said to the young man. He watched as she swung her long legs into the car, and looked back at him and he quickly turned away not wanting her to see his rising attraction. Jade smiled to herself, "Do I still got it going on or what?" *Humpf,* she thought soberly, *don't forget what Naiyah said or you'll have it going on alright.* Jade found the drugstore with no problem; the concierge had given perfect directions. She walked up and down the aisles until she reached the one with lubrication and condoms. "Oh my gosh, look at all this—ribbed, night glow, vibrating, how does anyone know what to choose?" Jade spotted a young couple moving down the aisle towards her, nervously and embarrassed she quickly left. She walked out of the store hurriedly, but turned and went back inside, realizing that, just maybe she *would* allow Ronnel to have her and if so, as her daughter so wisely pointed out, she would need to be ready. "Excuse me," she said to a nearby stock clerk, still a bit embarrassed. "Would you mind assisting me?"

"Not at all ma'am, how can I help you?" the young woman asked.

"I need to purchase prophylactics." Jade said stiffly. "But there are so many to choose from. Can you recommend something that isn't too intrusive, you know," she said demurely, something with the feel of natural skin, but effective?"

"Sure," she said turning towards the shelves, attempting to hide the embarrassing grin, now spread across her face. "Let me show you these over here, they're called thintensity and are very popular for their natural feel." Scrunching up her nose, Jade thanked the young lady and walked proudly, but discreetly to the check out counter, with her twelve pack of thintensities hugged closely to her chest. She left the store, feeling both satisfied and quite responsible.

"Hi, it's Jade," she said answering her cell.

"Sweetheart! Baby where are you?" Ronnel asked. "I got back early and immediately started to worry when I couldn't find you anywhere."

"Oh honey, not to worry," she replied feeling herself melt from the warmth and gentle concern she heard in his voice. "I'm fine, I just decided to take a drive in town to check things out."

"Fine, baby, just leave a note next time, don't scare me like that, here I was thinking you were somewhere on the premises. I looked everywhere for you."

"I'm sorry, Nelly," she said playfully. "I'm on my way back; I'll see you in a few."

"Good, I've already made arrangements for dinner."

"Wonderful, should I dress up?"

"It's up to you, you can dress up or down, it's an intimate affair actually, just you and me baby."

"Oh, so it is special, I can't wait," she said, patting the nondescript brown package on the seat next to her. Jade began to feel tingly all over, not knowing what the rest of their time together in San Diego would bring and especially what tonight might hold. She thought back again to her first time with Ronnel, how inexperienced and nervous they both were, yet how sweet the kisses. Their passion was explosive, she remembered, yet they burned together like quiet fire. "I'm ready," Jade thought aloud, as she rushed back to the Grand Del Mar. By the time Jade returned, Ronnel had already taken a very long hot shower and was relaxing on the sofa with a Hennessey and coke. "Baby, relax and take your time. I ordered a meal fit for a king and queen to be enjoyed right here in the privacy of this magnificent suite."

Blowing him a kiss, she said, "Let me put my things away and I'll be right back to join you." When she left the room, he got up and tuned into a mellow jazz station on the radio. His arms were outstretched when she returned and she couldn't help but glide right into them. "I never thought I'd find you in my arms again," he whispered. "I hope this never ends." She looked up at him, something in his voice sounded puzzling, but she shook it off and kept moving with him to the music. "I wanted you all to myself," he continued, "so I thought we'd have dinner alone and if you want, later we can join some of my colleagues for cocktails and conversation in the lounge."

"Sounds good, let me go get ready," she said standing slightly on tiptoe to kiss him on the lips. Ronnel hummed, enjoying the music and the inhibition lowering drink, while Jade luxuriated in the bath. By the time she returned, he was dressed in a lightweight pair of linen slacks and matching short-sleeved, buttoned-down shirt. Jade was wearing a long, flowing back-baring halter dress with high-heeled sandals. The sun was just beginning to disappear behind the horizon and candlelight twinkled everywhere. She looked for Ronnel and found him on the balcony with a waiter ready to serve their dinner. "Well, good evening," she said to the server who politely bowed his head in response. Ronnel took her hand and kissed it lightly. He then pulled out her chair so she could sit.

The evening was everything Ronnel said it would be. They laughed and talked and drank in the very essence of one another. After dinner and dessert, their waiter served them after dinner cordials, cleared the table and left them to themselves. "Come, sit with me over here," Ronnel said to Jade. They moved to the other side of the balcony where the water crashing lightly against the rocks below could be heard. "So what's next?" he asked.

"What do you mean?"

"I don't know, you've been a wife, a mother, I was just wondering what's next for you on this life's journey?"

"I don't know really, what about you?"

"I don't know either, what I do know though, is that I'm getting older and I want to make a real difference in someone's life. That usually means in the life of a child, but I'm too old to have any of my own."

"Oh, you are not," she said.

"You don't think so?"

"Of course not, your heart is so full of love, you'd be a terrific father."

"I thought so too once, but it didn't happen for me and my wife when we were married. How does being mother to Naiyah and Nathan feel?" he asked. "They're both really special people, I love being their mom."

"Yeah, they're really quite lucky to have you," he continued, "how do you think you'd feel being mother to our child, had you kept it, instead of giving it away," he asked staring directly into her eyes.

Jade's eyes grew wide. She couldn't blink—she felt trapped, betrayed, somehow, but she didn't know why. Finally she said, "What are you asking me, Ronnel?"

I guess what I'm asking is, why did you give my child away without talking to me about it. Jade, what gave you the right to play God and make that decision for me? You have no idea the anguish I've suffered because of this." Jade could no longer look at Ronnel. There truly was pain etched onto his face like daggers. She didn't know what to think or how to feel. She wondered how long he'd known and why Wilhelmina hadn't revealed that she told him, and she didn't understand either, why she thought she wouldn't have, after all, Ronnel's her brother and isn't blood supposed to be thicker than water? "Was this a set-up" she asked, "did you know all this time, that you planned to ambush me with this barrage of questions? Why are you trying to hurt me?" she cried.

He grabbed her to him forcefully, "Are you so full of pride that you really think it's all about you? Did you hear what I said? I've been hurt to my core over this, Jade. Doesn't that mean anything to you? You think I want to hurt you, that's the last thing I want to do. I love you, Jade, from the bottom of my heart, but I can't deny that I've been hurt deeply by the fact I have a child that I can't be a father to. Do you have any idea how that makes me feel, do you understand that I've been tormented by this ever since I found out? Evidently not," he said raising his voice, with veins popping out from his temples "you make me think you don't care about how this has hurt me."

Jade was stunned. She couldn't have seen this coming nor did she know what to say to him. It was wrong of her to exclude him, but she couldn't have known that it mattered to him.

Ronnel wanted to grab Jade by the arms and really shake her, but he remained in control. "Do you understand what you've done? You've taken away a precious part of my life; you created a massive hole that I can never fill. I can forgive you almost anything, baby, but this thing right here, I don't know." By now they had moved into the living area of the suite and, without warning, Ronnel broke down and began crying like a baby. Sitting on the sofa, he hung his head between his legs. "Somewhere in this great big world is a young man or woman who looks like me and carries my DNA, but I will never know them—they will never know me," he cried. Jade was getting frantic. She didn't know what to say or do. Nothing could possibly make this better, so she grabbed her purse and quietly walked out.

Once outside in the hallway, she fell against the wall from the staggering blow of what her action had done to him. It made her feel ashamed—like a murderer. His hope of having a son or daughter was murdered by the choice she made. She couldn't even console him with the knowledge of whether it was a boy or girl. She didn't want to know herself, so she insisted that she not be told, nor that the baby be brought to her after delivery. Instead, she wanted a completely clean break and anonymous adoption. She wept heavily as she let her own grief consume her. After a while, Jade ducked into the ladies room next to the lounge to compose herself and freshen up before going in for a drink and to commiserate with anyone willing to listen to her tale of woe. She sat at the bar for a good while drinking gin and tonics when a woman came over. "Honey, you look like you've lost your best friend," she said touching Jade gently on the arm, hoping to convey concern.

"I feel like I have," she said without looking up. The woman continued, "Acknowledge your part," she said, "and honor the truth of your role in it and *your* need from it."

Jade looked up to say thanks, but the woman had already turned and was walking away.

Jade settled her bill and went out to sit by the pool "my role, my need" she whispered turning those words over and over in her head. "Self-preservation, pure and simple, but need, I need to go another way, I need to ask the question—what *are* Jade's terms, Jade's truth and can she stand up for them?" When she returned to the suite she found the lights out and the door to Ronnel's room closed. She removed her clothes and went in for a shower. Afterwards, she put on a silky robe and placed one of the small round packets in her pocket. *"Right now, Jade needs some healing,"* she sighed. She knocked lightly on the door, and when he didn't answer, she walked in and, dropping her robe to the floor, slid in under the covers with him. His breathing was steady and his heart beating softly, as she moved closer, she knew he needed healing too.

XXXXIII

Leaving on a Jet Plane—II

The east coast was experiencing spring thaw and in northern California, they were experiencing the same. Weather stations in California were watching for signs of severe flooding, which they also experienced last year. But the weather was the furthest thing from Naiyah's mind, as she finished packing for her trip to New York to meet Mr. and Mrs. McCoy. She found herself pacing from time to time, absent-mindedly strumming her fingers on the dresser top. Her recent, wonderful and inspiring visit with Mani seemed a distant memory. "I really don't want to do this," she said to Faith as she came into the room.

"Don't be silly, Izzy, you have to."

"I know, but I'm nervous about it."

"Relax, they're going to love you."

"I wouldn't go so far as to say that, especially where Mrs. McCoy is concerned; she loved D'yanna and, like I told Lijah, I doubt that she holds me in high regard."

"Relax," Faith said again, "your mom will be there with you and hasn't Elijah made it quite clear that he chose you, so really, what his mother thinks doesn't much matter. Besides, didn't he tell you that his mother wants what he wants?"

Naiyah nodded, placed the last item into her travel bag, and zipped it closed. Hoisting herself up on the bed she said to Faith, "Life's amazing, isn't it? Funny how we find things we're not even looking for," she

229

continued, referring to this new and precarious relationship with both Elijah and his parents.

"Yeah, but turn that around for a minute," Faith said philosophically. "How often is it that what we find is almost always not what we want, but just as sure as day follows night, is definitely what we need? Look at your situation for instance, most definitely, you wouldn't have chosen this time to become a mother, but it seems precisely what was needed to create a deepening relationship between you and your own mom. It brought Mani back into your life and, what an added bonus, you have the support of a man who loves you. That's pretty good, wouldn't you say?"

Naiyah smiled at Faith and shook her head. "I'm glad you got to meet Mani," she said.

"Me too, it was really nice, cool even. I like her a lot, she reminds me of myself a little."

"*Really,* in what way?" Naiyah asked, anxious to hear how Faith thought she was like Mani.

"She parts like a river around a rock," Faith said without expression.

"What in the heck does that mean?"

Faith laughed, "It simply means she flows—like water, she just keeps moving."

Naiyah thought for a second. "Yeah, now that you mention it, I can see that, although I doubt she was partin' like a river back when she was mad at me all those years."

"Oh, yeah she was; I think she just reached a waterfall and redirected for a minute, that's all."

"Hummm," Naiyah said.

"Another cool thing about Mani," Faith said, "is that she's nothing like these immature chicks around here who think their friends can only be friends with them."

"Yeah, you dug that?"

"That is cool," Faith continued. "She's not threatened, she knows where she fits and she's comfortable with it."

"Well," Naiyah said, "I'm flying out early in the morning, and thanks again for offering to drive me to the airport. I'll call you over the weekend, once I confirm my return."

"That's cool," Faith replied, "try to get some rest, I'll see you in the morning. I'm going to hang out with friends down at the poetry salon."

XXXXIV

Relaxing at Elijah's

Naiyah sat watching people rush by while waiting for Elijah at JFK International, and then her phone rang. "Hi, it's Naiyah," she said, taking a break from the amusements.

"Hi, Izzy, it's Mani, where are you?"

"Hey Mon, I'm at the airport waiting on Elijah, what's up?"

"I'm calling to tell you I'll see you later. I spoke with Ms. Jade this morning and I'm coming with her to the McCoys' this evening."

"Oh, good; I need all the support I can get," she said, waving at Lijah when she saw him approaching. "See you soon—love ya, Mani, bye!"

"Hey love," Naiyah said, easing comfortably into Elijah despite the extra cargo she was carrying. "It's time to make it or break it; there's no looking back now," she whispered. Elijah didn't respond, instead he cocooned her in his protective embrace. They stood enmeshed for several minutes, while Elijah tried to pour himself into her and the child she was carrying, imagining them fusing together as one. After a while, with outstretched arms, he looked at Naiyah, taking in all the beauty and possibility standing before him.

"That's right, sweetheart—make it or break it, but my money's on making it. I have faith in the moment; I believe it's our time." He kissed her on the forehead. "Let's go for a chai latte," he said, "then we can get your bags and head into Brooklyn."

"Sounds great," she said locking arms and step with him. Elijah hoped she would find his place okay, and that no lingering traces of

Dee remained, that might upset her. He'd begun clearing the place of D'yanna's scent and presence right after their blow-up at Junior's. He was quite satisfied and hoped Naiyah would be too, even though she had no idea to what extent D'yanna had shared that space. "This is amazing," he said, "here we are getting ready to be about what I wanted us to be for so long, and getting to do it as grown-ups, ha" he chuckled, seeming to grasp for the first time how truly amazing it was.

Naiyah nodded, "Humm, yes—it's good, isn't it?" She played with the end of the intricate French braid running down her back for a moment, inhaling and exhaling deeply but steadily, taking it all in.

Elijah reached into his coat pockets and pulled out a box from each. He quietly placed the boxes in front of Naiyah. "What have we here?" she asked, eyeing them with interest.

"Go ahead, open them."

She gasped when she saw the simple but exquisite gold, diamond and pearl ring. Her eyes began to fill with tears, "Oh Lijah—Lijah, it's beautiful... I wasn't expecting anything, especially not a ring this beautiful."

"I intend it as a symbol of my love, and promise, when the time comes that we're officially engaged, then you're really going to cry; now go ahead," he directed making a gesture towards the other box sitting in the middle of the table between them. He looked at her with eyes full of love and appreciation.

"Oh Li," she breathed, "I really don't know what to say."

"Don't say anything, just open it."

She removed the ribbon slowly and lifted the lid. She gasped again as she admired the 14k white gold and diamond Tennis Bracelet alongside the beautiful 14k gold, cultured pearl and diamond ring, which when paired together, looked like a matching set.

"Oh my God! Oh my God!" was all she could say as she sat stunned, looking at the beautiful displays of affection Elijah had just lavished on her. This was the first really expensive gift she'd ever received from a man and, without a frame of reference, really didn't know what to say. It was beyond her to feign speechlessness or absolute shock and surprise. This was no joke; she was indeed speechless, shocked and surprised.

"Close your mouth," Elijah kidded, "and get used to it, you're my Nubian Queen and I'm always going to treat you this way; you're my heart, Ny, you just don't know," he said looking at her with obvious desire.

Naiyah sat and couldn't move. She closed her eyes and prayed silently, *Lord, please bless me to be worthy of this man's good love and demonstrated faith in me.*

When they reached his apartment, Elijah led the way inside. "It's nice," Naiyah said, "the chocolate leather makes a masculine but soft statement."

"Isn't that an oxymoron," he joked.

"Is it?" she teased back. Elijah grabbed her bags and took them to the back. When he returned, he took her in his arms again and this time he kissed her deeply. "Oh girl," he said, "it is *so* good to see you. It's been really hard knowing how close yet so far we are to being together as a family—with a little one no doubt, yeah yeah," he sang. "Wasn't it Dinah Washington who did *What A Difference A Day Makes?* I know that's right," he said letting go of her to place a CD in the changer. "Is there anything in particular you want to hear?" he asked.

"Oh no, whatever you choose will be fine," she said, looking around. "I like how you decorated the apartment, love, there's a nice balance between the masculine and feminine." Though she was curious about the decorator, she was wise enough to leave it at that. She thought better of pursuing the question because she knew she might not be able to handle the truth. "Thanks sweetheart, I do have a bit of a feminine side," he lied. Changing the subject, Naiyah placed her arms around Elijah's neck. "I noticed, love, you took my bags to the back; you're not planning on my staying here with you, are you?"

"Ww-what?" he stammered.

"You heard me," she said smiling, "you know I'm not staying here alone with you in this apartment. What would our parents think? Never mind," she continued, "it doesn't matter; you know I'm not that kind of girl."

Elijah looked at her curiously. "Aren't you carrying my baby, oh, I thought so," he teased.

"Shush your mouth," she said playfully pushing him, "and here I was thinking you made proper sleeping arrangements for me. By the way, my Mum wants to have lunch with me tomorrow while I'm in town. I can go home with her this evening and come back over tomorrow; will that interfere with anything you have planned?"

"Not exactly, but I was hoping we'd have some time to spend with *my* parents, just you and me, and I certainly want some time with you to myself," he said pitifully.

"Oh honey love, of course, of course we'll have time together, and yes, I agree we should visit your parents without my support group's influence," she laughed.

Elijah was relieved that she was in agreement and he laughed too. "Come over here," he said, reaching for her hand, "sit down with me a minute."

"Can I have a glass of water first?" she asked following him to the sofa. He dropped her hand and went to retrieve a bottle from the fridge. When he returned she sipped a little, then burrowed herself under the arm he'd casually draped over the back of the sofa.

"Well, you know, Ny," he said "I've noticed a change in you, a nice one if I must say so myself. You're more settled, relaxed even."

Naiyah, looking straight ahead, immersed in the soft music, simply replied "Yes."

"What's up with that," he continued, lightly stroking the top of her head, "I'd like to think I had a role in it somehow."

"Yes and no," she said. "With maturity comes a degree of acceptance, and I'm learning to accept some things about myself and my life. And you, Lijah, in this short period of time have given me a place, where I can be vulnerable, a place I never knew I could inhabit, even though I wanted too so badly, but more importantly I'm learning to rely on the God my YaYa tried so hard to introduce me to. What you notice is my emerging liberation," she said nodding her head as if it were an epiphany.

"Go on, girl with all that deep ethereal stuff," he joked. Elijah drew his arm around to cup Naiyah's nose with his index and third fingers and began stroking it. "You have the cutest little nose," he said, "you're beautiful. Whenever I see you, I almost can't take my eyes off of you. I know our baby will be beautiful too, I can't wait," he said.

"Me neither," she replied pulling away from the grasp he had on her nose, "but probably for different reasons than you," she laughed.

He placed his hand on her belly, "Yeah, I know."

"Lijah, tell me," she said, "what if I didn't make that fateful phone call to you last fall, what do you think would be happening now?"

Elijah hung his head. "I probably would be picking out my tuxedo and making wedding plans with D'yanna," he said shamefully.

"What's that strange look on your face all about?"

"I don't know, I guess I still can't believe I was going to marry her *and* for all the wrong reasons, but worse, that I wasn't on the up-and-up with you, so I feel ashamed," he sighed.

Naiyah took his hand in hers and held it. "If it helps any, remember I wasn't on the for real tip with you either." They sat in silence, except for the soft music playing in the background.

Finally Elijah said, "We need to get ready to go over for dinner with my folks and, for the record, Ms. Izzy Harland, I'm not happy about your decision to go out to Long Island tonight."

"Izzy Harland, you never call me that, that must mean you *really* aren't happy."

"Look at this face," he said with lips turned down, "but really though, the more I see of you, the more I know about you and I'm seeing the Izzy side more and more—the playful side," he said.

"We've said it all along," she replied, "it won't be easy, but I promise you, you'll see, it'll be worth it. Every breath I take will be to make you and our child happy."

XXXXV

Meeting His Parents

"*Mother,* this is Naiyah Harland," Elijah said upon entering his mother's kitchen, "where's Dad?"

"Down on the avenue, he'll be back in a few. Hi honey, come on in," she said warmly. "Did your mother come with you?"

"No Ma'am, but she should be here any minute."

"Aren't you a beauty," Esther remarked, reaching out to give Naiyah a hug. "Thank you," Naiyah said shyly.

"Go hang up her coat, Eli," Esther continued, pulling a chair out for Naiyah. "Come baby and have a seat, keep me company until my husband and your mother get here. It's nice to finally meet you."

Until Elijah joined them, there were a lot of awkward and empty spaces in the conversation. "Uhmmm, the food smells some kind-a good," he said looking over his mother's shoulder hoping to lighten things up.

"So Naiyah what was it like growing up on the Island with all that space and clean air?"

"Actually quite nice, I love Long Island," she said. "I guess you can say I'm a beach bum," she laughed, "that's how I spend my summers."

"And your falls," Elijah interjected, turning to his mother. "She had me out walking on the beach when she was home for Thanksgiving, as cold as it was." Just then the doorbell rang and Elijah went to greet Jade and Mani. "It's good seeing you again," Jade said, lightly kissing him on the cheek. "Thank you, Ms. Jade, so nice to see you too, hi, Mani," he said, offering her a hug, "let me take your coats." He showed them into the living room. "Be right back; Naiyah and my mother are in the kitchen, I'll get them."

The conversation between Jade and Esther was effortless and smooth. Though each was an advocate of their own child, it was obvious they had a mutual like and respect for one another. However, at the end of the day, it was the unborn child that garnered all the defense and attention. Mr. McCoy came in shortly after with a beautiful bouquet of flowers for his wife and a box of Godiva chocolates for Jade. Seeing the fully round Naiyah he said jokingly, "And you, my dear, get to have my son." His comment brought hearty laughter to everyone and reminded Naiyah that she had brought monogrammed guest towels as a hostess gift. "I almost forgot, Ms. Esther, I have something for you also."

After opening the gift bag handed to her, Esther fawned over the lovely towels with the gold lettering and knew exactly where she'd put them. "Thank you so much, baby," she said.

Jade winked proudly. "Well, that's not all, I have a small token as well." She reached into the oversized bag at her feet, retrieved a wrapped package and placed it in Esther's hand. It contained elegant stationery with matching return address labels with the McCoys' names on them.

"Oh my," she said, displaying signs of embarrassment from all the attention, "how very nice, you really didn't have to. Come," she said, wringing her hands and turning one way then the other, "dinner's ready to be served. Let's all go to the table."

Throughout the evening, pleasantries were exchanged and the night turned out to be an enormous success. Now knowing Naiyah's position on staying over at his apartment, Elijah confirmed that she'd be staying the next night with his parents. Jade was relieved to hear this.

On the drive home, Jade, Naiyah and Imani, recapped the evening, and all agreed it went very well. "You're not going to have any problem out of Esther McCoy," Jade said turning to Naiyah, "she likes you; you can tell."

"Keep your eyes on the road, Mum."

"Yeah," Mani chimed in, "she does, Izzy, and Mr. McCoy's pretty cool too, he's got a sense of humor, I like that." Naiyah smiled feeling like a flower in full bloom. "Mum," she said, "Let's call Nathan before going to lunch tomorrow. If I could, I'd also like to see Poppy. Want to join us, Mon?" she asked looking back at her friend.

"No thanks, you two go and have fun; I'm going on campus to get some lab work done," she said.

"Sweetheart, what about after lunch, what's the plan for getting you back to Brooklyn?" Jade wanted to know.

"I thought you'd take me to the commuter rail station near the airport, if you didn't mind."

"Sure, that'll work," Jade said.

"Izzy, if I don't see you, have a safe flight back," Mani said getting out of the station wagon and turning back to hug Naiyah once she opened the door. "Thanks for a nice time, Ms. Jade, good night. Love ya, Izzy—be well."

"Smooches," Naiyah said, blowing her a kiss.

XXXXVI

The Baby Came

"**Sweetheart,** how about joining me for a nice cup of chamomile tea before we turn in," Jade offered once she and Naiyah were in their nightclothes.

"I don't think so, Mum, but you go ahead."

"Okay," she said looking at Naiyah, "join me in the nook, let's chat a minute. Are you alright?" she asked, noticing an uncharacteristic reticence in her daughter.

"I'm okay, I just didn't get much rest today. I feel a little knotty in my belly and a bit fatigued, it must be from all the excitement. Don't worry; really, I'll be fine." Jade and Naiyah lingered a few minutes more before saying goodnight and going off to bed.

Later, in the darkest part of the night just before dawn, Jade heard a gut-wrenching scream "Ooowwwwl, oh Mum, Mummy, please!" yelled Naiyah from down the hall.

Frantic, Jade stumbled instinctively down to Naiyah's room, breathing laboriously. "Naiyah, honey!" she shouted. "What's the matter, what's wrong?"

"Please," she screamed, now in a cold sweat, "it feels like a sledge hammer is waging war in my belly. Oh God!" she shrieked.

"Okay baby, okay," Jade said, rushing to her side, not knowing what to do. She wiped Naiyah's forehead and began applying light pressure to her abdomen. When she did, she felt a hard thump against the palm of her hand. "Oh Lord Jesus," Jade wailed, "help us, please! Alright now," she continued, trying to gain her composure, "I'm calling an ambulance now; afterwards, I'll call your father."

On the way to the hospital, Naiyah moaned loudly in obvious discomfort. When Jade called him, Lucky didn't pick up the phone, so she left an explicit message that he should meet them at the hospital as soon as possible. She'd call Turquoise later when the hour on the west coast was more reasonable.

Jade waited while Naiyah was examined.

As the hours passed in what appeared to be slow motion, Jade grew more and more anxious. Finally, a doctor was standing before her. "Mrs. Harland, I'm sorry, we had to take the baby."

Jade shot straight up. "What does that mean? What are you trying to tell me?"

"Please, Ma'am, please calm down, your daughter's in great distress and so was the fetus. Fortunately, she was far enough along, allowing us to take the baby by cesarean."

"The baby?" she inquired weakly.

"It's hard to say, Mrs. Harland," the doctor said reassuringly, "it's going to be touch and go for a while, at least until we know what's causing her distress."

Jade began to sob. "Her," she said through her tears, "did Naiyah have a baby girl?" she asked.

"Yes Ma'am," the doctor said sensing that somehow this must be a silver lining. He added, "And we're going to do all we can to see that she thrives."

"Thank you," Jade cried, "thank you so much. I'll be right here waiting for any updates and, as soon as it's okay to see my daughter, please be sure to let me know."

"Of course," the doctor said in a gentle tone.

Jade tried to reach Lucky again but still no luck. Naiyah lay in the dimly-lit, sterile smelling hospital room on a litter, weeping her eyes out, afraid to go anywhere near the question *why*, realizing on an unconscious level that she knew the answer. She laid her hand on her chest trying desperately to calm her racing heart without success. When she gathered enough strength to stop weeping, her heart became steady, but then her thoughts galloped wildly out of control. She was utterly exhausted and thought she was hallucinating when she heard a whisper. She thought she heard someone say, *"Surrender; there will not be many more chances. My benevolent grace will not endure. Trust that I am with this child and so also, I will be with you."*

XXXXVII

The Weight of It

"**S**weetheart, Naiyah, baby, it's Mum," Jade whispered.

Naiyah lay facing the wall and didn't respond at first.

"Naiyah," Jade said again. "Oh baby," she said, rushing over when Naiyah turned to face her and she saw her eyes were almost swollen shut from crying. "It's going to be alright," she said as reassuringly as she could.

"I messed up," Naiyah wailed, thrusting her hands up to cover her face.

Jade reached over and gently took her hands down. "Calm down and think for a minute—if YaYa were here, what would she say?" Jade asked.

The question was enough for Naiyah to pause and focus. "She would say God does all things well. I think she'd also say, if He allowed it, I can bear it."

"Good," Jade said excitedly, "good; focus on that until we know more."

The doctor came into the room a short while later and the grave look on his face told them this wasn't good. Jade sat down as he approached Naiyah.

"We've made your little one as comfortable as possible, but we're dealing with two critical issues," he said. "Please don't be alarmed, we have to give you the worst-case scenario just so you know all you're dealing with."

"Please, doctor, just tell me what's wrong with my baby."

"Ms. Harland, your little girl is going through substance withdrawal, which is serious enough all by itself. She also has VSD, Ventricular Septum Disease."

"Oh no, please no," Naiyah gasped.

"Lord Jesus, Mary and Joseph," Jade said, standing to take Naiyah's hand. "Substance abuse?" she repeated, looking at Naiyah. "What kind of substance and what on earth is Ventricular Septum Disease?" she asked, about ready to hyperventilate.

The doctor looked from one to the other for a sign it was okay to continue. Naiyah nodded. "There's alcohol in her bloodstream and small traces of a narcotic which we suspect is cocaine."

Jade could not believe what she was hearing. "And this VSD, is it related to the alcohol and drugs?"

"It may be or it may be an independent abnormality, it's not conclusive at this point," he said, "Again, rest assured we will keep you apprised of all developments."

"But what is it?" she pressed.

"Pardon me, Ma'am," he began, with the somber expression returning, "VSD is a hole in the heart and its repair depends on the size, which we're still trying to determine."

Both Jade and Naiyah were speechless. After the doctor left, Jade thought a minute because she didn't want to say or do the wrong thing. Looking back, she knew she and Naiyah had traveled a long way in repairing their relationship and felt she shared some of the blame for her substance abuse. "Okay," she said finally, "I don't know why, but we've been dealt another hard one, but we'll get through it," she said, wiping the tears from her little girl's eyes. "Naiyah Isabella, when you were born, Mama Sadie said you were special, that you should be consecrated to God, so we let her name you Isabella. It may sound crazy, but I had faith in what she said—I still do, so don't worry, this will work out fine. We just have to believe, even though we can't see to the end of the matter," she said, giving Naiyah a bright smile and a hug.

"Yes Mum," Naiyah sniffled, "I believe."

"Alright then, get some rest, I'm going to step out and try to reach Auntie Aqua." Realizing they hadn't called Elijah, she asked, "Honey, do you want to call Elijah or do you want me to do it? Never mind, just put your mind at ease, I'll take care of it."

"Thanks, Mum," she squeaked. Because I can't, I'm nowhere near ready to deal with him.

"Rest," Jade said again, "I'll be back in a minute. I wonder what's keeping your father." Passing a nurses station, Jade noticed the time. *Good,* she thought, *the cafeteria's open, perhaps now I can get a cup of tea to calm these jangled nerves.* Feeling the vibration of her phone, she dug in her bag to retrieve it.

※

"Oh honey, I'm so sorry," came Wilhelmina's voice at the other end, "I had no idea Ronnel had all that bottled up inside of him——"

Before she could finish her sentence, Jade cut her off, "Willie, I don't have time for that right now, I'm dealing with a much bigger crisis at the moment, let me call you back okay?" she said abruptly snapping the phone closed.

"Qua, I know it's early, but I waited as long as I could."

"What happened, where are you?" she asked, feeling panic rising.

"I'm at the hospital with Naiyah; the baby came early this morning."

"What! Please say you're not serious; Izzy couldn't have been more than about thirty-two weeks or so, could she?"

"If that's close to eight months, I guess, but I'm sure you know better than me."

"So what happened?" Turquoise wanted to know.

"It all happened so fast. After dinner with Elijah's parents, she just started feeling poorly. The next thing I know she was in acute distress, screaming at the top of her lungs."

"Is the baby okay?"

Jade sat down, turning her back to the other cafeteria patrons, and whispered "No, she's bad off, really sick."

"Are the complications the same as is normal for most preemies?" Turquoise asked with concern.

Jade lowered her head. "Qua," she whispered loudly, "she's withdrawing from alcohol and drugs, plus she has something wrong with her heart, something called VSD."

Turquoise dropped the phone and screamed, forgetting totally that Johann was sleeping soundly right next to her. "Oh Sissy—Sissy, I'm so sorry. Oh Lord," she cried, "what's going to happen to the baby, is she going to live? Oh Lord, oh Lord," she said over and over. "How are you holding up, is Lucky there, what about Izzy?" She fired one question after another, her only defense from being completely consumed by the grief threatening to overtake her. "How is Elijah taking this?"

"He doesn't know yet. I have to call him next."

"Okay listen," she said more calmly, "just tell him the baby came early and don't give him all the details yet. Wait till he gets to the hospital. Under the circumstances, I doubt if Izzy will be able to return to school before the semester ends, so I'll see what I can do from here to get her assignments and arrange for her to finish up independently. I'll be in touch soon, but keep me posted if there are any new developments."

"Okay."

"Jade," Qua said, "I'm proud of you, you're doing fine, just stay strong."

"I will," she sighed, "I have to; because today I don't get to choose," she laughed.

"Oh wait," Turquoise yelled before Jade could hang up. "Did she name the baby yet?"

"I don't think so; she didn't say anything to me."

"Tell her to wait till I call back, I believe I have the most appropriate name for your granddaughter, that I hope you both and Elijah, of course, will consider."

Jade smiled and thought to herself, *Is she for real?*

XXXXVIII

It All has Meaning

Returning to the room, Jade noticed the litter was removed and Naiyah was now sitting up in a regular bed. "Sweetheart, I spoke to Elijah, he and his mother are on their way."

"Thanks. What about Auntie Aqua, you talked to her too, right?"

Jade nodded, "Naturally she's as upset as we are. She said something about having a name for the baby and was hoping you didn't already choose one."

Naiyah shifted to face her mother. "No, we don't have a name yet. I haven't even thought about it and Lijah probably doesn't care one way or the other."

"Would you consider giving her a name Auntie Aqua comes up with?" Jade asked.

"After what you told me about how my YaYa gave me the name Isabella, sure I'd consider it."

Jade smiled, happy that Naiyah was open, despite the difficult situation they faced.

"What did you say to Lijah?" Naiyah wanted to know.

"I took Qua's advice and just told him the baby came early."

"I guess I'll have to tell him the truth when he gets here," she said.

"No you don't."

"Why would you say that?" Naiyah asked, looking surprised.

"Sweetheart, I'm not an advocate for withholding the truth, but maybe you won't have to say anything to Elijah about the substance issues."

"Mum, how on earth do you think I can get away with that?"

"I don't know, Naiyah, I'm just saying. Premature births bring special circumstances all by themselves. Maybe, just maybe, the fact the baby is almost two months premature, maybe it's all he needs to know. But I know what——"

Naiyah stared at her mother not knowing what to expect, but knowing it would be an absolute miracle if she was to escape some hard word coming from her. "What?" she asked weakly.

Jade tempered her words, "What I know is, if you have a problem, be it big or small, you've got to get help now, right now. I understand, Naiyah, believe me I do; but it's not about you anymore, it's about your daughter who's in the nursery at this very moment fighting for her life."

"I don't think I have a problem, but I do admit to partying while I was pregnant, more than I should have."

Jade didn't respond. There was no need; the cat was out of the bag and Naiyah would have to deal with it.

"Mum, I promise you, I'm taking care of it. I know what I have to do."

"Okay Naiyah," Jade said, "we have a tiny little one who needs us. She doesn't need her mama fighting demons with drugs and alcohol, okay? Take care of it, that's all I'm going to say."

Elijah and his mother arrived not long after, rushing into Naiyah's hospital room and finding her resting seemingly well, with Jade sitting nearby, her eyes closed. Jade had spoken with Mani, who promised to stop on her way home from school and Lucky would get there as soon as he could. He was out of town when Jade's call came. When they spoke, she assured him everything was under control.

Meanwhile, Naiyah, who'd also drifted off briefly, imagined herself sitting comfortably in her YaYa's kitchen. Her imagination transported her into a picture of virtual reality such that her senses picked up the fragrances of patchouli and sandalwood all about, fragrances her YaYa wore often. She saw that YaYa was wearing a bright yellow dress. It reminded Naiyah of noontime, when the sun is at its highest and brightest. *"Stand still, granddaughter and know that He is God. You are free; the Son has set you free. Set yourself free. Tell the young man the truth; don't start out on an unstable and misleading foundation with him. It indeed will crumble.* "But YaYa, how——" she began—when next she witnessed an incredible sight, the dress appeared to turn into a flame which began moving toward lush vegetation in a sweltering desert. Yet

Naiyah continued sitting at YaYa's table, without blinking. The lovingly bathed vegetation, she noticed, was lush, an oasis. Naiyah swallowed involuntarily, not realizing she'd been thirsty, but recognizing the thirst had somehow been quenched.

❦

Turning to face Elijah she cried, "Oh love, sweetheart, forgive me, I'm sorry, so sorry."

"Ssssh," he said, taking her by the hand, "whatever the reason, it's going to be okay."

"Honey," Esther said, moving to the other side of the bed, "I'm sorry for insisting that you travel this late in your pregnancy; Elijah warned me that it may not be a good idea."

Jade stood up and joined them at Naiyah's bedside. She put her arm around Esther's shoulder to comfort her. At the moment, she couldn't bring forth any comforting words to express to this brokenhearted grandmother.

Elijah, taking charge of the situation, said; "Mother, take Naiyah by the hand," and he reached out his other hand to Jade. *"Father,"* he prayed, *"we have all made mistakes. In the name of your Son, the Lord Jesus Christ, we pray for forgiveness. We lift up the innocent baby you have entrusted into the care of us, gathered here within this circle. We pray, Father, that you will bless her right now as only you can with your hand of healing and protection. We pray that you won't hold the sins and foolishness of her parents, of whom I am one, against her. In Jesus' name we pray, Amen."*

"Amen," they each said conclusively.

"Esther, come," Jade said, once again taking her by the hand, "let's go for a snack while the two of them talk."

When they were alone, Naiyah took a deep breath and swallowed hard, "Lijah our baby is really sick."

"Yes, sweetheart, I'm sure; she's almost two months premature."

"Yes, but she's really sick." She didn't know how else to tackle this problem but to approach it head on. "She's facing some serious complications in addition to her prematurity."

Elijah felt something in his stomach that set off a chain reaction: his heart began to race and perspiration was now forming over his top lip as it always did when he got nervous. "What does that mean?" he asked, his voice cracking a little from the weight of fear rising within him.

"Elijah," she continued, "I've put our child at risk. While I was carrying her, I drank alcohol and used a little cocaine, and it's affected her, the doctor says, but to what degree, they're not completely sure."

"How much do you know?" he asked calmly.

"She's going through substance withdrawal, but he did say she doesn't have a lot of substance in her system," she added quickly. "She also has a small hole in her heart that has to be repaired."

Elijah stood up and walked quietly out of the room. All of a sudden it felt like all the air in the room had been vacuumed up just from the few words Naiyah had spoken, and he desperately needed some air. Though he knew better and would never have done so under normal circumstances, he ducked into an unoccupied handicapped restroom. There, he let out a silent scream and broke down into waves of uncontrollable sobs. With his head bent low, he let the snot running down his nose and his unchecked tears form a puddle at his feet. He stayed there releasing until he was spent. After a while, he stood and splashed water on his face and then returned to Naiyah's beside. Finally, he said, looking her straight in the eye, "I'm angry, Naiyah, mad as hell, but my anger won't change anything. We can't duck what's happened, so let's just gird up and deal with it."

"I hope you can forgive me one day. I'm so sorry and can't begin to tell you how ashamed I am."

"I won't hold this against you, that I'm sure of, but how quickly forgiveness comes, I can't say." When Naiyah began to cry, Elijah reached over the bed rails and tenderly took her in his arms. "I love you," he whispered, "that won't ever change and I love the baby girl you gave me; only God knows the reason this happened," he said with sincerity and conviction.

Jade and Esther walked in smiling. "Are you ready for this?" they asked in unison. "We have a name for the baby," Jade said with delight, Esther shaking her head enthusiastically in agreement. "Qua called back and said this baby girl's name, means *helped by God*, isn't that perfect?"

"I like that," Elijah said kissing Naiyah on the forehead.

"Well, what is it, Mum?" she asked, feeling a bit hopeful.

"It's Azaria," they sang.

"A-za-ria?" Elijah asked speaking phonetically.

"Yes, Azaria," Esther replied, "and we like it," she said pointing to Jade and then back to herself.

"Isn't that a boy's name?" he asked.

"No, you must be thinking of one of the three Hebrew furnace boys in the Bible whose name is spelled Azaria with an h on the end."

Elijah stared at his mother in disbelief. "How do you know that?"

"I looked it up right here in my pocket Bible after Jade's sister told us where to look."

"Sweetheart," he said turning to Naiyah, "I like it too, it works, but I have one request."

"Anything, just name it."

"I want her middle name to be Esther, after my mother."

"Of course, I think that's great. She'll be Queen Esther, *helped by God*," she laughed.

"Good, very good," he said turning to Esther. "Mother, have you seen her yet?"

"Oh son, yes," she said raising her hands to her mouth, "she is absolutely beautiful, let me take you to her."

"So, how'd it go?" Jade asked after they'd left.

"He was devastated," she said, adjusting the bed sheets.

"What did you tell him?"

"Everything," Naiyah said smiling, happy that she'd been honest. "I told him everything."

"Well," Jade asked, raising her eyebrows.

"In time, he'll forgive me, I'm sure and we'll move on," she replied confidently.

"That's my baby girl," Elijah announced proudly when they returned, "there isn't a child in the world more adorable," he said standing tall and puffing out his chest.

"I heard that," Lucky said, walking in with a box of cigars. "That's my granddaughter you're talking about; don't think you're the only one with bragging rights," he said, laughing heartily while gripping Elijah in an affectionate bear hug.

"Mr. Harland, wow, I'm glad you're here. Mother, this is Naiyah's father, Lemuel Harland."

Reaching out to shake Esther's hand, "Please, call me Lucky." Turning to Jade, he said in a loud, playful voice, "Congratulations, Grandma, can I give you a hug?"

Jade tried ignoring him, but he wasn't having any of it, not today anyhow. "Let me get a hug, Grandma," he asked again, reaching out to her.

"I don't know what she'll call me, but for sure it won't be Grandma," she replied squirming away from him.

Esther smiled, "Grandma is fine by me."

"Baby girl," Lucky said moving over to Naiyah, "you did it, congratulations." He turned and left the room, returning with the largest bouquet of yellow and lavender long-stemmed roses which reminded Jade of the weekly floral arrangements he used to have delivered to her. "Whatever you need, sweetheart, don't worry—I got you, I mean after Elijah, of course." They all laughed easily. "Izzy, how about coming home with me after you're released, would you like that?" Lucky asked.

Esther looked questioningly at Elijah, who whispered, "It's short for Isabella, her middle name."

"Oh," she mouthed back silently.

Jade's head jerked up abruptly from the rummaging she was doing through her bag. She hadn't expected this curve, and waited with baited breath for Naiyah's reply.

"Poppy, you know I won't be able to return to Stanford for a while."

"Izzy, we haven't had much time together lately," he said, "and I'd love the company."

"Isn't Analise coming back?" Jade shot in.

"No," he said sharply, without looking at her.

"I kinda like the idea," Naiyah said. "You know I'll be bringing a crying, sick baby after Azaria's released. Oh Lijah," she said, "by the way, love, we need to see if you can still sign the birth certificate before you leave."

"Azaria," Lucky repeated, picking up on what Naiyah said.

"Yes, Poppy, we're going to name her Azaria Esther McCoy."

"Cool, that's nice."

"Azaria means helped by God," she said.

"Good," he said "even better, Big Sadie would be very pleased."

XXXXIX

You Need Help, Start Here

"*Good Morning*, Ms. Harland, I'm Doctor Sage, a Psychiatric Social Worker on staff here, can we talk for a few minutes?"

Naiyah shrugged with disinterest, trying to abate her feelings of discomfort.

"I don't need my head examined, do I?" she asked nervously.

"You tell me," Dr. Sage said, moving closer. "Let's just cut to the chase and save ourselves a little time, is that okay with you?" she asked.

"Sure, we may as well," Naiyah said, looking everywhere but at the doctor.

"First, Naiyah—may I call you Naiyah," she asked politely; once getting the nod, she continued, "I want to say how very sorry I am about baby Azaria's challenges. Everything that can be done is being done and I believe in time she'll be able to function fairly normal, without much help."

"What kind of help?" Naiyah asked in a more conciliatory tone.

"Well, it depends, there may be some hyperactivity issues, or she may need special help in school due to mild learning disabilities, again, it's still pretty early. I'm just saying, guardedly, that I don't think her problems, over time, will be as severe as the doctors thought at first."

"Thank you, thank you, oh thank you for those encouraging words," Naiyah squealed.

"I thought that might make you feel a little better, but," she said reestablishing a professional distance, "we need to talk about the reasons you felt the need to indulge in risky behaviors, knowing full well that you were putting your baby in jeopardy." Before long, the censors were off and the floodgates once again open. Naiyah released all the hurt and uncertainty she'd been carrying. Dr. Sage sat quietly, occasionally nodding her understanding. When Naiyah had finished, Dr. Sage stood up, and moving over to the bed, she touched her hand with gentle reassurance. "Thanks for your time," she said, "I'll be writing up my assessment for your discharge summary. If you'd be willing, I'd like to refer you to someone privately who does shadow work."

"What's shadow work?"

"Simply put, it's discovering those things in our personality that we hide deep within our subconscious. They're usually the kinds of things we're afraid or ashamed of or feel weakened by, but they insist on being heard and they can't be denied. It's my guess you have denied parts of yourself. It's time to let them emerge and become fully integrated into the special person that you are," Dr. Sage said.

Naiyah smiled sweetly and broadly, "Again, I thank you, Dr. Sage."

"Be well, Naiyah, I'll be in touch."

XXXXX

It Isn't the End

"*Sweetheart,*" Jade said when they'd reached the house, "I was wondering, now that things are settling into a nice routine, wouldn't you like to have a party to celebrate?"

Naiyah followed her mother inside, going straight to the kitchen to put Azaria and her car seat on top of the table in the breakfast nook. While unbuttoning the baby's sweater, she asked, "A party?"

"Sure," Jade said, "it'll be fun and it's time to celebrate. You have your degree now and, at two months, the baby's finally beginning to gain weight. I think it's a great idea, don't you?"

"Yes, Mummy, it is, and believe me, I'm really glad you thought of it, but really, I think I'll pass."

"Aaahh Naiyah, we could get new party dresses and invite all of your friends and just have a good old time."

"Thanks but no," she said very directly, "but maybe in January when I start graduate school."

"Oh, all right then," Jade said taking Azaria out of Naiyah's arms, "she's the tiniest baby I've ever seen."

"I know, it's scary, isn't it?"

"How's Lucky around her?" Jade wanted to know, interrupting the lullaby she was softly humming.

"Mum, you should see him, he's so funny. He carries her around on a pillow and sings to her all the time."

"Has Analise been back since you got there?"

"You've got to be kidding, and it's not for a lack of tryin' on her part, but Poppy is so over her."

"Is he really?" Jade ventured.

"Oh stop, don't feign ignorance with me, you know good and well what my Poppy wants." Jade's smile wasn't lost on Naiyah. "Um-hum, I knew it."

"Knew what?"

"Mum, just quit it, don't make me go there."

"Let's change the subject, shall we?"

"Okay, but you started it, don't forget," she laughed.

XXXXXI

In the Beginning... Really

She was tiny and petite in stature, but there was no other remarkable sign to suggest Azaria would be handicapped. If love were a healing balm, she would surely be healed from the overflowing abundance she received from her parents, each of her grandparents, and her Uncle Nathan. As the months passed, she grew stronger and her doctors became more and more encouraged. Her hyperactivity was the most noticeable sign of the fetal alcohol syndrome, but with treatment and monitoring, her doctors were confident, she would live a full and productive life. Naiyah, now working a part-time job, at a local brokerage house as an intern, was adjusting well to motherhood and the break from school. She started spending more and more time with God-mommy Inez and joined the Bible Study Group at her church. Meanwhile, Elijah was working on subletting his apartment for his upcoming move to Boston in the fall, to start law school. This was an exciting time for the couple. The baby was growing in leaps and bounds; Elijah was promised a huge stipend for each year it took to earn his Jurist Doctorate degree, along with several other scholarships, and Naiyah was beginning a small ministry of her own, speaking to women's groups about her deepening faith in the power of God to deliver, heal and set free.

"Baby, I'm really proud of you," Inez said one fall evening getting into Jade's Mercedes station wagon, when Naiyah came to pick her up for Wednesday Night Bible Study. "Sharing your testimony and talking to the young women one on one about how the Lord is helping you and your baby, is making a difference in some of their lives."

"I can't take any credit, God-mommy. I'm just grateful my life is changing, even though I'm still struggling."

"Don't you worry about that, just take one day at a time. The Lord isn't going to leave you, and from what I can see, that young man isn't going anywhere either," Inez reassured.

Naiyah laughed as they pulled into the church parking lot, "Speaking of the young man, he's coming home for a visit this weekend and Zari and I are going into the city to see him."

"Oh how nice, baby, will you be driving in?" she asked.

"No, since we're staying over the weekend, we're going to take the train in."

"You be careful, Naiyah, you know how crazy those city folks can be. Don't let that baby out of your sight, anything can happen."

"I'll be careful," Naiyah said opening the door to the church for her godmother. "When I get back, Zari and I will come for tea and tell you all about it."

"Okay baby," Inez said kissing Naiyah's cheek lightly.

❦

The next morning, Naiyah was up early, getting ready for the trip to Brooklyn and the visit with Elijah.

"Izzy?" Lucky called.

"Yes, Poppy," she answered.

"How are you and Azaria getting to the station and when are you coming back?"

"It's such a gorgeous Indian summer day, I thought we'd walk."

"Look," he said, with parental concern in his voice, "that baby is susceptible to getting any and everything; make sure she's wrapped up good when you take her out of here."

"I will, Poppy."

"By the way, Izzy, didn't I hear you leave out last night?"

"Yes sir, I stepped out for just a minute. One of my friends stopped by and I went to the car to holla."

"To holla," he said, looking at her as if she'd lost her mind, "little girl please, I know your mama raised you better than that."

Embarrassed, Naiyah dropped her head.

"And," he continued, "even if I am in the house and Azaria's asleep, don't you dare walk out of here without telling me," he said with much bass in his voice.

"Yes, Poppy," she said contritely.

"Alright then; now, when again did you say you'll be back?"

"We'll be back Sunday afternoon."

"Have a good time then and give my best to Elijah and his parents. See you later, I love you," he said opening the door to leave.

Naiyah blew a kiss, though his back was now facing her, and turned her attention back to the cooing baby Azaria. "It's time to go see Daddy and your Ma-G," Naiyah sang to the baby, whose dark piercing eyes were fixed squarely on her.

Elijah drove in from Boston the night before, arriving just in time to have dinner with his mother and father before turning in for a much needed full night's sleep.

"How'd you sleep, son," Esther asked, greeting Elijah who strode into the kitchen walking straight and tall like the highest ranking captain of any installation. "I slept like a lamb," he said drawing her into an affectionate embrace. "Thank you, mother I was dog tired and it sure felt good to sink into the feather bed, riding on a cloud off to dreamland."

"Boy, please," she laughed "what's with the drama?"

He laughed too. "I'm just so excited, I haven't seen my girls in a month and I can't wait."

"Help yourself to the coffee on the counter and tell me what else I can get you for breakfast."

"I haven't had an omelet in quite some time, may I?"

"Absolutely, I'll make your favorite," she said while reaching for the now ringing phone, "Hello, oh hi baby, just a minute, he's right here," she said handing Elijah the telephone.

Smiling broadly he reached for it, knowing Naiyah's voice would greet him on the other end, to confirm their arrival time. "Hello, sweetheart," he said brightly.

"Yes, baby boy, I'm your sweetheart."

Elijah shot a gritty look at his mother who dropped her head, now giving her full attention to the omelet she was making. "Excuse me, I was expecting a call from someone else, what do you want, D'yanna? I'm busy right now and really don't have time for this; and anyhow, how did you know I was in town?" he asked, his dark eyes blazing a proverbial hole into his mother's back.

"Now is that any way to act towards your fiancée, baby, you're killin' me and trust, in case you really don't know, let me school you, I know every move you make," she said with wicked laughter. "C'mon, B.B., come on over and get my cookies, they're hot, straight out the oven."

Trying with all his mental power, Elijah wasn't able to command his lieutenant to remain at ease. The fact that D'yanna was scaring him with her crazy stalker talk, the thought of her "hot cookies," and the mental picture it conjured up caused an involuntary reflex.

"Ditch that schoolgirl chick and come to Mama."

"I told you before, Dee—don't make me. I've got to go now and please don't call me anymore," he said sternly, taking the cordless into the living room, not wanting his mother to see how much D'yanna's call had affected him.

Before he could hang up, she shouted, "I won't stop calling, Elijah. I'm not going to quit until I get you back, you belong to me, not her."

"Oh God," he cried, "why this temptation?" he said before slamming the phone down.

XXXXXII

But You Have to Surrender

"*You are my sunshine, my only sunshine, you make me happy when skies are gray...*" Naiyah sang. "You're so sweet, my little sweetie sweetie," she said to Azaria, who was now smiling brightly trying to figure out what her fingers were supposed to be doing. "Let's go see Da," she said putting on Zari's jacket. "This might not be warm enough," she thought aloud. "I better get a sweater too, just in case. What a glorious day," she said to the baby, basking in the sunlight, taking in the beauty of the crystal blue, cloud filled sky as they walked to catch the train. "Utterly glorious," she said.

As the express train traveled west, Naiyah rested her head on the backrest, while Azaria slept peacefully. She thought, *That dang Strong, he always comes through in the cut.* Arriving at the station, she knew they had thirty minutes before their connecting train left Jamaica, bound for Brooklyn. "Thank you," Naiyah said to the man who handed her the baby's stroller from overhead. Approaching the Hunter Avenue side of the platform, Naiyah spotted a small group of harmless looking schoolgirls. "Excuse me," she interrupted, "can I trouble you to keep an eye on my baby, just for five minutes, while I run to the restroom?" she asked.

"Sure, go ahead, we'll watch her," one of them replied. Naiyah trotted to the bathroom, daring not to leave Azaria too long. She berated herself the whole way, but she didn't turn around. *Just one more line,* she thought closing the door to the stall. As she sat, preparing to snort the cocaine from the aluminum wrapper, she asked herself, *what am I afraid of,* why *am I running?* These were questions, the therapist specializing in shadow work, whom Dr. Sage referred her to, had asked her over and over. In that, instant Naiyah recognized herself for the first time. She understood what her YaYa had tried to tell her all those many years ago. She was running from the light which brought life. "I am light," she breathed, "I have to shine for Azaria if she's to have life. That's it, my YaYa knew it—it's Azaria, God is helping her through me, that's why he kept saying surrender. The time is now; not tomorrow, not the next day—now, right now. Oh my God!" she screamed. "Azaria!" She balled up the foil and threw it in the toilet, grabbed her things and darted out. Out of breath, she reached the platform just in time to see the doors to the train closing behind the group of schoolgirls to whom she had entrusted her baby's welfare. She reached the stroller just as a transit cop was about to approach it. She grabbed the stroller handle and hurried down the platform. With tears streaming down her face she cried, "Yes, Lord, I surrender."

Guide for Book Clubs

Book Club Discussion Questions for the Novel, Tahitian Pearl

Discussion Questions:

1. Did the book demonstrate clearly the impact of YaYa's death on Naiyah? Explain?

2. What, in your opinion, could have influenced a different result of that impact?

3. Would you have handled the situation in the smoking room between Jade and Naiyah differently? Why or Why not?

4. Were you certain Nathan was, what he insisted he wasn't? Why?

5. Were Lucky's reasons for taking up with Analise acceptable? Why or why not?

6. What do you think the real reason the intimacy between Jade and Lucky waned? Is settling into routine a good reason, as alluded to in the book?

7. Do you know women like Turquoise? If so, how do you relate to them? Why?

8. Do you think Elijah will honor his commitment to Naiyah?

9. Though the book doesn't explore this, if he does honor the commitment, do you think he'll remain faithful?

10. Was D'yanna a likable character? If so, what did you like most about her?

11. Did Danny (aka Strong) have any redeeming qualities? If so, what were they?

12. Was God Mommy Inez too forceful or not forceful enough in the spiritual counsel she gave to Naiyah? Explain?

LaVergne, TN USA
09 September 2010
196491LV00008B/73/P